Only Two Letters In Orroroo

Also by Margaret Visciglio and published by Ginninderra Press
Blue Roses of Orrorroo
On the Edge
Terra Nullius

Margaret Visciglio

Only Two Letters In Orroroo

To my father, Charles Robert Burge, my hero of Kokoda.
And to my sister, Pamela Anne Buik – how I wish you could read this
book.

In 1892, the people of Orroroo petitioned the head of Posts and
Telegraphs, Sir Charles Todd, for a post office for the town. He
responded that a post office would never be needed as there would
only ever be two letters in Orroroo.

Only Two Letters In Orroroo
ISBN 978 1 76109 084 1
Copyright © Margaret Visciglio 2021
Cover photo: Sheep at Bullyacre by Margaret Visciglio

First published 2021 by
GINNINDERRA PRESS
PO Box 3461 Port Adelaide 5015
www.ginninderrapress.com.au

Contents

Preface

Many people who read *The Blue Roses of Orroroo* asked me what happened next. I said that I didn't know – it was a work of fiction. But they persisted, so I began to wonder too. Eventually, my curiosity got the better of me and I decided to take up the story of Rose's life after fourteen years had passed.

Some things haven't changed. Rose is still stubborn, irascible and guilt-ridden. And now she has something else to be guilty about. There is a new character, Danny, who is the putative twin of Mary's daughter, Rosemary. Remember we are talking about 1928/1929, and mores, even for a strong woman like Rose, were stricter then.

World War Two has begun. Rose worries about members of her family away in various theatres of war across the globe. Japan advances southwards. Despite the reassurances by politicians that Fortress Singapore will protect our nation, the fear of invasion looms.

Although Postmaster General Charles Todd joked there would never be more than two letters in Orroroo, many letters arrive for Rose from far-flung lands. A letter written in Darwin after the bombing does not arrive because all communication with the Top End is forbidden lest the populace panic.

The novel is told not only from Rose's point of view but also from the points of view of other voices. This was an experiment for me, and I will leave it to you, the reader, to judge whether the method succeeds. Yes, and Rose and Pask marry, but their wedding is overshadowed by Pearl Harbor.

The Papua New Guinea sequences incorporate many stories told to me by my father, Charlie Burge, who fought on the Kokoda Track. My homage to him and to all the men who endured the green hell of the Pacific.

The bow and arrows given to Charlie by the cannibal chieftain in the book hang over my mantelpiece. The pig incident happened; we never ate pork at home. Other stories, including the incident of the white mist, are products of my imagination, but my father certainly suffered from PTSD, evidenced by his waking at night screaming, which he tried to explain by saying he had malaria. The white mist incident is reprehensible to us now, but it would have been impossible to take and guard prisoners on the Track, and I can imagine horrors happened.

For other settings, I have done extensive research both in books and on the internet. Not all sources agree. Undoubtedly, mistakes will be found, and I apologise for any obvious ones. I have tried to be correct, but I am a novelist, not an historian.

Thanks, as always, to my long-suffering husband, Frank, who called piteously and often from the kitchen, 'Where are you?' The answer wasn't always Orroroo – sometimes it was the Middle East, sometimes Britain, sometimes the jungles of Papua, and once, disconcertingly, Belsen. I was glad to leave Belsen.

Thank you too to Stephen and Brenda Matthews who agreed to publish *Only Two Letters* – Brenda said she cried a lot, laughed a lot and learned a lot when reading the manuscript. I hope she, and all the people who encouraged me to write the sequel, enjoy the story too, because unless a page is worth turning, it should never be penned.

I wrote the book partly because I fear the younger generation is becoming unaware of our past, and I know that unless we remember our history we are doomed to repeat it.

This is not a war novel; it is an anti-war novel. Lest we forget.

Margaret Visciglio, 2021

1

Tuesday 14 January 1941
Rose Walsh – Norwood

I felt the blast of heat as Danny opened the door.

'Gran, I got two sixes,' he yelled. There was a thud as he tossed his cricket bag into the corner by the icebox.

A couple of belligerent blowflies zoomed through the door behind him. They put me in mind of the German bombers flying over London I'd seen in the newsreels at the movies. Nasty, aggressive brutes both: the Nazis and the blowies.

It would be night in London now. Black skies and searchlights reflected in the silver ribbon of the Thames. And young Bob and his mates high above the city, in their little Spitfires, darting through the frozen darkness, hunting the Huns. Or being hunted by them.

The blowflies veered and flew in formation towards me. I threw the tea towel in their direction and missed. I hate blowies. Up at Orroroo, I've seen what they can do to sheep. There's nothing worse than a fly-blown sheep.

But I hate the war even more than I hate blowies.

Because of the war, Bob's risking his life in England and my Brian's away with our army fighting for some worthless bit of sand in the Middle East. I took a deep breath. Come back to earth, Rose, get a grip on yourself, woman.

'Shut that door, Danny,' I said. 'The flies are coming in. The fly swat's on the table.'

'It's hot as Hades out there, Gran. Near a hundred, I reckon.'

I turned off the gas, lifted the pressure cooker from the stove, sat it in the sink and ran water over the lid. 'It's been hot for days,' I said. 'Heat-wave. You get them in summer. Happens every year, or so I've noticed.'

'I've been dying for a cold drink all the way home, Gran,' the kid whined. 'Did you hear me say I got two sixes?'

'Yes, Danny. Well done. Pour yourself a drink. That's what Don Bradman would do.'

'It's even bloody hot in here, Gran. And you're making it hotter with your cooking. Why couldn't we just have a fritz sandwich for tea? It's too hot to eat anyway.'

Danny ripped off his shirt. A button clinked as it hit the lino. An-other job to sew it back on, I thought. I caught the words 'doesn't care, doesn't give a bloody shit about me', so I turned and glared at him. I did care, but my hands were full and his were empty.

'How many times have I told you not to swear, Daniel Aloysius Mudge?' I demanded. 'If you talk like that around Father Flaherty, you're in deep shit. And you watch your mouth when your Uncle Joe gets back from Perth, too. It'll be Easter before we know it. You and Rosemary are getting confirmed at Easter, remember?'

I put the pot on the draining board and opened the lid, released the pressure and lifted the lid of the cooker. Through the steam that poured out, I saw Danny's face glowing red as the brisket in the water. I felt a stab of sympathy for him. But it was hot in the house, too, not just out-side. And I'd been hard at it all day working, not playing cricket.

Fritz sandwich for tea, indeed. If I served that up for a meal, I'd never hear the end of it from him or from Amy. Besides, Mary's hus-band's a butcher and I know what goes into fritz. Lips and arseholes, mainly. Bits of meat that had fallen on the floor, still coated with saw-dust when it went into the mix.

Kids! Would confirmation improve him or Rosemary at all? I doubted it. The twins were getting a bit old for confirmation, but Mary couldn't get away from Mount Gambier until Easter, what with the butcher shop and the baby, and of course we'd had to wait until Joe could get home from the west.

'Uncle Joe's all right, for a priest,' said Danny, probably reading my mind. No privacy in this house. 'Not like Father Flaherty. Rosemary swears worse than I do. She just doesn't do it when anyone's listening. Rosemary's sneaky.' He bent over the kitchen sink, turned the tap on, sloshed water over his face and forearms. 'That's better. Could you get me that drink now?'

'Swat those flies, Danny,' I ordered. 'And help yourself to a drink.'

'I like it better when you pour it for me, Gran. I'm really tired.' He plonked himself down on the nearest chair and looked at me expectantly.

So am I, I thought. Tired of running myself ragged for this family, tired of worrying about the future, tired of feeling guilty about the past.

I lost my grip on the meat and it plunged back into the pot. Drops of hot liquor hit my face. There's penance for my sins, I thought. I blotted the greasy water off my chin with the tea towel. Do it again, woman, I ordered myself. Only do it properly this time.

That sounds like bloody Michael talking, I thought. It's high time I put that bastard, and the way he used to carry on, out of my mind completely. These days, I can do what I want, how I want, and when I want. Except when it comes to this family, of course.

'I'll get you a drink in a minute,' I said.

I reached for the dish to sit the brisket in. The flies headed towards the meat even though it was still half covered by the hot water.

'You buggers aren't laying maggots on our dinner,' I yelled, waving them away. 'Filthy bloody bastards.'

'You're swearing now, Gran,' said Danny with a grin. 'Will that drink be much longer?'

'How're you doing with the blowies?' I snapped.

Danny sighed and resumed the hunt, waving the swat furiously but ineffectively.

I turned back to my own task. The water splashed as I dropped the beef back into the pot. This time, it was my hand that was scalded. I used a word I've heard Pask's shearers say when they cut too close to a sheep's skin and the animal bleeds. I hoped Danny hadn't heard me say that word. He'd recognise it because he helps with the shearing, too. The kid was running about the kitchen wildly waving the fly swat at the blowies, so maybe he hadn't heard.

I jabbed the fork into the brisket a bit harder so the meat wouldn't fall again on my next attempt. You're getting old, Rose, I told myself, if you can't even manage a simple job like this. It's the arthritis, that's the problem. I used to be able to do a full week's wash every Monday for six kids plus Michael and me, boil the whites in the copper, heft them out, rinse them with Reckitt's Blue, starch them, put the lot through the mangle, hang it out, use the rest of the water from the copper to mop the lino and do a batch of scones as well before the family got home. These days, it takes me all day just to do the washing for the three of us.

I lifted the meat clear and put it on the plate. I covered it with the tea towel in case more flies snuck in when Amy got home from the munitions factory at Hendon. She'd complain about having to eat a hot meal on a stinking hot day, but she's always whingeing about something. I'll make sandwiches for their lunches from the leftover brisket tomorrow.

'I need that drink, Gran,' Danny whined. 'I'm real thirsty. Look, I killed one of those flies. It's there, on the table next to the meat. The other one landed on the flypaper.' He waved the swat at the curl of brown sticky paper that dangled from the light fitting.

I was pleased to see the blowie beating its wings desperately as it tried to escape the insect cemetery. I don't like cruelty, but I make an exception for insects. And snakes. And rats. And Germans and Japs. And politicians.

'For goodness sake, help yourself, Danny. Get a glass out of the dresser. The big jug's in the ice chest with the lemonade I made this morning.'

I dumped the cabbage and carrots I had chopped earlier into the pressure cooker and ran more water in. I'd have one less saucepan to wash and there'd be flavour from the meat in the veg, even if it made the cabbage a bit greasy. Now I just had to peel and boil the spuds, make the parsley sauce and the meal would be ready.

Danny opened the icebox and picked up the jug. 'The water in the tap at school was putrid, Gran. No one could drink it. It was real hot at school, but it was even worse out on the oval at cricket practice. I reckon I'm dehydrated. The coach said that happens to cricketers.' He looked about as if expecting a glass to waft out of the cupboard and fill itself automatically.

'Did you get a glass from the dresser?' I asked. 'Can't you do anything for yourself, Danny? Amy's exactly the same. Slavery was abolished years ago, you know.'

He sighed, found a glass and filled it, spilling half the liquid on the table. He glanced at me and grabbed the tea towel to mop the sticky drink up before raising the glass to his lips and swallowing. I opted not to notice.

'Gran, the coach says I'm real promising. My bowling just needs more work.' He gulped the liquid and added, 'Trevor Wallace fainted because it was so hot. The coach says he's got heatstroke. I felt crook but I didn't pass out. I reckon Trev's a wuss. I wouldn't let a bit of heat stop me playing cricket.'

'You'll definitely be another Don Bradman when you grow up,' I said, smiling as I gave in and poured another drink for him. 'You'll beat the stuffing out of the Poms one day.'

'I just want to be another Uncle Brian,' Danny said, quaffing his drink and holding out his glass for a refill. 'He's my hero. Played Sheffield Shield cricket, and now he's off fighting the Vichy French in Syria. Uncle Charlie says Uncle Brian's been to Damascus, just like Saint Paul.'

But I bet Brian didn't see any visions on the road to Damascus, I thought. Only sand and rocks and Arabs and bloody Vichy French shooting at him. Did death appear to Brian in the dust storms? Please, God, keep my boy safe. And he's wearing khaki shorts and it's freezing out there in the desert at night.

I've only had the one letter from Brian since he reached the Middle East. He never was one for writing letters. Not like Charlie. But in his letter Brian complained of the cold and said that even though our boys were wearing every stitch of clothing they owned, it didn't help much. He said the British had great coats, but the Aussie 7th Division AIF didn't get kit like that. I remember our lads had the same sort of treatment from the Poms in the Great War. Look what happened at Gallipoli, for example. Bloody Churchill.

'Well,' I said, 'if Uncle Brian's your hero, you ought to respect his cricket bag better. I saw how you dumped it on the floor. He lent it to you, remember? He'll want it back in good condition when he comes home.'

The back door opened and slammed.

'Is that lemonade Danny's drinking? I need a cold drink more than he does. I've been doing my duty for king and country and I'm almost dead. It must have been well over the century in that rotten factory and then I had to swelter on a stinking trolley bus from Hendon and I almost died of heat exhaustion on a horrible smelly tram to get back here to Norwood. I nearly cooked. I never should have quit my job at Myers.' Amy grabbed the dishcloth out of the sink and wiped her face with it.

'Don't do that, Amy. You'll get make-up all over it. I wash the dishes with that dishrag.'

'You've got no idea what it's like sitting on a hard metal stool, in a hot shed, making bullets all day, Mum. What we munitions workers need is a union. No one gives a damn about the workers.'

'There's a war on, Amy,' I said, getting the potatoes out of the veg rack.

'I know that. That's all I ever hear. All the overhead fans in that shed do is move hot air around. I'm sweating like a pig. Why haven't we got a fan?'

'Because I'm not spending the money on one. Or on the electricity to run it if I did have one.' I mopped my forehead with the dishcloth that Amy had dropped on the table, wishing I had bought an electric fan at that sale when Mrs Williams next door got hers. It's all right for some, I thought. That woman's got more money than sense. It gets hotter at Orroroo, though, than down here, and Pask hasn't got a fan.

Amy kicked off her shoes, flopped down on a chair and put her feet up on the chair next to her.

'Your feet stink, Amy,' said Danny.

'You smell like a septic tank, Danny,' said Amy. 'Even when you've just had your bath on Saturday. Pour me a drink before I definitely expire completely, Mum.'

The bullets you're making in that factory will definitely cause some mother's sons to expire completely, I thought. And somewhere in the world another girl is making bullets to kill my boys.

Please, God, let Brian come home safely soon. Please God, keep Bob safe. Please, God, make this stupid war end before any more of my boys go away. What if it lasts until Danny turns eighteen? He's thirteen now, fourteen in August. But he's tall like his father. What if he decides to lie about his age and enlist?

'I scored two sixes today, Amy,' said Danny. 'And the coach says I've got real potential. Very promising, he says. He says I've got a terrific future in cricket as long as I practise my bowling.'

'Just as long as Hitler doesn't wipe us all out first,' said Amy, shrugging. 'Or unless the Japs do it instead.' She laid the back of one hand to her brow. She's seen some film star do that for dramatic emphasis, I thought. I wasn't sure which one, but Amy's always at the movies. She knows all the stars' names. I still fancy Rudolf Valentino. The moving pictures haven't been the same since he died back in 1928.

'Mr Williams says the Japs are coming south, so probably none of us have a future, actually,' Amy sighed. 'Unless I keep sacrificing myself in the munitions factory. Is there any more lemonade, Mum? This jug's empty.'

We're complaining of the heat and Brian's stone cold, I thought. It's winter over there.

I got the other jug out of the ice chest and poured more lemonade.

'Amy, you said the money was better in the munitions factory. You were only making twenty-six shillings a week in Myers and you're getting two pounds one shilling and sixpence in the factory. And, as I recall, you said you wanted to do your bit for the war effort.'

'All those posters in the shops said everyone should be helping the war effort, but I wasn't going to wear overalls and dig for spuds. Jen and I thought the munitions factory would be an easier option than the Land Army.'

Brian didn't look for an easy option, I thought. Neither did Bob. But I kept my mouth shut. It's useless arguing with Amy.

'And, yes,' she agreed, 'I did like the idea of the extra money at the munitions factory too. But it wasn't the middle of summer when I started work there, was it? No one told me it would be hot in that place. It's just a big shed with concrete floors. Pask's shearing shed is heaps better than the munitions factory. His sheep live the life of Riley. Once it gets hot where I work, it stays hot.'

She emptied the glass and held it out for a refill. 'Now the supervisor says we have to wear these ugly scarves on our heads because some stupid girl got her hair caught in the machinery and half her hair was ripped out.' Amy screwed up her face at the memory. 'It was awful, Mum. There was blood everywhere and she screamed as if she was being skinned alive.'

'I suppose she would.' I said. 'Was that someone knocking on the front door? Could you go, Amy?'

'It's probably just Mrs Williams. I need more lemonade.'

'She always comes to the back door. I still have to peel the potatoes for the mash and pick some parsley for the white sauce. If there's any left alive in this heat. Can't you see who's there?'

'I can't move. I'm in my death throes from those rotten bullets. Danny, you go.'

Danny shrugged his shirt back on and ran down the hallway, swinging his arm, bowling an imaginary ball at imaginary stumps. He was back an instant later, pale and clutching his throat as if he was about to vomit. He shuddered, looked at the floor and whispered, 'Gran, there's a telegram boy at the door. He wouldn't give the envelope to me. He said he has to give it to you. It couldn't be bad news about Uncle Brian, could it?'

'Brian's in Egypt, isn't he? He'd be safe there because the Poms own Egypt. Maybe we've won the lottery,' said Amy, hopefully. She sat up a little straighter in her chair and looked at me expectantly.

'The Poms don't own Egypt, it's a protectorate.' said Danny, looking about furtively as if he was giving away a state secret. 'They're protecting it because of the Suez Canal, so the Germans and Italians and the French don't get their hands on it. Not the good French, the rotten ones. And Uncle Brian's not in Egypt now, the AIF's marching through the desert on their way to Tripoli, Uncle Charlie told me.'

He grabbed my arm. 'You'd better get the telegram, Gran. I reckon it's important.'

'It has to be about a lottery ticket,' insisted Amy. But her voice shook, and I could see her eyes were filling with tears.

'I never buy lottery tickets,' I said, fighting off sudden nausea. 'Mick was the only gambler in this family. If there's a telegram, it's bad news.'

I took a deep breath and forced myself to walk up the hallway. My knees trembled as I neared the front room. The photographs of my two brothers, Patrick and Daniel, clad in the uniforms of the Light Horse in which they had gone off on what they called 'The Great Adventure' hung over the mantelpiece in that room. Those two boys never came back from France. My dead husband Michael, whose photo hung between my brothers' pictures, came home, although he was never the same man I'd farewelled in 1914. And all of them had fought to save France, so why was Brian fighting against the French now? Why were there good French and bad French? Politicians were crazy.

I paused at the entrance of the room. Was there a dead mouse in there? There was just the faintest whiff of corruption in the air. It was that same putrid stench that had driven me mad in the weeks after Michael had died, a smell that had had me pulling all the furniture out to check for rotting rats. I didn't find a rat back in 1928 and in the end, I decided the stench was the residue of my husband's body. His legacy. The front room was stifling hot then and it was the same now. He had lain there overnight before the funeral, but the boys insisted the lead-lined coffin Michael was brought back in from Mount Gambier would have stopped any odour. They said the whack I had given the coffin with the axe hadn't penetrated the lining, just damaged the wood.

The boys still won't let me live that down, even though it was nearly fifteen years ago. But back then I'd needed to see whether my husband really was in the box. I knew he was untrustworthy, and I was right about that. Of course, these days I'm confident that Michael's dead and buried and not coming back. I'm not mourning him these days.

Back when Michael died, no one else in the house could smell anything. Just to shut me up, the boys opened all the windows in the house and even checked inside the piano for dead rodents. I washed the floors with disinfectant and then in desperation I filled the place with roses. Eventually, either the stink went away, or I got used to it. You can get used to anything in the end, and there were distractions enough in the weeks after Mick died.

Now, the reek of death was back. The miasma wafted from the darkened room like a grey cloud, seeped around the house from the skirting boards up to the picture rail, pursued me as I inched my way down the hallway towards the front door that barricaded the heat. The house was at siege against summer and death.

I knew the smell of corruption and a telegram meant that Brian was dead. If it was about Bob, the telegram would have gone to Pask at Ororoo.

I don't pretend to have the second sight, although Mrs Williams always says there's something fey about the Irish. Of course, I'm Aussie to the core, second-generation Aussie, but there's a lot of Irish in me.

A furnace blast of hot air from hell hit me as I flung the door open. Speak of the devil...

Mrs Williams from next door stood on her veranda trying to look interested in the one solitary cloud that floated in the glaringly blue sky. She didn't fool me. That woman never missed a trick. She waved her hand. 'Hot enough for you, Mrs Walsh?' she called. 'Reckon that cloud means there'll be a storm?'

I pretended not to hear her or see her, knowing the old biddy had seen the telegram boy and guessed what the message in the telegram was. Everyone knew the contents of wartime telegrams. We all prayed the telegram boy wouldn't knock at our door, that he would pass us by like the Angel of Death passing by the Hebrews' doors in the Old Testament. Better anyone else than you. It had been exactly the same during the Great War.

'Can I do anything to help, Mrs Walsh?' I heard my neighbour call.

I shook my head. What could anyone, even God, do?

The telegram boy stood on the veranda mopping sweat from his forehead. I reached for the telegram, but my arm didn't seem long enough. The boy thrust the envelope at me. I grabbed it and slammed the door in his face. My numb hands clutched the paper.

Somehow, I staggered back past the room from which the dead faces in the photographs glared. They accused me of betraying my son to share their fate. Mud or dust, what was the difference?

Days later, when I was slowly coming to my senses, I wondered whether anyone ever thanked telegram boys when they delivered their messages. Or gave them a cool drink. That kid had a rotten job when you thought about it. Almost as bad as making bullets.

Did Amy have any idea what she was really doing in the munitions factory? Was it worse to kill a boy's body or to kill a parent's hope?

I leant against the wall for a minute with the envelope crumpled in my fist. Then I limped down the hallway to the kitchen. Danny must have pulled out my chair because he was standing behind it, holding it for me. I glanced at him and decided he was clinging to the chair so he wouldn't fall over. His face was whiter than the cricket get-up he was wearing.

I slumped down on my seat. I dropped the telegram onto the table in front of me and stared at the window over the sink. I couldn't bring myself to look at the yellow envelope before me.

'Aren't you going to open it, Gran?' Danny asked, his voice quivering.

I shook my head. 'In a moment,' I said. It was a mad idea, but somehow, I believed that Brian wouldn't really be dead until I read the official announcement.

It was always Brian who jumped or fell off things or got black eyes fighting in the schoolyard. But there was no saving him now. Why had he volunteered to go to war? He didn't even wait to be conscripted. He joined the army as soon as bloody Mr Menzies made his 'melancholy duty to inform you' speech back in 1939. Men were mad. All men were mad.

And I don't care what anyone says, that war was on the other side of the world. Miles away. It wasn't even our war. Something to do with some little country being invaded. Poland, or Belgium or whatever. I didn't even know where those places were, and I didn't want to know. Our men were going off to fight overseas when we would soon need them here in Australia. War was headed our way too. I read the newspapers. I listened to the wireless. I knew.

Everyone except the politicians knew the Japs were rattling their swords, wanting to expand their territory. Years ago, the wharfies had rioted because of Pig Iron Bob Menzies selling our scrap metal to the Japs – I remember the unionists saying back then that that metal would come back at us. I bet that Japanese girls just like Amy were working in munitions factories turning our pig iron into weapons right now.

The brisket under the tea towel on the table in front of me smelled like a rotting corpse. Must be the heat; or had a blowie crawled beneath its shroud? Was the dead meat crawling with maggots?

My Brian, my crazy son. Joined up because he said the army offered a secure job and the chance of adventure. I knew jobs were scarce, things had been tough ever since the Depression started, but I reminded him that you only get one life. I told him to stay alive a bit longer. Every moment is precious. He laughed. Like all young men, he knew he was immortal.

Young Bob, Pask's son, was just as foolhardy as Brian, but I suppose he could justify going off to fly Spitfires to save Britain because his mother was a Pom. And because he was aviation mad. Bob would go miles for a chance for a joyride in an aeroplane. His hero was that Hubert Wilkins who flew just about everywhere including across the Arctic. 'Sense of adventure', *The Advertiser* called it, and said Wilkins was a thrilling hero and an inspiration to our youth.

I bet his Mum, Pask's dead wife Elsie, wouldn't have been too inspired about Bob going to war, though. Pask certainly wasn't thrilled. Neither was I, and Bob wasn't even really my kid. It just felt like he was mine because I had brought him up. Why did anyone have sons, anyway, when they grew up to be cannon fodder for politicians?

'Mum,' Amy was asking. It sounded like she was a long way away or if she was talking underwater. 'Mum, do you want me to open it for you?'

'I can't see in here,' I said. 'Maybe I should take it outside. Only it's so hot out there.'

'I'll put the light on,' Danny said.

'Don't waste the electricity. I'll be all right in a moment. When my eyes adjust. It was sunny when I opened the door and I got dazzled. I have to get used to being in the dark again.'

I remembered how the light went out of the world when my brothers died. The sun must have risen every day as it always did, but it was dimmer in our house and I don't believe light never shone again in my mother's soul, although as time went on, my eyes slowly recovered. Of course, I was just a girl back then. My dead brothers were just boys, too.

One generation dies, another one grows up, and God then allows another war to happen. Why? Was God really in charge, or had He gone on holidays and let the Devil take over running the world? Was there really a god, anyway? Had Father Flaherty and his mates made up the whole story and it was like Father Christmas that you stopped believing in when you turned seven or so?

'She can't see because she's crying,' Amy told Danny. 'It might say

21

he's missing in action, Mum. Not every telegram says they're dead. Last week, Jenny – she's one of the girls at the munitions factory – her mum had a telegram saying Jen's brother Jack was missing in action. Then the next day they got another one to say his legs had been blown off and he's quite all right and coming home on the next troop ship. If Brian's missing in action, he'll probably come back wounded or something.'

'My mother got telegrams when my brothers were killed,' I said. 'First Daniel, then Patrick.' But I could hardly hear my own voice, and I wasn't sure if the kids knew I had spoken.

They were looking at each other and they didn't answer me.

My eyes were sticky, wet with tears but they were thick tears like Clag glue. It was like trying to see underwater, which I did try once, years ago, when Michael took me swimming at Glenelg, and I didn't know that salt water stung your eyes, so I opened them. I'd only been to the city baths before then and it was fresh water in there with some chemical in it that got up the back of your throat and stung. Funny how a memory can come back when you don't expect it. My throat was closing up now just as it had back at Glenelg.

Saliva filled my mouth and I had an urge to spit it out onto the envelope, but I thought that would be disrespectful to my dead Brian's memory, so I didn't do it. I swallowed hard. My nose was running so I pulled the tea towel off the brisket and blew my nose on it. I was leaking at the seams like a sinking ship, going down like that *Titanic* that was supposed to be unsinkable.

'When they say soldiers are missing in action, it usually means their bodies haven't been found. Blown to smithereens,' I said. My voice didn't sound like me, even to my ears. Unless my ears were clogged with tears as well so I couldn't hear properly.

Danny was stroking my hand and muttering something, but I wasn't listening to him.

'My brothers' bodies were never found. All we knew was that they were killed on the Somme. In the mud. And they went there to save the French. But Brian was fighting against the French. I don't understand any of it. The Great War was supposed to be the war to end all wars. What happened?'

'Uncle Charlie says it's not the real French that Uncle Brian's fighting,' said Danny. 'It's those Vichy French who are on the Germans' side. Uncle Brian's fighting the French Foreign Legion. Uncle Charlie says they're the dregs of humanity and they come from all over the world. Don't you remember that film, *Beau Geste*?'

'That was a really good film,' said Amy brightly. '1939, wasn't it? Gary Cooper and Susan Hayward. It got heaps of awards.'

'Well, you remember what a pig that Sergeant Markoff was? He was horrible to Beau and his brothers. Real brutal. Uncle Charlie says that's exactly what the Foreign Legion's like.'

I felt as if I was about to explode.

Amy must have sensed it, because she interrupted Danny. 'Mum probably doesn't want to hear this, Danny. It's not helping her to think about Gary Cooper suffering in the desert.'

'Yes, she does want to hear it,' insisted Danny. 'Some of the legionnaires don't speak French at first but they had to learn it. French is a rotten language. All those verbs and tenses and genders. Bloody stupid. Tables and chairs are female, I think. I'm doing French and I hate it.'

'Shut up, Danny,' shouted Amy. She punched him on the arm. 'You're talking crap. Stop it.'

Danny shook his head. Once Danny starts on a subject, you can't shut him up. His dad is much the same, although it takes longer to get him started. 'The Vichy are traitors. The real French are the Free French led by General Charles de Gaulle.'

Suddenly it was all too much. I pounded the table with my fists. 'Brian's dead and all you two can do is talk about Gary bloody Cooper,' I yelled. 'What's wrong with you both?'

Danny put his hand on my hand, his eyes full of concern. 'Do you want me to go and get Uncle Charlie, Gran?' he asked.

'Now that's a really good idea,' said Amy. 'It's the only sensible thing you've said so far. Charlie should be home from work by now. They probably knocked off from bricklaying early because it's so hot. You get Charlie and I'll put the kettle on and when Charlie gets here Mum can open the telegram.'

Danny ran out the door to get his bike.

'Charlie'll know what to do,' Amy told me. She was holding me and rubbing my back as if I had some sort of lumbago. 'He'll be here in just a minute, Mum. Isn't it a good thing that he and Phil live just around the corner in Harry's house while Harry's up in Darwin with the cops? Don't you pay any attention to that stuff about the Vichy French and *Beau Geste*. Danny's been watching too many newsreels and reading the papers and nattering with his mates at school.'

I knew Amy was talking, but my eyes were on the window, watching Danny whizz past on his bike, up the gravel to the front of the house, then round the corner on his mission to fetch Charlie. His shirt was flapping in the hot wind because of the missing buttons.

Amy kept nattering desperately. 'It's all nonsense. No one in this family is going to be hurt by this stupid little war. Anyway, I saw a news-reel at the movies and I'm sure it's the Italians in that part of the desert, not the French, so Danny's wrong about that, too. The Italians wouldn't be as ferocious as the French Foreign Legion, would they? The Pope's Italian, isn't he? So Brian will definitely be OK.'

Amy was talking very fast and very loudly and her voice was un-steady. I had the feeling that she knew what she was saying didn't make sense any more than Danny's conversation had, but that she couldn't stop herself talking.

She rambled on. 'Brian's probably all right, Mum. The telegram might just say that he's wounded, only not too badly. Maybe he's had an arm, or a finger shot off, or something he doesn't really need. Not on his bowling hand, though. Probably just a finger or two on his left hand. Not even his legs, like Jen's brother, Jack. Just something uncom-fortable but not dangerous, like his willy, or a couple of toes so he can't march through the desert now, and he's no further use to the army so he's being sent home to get better.'

I shook my head in disbelief at her stupidity, but there was no stop-ping Amy.

'Pask lost an eye in the last war, didn't he? But it didn't cause him any real problems, did it? He's still shearing sheep and running his farm up at Orroroo. Men don't have to be in one piece to get stuff done. And Charlie will be here soon. Charlie always knows what to do.'

'There's nothing anyone can do,' I yelled, as the dam broke and I burst into real sobs. I banged my fist on the table again and the envelope rose into the air and then wafted down gently and settled on the cloth as if to let me know that it wasn't going to go away.

'Brian's dead and it's all for nothing. Who cares about bloody Syria anyway? If the Germans or the Italians or those Vichy French want it, they're welcome to it. We shouldn't be worrying about them. We should be worrying about the Japs. They're on their way south to invade Aus-tralia. Those damned Vichy French gave them all the bits that France owned in Vietnam and now they want more. It was on the wireless. Mr Roosevelt was complaining about it.'

'The Japs'll never get past Singapore, Mum. It's called Fortress Sin-gapore, remember? Mr Menzies and the Poms won't let them anywhere near us. Don't cry like that, Mum. Charlie will be here soon.'

'I might as well as know the worst before he gets here.'

I took a deep breath to stop my body heaving, grabbed the envelope and tore it open. I read the words aloud.

Deeply regret to inform Stop Private Brian Ambrose Walsh 7th Ar-moured Division AIF missing in action Stop At Battle of Bardia 6.1.41 Stop Further communication follows Stop

I didn't bother to read who had sent the telegram, but it must have been someone in authority. Some officer who had sent my boy to be murdered by the French and Germans and Italians. Some officer whose job it was to sit calmly and safely behind a desk with a cup of tea beside him, writing telegrams to the mothers of boys who had been killed, and who would never be shot at by bullets made by girls who worked in munitions factories. Someone who would survive this war and go home to their family without a scratch on their body, probably wearing a row of medals on their spotless uniforms. Someone who knew how to write brief notes punctuated by the word 'Stop'.

'Stop, stop, stop,' I shrieked and buried my face in my hands. I didn't hear the back door open. I only knew Charlie was there when I felt his arms around my convulsing body. There was a sound like a banshee wailing. I looked up and saw that Danny was clutching Brian's cricket bag to his chest and howling as if his world had ended.

'Charlie, thank God you're here,' wailed Amy. 'Brian's missing in action in Syria. Mum says that means he's dead. But that can't be true, can it? Say it's not true, Charlie! And how are we going to tell Annie?'

2

8 April 1941 – Norwood

'Careful now,' I warned Amy as she tilted the whiskey bottle towards the cake mix. 'There's a...'

'I know, Mum,' she interrupted. 'There's a war on. I'm sick of hearing it. Wars are all anyone talks about. This war we've got now and how awful it was in the last war and how the Poms are suffering over in Pommyland and how we're all going to suffer here soon.'

I resisted the urge to kick the girl. Stay calm, Rose, I told myself. Brian always says Amy's spoilt. Brian always *said*, I reminded myself. Past tense. He won't be saying it any longer. I took a deep breath to stop the sobs rising. Brian's been dead for nearly three months now. How long would he have to stay in Purgatory if he's stuck there? If there is a Purgatory, if there is a God. If there is a God, why did he let Brian die?

'Mrs Williams says the war won't last much longer. She says it'll be over soon,' Amy said.

I gritted my teeth. 'That's what everyone said about the last war. Mrs Williams is wrong. No one knows what's going to happen. Probably not even Mr Menzies knows. And that dill Menzies should be here, not over in England.'

Amy nodded. 'Mr Williams says Mr Menzies is staying over there because he wants to be part of Churchill's war cabinet, because he thinks he'll get a knighthood if he does that. Mr Williams doesn't like Mr Menzies much either. He says Mr Fadden ought to be the prime minister because he's running the country while Menzies is swanning around in London. Mr Williams said Mr Fadden is doing all the work and he ought to get the credit for it.'

'Whatever,' I said, tired of the discussion. 'Let's just make the cake, shall we? It's got to be special because Joe's coming home. Only I know he'll be off back to Perth before the Holy Oil of Chrism is dry on the twins' heads.'

I beat the mixture so hard that bits of the stuff flew out of the bowl and landed on the table. I scraped it up and plonked it back with the rest and gave it another thrashing. Amy bent down so her face was between me and the dish. If any more of the mixture went flying again, she would cop it all over her face.

I lifted the wooden spoon and let the cake mix droop off it, testing to see if it was ready.

Amy grabbed my hand. 'You still haven't accepted that Joe's got a life of his own, have you, Mum? You've got to stop clinging to people. You've got to let go. And just stop brooding over Brian's death while Joe's here, at least. You've made everyone's life a misery since you got that telegram.'

I glared at her. How dare she speak to me like that? She bit her lip, but then she continued. Once Amy's made up her mind to say something, she keeps going no matter what. Michael was the same.

She must have realised she had gone too far. She patted my hand and smiled at me. I didn't smile back. Ungrateful hussy, I thought. After all I've done for her.

'I don't want to be nasty; I mean we all feel sorry for you, Mum, but we all feel rotten enough about Brian without you making it worse. So just buck up a bit and look happy for a change at least until after the confirmation. Don't spoil a happy occasion.'

Silly young flibbertigibbet, not a care in her head except which dress she was going to wear when she went to the Odeon to see the latest movie. What did she know about life and death? At her age, I was a married woman with a baby. Brian was right: she is a spoilt little minx.

The urge to thump Amy grew stronger. All the kids deserved a good kick for ignoring me. I'd had no say about what Brian did. He made up his mind and off he went. First to war, and then to heaven, if there was a heaven. Or to Purgatory for a bit. Or maybe worse. Impossible, Rose, I told myself. He's in Purgatory, for sure. But Brian was no angel, even I knew that. Maybe it's all bullshit. Maybe there's no life after death. Where's the proof? And how much letting go did Amy or God expect from me? I don't care what God says, Brian was a good boy.

'One of us has to go,' Brian had said. 'Harry can't go, because he's married with kids, plus he's a copper up in Darwin, so he's doing his duty for the country.'

'So marry Annie!' I had screamed at him. 'Have kids. Heaps of kids. See what it's like to spend your life worrying about kids. Annie loves you, she'd marry you at the drop of a hat, Pask thinks you're wonderful, you'd be classed as a farmer in a reserved occupation and you'd be doing your bit for Australia, producing wool and meat. And staying alive and having kids to provide another generation of Australians so they could be sent off to some other stupid war. Cannon fodder, that's what we're breeding.'

But of course, he didn't listen to me. And adventure called.

'You're looking all funny, Mum,' said Amy. 'Stop thinking about Brian. Just concentrate on mixing the cake.'

Oh, God, I thought. What will happen if the Japs keep coming down towards Australia? They've signed some sort of agreement with Germany and Italy, and if the Germans are sinking our ships just off our coast, things can't be too good. Harry's in Darwin. They'll get him first. What would the Japs do to Amy? Or Annie?

But Brian was still hammering away in my head, justifying why he was the one who had to go to war.

'Joe's a priest so he can't go,' Brian had added, 'and Charlie had that pleurisy, so they wouldn't take him anyway. Soldiers with crook lungs aren't much use, are they? And he's married, so he's got to stay here with Phil. One of us has to go. Annie said she'll wait for me. She's too young to get married anyway. Not even twenty yet. I've signed up, Mum. It's too late to back out now.'

'I can mix it if you don't want to do it,' said Amy. 'I watched you do it heaps of times. Why don't you sit down and have a cup of tea and let me take over?'

'Not yet,' I said. I'm not that old yet, I thought. 'We'll have a cuppa when the cake's in the oven.' But Brian was still clamouring away in my head.

'I won't be away long, Mum,' Brian had said. 'This is my chance to see the world and have a decent job for a change. With good pay. I'll be back eating your fruit cake before you know it.'

I shook my head. Come back down to earth, Rose, I told myself. You're flying higher than young Bob in his Spitfire. It must be fumes from the whiskey. Bob's the same age as Amy and he's in danger too. Twenty-three years old and could be dead at any minute, just like Brian.

Why do wars have to start when people are young? Why should the youth of every generation sacrifice the best years of their lives? I bit my lips to stop them trembling. My mouth was full of the metallic taste of blood. I swallowed hard.

'Joe hasn't had one of my cakes for two years since the Jesuits sent him to Perth,' I told Amy. 'Just take it easy with the whiskey. It's hard to get hold of it these days, you know. Charlie went to three pubs before he found this bottle. Because it comes from Scotland or Ireland and there are submarines out there sinking merchant ships.'

'Everything's hard to get hold of,' said Amy. 'Clothes, for example.'

I nodded. It was no use talking to Amy. When she wasn't at work at the munitions factory, she spent hours at the sewing machine trying to revitalise her old clothes. She was trying to look like the actresses in the latest Hollywood films. Why did she bother? These days there were so few decent boys left around here. And I didn't like of the look of the ones that were still lurking in the undergrowth.

'Rosemary and Danny are very quiet,' said Amy. 'I never trust them when they're quiet. What are they doing?"

'They've declared a temporary truce,' I said. 'They're sitting together in your dad's old chair in the front room, listening to Phil playing the piano. That sounds like the start of "Danny Boy". Charlie will start singing any minute now.'

'It won't last,' said Amy. 'They'll be at each other's throats again any minute. Rosemary always starts it, you know. Danny puts up with hell from her. He says she ought to be declared Australia's secret weapon and be sent off to fight Hitler. He says he can't wait for Mary to take her home again.'

'We all know what Rosemary's like. Just a couple more drops of whiskey,' I said. 'Steady, now. You just spilt some on the table.'

'But come you back…' sang Charlie, 'When summer's in the meadow. Or when the valley's hushed and white with snow.'

My eyes misted with tears. I sniffed hard in case Amy noticed. I always try to keep my emotions to myself. Well, most of the time. But 'Danny Boy' always has that effect on me, especially when sung by Charlie. Next, he'd be singing about flowers falling, and that makes me think of my son Brian falling in the desert in Syria. Michael used to talk about flowers falling when he talked about men dying in the Great War. He said it was an analogy. Mick knew about analogies and stuff like that. Educated, but rotten to the core.

'More flour, Mum?' asked Amy. 'The mix looks a bit runny.'

'Just a smidgeon,' I said. 'That should do it.'

I paused, certain that I had heard the front door open. I wouldn't have heard it over the music unless I had been listening hard, unless I had been expecting it. Hoping for it.

That's Joe, come back all the way from Perth for the confirmation, I thought. He'll be absolutely stuffed. Worn-out from travelling. Three, or was it four changes of train because of the different gauges of the train track just to get from Perth to Adelaide as well as that long crossing of the Nullarbor? It can't be easy climbing in and out of trains wearing a long black Jesuit cassock. Why did the Western Australians have to pinch our South Australian priests? Didn't they have enough of their own? Why in heaven's name did Joe decide to become a priest? Bloody Flaherty. Bloody Catholic Church.

And then the nerve-frazzling car ride, courtesy of Father Flaherty, from the Adelaide railway station to Norwood. Flaherty shouldn't have a licence the way he drives. Of course, it saved Joe a trolley bus ride, so we ought to be grateful Flaherty was picking him up, but as Charlie said, the clergy get a special fuel allowance so they can travel about consoling families whose sons have been killed. Joe denies it, but I still say Flaherty's to blame that Joe became a priest. That bugger must have brainwashed the kid, said God loved him. If God loved people, why did He let wars happen?

Michael would be spinning in his grave if he knew his son was wearing a skirt. Michael hated the church, especially after that business with Mary. Of course, the hatred was also because of Michael's guilty conscience, too. What he had done was enough to make you hope there was a heaven and a hell just so that Michael could be in hell. The deepest, hottest bit of hell.

If that had been Joe opening the front door, he would have come straight to the kitchen. He would have known where to find me. He hadn't come, so I must have only imagined the door had opened. But he would be here soon, I knew. He would have to arrive soon, Good Friday was on 11 April, and the twins would be confirmed on Easter Sunday. Just days away.

'And you will find the place where I am lying,' sang Charlie. 'And you will bend and tell me that you loved me, and all my grave will warmer, sweeter, be.'

Brian won't be coming to find the place where I'm lying, when I'm dead, I thought. And I'll never find the place where he's lying, either. He's out in the desert somewhere near the borders of Syria and Iraq, wherever that is. Some God forsaken bit of dirt. His body's probably mummified in the hot sand, like that dried rat I once found in Pask's woodshed up at Orroroo.

But Brian said Syria was colder than Hitler's heart. Especially at night. I'd like to get my hands on Hitler for just half an hour. And as for a grave being warm or sweet, that was a load of rubbish too. Graves are smelly, dark and cold. And lonely.

'Mum, if you keep beating that cake mix like that, you'll wear a hole in the basin. What are you so upset about?'

'Nothing,' I said. 'I'm not upset at all. Everything's fine.'

I've just been told that I've been making too much of a fuss because my son is dead and I couldn't even give him a decent funeral. Yes, everything's just fine.

Was it better to have your body mummified like an Egyptian or to go putrid and mouldy like the bodies of my brothers, Danny and Pat, whose bodies rotted in the cold mud of France? Either way, you're dead. Look how many of our soldiers died in the last war. The war to end all wars, the politicians had called it. We vote them in, and they lie to us. Truth is the first casualty in war, Michael used to say. Of course bloody Michael came back from the Great War, though; turned up like a bad penny.

But if Michael hadn't come back from the war, I wouldn't have Amy, would I? And she is my beautiful Amy, even if she is a dill. Actually, she's a total nitwit, but she's still my Amy, helping me to make this cake, standing beside me at the table, brushing her lovely auburn hair away from her face. She might not be the cleverest girl in the world, but she's certainly one of the prettiest.

How could she see to work in a munitions factory, making bombs and bullets to kill people, with her hair always falling across her eyes? Munitions. Even those enemy boys had parents who loved them and who would miss them when they died. Since I had lost Brian, I felt sorry for anyone whose sons were killed. Even the parents of the foe. Not their fault that their sons enlisted, any more than it was mine that Brian enlisted.

Despite being homicidal, Amy looked like an angel; she had done since the moment she was born.

Although, thinking back, when Amy was born, it seemed like the end of the world. Dreadful for Mary, and dreadful for me, too. Still, now I couldn't imagine life without my Amy. And Mary had forgiven me for taking her child away from her. After all, I had done it for everyone's good. You couldn't expect a child to bring up a child. Mary was a saint.

I'm no saint, though. Would Pask forgive me for what I had done, was still doing, to him? Lies to cover lies. Would I ever forgive myself? Has God forgiven my sins? Is that why He took Brian away – because of my sin over the Danny business? But Danny's birth was a miracle, a gift from God. So where was the sense of it all? Was the world mad? Was God mad? Heaven forfend, was I mad?

'I think it's mixed enough, Mum. Can we put it in the oven now?'

Amy put the paper-lined, greased cake pan on the table and looked at me, waiting for me to ladle the mix into it.

The piano and Charlie's song stopped in mid-verse. There were footsteps and loud voices, as though dozens of people were all talking at once.

I rested the spoon against the mixing bowl and smiled at Amy. 'Joe's back,' I said. 'I thought I heard the front door earlier, but he's definitely back now.'

'And Father Flaherty's with him,' she replied. 'I just heard his voice, too.'

I sighed. Wouldn't you think even Terence Flaherty would be sensitive enough to realise a family would want a bit of privacy when the prodigal son returned from exile? No, I realised, Flaherty wouldn't pass up the chance of free tea and food and, hopefully, a bit of salacious gossip that he could pass around the parish to earn himself more entertainment.

If Flaherty was here, we would have to be on our best behaviour. At least until he was out the door. A bit of restraint, a bit of self-control would prevail in the Walsh household, especially where I was concerned. I straightened my back and put a serious but serene smile on my face.

There was silence in the front room.

A head appeared at the kitchen door. Beneath the head, I saw a khaki uniform. Was it Brian come back from the dead?

Flummoxed, I looked again and saw Joe's face, smiling apprehensively. There were two shiny crosses on the lapels of his tunic.

I picked up the heavy mixing bowl and hurled it at his head.

The basin hit the doorpost with a thud and exploded. A rich spicy odour filled the kitchen. Joe ducked, but the thick fluid spattered the stiff new uniform that he wore. Amy shrieked. The rest of the cake mixture, embedded with yellow shards of china, ran slowly down the wall.

Joe grinned, shrugged and wiped sticky goo from his peaked officer's cap with his hanky. I saw that even his hanky was khaki. Bloody army issue. The army was thorough, I could see that.

'I knew you wouldn't be pleased, Mum,' he said.

'That was a wicked waste, Mum,' Amy accused, 'especially with a war on.'

I grabbed the bottle of whiskey from Amy's hands and took a long swig. I choked. When I got my breath back, I began yelling.

'Pleased? You thought I wouldn't be pleased, Joseph Thomas Walsh? Isn't it enough that you had to go and become a bloody Jesuit? Isn't it enough that your brother Brian is mouldering in an unmarked grave out in the heathen sand, and won't be marrying little Annie, and young Bob is off flying Spitfires to defend England because his mum was a bloody Pom? How do you think it makes me and Pask feel that our kids have gone off to fight in a war that isn't even our war, yet? And you're supposed to be a priest. What about "love thy neighbour" and "turn the other cheek" and all that sort of thing?'

I took another swig of whiskey for medicinal purposes because I felt a bit faint, then I thrust the bottle of whiskey back into Amy's hands and fell to my knees, scrabbling to gather chunks of china from the floor before Mary's baby, little Kathleen, came crawling out of the bedroom and cut her knees.

'And this was my mother's bowl. Look what you've made me do. Why do you want to go and get yourself killed by bloody stupid Vichy French or Arabs or Germans or Italians or whatever other wogs they've got over there? Why can't you just be patient and get yourself killed by the Japs the same as the rest of us?'

Joe slunk over to my side, one hand still clutching his now grimy officer's cap, his other hand hovering uncertainly over my head.

'I wouldn't give her absolution, Joe, if that's what you've got in mind,' warned Charlie, who stood in the doorway smirking. 'Especially with another priest present as witness.'

I looked up to see Father Flaherty gawking at the scene and Phil cringing in horror beside him. The twins jostled for position to get a better view of proceedings. Father Flaherty shook his head. I could read his expression. I knew he was unwilling to believe that such indignity could be offered a fellow priest; however, if that sort of behaviour could take place anywhere on earth, the depraved Walsh household was where it would happen.

'Quick, hide the whiskey,' I whispered urgently to Amy. 'You can't trust Flaherty around whiskey. He'll decide he needs consolation.'

She thrust the bottle into the nearest cupboard and slammed the door shut.

'Joe, Joe!' shouted Mary. She dashed into the kitchen, thrusting little Kathleen into Phil's arms as she pushed past the group in the doorway, and hastily buttoning her dress to cover her lactating breasts as she threw her arms around her brother. 'It's so wonderful to see you again, Joe,' she sobbed. 'Now we're all together again under one roof. Except for Fred and Paddy, of course. They had to stay in Mount Gambier because of the butcher shop, so they couldn't come for the confirmation. And of course,' she added, with a defiant glare at Father Flaherty, 'Fred's not a Catholic anyway, although he's agreed to the twins being confirmed.'

Fred wouldn't have come even if he had managed to find someone to mind the shop, I thought grimly. Fred thinks I'm crazy. Charlie had explained to me patiently that under the circumstances this was a perfectly reasonable opinion for Fred to hold.

'No man likes to find a cuckoo in his nest, you know, Mum.'

But it wasn't as if I had expected Fred to raise the kid. All I wanted was his name on the birth certificate. How hard is it to sign your name, after all?

Yes, I thought, we're all together under one roof except for Fred and

Paddy down at Mount Gambier, except for my dead boy Brian who will never come home again, and for my eldest son Harry, his pregnant wife Mavis and their two kiddies, Micky and Nathan, who are up in Darwin in the cyclone season with the Japs probably right on their doorstep despite what all the politicians say about Fortress Bloody Singapore, and except for Pask and Annie who're up at Orroroo. And young Bob, getting shot at by Germans in London. And, except, of course, for my late husband Michael, but I wouldn't have wanted him here anyway for all the tea in China.

3

Later the same day – Norwood

While I calculated the amount of tea that would be used to provide Father Flaherty with two or three cups of steaming stimulant, Amy put the kettle on. That priest was fond of sugar, too. Three teaspoonsful of sugar, as I recalled. And he would expect a good solid splash of milk, as well.

I wondered whether Pask's cow was still giving milk up at Orroroo. There was a drought on, so it might be hard to feed her. I hoped she hadn't had to be slaughtered. I was fond of Pask's cow.

Bloody God, when you thought about it. Not bad enough having a war but He had to send us a drought as well. Was He really on our side, as the politicians and the priests kept telling us? Maybe He was really on the enemy's side. Did Germany or Japan get droughts?

More to the immediate point, how was I going to scrounge enough ingredients to make a cake to replace the one I had thrown at Joe? I might have to borrow from Mrs Williams, and I hated doing that. Bad enough lending her stuff, although I will admit she always paid it back. Of course, I was never quite sure if she was actually in need of that cup of sugar she kept borrowing or whether it was just an excuse to get into my kitchen and stick her nose into my family's affairs.

Mary and I wet a couple of dishcloths and sponged the mess from Joe's chaplain uniform while he explained how he had wrestled with his conscience and decided that it was God's will that he accompany the army into battle to provide spiritual guidance to the men. It was his duty to God and humanity. He was needed more overseas than in Perth or Adelaide. You don't know how very much you are needed in Adelaide, I thought. But I didn't say it because I was getting enough black looks from everyone, including Flaherty, already.

Father Flaherty listened with approval, nodding from time to time. 'Joseph will be a prince of the church one day, Mrs Walsh, you'll see,' the priest assured me. 'Despite missing out on his good father's influence and of course the terrible adverse family environment he has endured over the years. A monsignor at the very least, if not an archbishop or cardinal. Dare we hope he might become the first Australian pope?'

'Popes are always Italian,' said Charlie. 'There might have been a French one once, I think. Dad mentioned him. Or maybe he was Spanish. Borgia, that was the name. Went around poisoning people.'

The priest glared at Charlie and continued his spiel. 'It's a blessing for you to have a son in the clergy, Mrs Walsh. It might even bring about your own salvation. I have high hopes of young Joseph.'

'My only hope is that he'll come back alive,' I said grimly. 'I don't particularly want my son to be a bishop or a pope, I just want him to keep breathing.'

'And with his languages, he'll go far,' Flaherty continued. 'Latin of course, and the French he learned at school, the Hebrew he did as extension studies in the seminary, and he told me just now in the car that he's studying German too.'

'Is that true, Joe?' I demanded. 'Hitler speaks German. Why on earth would you want to learn German?'

'Just for interest,' said Joe. 'It could be useful when we win the war. I enjoy learning other languages. Keeps the brain active.'

'If any foreigners want to speak to me, they can learn English,' I said. 'Waste of time speaking anything else. Ungodly lot, foreigners.'

'Perhaps young Amy might also consider life as a nun,' said Flaherty, probably inspired by my mention of God. He smiled up at Amy as she provided the second cup of tea he had demanded. 'Have you considered a vocation, my dear? A convent is a very peaceful place. A refuge from turmoil.'

Turmoil. So that's what he thinks of my home. A place of turmoil.

I glanced at the spots on Joe's uniform. Maybe this house is a bit tumultuous at times, but we're happy here. Sort of happy. And it's not boring, which I bet Flaherty's childhood home was. And as a convent would be.

Amy shuddered. I tried to imagine her in a nun's habit and couldn't. I knew she was thinking the same thing. For starters, they would cut off her hair and she would lose the Veronica Lake look she was cultivating.

'No, she hasn't considered it, and no, she won't be considering it,' I snapped. 'One vocation in the family is enough. It's one too many, in fact.'

The priest turned his attention to the twins, scrutinising them carefully. I resolved not to let him get his rotten hands on Danny in any way, shape or form. And if Flaherty was considering Rosemary for a religious career, he was making the biggest mistake of his life. Unless she took the name Sister Mary Lucifer. On the other hand, that could do the church the world of good...

'Goodness,' he said. 'I don't believe I have ever seen two such dissimilar twins in all my life. It's hard to believe that the pair of you are even brother and sister.'

I tried to stop my face from twitching, but I couldn't control it, so I turned away and picked up a biscuit. It was the last one on the plate, and I knew the cleric had been eyeing it, so there was an element of viciousness about my taking it. I was annoyed that the bugger was there at all, and furious that he had witnessed the business with the cake mix. Some things ought to be private, for goodness sake. And how dare he imply that this was not a good Catholic home? A bad influence, that's what Terence Flaherty was.

'You, Rosemary,' said Father Flaherty in an avuncular manner, 'are the very image of your dear mother at the same age. Just before she suddenly disappeared for a number of years and went down to Mount Gambier for unknown reasons.' He looked at me and then at Mary, suspicion on his face. 'I have never worked out why your dear parents sent you away like that, Mary.'

And if you think I'm going to enlighten you, you're wrong, I thought.

He looked back at my granddaughter. 'So Danny is your twin brother, is he, Rosemary dear?'

Rosemary shrugged.

The priest pursed his lips and continued to address Rosemary. 'It's a most peculiar thing, but I must say that Danny doesn't look anything like anyone in the Walsh family. Not even your grandfather, Michael, of blessed memory. Danny must resemble his father.'

'Danny's nothing like Dad,' snapped Rosemary. 'Dad's not very tall and he's a bit tubby. Just look at Danny. He's like a beanpole. And Dad's got fair hair and Danny's dark. Not even ginger like most of the Walshes. Danny doesn't look like anyone I know, either. He must be a throwback. I asked Dad, and he said maybe he's a creature from the Irish bogs.'

There was silence in the room. None of us adults could bear to meet each other's eyes. I glanced at Danny. He looked sullen, which was fair enough. I hadn't held a high opinion of Fred before, but hearing that he thought of Danny as a creature from the Irish bogs had driven him even lower in my opinion. But Mary worshipped Fred. I thought it best to change the subject.

'The twins say they have chosen their confirmation names, but neither of them want to tell us what they are yet. Perhaps now might be a good time to tell us what they are.' I looked at Rosemary expectantly.

'I'm taking the name Barbara,' said Rosemary. 'Saint Barbara's the patron saint of explosions. I like explosions.'

Why aren't I surprised, I thought. Saint Barbara is a good saint's name for a girl like you. From memory, I knew Saint Barbara and her father had a disagreement, but I couldn't recall what it was over. He probably wanted her to get married and she wanted to stay a virgin. Most female saints' stories run along those lines. They all aim to be virgins. Fixated with it, they are. I've got a feeling a bathhouse was involved in her story, which is unusual for saints. You don't often hear about their ablutions. Anyway, her dad beheaded her, so she had him struck by lightning in revenge. Which sounds both pretty far-fetched and nasty on all sides. Now that was a tumultuous home life. But if she was already dead, she must have organised the lightning from heaven with God lending a hand. In cahoots with God, of course. That was predictable. He's got a soft spot for virgins, what with His mother being one, of course.

I couldn't look St Barbara's story up, because I had burned my copy of *The Lives of the Saints* years ago, even before that business with Mary. There were some really disgusting tales in *The Lives*. St Barbara's story was pretty mild, by the general standard prevailing in the book. To tell the truth, I haven't read any religious books since I discovered James Joyce's *Ulysses* on Michael's bookshelf. It was hidden but I found it when I was dusting. That novel beat *The Lives of the Saints* for dead. And it was set in Dublin, too.

'She's not only the saint for explosions,' Joe corrected Rosemary. 'She was a martyr and she's the saint for miners and military engineers. And also for lightning. And for mathematicians, but I'm not really sure why they're included.'

So I was right about the lightning, I thought. God can be a nasty bloke at times when it suits Him. I remember Michael mentioned the Greeks had a god called Zeus. Michael said Zeus struck people down with lightning all the time. Michael said the original Ulysses was Greek, but I'm wasn't sure how it all fitted together. I didn't have Michael's education, though. I just enjoyed the fornication in Joyce's novel. I've always enjoyed a good fornicate. Everyone fornicated in *Ulysses*, from memory.

Rosemary shrugged. 'I like the name and I like explosions,' she insisted, grinning in a complacent sort of way.

I glared at her. I saw you pinch Kathleen to make her cry when you thought I wasn't looking, I felt like saying. Only I didn't say it because I didn't want to upset Mary, which was why I had kept quiet at the time. And I caught you pulling the cat's tail, too. You got yourself scratched and you didn't get any sympathy from me although you squawked louder than the cat did. The quicker this confirmation is over and done with and you are packed off on the train to Mount Gambier again, the better. Fred is welcome to you. I'll miss Mary and little Kathleen, but I won't miss you, twin or no twin.

'I think explosions are terrific,' the girl said defiantly.

'What sort of explosions?' asked Charlie dubiously.

'Bombs,' said Rosemary with relish. 'Big bombs. I like those newsreels at the movies with the planes dropping bombs. Bang! Crash!' Rosemary waved her arms about to indicate the direction and force of the explosions.

Flaherty, who was sitting close to her, ducked and put his hand over his teacup to protect it. Even so, the tea sloshed into the saucer and I hoped it wouldn't end up on the Axminster carpet square.

'And the anti-aircraft guns shooting at the planes. Whoom! Boom! And the dogfights between the planes. Whizz! Whack!' She clapped her hands to illustrate how the planes collided in mid-air.

I felt sick. Pask's son, Bob, was a pilot trying to save London from the Germans. The death rate for fighter pilots was high. I wanted to slap Rosemary, but I was so disgusted that I didn't have the strength to raise my hand. It was Mary's job to sort this kid out. And sorting out was what the rotten little sod needed.

'When explosions happen, people die,' I managed to say. 'Lots of people are dying in London because of bombs. Last month Buckingham Palace got bombed. Princess Margaret could have been killed. Don't you care about people dying?'

'Princess Margaret's an Anglican,' said Rosemary, with contempt. 'So's the king and the queen and Princess Elizabeth. Most people in London are Protestants. So I don't really care about any of them.'

'Your father is a Methodist,' gasped Mary. 'I'm ashamed of you, Rosemary.'

'That's not a nice attitude, Rosemary,' said Joe sternly. 'I would like you to consider what you have just said. Examine your conscience.'

'Yes, maybe you ought to go and work in the munitions factory with your Auntie Amy,' I suggested. 'I worry day and night that she might get blown up in an explosion. Munitions factories are dangerous places.'

'I just like seeing the explosions,' Rosemary protested. 'I bet everyone else does too. They just don't want to admit it. It's really thrilling when there's that big flash against the dark sky and there's a loud bang and stuff flies everywhere.'

'Your dad and I told you to stop talking like that, Rosemary,' snapped Mary. 'It's disgusting. Everyone is fed up with the way you carry on. It's not ladylike at all. And it's embarrassing, too. Especially when we're out in public, like the other night at the movies. That was awful.'

'What did she do?' asked Phil, whose face had gone white.

I remembered that her brothers were away with the navy and no one knew exactly where they were. The censorship was getting worse. There were posters everywhere saying 'Loose lips sink ships'. Someone ought to sew up Rosemary's lips. She must have the loosest lips in Australia.

'She started cheering when the newsreel came on showing the latest war news, which was all about the Blitz. Fred tried to shut her up, but she made such a noise that we were asked to leave before the main movie came on. And I really wanted to see that film, too.'

'What film was it?' Amy asked.

'That latest Veronica Lake movie, *I Wanted Wings*.'

'What a shame. That was a terrific picture,' said Amy. 'I love Veronica Lake's hair. I'm trying to get mine to hang over one eye the way hers does, but it won't stay in place.'

'You've almost got it right,' said Mary, looking closely at Amy's hair. 'Perhaps if you wet it and pin it up at night with bobby pins, it might stay in place.'

'I've been doing that. It looks really good when I first get up in the morning, but then it sort of flops down.'

'Have you tried using curling tongs?' asked Phil. 'Only you have to be careful because it's easy to singe your hair if the tongs are too hot.

That happened to my sister Dora and she actually lost a whole lock of hair.'

'Mum won't let me heat the tongs on the stove because she says it's a waste of gas.'

'And you, Danny, what patron saint have you chosen for your confirmation?' asked Joe, possibly because he thought, as a man of the cloth, he ought to appear interested in his nephew's religious ideas, or perhaps he wanted to divert attention away from the feminine conversation centred on frivolities and films. He might also have wished to prevent further interventions from Rosemary, whom he obviously had judged to be a difficult sort of girl likely to cause further cataclysmic social explosions.

'I'm taking the name of St Ignatius of Loyola,' said Danny. 'One,' (he held a finger up to enumerate his ideas) 'because there's a war on and Ignatius was a soldier, and two,' (another finger was elevated) 'because he started up the Jesuits and you're a Jesuit, aren't you, Uncle Joe? So it keeps it in the family.'

'That's great, Danny, that's a very well-reasoned argument,' said Joe. 'Worthy of a Jesuit. That's the sort of thinking we were encouraged to do at the seminary.'

Father Flaherty nodded his agreement.

Oh no, I thought. You're not going to persuade my Danny that he's got a vocation. Perhaps I ought to take Danny up to Orroroo again to get him away from religious influence. Of course, there was that Father Travers up there, but he was over at Pekina, in what people called Vatican Valley, not actually at Orroroo, and anyway, Father Travers was quite a civilised priest in comparison to Flaherty.

I glanced at Danny, who was gazing at Joe with the same sort of hero worship that he had bestowed on Brian. Yes, a trip to Orroroo was definitely on the agenda. Danny never needed persuasion to go and visit his Uncle Pask, and Pask would be overjoyed to see us.

'Only, what am I supposed to call you?' asked Danny. 'Do I call you Uncle Joe or do I call you Father Joe?'

'Call him Uncle Joe,' I said quickly. We've got enough confusion in this family already with who was whose father and who was whose mother without Danny calling Joe Father, I thought. The boy thought he was Joe's nephew, but was he in fact Joe's brother? Well, half-brother, perhaps. Yes, that was more like it. And Mary, of course she was Amy's mother, but she was also Amy's sister. So Danny was actually Mary's brother and also probably her nephew, I think. What was written on birth certificates wasn't always right. People's reputations matter more than keeping bureaucratic documents accurate.

Although officially Amy was my daughter and she called me Mum and believed that Michael was her father, it wasn't actually so. He was her father, of course, but because of the unspeakable sin he had committed all those years ago, he was also her grandfather. Incest is about as evil a sin that anyone could commit. I still imagined Michael's soul writhing in Hell whenever I looked into the flames of a wood fire.

It was far worse than anything you would find in *The Lives of the Saints*, when you thought about it. My head hurt just thinking about it. I had tried, over the years, to believe that it had been Michael's experiences in the Great War that had made him do what he had done, but I had never succeeded in forgiving his behaviour towards our daughter, and I never would succeed.

War doesn't just kill people. The residue, the scars of war, linger for generations after the initial slaughter.

Perhaps Mary's husband, Fred, was right – there was something slightly eccentric about this family. It would be nice if we could get back to normal. Forget the past and live for the future. That is, if any of us had a future, the way the world was going. And the Japs would come south. Manchuria wouldn't satisfy their hunger for conquest. Mr Williams told me that and I knew he was right.

'I'd like another cup of tea, Amy,' I said. 'And then we'd better go back into the kitchen, find another mixing bowl and start making another fruit cake for the confirmation. I think I might be able to scrape together enough stuff to do it if we go through the cupboards with a fine-toothed comb.'

But, as the children's nursery rhyme says, when we got there, the cupboard was bare. Flaherty departed to spread salacious gossip to his parishioners soon after, so we sat with another cup of tea and enjoyed Joe's company in peace before I went next door to do some scrounging.

4

1 May 1941
Rose Walsh – Norwood

'I won't miss Rosemary at all,' Danny had said when we farewelled Mary and her family at the railway station as they left for their home in Mount Gambier. 'I mean I'll miss Mum, I always do, and I'll miss my little sister Kathleen, but I won't miss Rosemary.'

I knew what he meant. None of us would miss Rosemary. But it was hard to say goodbye to Mary and little Kathleen. It would be a long time before we saw them again. Christmas probably. At least we had had Easter and Anzac Day together. Mary and I would both write letters, but a letter isn't the same as a cuddle.

I hoped that Kathleen wouldn't be too influenced by her sister as she grew up. I had almost suggested to Mary that she leave the baby with me for safe keeping. But I didn't dare. There had been too many children stolen in the past, inside this family and outside it. And to be frank, at fifty-nine I didn't think I could put up with another kid in the house permanently. There's a good reason why God sent the Change to us women, and nappies and babies crying at night is it.

Not long after Mary's departure, and with my eyes still shedding more tears than I knew they could hold, Joe, with a carefully packed and sealed fruit cake in his kitbag, went off on his crusade to save the souls of the AIF. I had had to borrow from Mrs Williams's pantry for that cake too, because my larder was right down to the dregs now. Any cockroaches that went looking in there for sustenance would have their bellies rumbling.

From what we read in the papers, food was getting short in England now, and all sorts of things were rationed. I hoped Bob wasn't hungry. Bob's always had a good appetite. He loves my fruit cake, too. Of course, full-on rationing could never happen here. Not in Australia. Although it was getting harder to get some things, because lots of things were being used for the war effort. And we were exporting food to Britain, too.

Would Joe be sent to Europe or to the Middle East? I was still mourning my Brian, and I was terrified that I might lose another of my boys. But it was out of my hands. If only this war would end soon, before Joe or Bob died on the altar of war.

I told Joe that the cake was for his personal use, but I knew it would be distributed right after the sacrificial host was handed out, to the first batch of needy men Joe said mass for. I was pretty sure there would be a resurgence of Catholicism in the troops when they sniffed that cake. It might even bring about a few miraculous conversions from Protestantism. Up yours, Henry VIII and Martin Luther, I mused.

It was after Joe left that I decided to reread the one letter that Brian had sent me from the desert. I waited until Amy was at work and Danny was at school so I wouldn't be accused of moping and upsetting them with my tears.

I sat on the bench outside the back door at my home in Norwood, the bench where I had foolishly spent hours weeping after Michael's death back in 1928. Now it was Brian's death I was trying to come to terms with. And would I be mourning Bob soon? And Joe? No parent should live longer than their child. It was unjust. But the world is unjust.

I opened the chocolate box with the pretty picture on the lid of a blue lake surrounded by trees, where I kept my most important papers. Michael's death certificate was in there, along with our marriage lines and all the birth and baptismal papers. And some letters. It was a pretty big box, for one that had once held chocolates. I really couldn't remember what chocolate tasted like. It was hard to get hold of during the Depression and I'd lost the taste for it afterwards. I sniffed the box, but it smelled more of old paper than of anything else.

The lake could have been the Blue Lake at Mount Gambier, except it was the wrong shape and was surrounded by tall snow-capped mountains. I knew what the Blue Lake looked like because I had spent six months down at Mount Gambier when Danny and Rosemary had been born. This lake looked more European than the Blue Lake and the trees were covered with red autumn leaves that were about to fall like the flowers Charlie sang about in 'Danny Boy'. The sky in the picture was a softer, more civilised blue than an Australian sky, with fluffy little white clouds floating peacefully in it.

There were white sheep in the meadow beside the water. Not brown, dusty sheep standing in desiccated fields like Pask's sheep up at Orroroo, but fat, pristine, gleaming animals raised on lush pastures. I didn't know where the lake was situated, but it had to be Europe. Perhaps Bob or Joe might see places like that, if they lived long enough. All Brian had seen was desert.

But if European skies were more civilised than Australian ones, why was Europe's soil so steeped in blood? Why did they keep having wars over there whilst we didn't have them here?

Unless you counted those half-forgotten, long-ago battles I had heard of between the white settlers and the Aborigines. Wars that were only whispered about in closed rooms. Pretty one-sided massacres, most of them. Spears and boomerangs couldn't have been much use against guns and smallpox infected blankets. I thought I could understand how the Aborigines must have felt when we whites invaded them. Because wasn't that just how we felt now that we were likely to be invaded too? Somehow that didn't seem to have occurred to anyone else. I wondered why. Wasn't there a poem by Banjo Paterson that said something about blood staining the wattle? It might be about to happen.

I picked up Brian's letter, which was the one laid carefully on top of a small pile that included the telegram announcing he was missing in action. Missing in action, I repeated to myself. That was a lie, but wasn't truth the first casualty in war? The telegram should have said he was dead, but of course that wasn't how these things were worded. The letter from his commanding officer was in the box, too. It said Brian had died gallantly, whatever that meant, and that a great victory had been won at Bardia with lots of Italians killed and captured and the loss of only a few Australians. Including, of course, Brian. No mention of the French; they seemed to have been blown away by the desert wind. Evaporated like a mirage.

Brian would be awarded a medal posthumously, the officer's letter said. It would be sent to me soon. Bullshit, I thought. You can stick your medal where the sun doesn't shine. I didn't want a medal, I wanted my Brian.

Even though it sounded traitorous, I would have preferred that the other side, whether they were Vichy French or Italians or whatever, had won and Brian had become a prisoner of war. It might have been uncomfortable or even humiliating for him, and he would have had to eat snails or macaroni, but at least he would still be breathing.

I put the officer's letter down and picked up Brian's letter.

The paper Brian's letter was written on was flimsy and the writing was already fading, although surely it hadn't been all that long since my son died. Was it because of the heat in the desert that the ink was faint or was it army issue ink and they were trying to save money by giving the troops cheaper stuff? The officer's letter was written in blacker ink on better quality paper. And it wasn't censored, either.

When I looked carefully, I could see a few grains of sand stuck to Brian's writing. There must have been a sandstorm blowing when Brian wrote it. I was careful not to touch the sand, because it might fall off, and it was the only physical contact I would ever have with the place where my son was buried. The words from 'Danny Boy' came back again and a shiver ran down my back. Someone walking over my grave, Michael would have said.

Of course, there were black marks all over the page where the censor had cut out any reference to where the letter was actually posted from, so that if the letter had fallen into enemy hands, be they Vichy French or German or Italian, there would be no danger of attack. But the troops' position would have changed by the time the mail had been dispatched, wouldn't it? And could the enemy read English? And Brian's handwriting was hard enough even for me to read, let alone some foreigner who wasn't his mother. He'd always been in trouble at school for his handwriting. More insanity. Official insanity is the worst kind.

There was enough of Brian's writing left on the thin paper to tell me that at first it was stiflingly hot when they first landed at Port Said. 'Hotter than it ever got at our place in Norwood, Mum, hotter than Orroroo, and even hotter than it was when Charlie and Joe and me went up the river that time in the Depression picking plums because that was the only place there was work.'

They had flimsy tents in the Middle Eastern desert, Brian wrote, and their uniforms were 'OK in the daytime, but it gets bloody cold here at night, and in fact it's getting cold during the day now too, so we put on every stitch of clothing we've got with us, and the blankets...'

The rest of that sentence was blacked out. Maybe the censor didn't like criticism of the quartermaster's supplies. Maybe the quartermaster was the person doing the censoring. References to the food, I noticed, were also blacked out. Brian had always been fond of his food. It was obvious he hadn't approved of his rations

'I lobbed a grenade into a nest of Vichy machine guns,' Brian wrote. 'Charlie would have been proud of me. It's nice to know that I haven't lost my touch. Us lads had a game of cricket the other day using a petrol tin for a wicket. The pitch wasn't too good because it's all just sand here, but I made a century. Tell Danny that, Mum. There was a bloody great explosion when I got that grenade in with those French bastards. Must have knocked them for six. Apparently, the Frogs, even Charles De Gaulle's crowd, don't play cricket, so they wouldn't have seen it coming. Biggest bang I've ever heard. It must have set off their ammo.'

Maybe that's where Rosemary gets it from, I thought. The interest in explosions.

'We used to play cricket up the river, too,' Brian went on. 'Mainly Charlie and me. When we weren't scrapping over crap. Seems silly now, the stuff we argued over. Joe used to sit around a lot, just thinking. I reckon that's when he started going religious. Not that he's all that religious, for a priest. He's a good bloke, our Joe. I miss you all one hell of a lot, Mum. I miss your fruit cake, too. If I catch it in the next attack which could be....'

I think the word that was blacked out might have been 'soon', because it was a fairly short bit of black ink, but even though I held the paper up to the sun and looked at the back of the page, Brian's writing was obscured by the censor. After the interruption I read, 'It was me that broke Mrs Williams's window with the cricket ball.'

He didn't have to confess that to me. I knew it. We all knew it. The whole family denied it. We said we were all down at the Odeon watching a Charlie Chaplin film at the time. A matinee. And Michael was away on union business so Brian didn't get a walloping for it.

There was more black ink, then the words 'Guilty conscience. Ask Joe to put in a word or two for me upstairs.'

That was all there was on the page, apart from 'Cheerio, give my love to all at home, keep smiling, your son Brian.'

I tried to smile but couldn't.

Folded carefully and sitting in the chocolate box under Brian's letter was that awful telegram from the War Office that had announced that my son was 'missing, believed dead'. I believed he was dead although his grave was still missing. Probably my boy didn't even have an actual grave. I was sure there had been another of those explosions both Brian and Rosemary enjoyed, and Brian's body had been rent apart and cast to the desert winds.

It didn't bear thinking about.

There was another letter addressed to me. It was from Brian's friend, Andy Gilbert. He said that he and Brian had agreed that whoever 'bought it' first would write to the other bloke's mum and fill in the details. He said that it was a real pity that Brian died when he did, because when the troops finally got into the port town of Bardia they found a whole lot of food and plonk that the Ities had stashed there, and the troops had enjoyed a real celebration. Got on the sauce, Andy said, and painted the town red.

One of the blokes found some actual paint in a shed, and they altered the names on the street signs. Via (which meant road in Itie) Mussolini was changed to Via Australia, that sort of thing. Andy wanted to call one of the streets Orroroo Road, because Brian was always going on about how he used to go to some farm at Orroroo on holidays and there was a girl up there that he knew Brian was real sweet on. Andy thought it would be nice touch, and something Brian would have done if he could, but as Andy didn't know the proper spelling of the name of that town, and he didn't want to look a dill in front of the other blokes, he didn't do it.

One of the chaps got hold of an Itie general's uniform and a white horse and rode around waving a sword. The Pommie officers went crook but our officers thought it was funny. It was one hell of a party and our Aussie officers just let the blokes celebrate. Brian would have really enjoyed himself if he'd lived that long, Andy said. Andy was real sorry Brian had missed the fun.

It was a strange sort of letter, but I know the chap meant well. I wondered if Andy had another mate now who would write to his mum if necessary. I hoped it wouldn't be necessary.

I reread the telegram but it didn't make Brian's death any more real to me. I put the telegram back in the box and, as I did so, I saw a pile of letters from Charlie, the envelopes postmarked from the Riverland (Mildura and Renmark) where he, Brian and Joe had spent months picking fruit when they lost their jobs back in 1929. Charlie was a prolific writer of letters. He had always kept me up to steam about the family in Norwood, back in the days when I had gone up to Orroroo to work soon after Michael's death.

During the Depression, the boys picked plums and oranges. Before 1929, they had apprenticeships, but there wasn't much work after the Depression hit. Brian, Joe and Charlie went fruit picking because they couldn't stand the idea of going on the 'Susso'. They had pride in themselves, my sons.

I still had some of Michael's money stashed away when the Depression started, because I have never trusted banks, but the kids told me to keep it 'for a rainy day'. That was a joke. There was a terrible drought during the Depression. It was lucky that there was enough water in the Murray to keep the fruit growing. Not that the fruit was worth much because people couldn't afford to buy it.

Pask's wool had sold for about seven shillings and sixpence a bushel before prices dropped but had only been worth ninepence when things went bad. Of course, the drought made things even worse. Pask had to slaughter sheep because there was no feed for them and the carcasses were worth nothing. It was a hot and hungry time for Australia. Lots of farmers lost their properties during the Depression, but somehow Pask had managed to hold on.

Funny how there was a drought back during the Depression and now we've got one when the war is starting. But isn't there a poem that talks about Australia being a 'land of droughts and flooding rains'. Nothing changes, really.

I was down at Mount Gambier with Mary for quite a few months during that time. I felt guilty I wasn't at Orroroo to help Pask because I knew he was struggling. I didn't have the courage to tell Pask why I had to stay there or what had happened down at the Mount. I will admit I felt ashamed about the situation I had found myself in, but I couldn't bear to add to his burden either. All these years later, I still can't tell him. There are lies of commission, and lies of omission, as the Church says.

I reread Charlie's letters from the Riverland. They were cheery, but I wondered what it was really like up there. I wondered, too, how much truth there is in letters sent home to mothers by absent sons, back then when he and the other boys were away working or now that Charlie and Joe are still writing from overseas.

I remember Michael quoting Shakespeare and saying, 'What a tangled web we weave when first we practice to deceive.' Deceit, of course, should have been Michael's second name, but we are all guilty to some extent. If there are lies in Charlie's letters to me, I am sure they were told with the very best of intentions.

5

January 1930
Charlie, Brian and Joe Walsh – near Renmark

'Jeeze, it's hot,' said Brian. 'I reckon it couldn't get hotter if it bloody tried. I reckon if we had a thermometer, it would burst. Is the water in that bag that's hanging on the tree cool, do you think?'

'Dunno,' said Charlie. 'I'm too hot to walk over to the tree to find out. It's even hotter here by the campfire, stirring this pot so you two won't go hungry tonight, so you can just stop whingeing, you silly bugger. All you do is bloody moan. The plum trees are too tall, the plums are too small, the bunnies are too old and too tough.'

'Charlie, this morning you were complaining about the lack of beer when it was so bloody early that the pubs wouldn't have been open even if we had money to buy it. Joe, you're nearest to the water bag. Could you see if it's drinkable?'

Joe rose wearily and lifted the canvas bag from its hook. He poured a little into his hand and tasted it. 'It's cooler than it was when we hung it up there this morning. Better than the water in our canteens, anyway. Brian, if you're hot, why don't you do like I did, and jump in the river for a bit? You'd feel a bit less sweaty and you'd smell better. If you leave your clothes on when you do it, you'd wash them as well as yourself.'

'Are you saying I stink, Joe?'

'That's what he's saying, Brian, only he's too well-mannered to put it like that,' said Charlie.

'Well, I've got news for you, Joe. Before you jumped in the water, you ponged of sweat and now you stink of river mud as well as sweat.

You can't have a decent wash without soap and we've run out of soap. And we can't afford to buy more.'

'At least my sweat's been watered down a bit,' answered Joe wearily. 'Sweat attracts flies and mossies, you know that. You'll be the one who gets bitten the most tonight if you don't have a swim. Charlie, you ought to have a wash, too. Mum wouldn't be too happy if she could see the way you chaps look and smell.'

'I already did. I had a dip when we got back from the orchard.'

'There's snakes in that river,' Brian said, 'only I suppose they don't bite you, Joe, because Jesus protects you.'

'That's about it, mate. Cleanliness is next to godliness.'

'Shut up, Joe. What's for tea, Charlie?' Brian asked. 'And don't say it's rabbit again and plums for dessert because I reckon I'll spew if you say that. Blimey, where's Mum when you need her? I keep thinking of her mutton stew and her fruit cake and even though my gut feels like it's shrivelled up to nothing, it still churns with longing at the memory of her cooking.'

'I've cooked up something special for you blokes tonight,' said Charlie proudly. 'Something real exotic and European. You wouldn't get better in a French restaurant. Dad probably ate stuff just like it when he was in Paris in 1918.'

'What is it?' demanded Brian eagerly.

'I've combined the bunny we snared this morning and some of the plums we picked today, and I've made a plum and rabbit stew.'

'Joe, you'd better start praying for Charlie, because I'm going to kill him.' Brian said, half lifting himself on one arm, then collapsing down again. 'As soon as I get the energy, I'm going to dong him on the head with his bloody saucepan, and while he's still seeing stars, I'll drown him in the river.'

'Forgive him, Brian. He knows not what he does. He's bloody bonkers. He can't help it. The heat's getting at him,' said Joe.

'Bloody hell. Joe's really found Jesus now. Quoting the Bible. He'll be having visions next,' said Brian.

'Or hallucinations. It's not just the heat, it's the work, and the fact that all we're eating is bunnies and plums. It's some sort of malnutrition,' Charlie agreed.

'It's the lack of cold beer. There's probably a lot of vitamins in beer. I don't ever want to see a rabbit or a plum again as long as I live,' groaned Brian.

'The plums'll be over soon,' said Joe. 'And then we'll start on the oranges. Not the navels, we've done them. It'll be the valencias next. Thank God for small mercies. You fill the bag quicker with oranges. And they don't leak juice all over your clothes.'

'But they're heavier. And I just know Charlie's going to cook rabbit in orange juice. I reckon I'm going to spew even before I eat tonight's concoction. It's a fate worse than death, as Amy would say.' Brian grabbed at his throat and pretended to vomit.

'We're earning a few quid, sending dough back to Mum and we're eating even if you don't like the grub. That's more than a lot of blokes are doing while this Depression and the bloody drought are on. The rabbit doesn't smell all that bad, really.'

His brothers sighed. Charlie was right. Maybe things would get better soon.

'Whose turn is it to write to Mum?' Charlie asked. 'She'll be expecting to hear from us soon.'

'It's your turn,' chorused his brothers.

'I wrote last time,' said Charlie. 'And the time before that as well.'

'Yair, but your letters are better than ours,' said Brian. 'I can never find anything to say, and Joe's letters sound as if he's swallowed a dictionary and it's stuck up his bum giving him constipation. You lie better than we do, too. You make it sound like we're having a bloody picnic up here.'

'I thought we were,' grinned Charlie.

Brian threw a plum in Charlie's direction. It lobbed into the open saucepan and sank to the bottom.

'Losing your touch, Brian?' asked Joe. 'We'd better set up the wicket and have a few hits after tea.'

'Wasn't really trying,' said Brian. 'Too bloody hot and tired. And I didn't want to upset the cook. How much longer before you serve that slop up, Charlie?'

'Come and get it,' said Charlie. 'And if you don't like it, bad luck, because whatever is left over gets eaten for breakfast.'

Memories, thought Charlie much later as he trudged along a track in a distant place. We didn't know it then, but those days up the Murray were some of the best days of our lives. We boys were together, Brian was alive and although there was hardship, we had no idea what fate and life were about to throw at us. Probably just as well, too.

6

2 July 1941
Rose Walsh – Norwood

'Rose, is that you? I've got to talk to you, love. It's real urgent.'

It was unusual for Pask to ring in the middle of the day. Daylight hours were usually spent chasing sheep. The evening was when he phoned, when it was too dark to be doing anything more urgent. The line was crackling but even through the background noise his voice sounded distraught.

'Pask, what's wrong? Have you had a telegram about Bob?'

'Telegram? What telegram? Rose, have you had a telegram about Bob?'

'No, Pask, they wouldn't send the telegram to me. He's your son, remember? I thought you sounded upset, and I wondered if you'd had bad news about the kid.'

Pask sighed loudly. 'No, it's not Bob that I'm worried about. Well, of course I am worried about Bob. In fact, I'm more worried about Bob than about anything in the world, to tell the truth. But right now it's Annie that's the problem. I can't say too much on the phone because it's a party line and you know how everyone listens in and then rumours fly all over the district.'

'What's wrong with Annie? She's not sick, is she? You know I always worry about her since she had the diphtheria that time. But she looked fine when I saw her last time I was up there. That was just before Christmas, wasn't it? Of course, it was. That was just before Brian was killed.'

'She's strong as a horse. Well, on the outside, anyway. I don't know if she'll ever get over losing Brian. She doesn't say much, but I reckon she's brooding about him all the time. Speaking of horses, I'm using the old horse and trap again now most of the time because petrol's rationed. I'm not getting one of them charcoal burners for the ute the government's been pushing. Tim O'Halloran put one on his Ford, and it stinks and makes an awful mess. The car's covered with sooty muck. Anastasia hates it. And charcoal's not that cheap, anyway. I reckon Australia's going to the pack, Rose. Bloody war.'

'It's not as bad as England,' I said. '*The Advertiser* says the rationing's terrible over there. I hope the Pommy air force is feeding Bob enough. And the blackout must be awful. Good thing we haven't got that here.'

'Yeah. I have to talk to you, Rose.'

'In a minute, Pask. I just wanted to tell you something. I still don't know where Joe is. Why hasn't he written more letters? I'm really worried.'

'At least you've got Amy. And you've got Danny.'

'Amy's fed up because all you can get now is grey or khaki wool and she wants to knit herself a cardigan. I don't know why she wants a new cardigan when the one she had last year is still perfectly good, but you know what she's like when she gets something in her head.'

I knew I was talking nonsense, but I hadn't spoken to Pask for so long my mouth was running ahead of me. I couldn't stop if I tried. I'd been Pask's housekeeper when his kids were small, and although there were no formal bonds between us, I often felt that we were an old married couple even though we hadn't tied the knot formally. We probably got along better than most married couples, come to think about it. And the fornication was still good when it happened. And there was Danny, too. He was an informal bond if ever there was one.

'So we're having to unravel an old pink one so she can make a jumper like one some film star she saw in a magazine was wearing. Danny's been roped in to hold his arms out so we can wind the wool around them to get the crinkles out.'

He interrupted me. 'Rose, I need you to come up here and talk some sense into Annie. She won't listen to me. She says she wants to go down to Adelaide, and if she goes away, I'll be all on my own, and to tell you the truth, Rose, I've been feeling pretty crook these last couple of months. Me legs and me shoulders are playing up bad. And me chest, too. Rheumatics, I s'pose. Or just old age. Or loneliness. Can you come back to Orroroo? Please, Rose. And could you bring the boy with you? I could use a bit of a hand around the place.'

'Danny talks about nothing else but coming back. Well, when he's not talking about Uncle Joe going off as a chaplain to the troops. We're not sure where Joe is, but he wrote that one letter and said he was in Port Said. He saw some big Aussie monument to the Anzacs over there, with horses rearing up.'

I sighed. Brian had landed at Port Said too, and seen that same monument before he had gone to that Bardia place where he got killed. Joe was following in his brother's footsteps. But not to Bardia, and not to the gates of Heaven, I hoped. I prayed.

I banged my fist against the wall, next to the wooden hanger where the phone hung. Where was Joe right now? A mother had a right to know where her sons were. Bloody army. Bloody war. Bloody politicians.

'Are you still there, Rose?' Pask asked. 'I heard a thud and then the line went sort of dead for a moment.'

A lot like my heart feels, I thought. I'd better try to sound cheery. Pask obviously needed cheering up.

'If I come back, Danny'll tag along even if he has to hide in my suitcase. Although he's getting a bit too bit to fit in a case now. He's really shot up lately.'

And I wanted to say, and he looks just like his dad and his big brother, but I couldn't bring myself to say it.

'He's always coming out with "Uncle Pask would be crutching now, or Uncle Pask would be shearing." I think he knows the sheep calendar off by heart, and it's got lambing, crutching, shearing on it instead of May, June and July.'

'Well, it's July now, love. We'll be lambing in spring. But I'll find him something to do before that gets going. I was thinking I'd teach him to drive the ute. I've been saving up my petrol ration so there'd be a bit of petrol put by. He's almost fourteen now, isn't he? Will be in August, anyway. Bob was driving at that age. Don't you remember how he used to tear around the paddocks like a madman?'

Yes, I thought, I do remember. And I remember how my heart nearly jumped out of my chest watching him, praying that he wouldn't hit a tree and kill himself. And now you're planning to let Danny do the same as Bob did. But boys will be boys.

And now Bob's whizzing around the night skies over England, chasing Germans in his aeroplane. That kid always swore he would fly a plane. He built little wooden model planes and hung them all over his room with fishing line. I was forever dusting them. It's dusty at Orroroo when it's windy, and it's always windy at Orroroo

I'll never forget how he went off to Port Pirie for the air force training course flying those Tiger Moths. I told him not to fly too high or too fast and he laughed and said when you got into a dogfight, the blokes who didn't fly high and fast got killed quicker than the other blokes did.

What if Bob gets killed? I bit my lip. Even one of our boys lost was one too many. And Brian was dead. My Brian was dead.

'Will you come, Rose? Will you come and talk to Annie?'

'I wasn't any good at talking Bob out of joining the RAAF, Pask. What makes you think I'll be any use with Annie? What does she want to do, anyway?'

'Well, I might as well come out with it, party line or not. I s'pose the whole district'll know soon enough. She's got it into her head that she wants to be a nurse. Wants to go and put the pieces back to together of all those lads who're getting themselves shot up. I reckon it's because of Brian getting killed. I reckon she feels guilty about being alive when he's dead. She says she can't stand being up here in the bush any longer. She wants to see the world. Wants to do her bit. Save Australia.'

Pask stopped talking. I heard him drawing a very deep breath. It took him a few minutes to get going again, and I kept quiet because I didn't want to stop him saying what he needed to get off his chest. And to tell the truth, I was flabbergasted. My little Annie, a nurse.

'She says she has to do something to make this war end before anyone else dies. She says if she'd been there she could have stopped him dying. Only she couldn't have done, not if he was blown to bits. And she's only nineteen, Rose, still just a kiddie. They wouldn't let her join up, would they? They wouldn't send her off to the war, would they?'

'Our little Annie, a nurse. Like Florence Nightingale in the Crimea,' I mused. It was a horrible idea. 'Good God, no, Pask. I've been worried about her ever since we lost Brian. I did wonder at one stage whether Amy might want to go nursing or something like that too, but she seems happy working at that munitions factory. Well, she's happier now it's a bit cooler.'

'The kids all want to be doing something for the war effort, I s'pose,' said Pask. 'But to tell the truth, I never thought of Amy being a nurse. Or either of the girls leaving home. Except to get married. And not yet. Not for years and years. I can't see Amy being a nurse.'

'No, Amy's really too selfish for that,' I agreed. 'And squeamish too. The munitions factory's more her cup of tea. I don't like her working there either, to be honest. There've been accidents. There was an explosion last week and some girl got hurt. But Annie going nursing would be awful. The army could send her anywhere. We can't let Annie do it.'

'That's what I'm worried about,' said Pask. 'I keep thinking about Bob over there in the Blitz and you hear stories about how many pilots get shot down. I don't want to lose him and I don't want to lose Annie. I still can't believe Brian won't be coming back. I really thought that war I fought in would solve all the world's problems, but it didn't work, did it?'

'I know, Pask, that's what I keep thinking. We all made those sacrifices in 1914 because we thought the Great War was going to fix everything, but now there's a whole new set of problems and they seem even worse ones than last time.'

I heard what sounded like a muffled sob at the other end of the line and I decided to try to change the subject a bit. 'All Amy's friends are doing something for the war effort, so I suppose Annie's thinking the same way. Maybe if she comes down and stays with Amy and works in the munitions factory, that might be enough for her. Then I could come up and stay with you for a bit. I'm knitting socks for the troops. Khaki wool of course.'

'Yeah, they'll be needing socks.' There was a sort of gulp at the other end, and then Pask went on. 'Never get enough socks in a war. So will you come back to Orroroo, Rose?'

Of course, I would. I owed it to Pask for the wrong I had done him, denying him his son. Not quite stealing the child the way Michael and I had taken Amy from my daughter Mary, but not far from it, either. I would go back to Orroroo and I would take Danny with me. Charlie and Phil would keep an eye on Amy, and Amy was an adult now, anyway. And Annie could come down and stay here with Amy. Annie was level-headed, not giddy like Amy. Chalk and cheese, really, but they got on well together.

I went and packed my bag and one for Danny too. He was almost fourteen now, old enough to leave school. Pask had told me there would be plenty of room for him at the Orroroo school if he wanted to go there, because enrolments had dropped as men enlisted and their wives moved away to stay with their families in Adelaide for the duration of the war. But Danny said he'd had enough of school and there was more to life than learning crap he intended to forget as soon as he got the chance.

I agreed. Danny would learn more useful skills from Pask than any school could teach him. Farming was a reserved occupation, wasn't it? Danny would become a farmer and wouldn't go to war. When Bob came back, he and Danny would help Pask out and maybe one day I would have the courage to tell the truth about the kid. And the war might end soon, although I didn't believe it would. But from what I had just heard, Pask needed me at Orroroo now.

7

17 July 1941
Rose Walsh and Daniel Mudge – en route to Orroroo

'Luftwaffe Airstrikes on Malta', said the headline in *The Advertiser*. 'Britain to rescue. Convoys despatched.' Further down the page I read, 'Clothing rationing extended in Britain'. I hope that doesn't happen here, I thought. Amy would go berserk.

I put the newspaper down and looked out the train window at the first flush of green in the paddocks. The Scotch thistles that we always referred to as blue roses weren't in flower yet; it was too early for that. Or maybe too late, with this drought. I sighed. The train was running late because it had had to sit in a siding while a freight train carrying stuff needed for the war effort chugged slowly past. Freight was more important than passengers these days.

Time and life passed too quickly, much faster than the trains travelled. More haste, less speed, my mother used to say. This race had left us all behind. If life was the Melbourne Cup, we would all be standing at the starting gate. It was too late for so many things. Brian marrying Annie, for example. Brian was always late for school. Michael used to say Brian would be late for his own funeral. But Brian didn't actually get a funeral, so Michael was wrong about that.

Brian would have really enjoyed himself at that party after the Battle of Bardia, Andy had said. But Brian wasn't in time for the party. Unavoidably delayed in transit. Stop thinking about that, Rose, or you'll be in tears again.

The sun was shining outside, gleaming on the early crops. They probably need a drop of water. Lately we had had nothing but rainy days back home, but there was always less rain at Orroroo than in Adelaide. Pask always talks about Goyder's Line and the fact that some of his farm is over it and a bit under it. Goyder knew what he was talking about, but it's a pity he put that damn line where he did.

My umbrella smelled musty because it hadn't had time to dry out between showers back home. It had been raining when we left home, but I doubted I would be using the thing much up here. I remembered a headline in *The Advertiser* a couple of days ago saying Stalin had announced a 'scorched earth policy'. Charlie said that meant that they weren't going to leave any crops around that the Germans could eat when they invaded. It would be easy to have a scorched earth policy in Australia, I thought. All you would need is a bushfire or a drought. Both happen regularly in this country.

Winter here probably meant summer in England. Something to do with the Earth's axis, I think Michael once explained it. I remembered a poem from school about daffodils and lonely clouds. From memory, Wordsworth wrote it. Bob wouldn't be doing any wandering about in the Lake District looking at flowers this summer. Nothing so peaceful. He would be up in the clouds in his Spitfire hunting Huns or escorting bombers towards Germany.

Bob's airfield was somewhere near London. We had all seen footage of the Blitz on the newsreels at the movies, with a solemn commentary about the gallantry of the RAF and the ferocity of the Luftwaffe attacks.

Was Bob all right? Pask said he had received a letter from the boy that, although heavily censored, hinted about the dark skies over the city pierced by flashes from the anti-aircraft guns and the long beams of the searchlights reaching high and criss-crossing above London, like white spears reflected in the silver Thames far below. The Germans seemed dead set on destroying St Paul's cathedral, but the Londoners were determined to save it, Bob said. It was a sort of symbol, a mascot for the city.

Bob had praised the bravery of the men who put out the fires caused by German incendiary bombs and admitted how cold and lonely it was up there in the darkness looking down at the burning town. And noisy, Bob said. Apparently, Spitfire engines are really loud. Bob said the engines were called Merlins, like the wizard in *King Arthur*.

Pask said there was a strange elation in Bob's words, as if he was almost drunk on adrenalin, which overcame any fear. Bob, Pask said, reminded him of the stories of King Arthur and his knights fighting fire-breathing dragons to protect fair maidens. The maidens, of course, being the citizens of London. It was quite a flight of fancy for Pask to say something like that. He wasn't usually given to such poetic ideas.

It was probably hearing about those Merlin engines that put that idea into his head. I remembered how he used to listen to me reading aloud by kerosene lamp light. In a cupboard, I had found a pile of books that had belonged to Pask's dead wife, Elsie, and there were poems by Lord Tennyson about King Arthur in the heap.

The Germans were bombing the regional cities of Britain, and now the RAF was going on the offensive, beginning to strike across the Channel. Bob had survived longer than many of his mates, but how long before his luck ran out? No wonder Pask was beside himself with worry.

I glanced over at Danny, who was slumped sideways against the green leather upholstery. He had fallen asleep in his seat. We had been around at Charlie and Phil's place most of last evening. The kid had driven us all mad. All Danny could talk about was what he was going to do at Orroroo, the yabbies he was going to fish from the dam, the sheep he would chase with Pask, the ute he would learn to drive. I bet he didn't get a wink of sleep last night. At least it had put the war out of the kid's mind.

Please, God, let it end before he's old enough to join up. And God save all my children. That includes Bob. And Annie, too, if she becomes a nurse.

It was just as well Danny and I were going to Orroroo to bring Pask back down to earth. It was a pity that we couldn't bring young Bob safely down to earth as well without him crashing from a great height, but you can only do what you can, and it's not much use worrying about things you can't change. Although it's easier to say that than do it. Worry comes naturally to a parent. And sometimes to a child when they feel abandoned.

'So just who is going to look after me?' Amy had demanded as Danny and I carried our suitcases out the door to catch the tram to go to the railway station. 'Who's going to cook my meals and do my washing, for example? Am I supposed to work all day and then come home and work all night housekeeping? What am I supposed to eat while you're away?'

'Just keep watering the choko vine and you'll have plenty to eat. You can even use choko instead of apple when you make an apple pie, you know.'

'Oooh yuk, Mum. You don't do that, do you?'

'Yes, all the time, and you've never known the difference. Don't look like that, Amy. It tastes exactly the same. You just put more cloves and cinnamon in. And there's pumpkins from last year stored in the shed and silverbeet and onions in the garden and the rhubarb's doing well. You can put choko in with the rhubarb to make it go further, too.'

'I hate chokos. You know I hate chokos. Horrible, slimy things. I hate cooking. All cooking. And washing up too. How long are you going to be away for? It's not fair.'

'As long as it takes,' I said wearily. I was just a bit fed up with Amy. 'It's about time you learned to cook and clean and look after yourself. You're twenty-three years old. I was married and had children by your age.'

'Well, there's no one around here to marry at the moment,' said Amy. 'They're all volunteering to go off to war and they're not even thinking about girls any more. They all just want to be heroes.'

I had a feeling there was a chap lurking somewhere in the background that Amy wasn't admitting to, but I really didn't want to know. She had been wearing a brighter shade of lipstick lately and there was a spring in her step that hadn't been there for a while. I wondered whether I was doing the right thing leaving her to her own devices, but I had told Pask I was coming and I'd told the school Danny was leaving for an extended period so I couldn't back down now.

'You know Annie's coming down to stay here with you for a bit,' I said. 'She's good at cooking and things. She's talking about becoming a nurse, but if she does sign up, she'll be training in Adelaide for a while before she gets sent away with the army.'

'I thought you were going up there to talk her out of that. It's a pretty stupid idea,' Amy said. 'She could be sent anywhere. And those army uniforms are shapeless. Really badly tailored. Why doesn't she just work at the factory with me? There's heaps of jobs going packing parachutes. I could get her in there. A girl I know said she pinched some silk from the parachute shed and made a blouse out it. It's only cream-coloured, but at least it's better than having to remake an old blouse and she embroidered flowers on the collar, so it looks quite nice.'

I shook my head. So that was the attitude of the girls who were supposed to be contributing to the war effort. I hoped there wouldn't be a blouse-shaped hole in some poor aviator's parachute when he bailed out of his burning plane. I hoped that Bob wouldn't have to use a parachute. How would you know when to pull the cord? What if he left it too late? What if the enemy shot at him while he was floating down?'

'I'll say Annie's my cousin or something. She's sort of a cousin in a way, isn't she? If Brian had married her, she would have been my sister-in-law.'

'She's not really your cousin, but you might as well say that if you like,' I said, picking up my case. 'Just don't do anything I wouldn't approve of. I've asked Mrs Williams to keep an eye on you.'

Why shouldn't Annie be described as Amy's cousin, anyway? I thought, as Danny and I boarded the train to Orroroo. The relationships in our family were unusual. A bit confused, really. Danny and Rosemary were officially twins, but that was only on paper. It had been convenient that my daughter Mary was pregnant with Rosemary when

70

I realised that I was pregnant with Danny. I was forty-five years old at the time, and when my periods stopped, I was certain that I was going through the Change, although I hadn't had the hot flushes that I had heard other women complain of. Just a cessation of the monthly curse, which at first came as a relief.

I was up at Orroroo at the time, and Pask had remarked that I was looking particularly bonny. I still remember his words. 'If you were a sheep, Mrs W, I would have said you were in lamb. Of course, you don't have any wool to speak of, but there's a glow about your whole body."

I was horrified when, just days after he said that, I felt a sort of squirming feeling in my belly. I almost dismissed it as wind. We had been chewing on a rather ancient sheep at the time and mutton stew usually gives me wind. Especially when the chops are a bit green. Of course, you give them a good wash in vinegar before you cook them, but when something is off, it's off.

After a couple of days, I knew it was true. It wasn't wind at all. I recognised it as the quickening, those first fluttery movements that a mother feels in her womb when the child begins to swim about. That meant I must be four or more months gone. I hadn't had any morning sickness, but I had never been very prone to that sort of thing with my other babies, so that wasn't too surprising.

But 1929 was a terrible time to be pregnant. There had been the crash on Wall Street over in America, which gradually spread world-wide just as the Spanish flu had spread after the Great War; in fact, just like this war was spreading now. Just like a bushfire, really. Embers fall and start a conflagration that gets out of control and destroys everything in its path. In 1929, businesses were closing, men were out of work and families were evicted from their homes. Some men who lost all their money committed suicide.

And to make matters worse, we had drought raging almost all over Australia. The Depression Drought, it was called. Misery piled on misery. The price of wool dropped, and I knew Pask was finding finances difficult.

I couldn't dump another burden on him. He had blown his last wool cheque on the ute, and he was a bit stretched as far as money was concerned. My pregnancy would have to be swept under the carpet.

The whole country was experiencing problems. My boys lost their jobs and went to the country picking fruit because they couldn't bear the idea of going on the Susso. I didn't blame them. They said they were humiliated by the idea of accepting help from the government so they tramped miles with swags on their backs, looking for work even though I kept telling them that I still had some of Michael's money stashed away under the chopping block near the woodheap in the backyard so we weren't going to lose the house. Our goods and chattels (whatever a chattel is) wouldn't be seized. Although that happened to lots of other poor people.

I would have been even more humiliated than my boys were about the Susso if I had had to ask Pask to marry me because I was carrying his child. He'd been proposing to me for ages. In fact, he had proposed to me not that long before I fell pregnant, but at that stage I said I wasn't ready. I had gotten used to being an independent woman. I couldn't go back on what I had said.

And as well as all the above, I wanted to bring shame on Michael's name by fornicating with Pask out of wedlock as often as I could. I know this sounds dreadful, but the thought of sinning really did heighten my sexual feelings. You wouldn't think sex would be better if it was illicit, but it is. There's nothing like a bit of anger to add spice.

I was enraged with Mick after I found out that he had made our daughter Mary pregnant. You wouldn't think it possible that a father could do a thing like that to his child. Incest! That's not a sin that's mentioned in the Ten Commandments or the seven deadly sins as far as I know, but probably only because Moses or whoever formulated the seven deadly sins never thought of it. Or maybe because it was a male (and God is male, isn't He, which I always felt stacks the cards against us females) who did the formulating of the original rules and not many males admit that sort of thing happens. But it does.

You can tell that the rules were against women because look how

Eve got the blame for those goings on in the Garden of Eden, when everyone knows it takes two to tango. Or whatever dance they did back in those days.

And then Michael acted as if butter wouldn't melt in his mouth and he sent poor Mary off in disgrace to Mount Gambier as soon as Amy was born. Blaming the victim for his own sin. The worst part of it all was that I was such an idiot that I didn't know what was going on, and I went along with his scheming. I'd had the wool pulled over my eyes long before I ever set eyes on a sheep.

Of course if I had told Pask I was pregnant and agreed to marry him, we could have gone over to Pekina and got Father Travers to perform a rush job of a marriage, and then I could have pretended that the baby had come early. But I knew my babies were usually a fair size and it would be hard to persuade anyone the kid was premature. The entire community of Orroroo would have been laughing behind our backs. I can only imagine how my family would have reacted. And Mrs Williams's tongue would have wagged even harder than Father Flaherty's. Distance would not have protected me.

In the end, I just couldn't face the shame of it all, so I jumped on a train and took off to Mount Gambier just to get away from everyone and everything. As though a bit more distance would help to sweep it under the carpet. It was a carpet with a bloody big lump in it, I knew.

'Is it much further, Gran?' Danny asked.

I jumped at the sound of his voice. I had almost forgotten he was in the carriage with me. 'You ought to know better than to ask that,' I said. 'You've been up and down this train track from Orroroo and back heaps of times. Since you were a baby. You should know the way like the back of your hand.'

'It's just that I'm getting pretty hungry,' the boy explained. 'It seems a long time since breakfast. Haven't you got some sandwiches or something?'

I pulled out one of the brown paper bags I had packed this morning and opened one. 'Would corned beef and mustard be all right?' I asked.

'Is there any fruit cake? I really like your fruit cake, Gran,' he whined.

'There's one in my bag, but I'm taking it up to share with Pask and Annie. You'll have to make do with sandwiches until we get there.'

Danny munched on a couple of sandwiches and when he had finished, I gave him *The Advertiser* to read. It would keep him amused for a while and I had my memories to keep me occupied. If he finished today's copy, I had more newspaper wrapped around the rhubarb plants I was taking up to put in the garden at Orroroo in case the ones I had put in a few months ago had died. Annie's a lovely kid but she doesn't always remember to water stuff. She's got enough to do as it is when I'm not there to run the place.

'The Luftwaffe is keeping the RAF busy,' said Danny. 'Bob must be buzzing all over England in his plane right now. The Hun won't know what hit them when he chases them. Uncle Charlie says the element of surprise is the best tactic in the air. Surprise is the best tactic in war, all round, actually, Uncle Charlie says.'

Mary and Fred had been surprised when I lobbed on their doorstep back in 1929. I said at first that I had come to help Mary through her pregnancy. But before too long, with my belly swelling up, and my clothes getting tighter each day, my predicament was obvious.

Fred wasn't impressed when I suggested that the easiest way out of the dilemma would be to say that Mary had given birth to twins. He said in his opinion there had been enough problems caused when Michael and I had passed Mary's first child, Amy, off as our own, although I still think it had worked out for the best. Well, that was my take on the situation, and even Fred agreed that Mary giving birth to a child and raising it on her own when she was still a mere child of fifteen wouldn't have been an ideal proposition. Of course, Amy's parentage still rankled with him, as it did with me. You don't expect or forgive incest in the family.

Father Flaherty was the only person I knew who described Michael as 'of blessed memory'. No one had ever told Flaherty about the true facts of Amy's parentage, and I would personally murder anyone who did. That went for Danny's parentage, too.

In a somewhat heated exchange, during which Mary wisely took young Paddy for a long walk, I reminded Fred that he wouldn't have had his butcher's shop if Michael hadn't provided the investment for it when Fred had married our daughter. Another evidence of Michael's deceit, because I only heard about that investment years later, but that was beside the point.

I will admit I used the words 'bribery' and 'mercenary', which didn't impress Fred one little bit. Fred said he had married Mary for love, not money, even though she had confessed everything to him. I said it wasn't as if Mary had chosen to have a child out of wedlock from an incestuous relationship, and Michael had forced her to go to Mount Gambier against her will. Mary had certainly not trapped Fred into marrying her.

Fred said he had been willing to overlook the shameful past because of his feelings for Mary. I commended him on his enlightened attitude, and perhaps he was a little mollified. A little, but not much.

That was the general gist of our discussion, although it wasn't the actual language Fred and I used. It was a bit like one of those dramas you hear on the wireless, the more lurid end of the spectrum. If our conversation had been part of an episode of *Dad and Dave*, for example, the volume knob would have been turned to maximum. The neighbours would have complained. To tell the truth, I was amazed that there were no irate people at Fred's door. They must be a tolerant lot at Mount Gambier.

Our hackles and feathers were a bit less ruffled by the time Mary and little Paddy came back to the house, although Fred has never looked at me the same way since.

Personally, I believe it was the idea of a dreadful scandal in the Mount Gambier community costing him customers that brought him round to my point of view. A live-in middle-aged mother-in-law having a child out of wedlock was not an appealing prospect for a man running a business in a small town. To use a bad pun, a lot was at stake. Another butcher's shop had opened not far from Fred's business, and a sausage price war was in progress.

During the Depression, sausages were a luxury to be savoured. The staples were tripe, liver and even lungs. Awful offal, as Amy calls it. I've tried calling pancreas sweetbread, but she still refuses it. Amy puts her nose in the air even when I serve kidneys or brains up. Our main luxury is brisket.

We get the occasional mutton roast up at Orroroo, when Pask kills one of the older ewes. Right now, I was looking forward to a bit of mutton, green or otherwise.

'Got any more sandwiches, Gran?' asked Danny. Then, 'Malta's been bombed by the Germans. But lots of German planes got shot down. And Belfast, in Northern Ireland, was bombed too. Better Belfast than Dublin. Do you reckon our side's got any chance of beating those buggers?' He glanced down at the paper again and said wistfully, 'If only I was a bit older, I could join up and do my bit. I bet the war ends before I'm eighteen.'

'Well, I hope it does end soon, and I'm glad you're still too young to join up. I'd put a brick on your head if I could, to slow your growth a bit. By the way, I don't think Pask will enjoy hearing you swear, Danny,' I said.

'I'll try to stop it, Gran. I don't think I do swear much around Pask, anyway. I learned lots of swear words from Rosemary,' he said, grabbing the paper bag of sandwiches I held out to him. 'She says it drives our mum mad and that's why she does it. She enjoys stirring poor Mum up. I reckon Dad's just about given up on Rosemary now. Rosemary says Dad hardly pays attention when she swears these days.'

It always made me shudder when I heard Danny refer to Fred as 'Dad', although I should be used to it. And I felt a frisson of jealousy when he called Mary 'Mum'. But that was how Danny had been trained and I had no one to blame for it but myself.

Poor Mary indeed, I thought. She didn't deserve a daughter like

Rosemary. She had had enough problems in her life without having to cope with a rebellious kid like that. I don't know what made Rosemary into the person she is. Could it be because the girl had been separated from her 'twin' all her life? But there was no close blood bond between Danny and Rosemary. They were cousins or maybe aunt and nephew or something more complicated. Or maybe they were both. But since she believed he was her twin, she might have all sorts of twisted thoughts. Who knows what goes on in kids' minds, anyway?

Judging by the way Danny was wolfing the sandwiches, food was the main thing in this particular kid's mind. I grabbed a sandwich myself before they all disappeared and then I took refuge in the past. Danny had picked up the newspaper again and became engrossed in the present.

Mary had given birth to Rosemary first, and we had persuaded Fred not to register the child until I had delivered my baby. It was Fred's idea to hasten the process by taking a trip out to the Umpherston Cave. He said there were some steep steps going down to the picnic grounds surrounding the cave. He suggested climbing up and down the stairs might bring my labour on.

I worried about those stairs. Mainly I was worried one of us would trip and fall because of our encumbrances. Mary had to wear a long coat with a cushion tied around her waist under it to hide the fact that she wasn't pregnant, and I had to wear a long coat minus the cushion to hide the fact that I was. Just as well it was July and cold down at Mount Gambier because we would have looked really silly if the weather was warm.

I knew it would be easy to get our heavy clothes tangled up in the bushes at the Cave Gardens and tumble down the slippery steps. And in July at Mount Gambier, it rained all the time and there was moss and slime to contend with.

But we couldn't let my pregnancy drag on much longer when one 'twin' had already arrived. Drastic measures were called for.

We packed a picnic lunch and left young Paddy with a friend of

Mary's for the afternoon, using the excuse that Mary needed a bit of quiet time before her baby was born. We had to smuggle Rosemary along with us, so we packed her in with the tightly closed thermos of tea and the sandwiches. I remember tucking her up in the wicker picnic basket and closing the lid gently on her.

As a newborn, Rosemary was quite a sweet little thing. They all are. I've never believed in original sin and, to tell the truth, that child seemed free of any taint until after she was baptised. Perhaps the holy water was contaminated in some way.

8

28 August 1929
Rose Walsh – Umpherston Cave near
Mount Gambier

'You sit in the van, Mary,' I told my daughter. 'It's cold and wet out there and you should still be lying in. It's only two days since you gave birth to dear little Rosemary. She might wake up and want feeding.'

'I've just fed her half an hour ago. She should sleep for a while yet.'

'Mary, I'll be all right. I don't want you to catch a chill. You just stay here.' I adjusted the blanket around her shoulders and made sure it covered her legs. I felt guilty about dragging her away from her fireside in this weather, but we all knew time was of the essence.

'I'd rather come out and make sure you don't fall over, Mum,' she said. 'Those steps down to the cave are wet and slimy. If you slip, you could fall all the way down and anything could happen. It's dangerous here for a lady in your condition, especially at your age.'

She glared at Fred, who was holding the door of the van open so I could climb out. 'This is a rotten idea. The rain's starting up again and it looks like it's set in. Why couldn't we just go for a long drive over a bumpy road?'

'I can't spare the petrol,' said Fred. 'Fuel's expensive. The Depression, remember? I have to watch how much I use. I've got deliveries to make.'

'I've got a delivery to make, too,' I said, holding onto the side of the van. I pulled my coat a bit tighter around me. 'Are there any other picnickers here?'

'Not likely,' said Fred. 'It's cold and it's wet and it's miserable. Everyone with any sense in their head is sitting home by their fire.'

'You stay here with Rosemary,' I told Mary. 'If she starts crying, someone might hear her and then our whole story would fall apart at the seams. I'll be all right. I've had heaps of babies before.'

'But you were younger then,' protested Mary. 'And you had them in a bed like a Christian, not in a cave in the middle of the bush.'

'She got herself into this and she'll have to get herself out of it,' said my son-in-law grimly. 'Unmarried mothers can't expect to have it easy.' He tucked a hessian bag under one arm and took my arm with the other hand. 'The stairs are this way, Mum. Can you run down and up them a few times, do you reckon?'

I didn't know about running, but I did my best to waddle as fast as I could. Down and up, down and up. And then down again and up again.

It wasn't a pleasant experience. The Cave Gardens are usually very pretty, but the roses had been pruned for winter so there weren't any flowers to look at. There was plenty of bracken and ferns of course; that sort of plant does well in the damp climate down at Mount Gambier. Water dripped off every leaf and most of it seemed determined to find its way down the neck of my coat.

You wouldn't think that there could be such a difference in climate around Australia, I reflected, as Fred, clutching my arm tightly, hustled me up and down the steps.

At Orroroo, there had been that awful drought and the grass had shrivelled so that there was nothing for Pask's sheep to eat; it hadn't been quite as bad at home in Norwood. No sheep to worry about there, of course, although we had just about emptied our rainwater tanks to keep the garden going, but down here around Mount Gambier in July, the middle of winter, there was an abundance of water and the cave gardens at Umpherston were lush.

I've become quite a seasoned traveller since Mick died, I thought.

'You need to hurry up a bit, work a bit harder,' urged Fred. 'Otherwise we'll be here all day. The rain's running down my collar and I'm getting soaked.'

I was already soaked and shivering. I looked down at my hand, the one I was using to holding the metal railing, and saw my fingers were white with the cold. Chilblains, I thought. If the temperature dropped any further, my hand would be frozen to the rail and Fred would have to prise it off. Or probably cut it off with whatever was in his hessian bag. I suspected he had his butchering tools with him and wondered whether that was what he was planning to use as birthing aids. I shuddered.

'It's not that cold,' said Fred impatiently, 'Move a bit faster and you'll warm up. There's nothing like a bit of exercise in a bracing climate.'

'That's all very well for you to say. You were born down here. You're used to this sort of thing. I'm a Norwood girl. Or maybe an Orroroo woman. And I'm a lot older than you are.'

'I don't think I'll ever get used to this sort of thing, or used to having you for a mother-in-law,' said Fred grimly. 'Not if I live to be a hundred years old.'

'Could we have a bit of a break and a cup of tea?' I asked. 'We must have been up and down these steps a dozen times already. My back is killing me.'

'That's a good sign, isn't it?' asked Fred mercilessly. 'If your back is hurting, maybe you're going into labour. This whole twin thing wasn't my idea or Mary's idea, you know. You cooked up this hare-brained scheme all on your own. We're nearly at the top now, so what if we turn around when we get there and go back down again and if nothing has happened by then, we'll come up the stairs, go back to the van and have a cup of tea and then start all over again?'

'You're a hard man, Fred Mudge,' I said, shuffling my feet as quickly as I dared on the moss-covered steps. 'I don't know what Mary sees in you.'

'Sanity and stability, I reckon,' said Fred. 'The sort of thing she missed out on when she was a kid.'

I was about to defend Mary's upbringing, but I doubled up in pain and grabbed at Fred's arm with the hand I had been using to hold the railing. A sudden warm wetness drenched my underwear. 'My water's broken,' I gasped.

'Good, said my son-in-law with what sounded like vast relief. 'There's the cave. There's a bench inside it. You were supposed to have the baby in the van, in decent privacy, like a Christian, but of course nothing works out as planned in your family, does it?'

The Umpherstone Cave wasn't my choice of a place to give birth, but I had to have this baby as soon as possible if we were going to pass it off as Mary's new baby's twin. Since Pask and I weren't actually married, the only way I could go back to Orroroo with a baby in my arms was to say I was looking after my daughter's child; she couldn't cope with twins and I was helping her out.

Right now, I was more worried about the birth than the consequences – as Mary had said, I wasn't young any longer. Forty-six is getting a bit long in the tooth to have a baby. Pask always slaughters ewes before they reach that stage of their lives. The way I was feeling, it seemed a good idea. A great kindness, in fact.

'Jesus, Mary and Joseph!' I yelled as the pains began. 'How did you give birth if you were a virgin?' I'd never thought about it before. Birth was bad enough without adding complications. Poor Virgin Mary. Poor all mothers.

'Can you lie down on the bench?' Fred asked, ignoring my Catholic ranting. He probably dismissed it as more evidence of my insanity. 'I've got some towels in this bag. I'll just spread them out a bit. I've got knives and the string I use to make sausages, too, so cutting the cord won't be a problem.'

He helped me to settle down on the towels. The bench was narrow, and I was wide, but it would have to do.

'You lie down there and try not to let anything major happen while I run up to the van and get the vacuum flask of hot water and the basin I brought to wash the kid in. We'll have to forget about the cup of tea until it's all over.'

'Tell Mary not to come down,' I called after him. 'I'll be all right. I don't want her to get upset.'

'Mary's upset already,' Fred yelled back as he loped up the stairs. 'It's a bit late to be worried about upsetting her now. Just don't do anything until I get back. Keep your legs together. Pity you didn't do that earlier, actually.'

At least it was a bit drier in the cave than outside it, I thought while I relaxed on the bench. When I say 'relaxed', I wasn't really relaxing all that well, because the pains were coming thick and fast without much respite between them. That, I hoped, meant the labour would be short.

There was a musty, mouldy smell about the cave. The place might be pretty on a sunny day. I suppose there was a sort of romantic atmosphere to it. A grotto, the sort that saints liked to appear in. Or Our Lady. Lourdes, Fatima, that sort of place. I didn't expect any holy manifestations and didn't know how I would cope if any came my way.

Thick creepers, probably crawling with spiders, hung down and almost covered the jagged entrance. Did bats eat spiders? I remembered someone had mentioned once that bats lived in the Umpherston Cave. That might account for some of the smell. I'd read somewhere that bat shit smells. There were swallows flittering about the entrance, but birds don't smell, although their droppings might if there was a lot of it. Chook shit stinks, and chooks are birds. I looked up at the dank stone walls and saw the little mud nests the swallows had built. I bet laying eggs doesn't hurt as much as giving birth, I thought.

Someone had told me the caves in Mount Gambier were limestone. I didn't know much about rocks, but the walls of my shelter were grey so that must be the colour of limestone. Despite the semi-darkness, little ferns and creepers flourished, clinging to the walls. Some plants don't need a lot of sunlight, I thought.

Another wave of pain took over and I gasped. I touched my belly. It was rock hard. I felt the contraction pass down from top to bottom. This baby was coming fast. Would Fred get back with the hot water before the baby came into the world?

Is this how the Virgin Mary felt when she gave birth to Jesus? Probably Joseph was away trying to persuade the innkeeper to part with some hot water or string for tying sausages with when her baby came into the world. She had a couple of cows and asses to keep the child warm with their hot breath. I didn't even have a bloody kangaroo.

'Bloody Pask!' I yelled, pulling my legs up to my belly in agony. I remembered I had cursed Michael in exactly the same way when I was giving birth to his babies. Had Eve cursed Adam like this? Did all women blame their men when they were in the throes of labour? God must be male, or women wouldn't have to suffer like this. Women were mad, going through this sort of pain just because men wanted a bit of pleasure. Why did I have to be born a female? Men got off scot-free from having kids.

Suddenly I remembered that my daughter Mary hadn't cursed at all when she had given birth to Amy. If she had cried out Michael's name, I would have found out the dreadful family secrets that had been hidden long before I had discovered them. Come to think of it, Mary hadn't made a lot of noise two days ago when she had given birth to little Rose-mary. I sighed. As I had often thought, Mary was a saint. I don't know who she took after, but it probably wasn't me.

The contraction subsided, and as the pain lessened, I remembered that after all I did have a part in getting myself into this predicament. It wasn't only Pask's doing. We had both had a part in making the bed springs creak in the farmhouse at Orroroo.

I looked at the cave walls again. The same person who had told me about the limestone had said that the Blue Lake was actually the crater of a volcano. That seemed hard to believe. You don't think of volcanoes happening in Australia. They have them in Italy, of course, because that's the sort of thing foreigners do.

Of course, the lake wasn't blue right now. It had been blue when I first arrived at Mary's home back in February but lately the colour had changed to a sullen grey. Apparently, that transformation happens according to the season. Like the cycle of birth and death. The lake had a lot in common with Fred, come to think of it. Bright and sparkly before I came to stay but changing to dark and gloomy as the months went by and the summer died.

The pains were just getting to the stage where I would have welcomed death when Fred, closely followed by Mary, arrived back in the shelter.

'I couldn't stop her,' said Fred, who was burdened with the wicker basket containing Mary's baby, as well as a couple of blankets. He looked for a slightly drier patch of cave floor and set the basket down carefully.

Mary opened it and peered inside. 'She's still sound asleep,' she said. She bent over me anxiously. 'Are you all right, Mum?' she asked. 'Are the pains bad?'

'No,' I lied. 'Hardly there at all.' Another wave struck me. 'God help me!' I screamed.

'Quiet, you'll wake the baby,' Fred said, lifting the basket lid again. He shut it again quickly.

'Which one?' I yelled.

'Let me have a look,' said Mary lifting the towel that I had covered myself with. 'Oh golly, I can see black curls. Not red hair this time. Young Bob's dark, isn't he? The baby's nearly here, Mum. Not much longer before we'll have both twins in that picnic basket. Can you push now?'

I heard a sort of metal grinding sound and looked up to see Fred sharpening his knives. 'Couldn't you have done that earlier when I wasn't looking?' I demanded. 'You make me feel like a sheep about to be slaughtered.' Then I shouted, 'Shit!' as another wave of pain engulfed me.

'Nothing like a freshly sharpened knife to encourage a bit of blood, guts and action,' my son-in-law said. He looked to be in relishing his preparations as he tested his blade with his finger. 'I have to cut the cord, don't I? I've got the sausage string ready. How much longer is this going to take?'

'How long is a piece of string?' I said.

'It's sausage string,' said Fred. 'I've got plenty.'

I moaned again.

Fred glared at me. 'How much longer will you be?' he demanded

'As long as it takes,' I gasped. 'Why?'

'The bats and possums live in here and they usually come in to roost when the sun goes down.'

Just as he spoke, I heard a squeaking sound and saw a couple of possums scamper across the entrance of the cave, tails held high. Then a small wallaby came bounding in, paused, saw that the shelter was occupied and scurried out again with a reproachful backwards glance.

'The baby's coming,' yelled Mary.

I could have told her that, but I was too busy pushing.

'It's a boy,' said Mary.

Fred grabbed the child by the feet and swung him upside down. He whacked the baby harder than I thought necessary on his little backside, and Danny announced his presence to the world with a yell that echoed around the cave. His cries awoke Rosemary and the 'twins' joined voices in what was probably their first and last joint venture. After that initial shared enterprise, there was little else they ever agreed on.

9

17 July 1941
Rose Walsh, Danny Mudge and Pask – Orroroo

'Uncle Pask's here. Look, Gran. He's over there with the horse and buggy,' said Danny tossing *The Advertiser* onto the floor. 'Let's go, Gran!'

'Pick that newspaper up and put it in the bag,' I said. 'Pask will want to read it. He likes the paper but he doesn't often get it. And when he's finished with it, we'll cut it into squares for paper in the long-drop loo, wipe ours bums on that picture of Hitler. You get our cases down from the shelf, Danny. You're taller than I am now.'

But Danny was already running down the carriage to the train's door.

'Daniel Mudge, you get back here this minute!' I shouted. 'The train hasn't even slowed down properly yet. Give me a hand with those cases.'

Reluctantly, the lad came back and hefted the bags down from the overhead shelves.

'He might think we've missed the train,' he explained. 'He might be sitting there wondering whether we're still back in Adelaide. He might think we've changed our minds or something.'

'He knows we're coming,' I said. The kid was always like this when we came back to Orroroo. Couldn't wait to get back to the farm. Couldn't wait to be home.

'Look, he's waving,' yelled Danny. 'He's seen us through the window. Come on, Gran, we can't keep him waiting. Come on, quick!'

'He won't go without us,' I said. 'Don't drop that bundle of rhubarb. The ones I put in last time might have died if Annie forgot to water them. Careful of that bag with the cake. Calm down, Danny.'

I glanced skywards as I climbed down the steps to the platform. It had been overcast in Adelaide, but the sky in Orroroo was clear. I expect Pask and the other farmers want rain, I thought; farmers always want rain, but it's so nice to see a blue sky again. We've crossed Goyder's Line, of course.

Pask gave me a quick hug and then helped me up on to the buggy.

'Was the buggy always this high?' I asked him. 'I used to be able to climb up without much help. My joints must have stiffened because of sitting on the train for a couple of hours.'

He grinned at me. 'We're both getting older, Rose,' he said. 'The time goes so slowly when we're apart, so we age faster.'

'I was here just before Christmas,' I protested. 'That's only six or seven months.'

'Too long, love, much too long. And the boy's grown at least three or four inches in that time. He's nearly as tall as I am now.

Pask looked older. Much older. Worn-out, in fact. There was more white in his moustache and, even though he had his hat on, I guessed his hair was thinner. His shoulders were more slumped than ever. Age does that to us. The RSL are right about age wearying us. Worry and sadness does its bit, too.

But he straightened up and grinned when Danny leaped up onto the buggy and shook his hand. I could see he was itching to give him a hug, but men can't do that to each other. Might give the wrong message. He patted the kid on the back, and then managed to plant a kiss on my cheek when I was safely on the seat beside him and Danny was looking the other way.

I always felt so appreciated when I was with Pask. He was nothing like Michael, who, I remembered, had once told me I was his chattel. He laughed when he found me looking it up in the dictionary and laughed even harder when he saw how angry I was when I understood what he had said.

Danny had tossed our bags into the buggy. Now he sat at the back with his legs swinging over the edge, just as Bob and Annie used to do.

'I hope you didn't have too long to wait,' I said, checking that Danny was surveying the landscape, before giving the old bloke a quick cuddle. It was so good to be seated high on Pask's cart, feeling the hard metal back of the seat pressing into my back, hearing the slow 'clop, clop' of the horse, with the horse smell in my nostrils and the dry dusty road ahead.

I waved the ever-present flies away from my mouth before speaking. 'Where's Annie?'

'Annie's back home. I had a bit of a wait, but it was worth it. You're always worth waiting for, Rose. The train was running a bit late.' Pask agreed with a smile. 'But you get that. There's a war on.'

'So they tell me,' I said. 'Charlie's been out training with the militia just about every night after work, and he goes off on camps every weekend too. They've stepped up the training, so it looks as if there's something happening that we haven't been told about. I'm still hoping they won't actually put him in the real army because of that pleurisy he had last year. And of course, he's married, too, and they weren't taking married men before. Only they might change their minds the way things are going. You can't put your trust in the future these days.'

Pask nodded sadly.

'We've got *The Advertiser* for you, Uncle Pask,' Danny said, turning back towards us. 'There's heaps about the war in it. Bob must be busy in England. I bet he's giving those Huns what for.'

'Yair,' said Pask. He sighed and lowered his voice. 'Annie's still talking about going nursing, Rose. She wants your advice, though. She keeps saying Auntie Rose will fix everything for her.'

'Amy's arranged that job for her in the factory,' I said. 'Packing parachutes. I'm just hoping Annie'll settle for that instead of joining the army nurses. She's too young, anyway. I don't like the idea of her going off overseas any more than you do. I thought she'd be here to meet us. Where is she?'

'She's got a roast on and she didn't want to leave it,' Pask said. 'She reckons you'll be half starved for a bit of decent meat. She said you need some good tucker after that rationing down in Adelaide. I reckon she wants to show off too. She's a good little cook, our Annie. Of course, she learned from the best cook in Orroroo, so she couldn't go too far wrong, could she?'

I could smell the roast as I climbed down from the buggy. Pask's three dogs were hanging around the back door, looking hopeful. When they saw Danny and me, they forgot about the aroma of meat and launched themselves at us, jumping up and down and whining, demanding attention. Pask aimed a kick at them, but it was a half-hearted, good-natured kick. I patted a couple of heads, and Danny stopped to scratch the ears of his favourite, Blue, before dashing in to hug Annie.

'Auntie Rose, it's so wonderful to see you again,' Annie said, throwing her arms around me.

I always love to see Annie smile. I remember a time when her smiles didn't come easily, but that time was past. There was just a slight air of wistfulness about her, though, and I knew that was because of Brian's death.

'Look at you,' I said, tears of happiness at seeing her again mingling with tears of regret that she would never be my daughter-in-law, never have Brian's babies. 'You get prettier every time I come home. And look how lovely and clean the house is. Even the windows are shining. You've been watering the garden, I can see that. And that roast smells marvellous.'

'I made scones, too, Auntie Rose. Although they won't be as good as yours are. There's some of that fig jam you made last time you were here, and I've got fresh cream from the cow.'

'It'll be a feast, love,' I said. 'And just being here's a feast for sore eyes anyway.'

Pask had a surprise for me. He barely waited for the hugs and kisses from Annie to slow down before he dragged me out the back to the lean-to where the laundry copper and trough stood. The lean-to had been extended and even painted cream, and now it comprised a couple of rooms. There was even a window cut into the corrugated iron with an actual frame and a pane of glass fitted. Glass louvres, An actual window that opened. I'd always had to leave the door propped open before, to let the steam from the copper out and get a bit of light to see what I was doing.

I was so astounded that I got the shakes and had to steady myself against the trough. For once, I was lost for words.

'Is it all right, then, Rose?' Pask asked anxiously. 'You didn't prefer it the way it was, did you?'

'It's amazing, Pask,' I said. 'It's wonderful. It was always so dark and stuffy in here before.'

He paused at the entrance of the second room and looked expectantly at me. I thought it would be a storage place for wood for the copper, but from Pask's attitude I realised there must be more to see.

He had such a look of expectancy that I asked, 'What's through the doorway?'

'It's Annie's idea. Come and look. Annie said you might be happier here if we sorted out the bathroom and lav a bit.' He flung open the door and I thought he was going to burst with pride. 'We pulled out all the stops to get it done before you got here,' he said proudly. 'Worked night and day. Used kero lamps so's we could see in the dark. Tim O'Halloran and the other blokes gave me a hand to dig out the hole for the septic tank, and then we ran some pipe in here and look, there's a tub that you can bath in and there's an actual lavatory that's got a chain to pull, just like the one you've got back in Norwood, so you don't have to go out the back to the long drop at night when it's raining.'

'A septic tank! And a bath and an inside lavatory. I don't believe it,' I said, shaking my head. I touched the edge of the bathtub as if it might be some sort of vision. A mirage of a bath that would disappear on contact. 'No more using the tin tub in the kitchen and baling the water out with the dipper.'

'I know you worry about snakes out there in the long-drop,' Pask said. 'There's no snakes in here. Well, if there are, you can see where they are.'

I glanced under the bath. Snakes have a way of lurking in unexpected places. You expect them in the woodpile, but once there was one in the cupboard where we kept the saucepans.

'It's a real farmer's special, this bath. I got it from Frank Byerlee's place. He put in a new bath a couple of years ago and he was using this one for a horse trough. Only charged me a few bob for it. Annie's scrubbed it out and put bleach in it so it's good as new. Well, there's a few stains, but you'll soon fix that, Rose.'

'Look at the feet, Gran,' Danny said. 'It's got those claw feet that look like dragon's claws. They're better than the lion foot ones on the bath at home. So I reckon this bath must be pretty special. Except one foot's missing and it's propped up on bricks. But it's a real beauty. You've done a corker job, Uncle Pask.'

I had seen the stains on the enamel, and I was planning on more bleach and maybe a good scouring with some dry sand. Then a rub over with kero, that ought to do the job. Kero will clean most things if used with plenty of elbow grease.

Pask was explaining the plumbing. 'You use the copper to heat the water for the bath. You have to use the dipper to put the water in, of course, but when you've finished, you just pull out the plug with this chain and the water runs out a treat. The silverbeet's growing real beaut out where the septic trench flows.'

Bob was pushing ahead of us, dashing into a smaller alcove. I heard a cranking sound and then rushing water.

'Don't waste the water, sonny!' Pask yelled. 'We've got a drought.'

Danny emerged looking a bit sheepish. 'I just wanted to see if it worked. I did have a wee.'

'You don't flush just for a wee,' I said. 'You could have done that on the lemon tree. Wee does lemon trees the world of good. Nitrate or nitrogen, I once heard.'

'The chain's not too high for you, is it, Rose?' Pask asked me. 'I used Annie to measure the height. She's a bit taller than you are now, but not that much. That pipe goes out to the septic, too.'

I was flabbergasted. No more chamber pots under the beds to empty in the morning. Well, it was a far step from the bedrooms to here, and Pask did get up a few times in the night, so maybe we'd still use the pots. But I could just dump the contents in here. But there would be no more weekly dragging the tin bath in, setting it up in front of the wood stove, taking turns to use it, and then ladling the water out afterwards. We'd still share the water, because as Pask said, there was a drought. Me and Annie first, then the blokes.

As Pask had realised, the lack of civilised ablutions was one of the reasons I needed to escape to Norwood occasionally. It's all very well being stoic and pioneering, but there are drawbacks to a Spartan existence, especially when you're getting up in years.

'I just might stay here for the rest of my life,' I said. I immediately regretted saying that because of the way Pask's face lit up. I like being at Orroroo, but I do like my own home too. And my independence, as well. It's a terrible thing to be torn in two directions.

'That's about the best thing I've ever heard you say, Rose,' he said, beaming from ear to ear. And he kissed me again. He didn't seem to care that Danny was poking about the lean-to, inspecting the pipes. Pask was usually careful not to touch me in front of the children, keeping up the idea that I was the housekeeper and family friend, so I was a bit surprised.

But we hadn't seen each other for a few months. Not since before Christmas, in fact. I knew he'd wanted me to spend Christmas with him and Annie, and I had half-wanted to do that too, but Amy had carried on so much I had gone back to Norwood to spent the festivities with her and the rest of the family. I was worried Charlie might join up and I wouldn't see him before he left for the war. Now I was glad that I had that time with the son who I had to admit was one of my favourites. I know mothers shouldn't have favourites, but Charlie is such a lovely lad. The tears welled in my eyes when I remembered he's joined up and now he's in danger too. Bloody war.

Pask was obviously feeling a bit emotional too, because he gave me another quick squeeze. I wondered if it was partly because Bob wasn't here. Bob was so far away. And of course, I knew that Brian's death had upset Pask. Brian was always one of Pask's favourites, especially because we had all hoped he and Annie's would be married one day.

'I always reckon my life's over when you get on that train and I watch it steam off to Adelaide,' Pask whispered in my ear. 'I know you've got another life down there, love, but I wish you'd spend more time here and less there, if you know what I mean.'

'The roast's about ready to serve up,' said Annie. She was standing by the door watching us. She must have seen everything, but she didn't seem to mind that her father had kissed me. 'I've been slaving over a hot stove all day, Auntie Rose, so you'd better say you're happy with my cooking. And I forgot to say before, there's an apple pie for dessert. We'll have the scones with a cup of tea later on.'

She's a good little cook, my Annie. She could teach Amy a thing or two. And she probably will, because she told me, while we were eating, that she intended to take up the offer of staying in the house at Norwood and to try out the job packing parachutes that Amy had found her.

'I'll put the bags away before we fall over them,' said Danny, after he had guzzled all the food he could hold.

There was gravy on his shirt, along with some of the cream that went with the apple pie, but that would wash out. I had a new, brighter laundry to work in now, so it would be a pleasure to do the washing.

Danny lifted his case and headed for the sleep-out where he usually slept.

'Wait on, sonny, it's a bit too cool out there right now,' Pask called after him. 'That galvanised iron loses heat fast this time of year. Annie and I were thinking you might as well use Bob's room, since he won't be back for a while. In fact, we both reckon Bob would be happy to know you were sleeping in his bed.'

Danny stopped dead in his tracks. 'Really?' he asked. A huge grin spread across his face. He looked from Pask to Annie and then back again. 'That'd be real good. Are you sure about it, though?'

'Yes, Danny,' said Annie. 'We are absolutely definitely certain about it. I've put fresh sheets on the bed and dusted all the model aeroplanes.'

'Thank you,' said Danny, his voice catching. 'That's just really, really, all right.'

'Thank you both,' I said, as Danny ran off toward Bob's room. 'He's thrilled to bits.'

'Well, we don't know when Bob will be back, do we?' Pask said. 'Or if he'll ever be back. Not the way this war is going. It looks like the Germans are about to take Leningrad. I heard that on the wireless yesterday. And the Japs are in Saigon, now. Things are bloody bad, Rose.'

'That's why I've got to be a nurse,' Annie explained. 'Because Australia is going to need nurses when things get worse. And things will get worse, we all know that. But I thought I'd try living in town for a bit before. So that I won't be a country bumpkin when I join up.' She gave me a peck on the cheek. 'Amy and I will be fine together, Auntie Rose, really we will. Dad says I'm too young to go nursing just now. He wants me to wait a while, so I'll do that. But I am going to join up, Auntie Rose. I owe it to Brian, too. And this war could drag on for ages.'

'Let's hope it'll all be over soon and that we win it,' I said. But I had a bad feeling that things were going to get worse before they got better.

Pask put my bag in my room. I wondered whether he would join me in bed tonight. I hoped he would. We're both getting a bit old, I reminded myself. But it's still good to have company in bed even if nothing much else happens. And with all the rotten things happening in the world, we both needed a good cuddle. When you're alone in the darkness, fear grows.

I felt a lot better about leaving Amy when I knew for sure that Annie would go down to Norwood and stay with her. I'd started worrying about Amy as soon as I got on the train to come up here. Ridiculous, of course. Amy's an adult woman now, with a job outside the home and a weekly pay packet. Charlie and Phil were just around the corner – at least until Charlie was sent away. They'd keep an eye on her. And Mrs Williams said she would be over there all the time to check on her. Amy didn't like that idea. She insisted she was perfectly able to look after herself, thank you very much.

But she admitted she would like Annie to be there. Two girls to-gether would be better off than one girl alone; they would have such fun together. 'Movies and dances,' Amy said, 'that's if there's anyone left in Norwood or Adelaide to dance with.' So I really should stop wor-rying and just enjoy being at Orroroo.

The only creature that didn't make me feel welcome at Orroroo was Pask's cocky, Solomon. That bird hadn't liked me when I first came up here, and the years hadn't mellowed it. It screeched and flapped its wings and raised its crest every time I walked past its cage. In the end, we tossed a hessian bag over the thing so we could sit with cups of tea on the bench by the kitchen door, relishing the cold crisp air, digesting Amy's excellent roast mutton and listening to the magpies in the trees as the sun went down.

'Another frost, I reckon,' said Pask. 'There won't be any rain for at least another week. We need the rain real bad.'

'When it rains, you say it's too wet to shear or whatever, and when it doesn't rain, you say you need it,' I said. 'I've missed hearing that eter-nal farmers' lament. It's so good to be back.'

10

28 August 1941
Rose Walsh – Orroroo

'I rang to say happy birthday to Danny and now you say he's out doing something to the sheep,' Amy shouted into the phone.

I held the phone away from my ear to save my eardrums. I thought she was being a bit unreasonable. Danny had a right to be out with the sheep if he wanted to be, even if it was his birthday.

'You'll just have to say happy birthday for me, then, and give him a hug if he'll let you.'

'You could ring back tonight,' I said. 'Only it's a bit expensive to make two calls in one day. There's a war on, you know.'

'I've noticed,' snapped Amy. 'He never lets me hug him anyway, and I don't suppose he lets you hug him either. He's a boy, after all.'

'Boys are like that,' I said, wishing I'd hugged Brian more often, but as Amy had observed, boys didn't approve of hugs.

'When's Annie coming down?' Amy demanded. 'I've had to tell them at the munitions factory she's been ill because they keep asking when she's starting work. I'm running out of excuses. The other day, my supervisor said if Annie's always ill she's probably not worth having anyway, and I had to lie and say it was her dad who's ill now.'

'Her dad has been ill,' I said. 'Pask's had bronchitis. Dr Watson said it could turn to pneumonia, but he seems to be getting better now. We've been really worried about him and Annie didn't want to go away until she was sure he would be all right.'

'Well, it's given her a chance to try out nursing, I suppose. So is Pask better now?'

'Yes, pretty much, although I think his chest still hurts from the coughing. We're going into town tomorrow. He hasn't felt up to going into town for supplies lately and we're nearly out of tea and sugar. He has to get his petrol ration or he'll lose it and then he won't be able to use the ute. He's teaching Danny to drive.'

'Mr Williams says it's getting harder to get petrol now. The army's requisitioning most of it for training. Oh, I just heard on the wireless, Mr Menzies isn't prime minister any more. Mr Fadden's getting sworn in tomorrow. I don't suppose it'll make any difference, though, do you? I mean, the war's still going on.'

'I think the war will go on for quite a while yet. At least Mr Fadden's here and not overseas.'

'Well, I'm sick of the whole thing. I just want to get back to normal. I'm fed up with working hard and coming home tired and having to cook and wash and stuff.'

'We all have to work hard. Danny's had to do most of the farm work while Pask's been crook. Not that he's minded. We had to practically tie him down to keep inside today long enough to blow out the candles on his cake.'

'Yes, that's another thing. I've missed Danny's birthday. It's no good, Mum, this business of being there half the time and here half the time. You've got a duty to me, too, you know.'

'You're twenty-three years old, Amy,' I said. 'You told me that it was time I realised that you're an adult and you said I had to learn to let go and let you grow up. Remember?'

'Well, yes, I do remember saying it. But Mum, I don't like being here on my own. I really don't like it one bit. This house makes funny noises at night. It's spooky. I never realised it before. I'm not getting much sleep. I've got dark rings under my eyes from lack of sleep. Phil noticed it the other day and asked if I've been out late dancing. And I haven't because I'm too tired to go out.'

'That's not like you, Amy. You're not even going to the movies?"

'I don't like the idea of walking home on my own. You don't know who's lurking in the bushes. There could be murderers or Germans or Japs or anything out there. And the house is getting me down. There's too much work for one person. So don't expect to see the floors shining or much dusting done when you get back.'

'The floors were shining and there wasn't any dust about when I left, Amy. The house shouldn't get that dirty with one person in it and there shouldn't be much dust about in winter.'

'Well, it doesn't rain every day, so there is dust. Especially on the piano, because no one's using it. Charlie's always out training and Phil's at her mum's place most of the time because her mum's been sick too. She fell over and broke her hip. She's bedridden.'

'Sorry to hear that. She probably won't get over it, will she? Pretty much a death sentence, a broken hip, when you're in your seventies.'

'Yes, the family's really upset. They're expecting her to get pneumonia. She's not tough like Pask, so it would probably kill her. But back to Annie: just when is she coming down? I'm sick of being on my own in this house.'

'She's had her bag packed for ages, but she won't leave here until Pask's better. But he went out today with Danny to look at the sheep. Pask said Danny's really good with the sheep. He says it's as if Danny was born to be a farmer.'

'Well, that's not really surprising, is it?'

'What do you mean by that, Amy?'

'You know what I mean, Mum. We all know that Danny's the image of Bob. And it was funny how he was born just nine months after you came back from Orroroo and how you happened to be at Mount Gambier when Mary had twins and the twins don't look anything like each other. Mrs Williams worked that one out, and she hardly knows Pask or Bob or Fred.'

'You're spending too much time with Mrs Williams. She's an old gossip and she doesn't know what she's talking about.'

'Who else have I got to spend time with, then? Charlie's always out training with the militia and Phil's at her mother's place most of the time. I'm lonely, Mum. You still haven't answered my question. When is Annie coming to Adelaide?'

'Probably next week. Depends, as I said. Are you looking after the garden?'

'Yes, your rotten garden's doing fine. There's a lot of weeds, but it's been raining heaps, so it's been watered. The silverbeet's gone feral and so has your horrible choko. I gave some to Charlie. I'm not eating them. Although veg is getting expensive now. Potatoes are a terrible price. Apparently, the army's buying most of them to feed the troops. Speaking of the militia, Charlie came around and pruned the roses, so that's done.'

'I'll tell Danny you rang,' I said. 'This phone call is expensive, so we'd better hang up. Write me a letter if you have time.'

I knew she wouldn't have time to write. I didn't feel like talking to her much longer. She's got a way of putting my back up. My guilt at being away from her was lessening by the minute. I felt sorry for Annie, who would be stuck living in the same house with her. I had a feeling that Annie would be doing most of the housework, since there was too much for one person to do. Amy would be back to her old tricks, saying she was just too exhausted after working at Hendon to lift a finger to help. I hoped packing parachutes wasn't as exhausting as making bullets seemed to be.

11

28 September 1941
Rose Walsh and Pask – Orroroo

'We'll go to the post office first,' Pask said. 'I have to get these ration tickets sorted out for the petrol and we'll pick up the mail while we're there. Save Colin Thomson a delivery. And then we'll see about the supplies and you can have a bit of a natter with the ladies in the general store while I sort out the feed for the chooks and stuff. I reckon you'll have a bit of catching up to do.'

'I've got to find out when the next train is, too, Dad,' said Annie. 'I've had my bag packed for a couple of weeks and I'm sick of not knowing if stuff is in my bag or in my cupboard. Amy said that job won't wait forever for me.'

'Yeah, I suppose you're right, love, but it's going to be hard to see you leave home. I still remember when Bob went.'

Annie patted her father's arm. 'So do I, Dad. Leaving home's part of life. Your parents must have been upset when you left home too.'

'I s'pose they were,' said Pask. '1914 was a long time ago, though. A lifetime ago. Mum shed a few tears but Dad never said much. I think he was proud of me, though he complained he'd be stuck with all the work.'

'Well, I'm here to help this time, Uncle Pask,' said Danny. 'I won't be going anywhere for a while. I can't join up until I'm eighteen and I just know the war will probably be over by then, so I'll miss out on all the fun.'

Pask nodded. 'With a bit of luck, sonny, you might be right. We'll call into the railway station on the way home.'

He parked the ute in front of the post office. It was a bit squashy in the car with the four of us, but Danny and Annie didn't take up much room, and Pask had lost weight since he had the bronchitis. My clothes felt tighter since I had come back to Orroroo even though I had been working hard. My back almost killed me at first, but I was getting used to the exercise. There were a lot of jobs like milking the cow that I didn't do back in Norwood. But there was more fresh cream too, and cream always puts the weight on. Thank God I was much too old to get in the family way again. I was amazed how frisky Pask had been before the bronchitis set in. He'd slowed down lately, which was probably just as well.

We were using the ute because Pask wanted to fill the tank up. He had a few jerrycans in the tray that would hold more petrol. Also, it was more convincing to be driving a vehicle with an internal combustion engine than a horse and cart when you were buying petrol. Strangers could be lurking – although that was unlikely in Orroroo. There was no privacy in a town this size.

'Hello, Mrs Walsh,', said Mrs Thomson in the post office. 'I knew you must be back, because there's a couple of letters here for you. One's from overseas. Got a foreign stamp on it. Egypt, I think.' She peered at the letters. 'This other one's postmarked Darwin. It'd be a bit warmer in Darwin this time of year than it is here, I reckon.'

'It's always warmer in Darwin than it is here,' I said. 'My son Harry says it's really humid up there. It'd be getting towards the build up right now and that's always nasty. He says once the storms start and it rains every afternoon, it's not quite as bad. People go mad this time of year from the heat and the humidity. Harry's a policeman so he has to deal with all sorts of things.'

Mrs Roberts nodded wisely. 'I've heard about that build-up. So now you've got another son in Egypt with the army, have you? Pask told us about Brian getting killed over there. We were real sorry to hear that. Brian was a nice young chap. Always had a chat with Colin and me when he came in here with Pask or Annie. He was always up here, wasn't he? Going to marry little Annie, I heard. And young Bob's over in England. Your boys are certainly doing their bit towards the war effort.' She rummaged in the pile of mail on her desk and held up an envelope. 'I've got a letter from England for Pask from young Bob, too.'

'Pask'll be in here in a minute,' I said. 'He saw a couple of his mates out the front and he stopped to say hello. He has to get some petrol so he'll bring his ration tickets in to be signed. I'll give him Bob's letter. He'll be happy about that because he's been worried how the lad's getting on.'

A door slammed. I heard feet running. Colin Thomson stuck his head into the pigeonhole-lined office where his wife sat.

'I've got to go out to Pask's place right away, love,' he said. 'A telegram's just come through for him. One of them official military ones. Christ, I hate delivering telegrams.'

I clutched the edge of the counter because the room was swaying. Please, God, no, I prayed. Please God, not another one of our boys. Not Bob. Not Joe. It couldn't be Joe. Padres didn't get killed, did they? Yes, they could if they got in the line of fire. And Joe would be likely to get in the line of fire if he felt he had to give the last rites to some dying soldier. Which, being Joe, he would do. But Colin said the telegram was for Pask. Oh, God, not Bob. Please God, not our little Bob.

'Colin, get a chair for Rose,' yelled Sue Thomson. 'She's swaying. She's fainted. Get some water.'

'Are you all right, Rose?' Pask said. His voice was distant, and it was hard to hear him over a sort of buzzing noise in my ears. Loud buzzing, like a swarm of hundreds of blowflies.

Squadrons of blowflies. blowflies flying in determined straight courses just as Messerschmitt planes do when the Huns are attacking a lonely little Spitfire with the intention of shooting it down and murdering the young pilot sitting in it, an Australian pilot who is defending his mother's country in a war that hadn't even come to his own country yet; a pilot who is wearing a flimsy white silk scarf and a leather helmet and a leather jacket with a woollen lining to keep the cold out over his blue RAF uniform. A lining that won't keep the fire out when the flames engulf the plane and it goes into a fatal spin like a Catherine wheel on

Guy Fawkes night and it spirals down through the black European sky to plummet into a cold alien earth far from the fields of Orroroo, falling out of the heavens, wings afire, like a bird in a bushfire.

Someone was slapping my face gently and fanning me with a copy of *The Advertiser* that would be full of more news about the war. 'German armies now have Kiev completely surrounded. American President, Franklin D. Roosevelt, orders the United States to shoot on sight if any ship or convoy is threatened. The US Naval Command orders an all-out war on Axis shipping in American waters.'

The slapping and fanning stopped.

From a great distance, it seemed, I heard Sue Thomson's voice say, 'There's a telegram, Pask,' and Pask say, 'No,' in a weak voice, and then I heard Colin shout, 'Oh, Christ, Pask.'

And the floor shook as a heavy body landed beside me.

Suddenly the room was full of people all talking at once.

'He's clutching at his chest,' Colin said. 'Phone Dr Watson. I reckon Pask's had a heart attack. I don't think he's breathing. Help me turn him on his side so he can breathe a bit better.'

'Dad!' screamed Annie. 'Auntie Rose!'

'Gran!'

That must be Danny, I thought. He sounded anguished. I tried to come back from wherever I had been, although I wasn't sure I wanted to be back. Not when I was certain that young Bob was gone. Two boys dead and the war hardly started?

Had Colin Thomson said Pask was having a heart attack? Why was Annie so upset? She hadn't even heard about the telegram yet. I struggled to sit up. Annie and Danny seemed to be wrestling together and trying to outdo each other shrieking. Pask was lying in a crumpled heap beside me. I could feel a scream rising from my own throat, and my arms were thrashing about although I wasn't telling them to do that.

'Take it easy, now, Rose,' said Sue Thomson. 'The doctor will be here soon. Colin's phoning the hospital and either Dr Watson will come over or we'll get Pask over there. Colin thinks it's Pask's heart.'

12

Later the same day – Orroroo

Dr Watson sent the ambulance to take Pask to the hospital. Annie, Danny and I followed in the ute. Annie drove. I didn't know that Annie could drive. It didn't seem right to see her behind the wheel. It's not a feminine thing, driving a car.

Of course, I had seen girls drive cars in the movies. And there was that woman with the red scarf who got strangled when her scarf got caught in the hubcap of her car. It must have been a very long scarf. That was back in 1927, just before I met Pask. Isadora Duncan, that was her. She was in all the papers and on the wireless too. I don't know whether she was driving, but she was very bohemian, so she probably was. I remember she believed in free love and communism and she was a dancer. I suppose that's why the scarf was red, because of communism.

Not that I'm saying Annie's communist or bohemian or at all inclined that way just because she can drive a car. And the only time I've seen her dance was when we went to the St Patrick's Day dance at Pekina and Brian was up here at the time and they did the 'Pride of Erin' together. They made a lovely couple, although I must admit Brian seemed better at cricket than he was at dancing. '

'I didn't know you could drive, Annie,' I said.

She must have heard the slightly disapproving note in my voice, because she turned to face me, which really worried me. It didn't seem good idea to take her eyes off the road when she was holding the steering wheel. Pask doesn't do that. He just talks while keeping his one eye carefully on the windscreen. He probably has to really concentrate when he's driving, I realised. Only having the one eye. I tend to forget that he's got that handicap.

'Dad taught me when he taught Bob,' she said. 'Only I never got much of a look in because Bob always wanted to whizz all over the place. Lots of girls drive cars, Auntie Rose. I'm quite good at it.'

'Oh, I'm not saying there's anything wrong about it, Annie. I'm just surprised, that's all. And it's a very good thing that you can, under the circumstances.'

'Uncle Pask's been teaching me to drive on the farm,' piped up Danny. 'But I've never driven on the road and I don't think I'm ready for it yet. The gears keep crunching when I drive and Uncle Pask says I have to learn how to use the clutch better. Annie's doing it real well. Uncle Pask says the clutch is a bit touchy on this ute.'

At the hospital, Pask was lying on a bed looking angry and twisting the sheet in his fists.

Dr Watson was standing over him with a deep frown on his face and his stethoscope to Pask's chest. 'Keep still, man,' he ordered. 'I'm having difficulty osculating your heart because you're moving constantly.'

'Is it a heart attack?' I demanded.

'It's difficult to say with certainty,' the doctor replied. 'He's never had symptomless phthisis, has he?'

'I don't know what that means,' I said. 'I only speak English and a bit of church Latin.'

'Tuberculosis, or TB to you,' said the doctor impatiently. He turned to Pask. 'You're a returned serviceman. That's how you lost that eye, isn't it? Lots of soldiers got TB in the trenches in the Great War.'

'No, I haven't got bloody TB,' said Pask angrily. 'I had a chest X-ray. And I'm not having a bloody heart attack either. I haven't got time for that sort of thing. I need to get back to my sheep.'

'It could be orf,' mused the doctor. 'One gets that from sheep.'

'He looks awful,' said Danny.

'Heart attack is increasing in incidence,' said Dr Watson gravely.

I supposed he was thinking aloud, because it didn't sound as if he was talking to us and he was gazing into the middle distance, not even really looking at Pask, whose face was getting redder and redder. Apart from his colour, I'd seen corpses that looked livelier

'As the population ages,' the doctor muttered. 'But this could be indigestion or a gallbladder problem. Of course,' he turned back to me, 'he has had that chest infection in recent weeks. Cyanosis is not present at the moment, and I haven't observed it in the past.'

'He had bronchitis and I made him inhalations with Vicks in the water. And a drop or two of kerosene.'

'I believe I've warned you in the past against using kerosene in a medicinal manner, Mrs Walsh.'

'Kerosene works a treat for bronchitis,' I insisted. 'My mum used to swear by it.'

The doctor's frown grew deeper. 'Now he has dyspnoea, collapse, pain and discomfort in the chest. Sometimes a pneumothorax can look like this. Or the pain could be angina. On balance, a heart attack is a real possibility.'

'Could you just speak English,' Pask croaked. 'I haven't understood a bloody word you've said since I got here.'

I patted him on the shoulder, relieved that he was still in the land of the living.

'On the other hand, it could be alimentary. Have you had flatulence?' asked the doctor. 'Were you agitated and anxious when this episode began?'

'Are you asking if I've been farting?' demanded Pask. 'Of course, I fart. We practically live on mutton. You'd fart too, if you ate mutton every day.'

I patted Pask's bare shoulder again. 'Try to relax,' I said. 'Let me do the talking.' I turned to the doctor. 'Yes, of course he was agitated. I'd just fainted and then Colin Thomson gave him the telegram about Bob and then Pask collapsed. You'd collapse if your kid was overseas and you got a telegram. Only human, I'd say.'

'Where is that telegram?' Pask demanded. 'I didn't open it. What's in it? I still don't know if young Bob's dead or alive. Have you got the telegram, Rose?'

'I don't want you to get upset, Pask,' said Dr Watson. 'If you have had a heart attack, you must stay calm and relax. Complete rest for at least two weeks. Just in case. Do you have pain in your jaw or arms or neck?'

'Yair, doctor. I do have pain there. To be honest, I reckon you're a bit of a pain in the neck. How would you feel if you were in my shoes? I want to know if my son's alive or dead. Where's that bloody telegram? I remember Colin handed it to me, but I don't remember anything else after that. I want to know if Bob's alive. Rose, find out for me. I must have dropped the bloody thing somewhere. Is it in your bag or in that ambulance?'

But the telegram wasn't in my bag. There were the three letters that Sue had handed me, but the telegram wasn't with them. It wasn't in the ambulance either. We phoned the post office and Colin was certain that Pask had it clenched in his fist when he left the post office. The telegram was nowhere to be found.

In the end, Annie phoned Colin Thomson and then phoned Adelaide to check what had happened. She was told that Bob's plane had been shot down over France. Bob had been seen parachuting down and now he was missing in action. I prayed that this time missing in action meant what it said.

Pask refused to stay in hospital. He said he needed to be where he could understand what people were saying. He said he knew just how Bob must be feeling if he was a prisoner stuck in France where no one spoke English and where you couldn't trust anyone. He said he was bloody well going home and if he died there that would be better than dying in a bloody hospital where they didn't know what was wrong with him anyway. And besides, if Annie wanted to learn to be a nurse, she could get some experience of it and then she would find out whether that was what she really wanted to do.

Dr Watson said he believed nursing Pask would put anyone off nursing as a career. He wouldn't take the responsibility for what happened if Pask went home. Wanting to be a nurse didn't mean Annie had the necessary skill set to care for anyone. It took a long time and a lot of discipline to become a trained nurse.

'Furthermore,' he said sternly, his mouth making a grim line on his face that could be construed as a smile, if indeed the bugger knew how to smile. He still remembered vividly how I had dosed the kids with kerosene that time when they had diphtheria. However, he said with a fatalistic sort of shrug, if this family had the stamina to live despite that sort of treatment, possibly Pask might survive being nursed by me and by Annie.

That was when I got really annoyed. I reminded him that I had saved Annie's life when I had performed the emergency tracheotomy on Annie on our kitchen table, back when she was choking with the diphtheria. 'And it worked and she's still alive,' I yelled.

'Yes,' the doctor admitted, 'I can see that she's still alive.' He turned away and I suspect it was because he was having trouble not laughing. 'Obviously,' he said, 'this family is made of extremely strong stuff. Phenomenal example of evolution, survival of the fittest, in fact.'

I wasn't sure if that was a compliment or not, so I didn't reply. Also, I had a feeling that believing in the theory of evolution was heresy anyway. 'Thank you for your time and trouble,' I said, with as much dignity as I could muster. 'I expect your fee is the usual two and sixpence.'

I found the money in my purse and put it on the mantelpiece. That's how doctors are meant to be paid, or at least my mother brought me up to do it like that. I had a feeling that two and sixpence had been the fee for a very long time, and I wondered whether a slight increase was warranted, especially if one believed in evolution, but under the circumstances Dr Watson couldn't expect more because he hadn't really done much, anyway. Waste of good money that could have been spent on kerosene.

Danny and me and Annie got Pask on his feet and we bundled him out the door. Pask was still grumbling imprecations at the physician as we left.

Dr Watson wished us all good luck, but he slammed the door behind us when we left. I had the impression he thought we were a mob of hillbillies and he was hoping we wouldn't come back. Some doctors have lousy bedside manners.

13

28 August 1941
Captain Joe Walsh – Port Said

Dear Mum,

I hope all goes well with you and the family. I know you said in your last letter that you were going back to Orroroo, so I will send this letter there. But I know Pask will return it to Norwood if, for some reason, you're still at home.

I thought I would write today because it is young Danny's birthday and he is in my thoughts and prayers, as are you all, constantly. Of course, you won't receive my missive for a while, but as they say, there is a war on so we must accept sacrifices.

I arrived here in Port Said a few days ago. The sea voyage was fine, although there were a few rough patches and some of the men were very seasick. I was fortunate to escape that, so I was able to spend my time visiting them and comforting them as best I could. I suspect homesickness played its part in their malaise, too. I will admit it is intimidating to know that you are so far from home and facing an uncertain future in a foreign land. There is, of course, an element of excitement, but there is also a real sense of loss. You don't realise how much you care about home, family and friends and just the actual country of Australia until you know that you will not be back for an extended period.

I decided to visit the Anzac Memorial yesterday. It is quite a tradition for us Aussies to do that. It made me think of Dad and of my uncles Patrick and Daniel who also passed through Port Said on their way to the Great War. Of course, the memorial was built long after their visits. But I am sure that Brian would have called in to see it, and so I felt closer to Brian there.

The memorial depicts two wide-eyed bronze horses, one rearing up and the other crouching down, with two chaps in the uniform of the Light Horse looking very brave and intrepid on the horses' backs. It is set on a granite plinth and overlooks the Canal.

Of course, the Suez Canal is one of the reasons we are here in this part of the world. If the Germans take the canal, it would make things very difficult for all of us. Our side couldn't send vital material and troops to Britain, and Britain wouldn't be able to send troops or materials to Australia. (I wonder whether that sentence will be censored, but I think it is common knowledge, so it probably won't be.)

A chap never knows how much of his letter will be covered in black ink when the family receives it. I have acted as censor a few times and I always feel guilty when I ink out stuff some poor fellow sweated blood and tears to convey to his loved ones. But letters have to be censored, so if you find a few black spots on the paper, be understanding, Mum.

I was sitting by the memorial when a little kid came over to me. He was skinny and dressed in shorts and shirt, so he wasn't one of the usual Arab kids that swarm all over the place here demanding anything they can get out of a chap. He pointed to the bronze soldiers in their Light Horse uniforms and then pointed to mine. He jabbered something at me, which sounded like French, so I thought I would try out my schoolboy French on him. It's amazing how many of the people speak French here, even the ones who aren't actually French. Port Said is a multilingual sort of place.

I asked his name and he said, '*Je m'appelle* François.' I asked where his papa was, and he told me Papa was in prison because he is Italian, and all the Italian men have been sent to a camp out into the desert for the duration of the war. This child could possibly be the youngest enemy I will meet, poor little chap. It must be hard on the kiddies, not seeing their fathers for two or three years or however long it takes for this war to end. But at least their dads are not being shot at, like our chaps are, and I'm sure the British will look after them according to the Geneva Convention.

Anyway, I gave him a threepenny-bit I had in my pocket, and the kiddie was over the moon. He turned it over and over and (I think) asked if it was the sort of money we used in Australia. He pointed to the cross on my tunic, so I blessed the kiddie and he put his hands together in prayer for a moment and bowed his little head.

Then he grinned and ran off to a group of women standing talking a bit further away and jabbered away at them, apparently excited that he had met an Australian padre. You could see the women weren't Arabs because they weren't wearing the draperies the Muslims wear, so they must be part of the European community that lives here. I wonder what their fate will be in this war.

We will be here for a few days, then we head off again. I won't say where we are going, because that is definitely not allowed.

By the way, that fruit cake you gave me before I left was very popular with the chaps. I miss you, Mum, and I miss your cake too. Give my love and my blessings to the family.

Your loving son,
Joseph.

14

20 August 1941
Flight Officer Bob Pask – London

Dear Dad,

You wouldn't believe how much it rains in Pommieland. And it's supposed to be summer here. They get scads more rain in summer than Orroroo does in winter. Or even Norwood does in winter from what Auntie Rose says.

I hope you've had a bit of rain back home. From what you said in your last letter, you need it, or the sheep will be getting hungry pretty soon.

The rationing here in London is getting worse. I really miss our good old Aussie food. Just the thought of a mutton chop makes my mouth water, even a chop that's getting a bit green and long in the tooth would do me right now. And if I could get my hands on one of Auntie Rose's fruit cakes, I reckon I would kill anyone who stood in the way.

Lately, we have been flying sorties out over the English Channel to France, protecting the Lancaster bombers that are giving the Hun what for. We have the odd dogfight occasionally and then there's the ack-ack. The Hun seems to have given up on bombing London at the moment, but there has been a bit of action up north in the industrial towns. Coventry was hit real bad. The censor might black that bit out, but you would have heard about it on the wireless. So you might as well leave it in, you silly drongo. (That was to the censor, not to you, Dad.)

We are hoping to give the buggers as good as they have been giving us. It is about time we turned things around and got our own back. Tell you what, you wouldn't believe the noise a Spitfire engine makes. A tractor sounds like a lamb bleating in comparison.

You get used to it, though, and we have earmuffs which keep the cold off a bit and deaden the sound a bit too.

Have you finished the shearing yet? You ought to get young Danny up to help out on the farm. And I reckon you ought to talk Auntie Rose into marrying you. You two have been together on and off for yonks and I reckon it's time you tied the knot and settled down properly. Neither of you are getting any younger. You might need each other to prop yourselves up on soon, the way the years are ticking over. I reckon we all know that Danny's actually your kid, although everyone tries to pass him off as Mary's. It's Fred I feel sorry for. And Danny.

It's about time you and Rose came clean and stopped trying to fool yourselves and us. Those bedsprings are pretty noisy and you can't keep secrets in a small house. You're not fooling anyone, Dad. We kids all know the facts of life, believe it or not.

The thing is, Dad, if anything happens to me, I want to know that my brother (well, I suppose half-brother, really) is there to keep an eye on you. You can't expect to be able to chase the sheep the way you used to at your age. You think about it, Dad, and give Rose a good talking to, and I want to hear in my next letter from you that she is Mrs Rose Pask now, not Mrs Rose Walsh any longer.

Best wishes and keep your chin up. Say hello to the sheep for me.

Bob.

15

15 September 1941
Police Sergeant Harry Walsh – Darwin

Dear Mum and all in Norwood, Orroroo and Mount Gambier,

I know you are at Orroroo now, Mum, but I'm sure you will send my regards on to Charlie and Amy down in Norwood and Mary at Mount Gambier and Joe wherever he is. In fact, to all the family. We are spread out a bit, aren't we? Say hello to Pask for me.

I hope you have heard from Joe and from young Bob and that they are OK.

Mavis and the kids are well and are looking forward to Christmas. Mavis's been out Christmas shopping already, although I think it's a bit soon. She says with the war on it will be hard to get hold of stuff nearer to Christmas and she doesn't want the kids to think Father Christmas has forgotten them. She's got stuff stashed in cupboards all over the house, so all we'll have to do it is stick it in their pillowcases on Christmas Eve and we'll be right.

I think it's mad having a hot dinner on Christmas Day in Darwin, but she's got her heart set on it. The roast chook, the spuds, the Christmas pudding and custard. The whole shebang. Just shows you how boring life is in the build up at here at the Top End when you start thinking about Christmas in September.

The new baby's not due until February but Mavis's pretty big already and I feel sorry for her because of the weather up here now. And she's not as young as she used to be, so I worry about her. I'd like to send her down to Adelaide to have the baby, but she won't leave me. She's worried about the Japs invading Darwin, but I keep telling her they'll never get past Fortress Singapore

We're all looking forward for the Wet to start, because the build up is its usual rotten self; it's hot and steamy and hard to breath because of the humidity.

Us coppers are kept pretty busy with the usual problems. The cells are full of blokes charged with being drunk and disorderly, but we usually let them out the next day when they have sobered up. We have to, because there wouldn't be room to keep them and stash the next lot in the next night as well. Standing room only.

We've had some Yankee sailors arrive and there's quite a few of their ships in the harbour too. They seem to feel the heat more than us locals do, and they all winge that the weather is topsy-turvy in Australia. Apparently, this time of year it is autumn or 'fall' as they call it back home. Their sailors don't seem to be able to hold their booze too well but they're not bad blokes on the whole.

You might have read in *The Advertiser* about a spot of trouble we had at the Victoria Hotel. Some blokes were playing football in the road outside the pub and caused a few problems and us coppers were called out. The Vic shut its doors and some soldiers went crook and broke in and pinched about sixty pounds worth of booze. Things were getting out of hand, so we asked the army to come out from Larrakia and they sorted the problem out. It was mainly soldiers who caused the problem, after all, so it was the army's job, not ours.

Still, none of us cops expected to see an officer leading a troop with rifles and bayonets in the streets of Darwin. It made the war seem a whole lot closer somehow. But with those Yankees and our own blokes here, we should be OK, as long as the stupid buggers stay sober. I thought I'd better write and let you know about it, Mum, in case you read about it in the paper and get worried. Everything has settled down again now. I hope everything is fine in your neck of the woods. And that the weather is better there than it is here, although I know it is.

Love and best wishes to all,

Harry and family.

16

1 December 1941
Rose Walsh – Orroroo

Annie should be almost finished with the milking, I thought. I filled the kettle and put it on the stove so she could have a cup of tea when she came in.

Then I heard a noise in my room. Well, I still called it my room, but actually since Pask had been ill, he had been sharing my bed. The excuse we made to Annie and Danny was that I could keep an eye on him better that way, but even when he had improved and begun going out with Danny to chase the occasional sheep, we kept sleeping together, although the bed springs didn't creak the way they used to fifteen years ago. Well, not as often and not as loudly.

But Pask had been very ill. There was always the possibility of a relapse, I told the kids, and you couldn't be too careful. The kids just shrugged and neither of them said anything, so I decided they didn't care one way or the other.

Just now, Pask was sitting at the table looking expectantly at the wireless on the mantelshelf. We had turned the wireless on because the news broadcast would be on soon, and we were all anxious about the war because things hadn't gone too well lately. Just the other day, the Japs had fired on an American ship and killed seventeen sailors, the Germans were heading for Moscow, although apparently there was a blizzard over there so that might slow the buggers down a bit, and Rommel was making a lot of trouble for our army near Tobruk.

I still didn't know exactly where Joe was, although since he had sent that letter from Port Said, Tobruk was a distinct possibility, so I was worried about him. And of course, I was worried about all the kids. We had had no more news about Bob's whereabouts, although Annie had asked the Red Cross to try to find out if he was in a German prisoner of war camp, and if so, could we write to him and send a box of comforts? I was planning a cake, of course. Harry and his family were in Darwin and the Japs were heading south.

After the thud from the bedroom, I thought I heard glass breaking.

'Did you hear a noise?' I asked.

'No, love,' Pask said, twiddling the dial of the wireless. 'Where's Danny? He always wants to hear the news. It'll be on in a couple of minutes.'

I found Danny in our bedroom. His back was turned to me and he was holding the photo of Bob in his RAAF uniform and trying to fit it back into its frame. I saw glass shards on the floor.

'What are you up to?' I asked.

Danny spun around guiltily. 'Nothing,' he said. 'It was an accident. I dropped it and it broke.'

'What are you doing in here?' I demanded. 'Ever heard of privacy?'

His lip thrust out petulantly. He used to do that even when he was tiny. When he was cornered, when he knew he was doing something naughty, when he was angry and defiant, that lip always came out. I felt like either smacking him or hugging him, I wasn't sure which. At fifteen, he was a bit big to smack. But I was cross about the photo being dropped and I was annoyed that he had intruded into my bedroom. That sort of thing would be embarrassing if there was underwear lying about.

I had a quick glance around and there wasn't anything like that. But I felt he should respect his elders. I was supposed to be his granny after all.

'I want to read Bob's letter,' he said. 'You let me read Harry's letter and Joe's letter, but you won't let me see Bob's. I reckon you've got it stashed in here somewhere, because I've looked everywhere else.'

'It's not mine to give you,' I said. 'Bob's Pask's son and Pask said he doesn't want you to read Bob's letter. I don't know where he's put it.'

'Stop lying, Gran. Or should I say Mum?'

'What?' I asked. Nausea made the last cup of tea I had drunk flow up my gullet and I felt dizzy too. Probably reflux, I thought. I leant against the door to steady my knees which were suddenly weak. 'What do you mean, Danny?'

'I know Pask's my dad and you're my mum. That Rosemary stuff's bullshit. She's not my sister and Mary and Fred aren't my parents. So that means that Bob's my brother, so I've got the right to read his letter. Where is it? The Germans might be torturing Bob or shooting him right now if they haven't already done it, and I want to know what he put in that letter. It might be the last time I read anything he writes. Hand it over, Mum!' He was yelling.

I heard the scrape of Pask's chair on the floor. Bugger, I thought, Pask's not that well yet. He doesn't need to be upset. He's still getting over that pneumonia or heart attack or whatever he had and he's not happy about Annie leaving home and going down to Adelaide. And she's going soon. Very soon.

'Stop it, Danny,' I begged. 'Just stop it.'

'What's going on?' asked Pask, putting his head around the door frame.

'Bob's my brother and I want to read his letter,' said Danny sullenly.

'How do you know he's your brother?' asked Pask. His face had gone pale, just like it had when he had that funny turn in the post office.

'Look at that,' said Danny, holding up the photo of Bob. 'Put me in a RAAF uniform and that's me in a couple of year's time. And you won't be able to stop me enlisting, either. I just hope this war doesn't end before I turn eighteen.' He glared at Pask. 'And you didn't even have the decency to marry my mother when she knew she was pregnant with your kid. You can't say you're not free to get married, so there's no excuse. You both cooked up that story about Mary and Fred being my parents.'

'Danny,' I began.

'Shut up, Mum. I know Rosemary's not my twin sister. She's probably not even a relation.'

'Yes, she is,' I said. 'She's your cousin or maybe your auntie or your niece. Or all of them, or some of them anyway. I'll have to work it out.'

Danny's face was incandescent with fury. 'Rubbish, Gran! You didn't want me, did you? I bet you tried to get rid of me and it didn't work, so that's why I'm here. And you know what? I don't want you either. You and Pask are liars and cheats and I hate you both. I'm going down to Adelaide on the next train and I'm going to try to enlist anyway. I look older than fifteen. Everyone says I'm tall for my age. If the army's desperate, they'll take me. And I reckon they're desperate now.'

I burst into tears. Pask put his arms around me. It wasn't the knowledge that Danny knew our secret, although that hurt. It wasn't his rage and his accusations. I could understand that. He was absolutely right. Well, he was right about me, not about Pask. Pask had wanted to marry me. I was the one who had invented the false parentage for our son. I deserved everything Danny said, but Pask didn't.

I sobbed as if my world had ended. And Pask held me and was silent. I think he was dumbstruck by the whole situation.

I just couldn't bear the thought of my baby going to war as my other sons had done. As Brian had done, as Joe had done, as Charlie would do soon if the Japs kept coming south. Because despite Charlie's history of pleurisy and despite the fact that he was married, soon every man would be needed to save Australia.

Eventually, when Danny had run out of steam, I took a deep breath and said, 'It was all my fault, Danny. I'm sorry. I'm really sorry. I just couldn't see what else I could do. Under the circumstances. It seemed a good idea at the time. Pask wanted to marry me when he found out. Only he didn't find out for a while. And I didn't try to get rid of you.'

In fact, I had sat in a hot bath with Epsom salts in it for long time, but I had been pleased in a way when it hadn't worked. Sort of, although I'd been terrified of having another baby at my advanced age, too. Danny didn't need to know any of that.

'Please, Danny, please don't go away. Please, Danny,' I sobbed.

'Son,' said Pask, finding his voice at last, 'it was all a mistake. A whole pile of mistakes. Everyone makes mistakes, and your mum and me, yes, we made a big mistake. But because of that mistake, you're here. So it was the best mistake I ever made in my life and I'm glad I made it. Your mum and me, we love you, Danny.'

Danny shook his head and glared at us both. 'I reckon actions speak louder than words. That's what Brother Bartholomew always says at school. I reckon the fact that you two tried to pass me off as someone else's kid means neither of you wanted me. I reckon the only people who might want me is the air force or the army or the navy. I bet I can get into one of them. And you're not stopping me.'

'You're too young, Danny,' I pleaded.

I tried to touch his hand, but he shook me off. Tears ran down his face. I had never seen him so upset. Not even when he came home from school that time saying Brother Andrew had caned him because he wouldn't dob in his mates for fighting behind the bike shed. Not even when Brian was killed. After his initial hysterics, he had been silent and withdrawn then and I knew he had tried to look as if he was bearing his grief like a man.

But now he was overwhelmed. And he expressed it by yelling his head off louder than he had when he was a toddler and Mrs Williams's dog bit his bum after he had tried to take a bone away from it.

'You've lied to me ever since I was born. You made me call you Gran instead of Mum. I really thought Rosemary was my sister even though I can't stand her. I had to call Fred Dad, and I couldn't understand why he didn't like me, why he never wanted to have me around. Even Paddy who was supposed to be my big brother didn't want to have much to do with me. Now I know why. He probably knows the whole rotten story. And I thought Mary was my mum and I was jealous because I could see she cared more about Rosemary and the others than she did about me. And she was happy for me to live with you instead of her, so that just proves it, doesn't it?'

'Danny,' I pleaded. 'Danny.'

'Bob's always been really nice to me, much nicer than Rosemary or Paddy and I reckon he guessed the truth.'

'Danny,' I whimpered. I grabbed his arm, but he shook it off.

'Bitch!' he yelled.

'Danny,' I pleaded, 'Danny.'

'I never could understand why I had to live with you instead of down at Mount Gambier with my own family. Or why I felt more at home in Norwood than in Mount Gambier. Now I understand everything. Every bloody rotten, stinking thing!' He ran out of the room and slammed the door behind him.

Pask looked at me and nodded sadly. 'I've always said this would come to a head one day, Rose. You can't sweep things under the carpet and not expect them to surface one day and bite your bum.'

'What are we going to do?' I asked. 'He'll never forgive either of us.'

'The only thing we can do is to give him Bob's letter to read, apologise as best we can, and hope he settles down. Bob's right, we ought to get married, Rose. Maybe that would fix it up for Danny, fix it up for all of us.'

Pask pulled the letter out of his shirt pocket. It looked pretty crumpled, so he must have been carrying it about since it arrived. I had read it when it first came, but I'd had no idea where it had got to since then. Now I realised that Pask was keeping it close to his heart, and I understood that he did this because he wished he could keep Bob there, too, although that wasn't the sort of thing a man would say.

When we have kids, we don't realise what we are letting ourselves in for. There is so much joy in being a parent, but so much pain, too.

We found Danny sitting at the kitchen table, his head resting on his arms, sobs racking his body.

Pask put his arm around the lad. Danny tried to shrug it off, but Pask wouldn't be fobbed off. Just for once, the kid would have to put up with being hugged. He patted the boy on the shoulder while cradling Bob's letter in the other hand as though it was the most precious thing in the whole world. 'Just listen up a bit, Danny. Your mum and me, we love you, son. We both love you, and I reckon you won't understand how much we love you until you become a dad yourself. Kids never understand that until it happens to them. And no matter how it looks right now, no matter how angry you're feeling, I reckon you love us too. So let's just have that cup of tea your mum's about to make.'

'Don't want tea, don't want anything from either of you,' Danny blurted out.

'Here,' said Pask, 'I'm giving you Bob's letter to read. Just handle it carefully because it means everything to me. We'd like to know what you think of what he wrote in it. And while you're reading it, your mum and me could listen to the news on the wireless, so we'll find out what's going on outside Orroroo as well. The whole world's got problems, son, not just us.'

Danny raised his head and glared at Pask. I could see that he believed that his own problems were bigger than any problems the rest of the world might have. But he reached out his hand and snatched Bob's letter from Pask and unfolded it. Pask held his breath. He was obviously terrified to let the missive out of his possession; I could see he was afraid that Danny might tear the letter up.

I put the kettle on and Pask slowly walked to the shelf and turned up the wireless.

'We'll just have a bit of a listen while Danny's reading Bob's letter,' Pask said, just as Annie walked from milking the cow.

She had shed her boots on the veranda. Now, although she must have already washed her hands in the cowshed, she slowly walked to the kitchen sink, and washed them again. She wiped her hands on her apron and looked around the kitchen at us. I could see that she had picked up the tension in the room. I knew none of us looked too happy.

'Is the tea brewed, Auntie Rose?' she asked. 'What's happened? Did they announce bad news on the wireless?'

Let her think it's something about the war, I thought. She'll find out soon enough about Danny. Although if Bob had worked everything out, Annie would know too. They were always chattering together, those two. Thick as thieves were Bob and Annie. She must miss him dreadfully. No wonder she wants to get away from this place. Did she secretly hate me? I must have been crazy to think I could keep secrets from anyone in this family. Danny was right to call me a bitch. A silly old bitch, that's me.

'Hush,' said her father. 'I think the announcer said something about Mr Curtin.'

'I can't keep up with who's prime minister these days,' said Annie. 'They seem to change more often than the wind changes direction. Menzies was chucked out and Fadden took over and now it's Curtin. All in the space of a few months. I bet that never happens again in all of Australia's history. Three prime ministers in such a short time. I wish people would make up their minds.'

I kept quiet and poured the tea. I knew Annie was chattering to give us time to calm down, and perhaps to give herself time to work out what had happened.

Danny kept reading and rereading the letter. He seemed to be having trouble taking in Bob's words, or else he was committing them to memory. I tried not to look at him, but my eyes kept straying his way. My hands were shaking. I spilt tea on the oilcloth-covered table. Annie looked at me and said nothing, but she reached for the tea towel and mopped up the tea. Then she gently took the teapot from me and poured four cups of tea, added the sugar and milk and handed them around.

'There was a no confidence vote because of the budget and Fadden got chucked out and the Labor Party came in. I reckon it'll be Curtin for a bit now, Annie,' Pask was saying. 'We'd better listen to what they've got to say. It could be important.'

Most of us looked towards the wireless set on the shelf. Except Danny, who was still absorbed in the words on the page he held in both hands.

'The prime minister, Mr John Curtin, has confirmed that the *Kormoran* and the *Sydney* fired salvos simultaneously, but the raider's first salvos destroyed the bridge and probably the central firing controls. There has been no direct information from the *Sydney*, which apparently sank with all six hundred and forty-five hands after an encounter on 19 November, three miles west of Carnarvon, Western Australia.'

'Is Phil's brother on the *Sydney*?' asked Annie. 'He's in the navy, isn't he?'

17

2 December 1941
Rose Walsh – Orroroo

I was still trying to catch my breath from the news about all those poor sailors dead in the *Sydney* (Phil's brother wasn't one of them, thank God) and thinking how their mothers and their sisters, wives and sweethearts must be feeling, when a letter came from Charlie that just about knocked the socks off my feet.

He must have written a week or so ago but Colin brought it (and some bills that we'll have to somehow find the money to pay) plus the letter we had been hoping for, one from the Red Cross that finally told us that they had located the prison camp Bob that was in. Apparently, Bob is somewhere in Germany, although they didn't say where. The important thing is that he's OK and being treated reasonably well, according to the Geneva Conventions, whatever that means, and now we'll be able to write to an address in Switzerland and the Red Cross will forward mail to him. And we can send him some comforts, which is a blessing. I started to plan a fruit cake for him immediately, and Annie's going to knit some socks and a scarf, because it must be cold over there.

Lately, Colin had taken to coming right up to the house rather than putting our letters into the kero tin at the end of the drive. He said he feels like a cup of tea by the time he gets out to our place, but I think he wants to check up to make sure we're all all right after that business with Pask's heart. Which is really nice of him.

Fortunately, Colin had left before I read Charlie's letter, because I almost had another fainting spell, just like the one I had in the post office at Orroroo when I knew there was a telegram saying young Bob was missing in action. Things are just happening too fast for me to keep up with, and my nerves are getting shot to bits by this bloody war. But never mind my nerves; it's my kids that I don't want shot.

Charlie was writing from Norwood, but he said we won't be able to reach him there much longer, but to write to that address anyway and Phil will put our letters in with hers and send them off to wherever he will be. I started to get worried when I read that, and I got ever more worried as I went further into his letter. I knew he had joined the militia, but I didn't think he would be posted anywhere, not with his health issues.

'I couldn't wait any longer, Mum,' Charlie wrote.

Things are getting pretty bad, we can all see that, and now with the *Sydney* and everything, I decided that I would have another go at enlisting. Australia needs all the men she can get. We've all got to do our bit. The army wouldn't take me before because of that pleurisy I had last year, but this time the doctors didn't seem to be so fussy, especially after I told them that I kept on playing football even when I had the tube to drain the muck out stuck in my side and I just pulled it out when I was on the field and put it back when the game ended.

One of the quacks said if I could do that, I must be fit enough to go to war. They put the Accepted rubber stamp on my forms. These days, they don't care whether a bloke is married or not, but I didn't tell them Phil's pregnant just in case they objected to that. Anyway, they didn't ask, and I didn't say.

And I don't think we've actually told you about that yet, Mum, either. So that's our really big news. Phil's in the family way, although it's only early days yet. Two months, we think. I don't know where I'll be when the baby comes, but I'm going to make sure that Australia's not run by the Japs when it does come, so I'm off to Queensland for some real army training in the jungle. Not just that militia stuff.

Congratulations to you and Pask for the wedding, and I reckon you'll want to send your congratulations to Phil and me for the baby. Wish me well for my army career too, Mum, even though I know you hate war. I'll do my best to stay out of too much trouble, but none of us Aussies has any choice now. The job has to be done.

Our very best wishes to you and I wish we could be there for your special day, but we will be thinking of you. I shouldn't say it, but the whole family thinks it's about time you two got hitched properly. What's it been, fifteen or sixteen years? Better late than never, as they say

All our love.

Charlie and Phil.

18

8 December 1941
Rose Walsh and family – Orroroo

'It's horrible,' said Rosemary. 'It's sort of lurking there, gathering itself to spring and devour someone alive. I won't be able to sleep with that thing in the house. And it stinks. Reeks of the cowshed.'

'It's a hat,' I said. 'It's just a hat sitting on the table.'

Danny nodded. 'Rosemary's right, it does look evil. I don't know how you could ever have put it on your head, Mum. It must be crawling with germs. Fleas, too, I expect.'

He and Rosemary grinned at each other. They seemed quite friendly now that they knew they weren't twins. Or even brother and sister.

Mary giggled. 'It's not exactly the height of fashion, Mum, even by wartime austerity standards.'

'I remember the first time you wore it, Auntie Rose,' said Annie. 'I thought it was lovely. It was just an ordinary hat until you put those blue roses on it. And I remember that blue dress you made me from the same material, and the blue shirts for Bob. And you made a little dress for Polly, my rag doll. I've still got Polly, after all those years. She's in my bottom drawer.'

'Pask doesn't really want you to wear it for the wedding, does he?' asked Amy apprehensively. She picked the hat up and sniffed it, then tossed it back on to the table in disgust. 'He must be mad. It does smell like cow. And it looks as if the cow's been sitting on it.'

'Shitting on it,' suggested Danny.

'It's been out in the dairy for a few years,' I admitted. 'It's bound to be a bit smelly. I thought we could unpick the blue roses and give them a bit of wash in Lux flakes and then maybe brush the hat with an old toothbrush and some kero. Leave it out in the sun for a bit. That should get rid of the smell.'

'You won't really wear it, Mum?' asked Mary. 'You're not serious, are you?'

I nodded. 'Pask says I should. He says its good luck to have something old, something new, something borrowed and something blue. And this is old and blue. Not borrowed, though. I bought it for Michael's funeral. Seven and six, I think it cost.'

'Can't you borrow something old and blue?' asked Amy. 'Have you got a hat Mum could borrow, Anastasia?'

'Pask's set his heart on this hat,' I said. 'I'm borrowing Anastasia's handbag, because it's new.'

Anastasia nodded, but I could see she was dubious about the hat too. Mrs Williams, who had invited herself to the wedding and who had come up on the train with Amy, Mary and little Kathleen, looked disgusted. She shook her head and looked towards Anastasia. She and Anastasia had become fast friends, which was a good thing, because Mrs Williams was staying with Tim and Anastasia O'Halloran. Our house was overflowing with wedding guests as it was, and we couldn't have fitted her in sideways.

Speaking of Mrs Williams, she had been a bit puzzled when she got off the train and found that she was in Orroroo in the mid-north of South Australia. Somehow, she had thought they were headed for Wallaroo, which she knew was near the sea. Anastasia told me my neighbour from Norwood had even brought along a bathing costume in case we would be visiting the beach.

'I don't think Father Travers will let you in the church wearing that hat, Rose,' Anastasia said. 'He wouldn't be able to keep a straight face and he'll get the wedding vows all wrong. You might end up not getting properly married.'

That, I thought, might not be such a bad thing. I was beginning to feel as if I had been railroaded into this wedding.

When I agreed to marry Pask, it was because of the pressure from Bob's letter and from Danny, who said he would only stay in Orroroo if his parents were respectable married people. And of course, from Pask, but he had been putting pressure on me to marry him since 1928, so I was used to ignoring him.

I still wanted to make Bob, Pask and most of all Danny, happy, but now I was beginning to have a few reservations about this whole marriage business.

Firstly, I was a bit annoyed because there was a rumour that the government was going to bring in widows' pensions next year. I didn't know how much money I would have gotten from that pension if I kept on being a widow, but I did know if I got married I would miss out on it. I was entitled to that money. I should have had it fourteen years ago. Bloody government. And with the drought and the war, we could use some cash.

As for being respectable, Pask and I had lived in sin all these years and no bolt of lightning had appeared to blast us to oblivion for sinning. God and the people of Orroroo and even most of my family were probably used to the idea of our fornication by now. Not that we were fornicating with as much vigour as we used to, these days. The years do wither some things, unfortunately.

But I was worried that, if we didn't get married, Danny might carry out his threat to run off and join the RAAF, the army or the navy. He was using all three services in turn to frighten me, depending on which one was suffering the most casualties on the current news story on the wireless.

In the end, I had agreed to go through with the wedding, although I stipulated that I wasn't going to go down to Adelaide and have Father Flaherty do the deed. I just wanted a quiet ceremony somewhere where no one would make a fuss and a song and dance about my nuptials. Or read me a sermon on my misdemeanours.

I even considered a registry office wedding, although I had a feeling that I would be committing a mortal sin if I tied the knot that way. It wouldn't be a sin for Pask, of course, because he wasn't a Catholic and non-Catholics don't commit sins, mortal or otherwise. Although, when you think about it, expecting me to wear that hat was a terrible sin. If I didn't know Pask better, I would have said he was having a joke at my expense. Or maybe at Father Travers's expense. Or the Orroroo community in general.

Wearing it might be a penance for my sins. I might even be absolved from sins I hadn't committed yet. It would be like walking barefoot across a paddock full of Scotch thistles.

Pask had been so happy when he found the damn thing hanging on a hook in the cowshed. He came in, twirling it on his finger and singing 'Here comes the bride'. 'You've got to wear this, Rose,' he said. 'You can't wear a veil, after all. Not when you've had all those kids. You're not exactly a virgin, love, so no one's going to expect you to wear white. But this will be perfect.'

'It's putrid, Pask,' I said. 'I used to wear it when I was driving Daisy in to be milked. It fell in the mud heaps of times. And in worse than mud, too. We've had three cows since Daisy. I stopped wearing it when we got Petal because she wouldn't settle down whenever she saw it. She was terrified of that hat. Once, she kicked a full bucket of milk over at the sight of it. So I hung it up on that hook, covered it with a hessian bag and forgot about it.'

'Well, it brings back good memories for me, Rose. And it's just the thing for the wedding. Something old, something blue. Two for the price of one, this is.'

He hadn't smiled like that since I agreed to be his bride. In fact, I don't think I'd ever seen a grin from ear to ear like the one he was wearing.

'I have to wear it,' I told them all. 'Pask has set his mind on it. He'll be upset if I don't. Father Travers will be all right. He's being nice about Pask muttering "bullshit" every time he goes for religious instruction, so I'm sure he won't complain about what I wear on my head.'

'Well, if we're going to have to resurrect this hat, we'd better fix it up in a hurry,' said Anastasia. 'The wedding's on Sunday. Did your fruit cake turn out all right, Rose?'

'Of course, it did,' said Pask, coming in the back door and tossing his hat onto the table beside the hat with the drooping blue roses. 'Do you remember this bonnet of Rose's, Anastasia? She's going to wear it for the wedding. Jeez, I hope we get a bit of a cool change before the day or I reckon I might have another one of them funny turns in the church.'

He saw the look of horror on my face and gave me a hug. 'Only kidding, love. I'm right as rain. Nothing's going to stop us getting hitched on Sunday. And then we're having that slap up do at the Pekina pub. People're coming from miles around for it. It'll be the wedding of the year. Our wedding is going to be the talk of the town.'

19

8 December 1941
Rose Walsh

The wedding wasn't the talk of the town after all. While the family had been discussing my hat, the Japanese had been bombing Pearl Harbor. I shuddered when I thought the bombs were probably raining down while we were planning the wedding. And then things got worse.

'They're playing "Advance Australia Fair",' I said, as Pask put the wireless on when we sat down to eat.

We had a lot of people around the kitchen table, what with our visitors up from Norwood. The country air seemed to make them hungry. Pask had killed an old ewe but perhaps we should have had a fatted calf judging from their appetites.

'They always play "God Save the King" before Mr Curtin does his talk.' I paused in the middle of dishing up the roast leg of mutton with baked spuds and silverbeet from the patch out by the septic tank. 'Not that I mind. "God Save the King" always annoys me when we have to stand up for it in the movies. Being of Irish descent, that is. It's nice to have a change.'

'Hush, Rose, I reckon Mr Curtin must have something important to say.'

Pask turned up the wireless and we all looked in its direction. As if that would make any difference, but it seemed to be important to see where the voice was coming from. It was so loud you would have thought Mr Curtin was sitting at the table with us.

I put the food back into the baking tray and sat it on the wood stove, hoping that it wouldn't dry out too much. It was more important to know our future than to fill our bellies. I was right; this was a really dramatic moment.

It was an important speech, too. Mr Curtin announced Australia had declared war on Japan because of the Japanese bombing Pearl Harbor. He said it showed the Japs were serious about invasion, as though we didn't know that anyway.

Afterwards, we all agreed he, or the radio station, had chosen 'Advance Australia Fair' instead of 'God Save the King' because this was the first time in history that we, as a nation, had declared war on another country without Britain telling us we had to do it. Being patriotic and independent at the same time, I suppose.

I agree it's time we made up our own mind about things, and the Poms aren't likely to be much use to us because they've got enough on their plate with Hitler, but I still don't like war. Especially when my kids are involved in it.

Mr Curtin said the priority of Australia has to be to secure the defence of Australia. He'd made speeches before, predicting that sending our men to Europe to fight Britain's war was exposing us to danger and the soldiers were soon going to be needed here. He was right. I was so glad we had got rid of Menzies and had someone in charge who wanted to save our country.

We all actually clapped hands at the end of the speech, although naturally we were terrified of what the future would hold. It had been bad enough knowing our boys were fighting overseas, but now Australia was at war it was closer to home, as it were. Pask went into the front room, where he kept a bottle of brandy for medicinal purposes (he says it beats kerosene actually) and poured glasses for us all. Even a taste for Danny and Rosemary, although Mary and I didn't really agree with that, but Pask said we were all in this together and they were going to have to grow up fast now.

We drank to victory and to Mr Curtin and to Australia in general. We cheered and hugged and shed some tears. I thought a lot about our boys, especially Brian and Bob and Joe and Charlie, who was up in Queensland training with the army.

I shed more tears, and then I looked at Annie and tried not to show how frightened I was, because her eyes were shining and I could see that she was even more determined to become a nurse and go off and patch soldiers together under a tropical sky or where ever the Army sent her.

Australia was at war now because of the Japs bombing a place no one had ever heard of before called Pearl Harbor, which is on an island called Hawaii that belongs to the Americans; so it was a big mistake on the Japs' part.

20

Sunday 14 December 1941
Rose Pask

Pearl Harbor was the topic on everyone's lips when they gathered outside the Pekina church on Sunday, and not our rushing into wedlock as Pask and I had thought.

And just like the mood around our table, the mood outside the church was both grim and elated. Grim because Australia was now engaged in a terrible struggle for survival against the Japanese but elated because now Mr Roosevelt had committed America to war. Now, everyone said, we would start to see things happen.

People were elated that Pask and I were getting married, too, but there was that undercurrent, that buzz of conversation that bore a faint air of distraction when the buggy arrived at the Pekina church. There were some furrowed brows as people gazed towards the war memorial across the road from the church and wondered whether their boys' names might be inscribed in the future on that war memorial.

Danny gave me away. I wished that Charlie could have come up from Adelaide to do that, but Charlie was somewhere up near Brisbane, training for battle in the tropics.

Although I had hoped and prayed that the army wouldn't take him because of the pleurisy he had had last year, I knew he was determined to join up. He'd never let the pleurisy stop him playing football. We told him he was crazy, but he wasn't going to let his mates down on the footy field, and I knew he wouldn't be letting them down when it came to a stoush against the Japs, either.

So many 'if onlys' went through my mind as Pask helped me climb out of the cart and Mary handed down my bouquet. I didn't intend to toss the bouquet after the ceremony, because I knew no one would want to catch a prickly thing like this. They would have to be mad; I was getting some bemused looks from members of the congregation who had noticed the unusual floral arrangement. And my hat too. There were a few smirks on the faces of a few Pekinians. And on Mrs Williams's face too. Bitch!

To distract myself and to attempt to keep a regal or at least a bridal smile on my face, I reflected on all the circumstances that had brought me to the Pekina church today.

If Michael hadn't died and left the family destitute, I would never have come to Orroroo back in 1928 as Pask's housekeeper; if he and the kids hadn't accepted me into their family or I hadn't come under their spell I wouldn't have stayed. If I hadn't gotten pregnant when I did, long after I had thought I could, we wouldn't have Danny. And if the war hadn't broken out, my Brian wouldn't be dead, and my other boys would be here today.

But here I was, and I was holding admittedly the most unusual bouquet of flowers a bride had ever carried.

Pask had gone out to the shed this morning and come back with a big grin on his face and a bunch of three of the biggest Scotch thistles I had ever seen, wrapped in hessian. 'Blue roses for the bride!' he said, thrusting the blooms at me. 'I've been keeping an eye on these for weeks,' he said. 'Even poured a bit of water on them to keep them going, although I never in my life thought I would water bloody thistles.'

I looked in the bottom drawer of the kitchen dresser and found a leftover scrap of the blue cloth that I had used all those years ago to make clothes for Annie and Bob, and also to fashion the blue roses to decorate my hat and take away its funereal aura.

I cut a strip of the cloth to tie around the hessian for luck. Mary had brought some white ribbons for Kathleen and Rosemary's hair and we tied the leftover ones to the bouquet too. In the end it looked quite impressive. Different, but impressive.

'It'll bring us good luck,' said Pask of the bouquet.

Now, as I walked towards the church on Danny's arm, I gave the horse a pat for luck as well. We were all going to need as much luck as we could get, and not just to get through this wedding ceremony. Australia was at war. Who knew what the coming months and years held?

If only this rotten war wasn't on, Joe would have been the priest who joined Pask and me in holy matrimony. Not that Father Travers wasn't a really nice chap. It was good of him to turn a blind eye to that calling of the banns rule. By rights, we should have waited at least two weeks while anyone who had objections to our marriage spoke up. Father Travers said anyone with objections had had fifteen years to speak up, so they could keep their mouths shut if they were unhappy.

And of course, it was Advent, and people weren't supposed to get married until after Christmas. But Father Travers said that, because there was a war on, rules could be bent. Father Flaherty would never have reasoned like that, Jesuit or not.

If things were different, Harry, as my eldest boy, would be giving me away, and if Brian wasn't dead, he would have grabbed my flowers and tossed them into the crowd, prickles and all, after the ceremony, probably aiming for Annie so she would catch them and be the next bride. With him as groom

If the war wasn't happening, Charlie would be singing 'Ave Maria' when Pask and I went in to sign the register, and he would have sung 'Danny Boy' at the reception. There wouldn't have been a dry eye in the house. If there was no war.

And Bob would be there, grinning beside his father and wearing in his buttonhole a flower (probably a Scotch thistle or one of the white roses from the bush by our back door) and being the best man, instead of being stuck in some freezing cold German prison. Now that we had the address from the Red Cross, Annie said she was going to write to him and tell him all about what Pask insisted on calling 'the wedding of the year'.

'No one has ever seen a wedding like this one,' Annie said. 'It's got to be the most unorthodox ceremony that's ever happened in Orroroo.'

'Or anywhere else either,' said Mrs Williams, surveying my hat and my flowers and the horse and buggy some of us had arrived in at the church.

I couldn't see why we shouldn't save a bit of petrol. No sense in making two trips to Pekina. Annie was driving the rest of the family in the ute and that ute was full including the back tray, so we couldn't have squeezed in even if we had tried. Call it sentiment or superstition, but I was happy that we were using the horse and cart, because Pask had been driving that cart the first time I had met him, back in 1928. Of course, the Dobbin that drew the cart was actually Dobbin the Third, but that was irrelevant. Same colour, same placid temperament, same farts that wafted up to the passengers.

'Best bridal bouquet the Pekina church has ever seen,' said Pask, inspecting the blue roses. 'And the best-looking bride, too.'

He had a white rose from our rose bush in his buttonhole, which spruced up his old suit a bit. I suspected he had worn that suit for his first marriage to Elsie, Bob and Annie's mum, all those years ago. It hung a bit loose on him now, because he had lost quite a bit of weight when he was ill recently.

We had put petals from the white rose into a little basket for Kathleen, Mary's two-year-old, to carry, so she could be a flower girl. It was Mary's idea that the kiddie could scatter them as I walked up the aisle on Danny's arm. Only Kathleen refused to do that. Instead, she kept them all until I was standing beside Pask at the altar, and then she suddenly pelted us both as hard as she could with the full contents of the basket and tossed the basket at us as well for good measure. It hit Pask on the ankle with surprising force and he winced.

The members of the congregation who were not already in stitches over my hat and bouquet tried not to laugh, but not many succeeded. Even I had to pinch myself to keep from giggling. All in all, I was feeling quite discombobulated, although all I had drunk was a bit of sherry before we left the farmhouse to give me Dutch courage.

My hat, even with its kerosene bath, was still a bit whiffy and a slight scent of the cowshed wafted from the black straw. I had tried to make the hat presentable, but I knew only Pask truly appreciated my efforts. The blue roses had been disassembled, washed and refashioned, and clung to the brim looking rather more garish than I had hoped.

I remembered that years ago when we were going to a dance at Pekina, Pask had said 'that hat will knock everyone for six', and it still seemed to have that effect. Or perhaps it was the bunch of Scotch thistles.

Father Travers impressed me with his ability to keep a straight face. Perhaps he was concentrating on the words and not on my attire, my bouquet, or young Katherine's behaviour.

'Do you, Rose Margaret Alma Walsh, take this man, Cedric Cecil Pascal, to be your lawful wedded husband to love, honour and obey?'

'Hang on a bit, Father,' interjected Pask.

'Your turn will come, Pask,' said the priest, finger raised in admonition.

'No, I've got an objection, Father,' insisted Pask. 'You asked if anyone had any objections. I've got one now, and there won't be any peace for anyone unless or until I speak up. Rose has never obeyed anyone in her life, although that bastard Michael who she was married to before I met her tried. Well, I'm not asking her to obey me. So, with all due respect, Father, you'll have to take that bit out or I'm not going through with this, even though I've been waiting for fifteen years for this day to come.'

There was silence. And then everyone started clapping and cheering.

'Well, if everyone feels that way,' said Father Travers, 'I'll have to bow to the majority. It's a bit unorthodox, but this is not an orthodox ceremony. We'll just stick to love and honour, if that's all right with everyone.' He gave a little bow in our direction. He was grinning from ear to ear.

I lost control, because I was imagining how Flaherty would have reacted, and I laughed out loud. Father Flaherty would never have made a concession like that. Thank God we had decided to be married in Or-roroo instead of Norwood.

'Do you, Cedric Cecil Pascal, take this woman…' Father Travers intoned.

'I bloody well do!' yelled Pask, not letting the priest complete his spiel.

'And about bloody time, too!' shouted Danny.

Pask didn't wait to be told, 'You may kiss the bride.' He just grabbed me and kissed me before I even had time to realise that now I was Mrs P, not Mrs W any longer.

21

24 February 1942
Police Sergeant Harry Walsh – Darwin

Dear Mum,

A bloke isn't supposed to give in – we're supposed to put on a show and keep going no matter what. But I'll tell you straight, since Mavis and the kids were evacuated on that bloody tub Koolinda just before Christmas (it was 19 December and there must be something about the 19th of some months, because it was on 19 February that the Japs hit us the first time), I've been down in the dumps. Real down in the dumps. I've never been so bloody miserable in all my whole bloody life.

It was bad enough watching my wife and kiddies go up the gangplank knowing anything could happen between here and Brisbane, what with the Japs bombing Pearl Harbor, and we all knew those bastards were heading south now and they'd be here soon.

One little calico bag each they got to put everything in for two weeks or more. If anyone tried to bring anything more on board, it got chucked into the harbour. There were a few arguments and I saw at least one box of family heirlooms join the crocs in the water. One old lady got hysterical and thumped a sailor real hard, but it didn't do any good.

Mavis was really upset because her Chinese friend, Mrs Lee, and her kiddies and their old granny were told they had to sit on the deck. All the Chinese got treated like that, even the pregnant women, because there were only cabins for white people. No shelter at all for the poor buggers, so I told the crew to sling up some tarps so at least they would have a bit of shade and it might keep some of the rain off. It's the Wet now and when it rains it pelts down up here. The copper's uniform must have helped a bit, because they did what they were told even though they weren't happy about it.

And Mavis's pregnant, too. I feel real bad about it now. We were happy at first to be having another kiddie but now I'm scared about her travelling down on that boat without me and then she's got the long train ride after from Brisbane to Adelaide. I should never have dragged the family up here to Darwin just so I could be a sergeant and have a bit of adventure in the tropics.

The money they were offering seemed good at the time but everything's dearer here because of the isolation so we weren't really any better off anyway. Mavis's been a real saint but I reckon the heat got to her. Always got heat rash. The kids were OK, but kids are OK anywhere. Young Mickey's going to miss the green frogs when he gets down south. Real fond of frogs, that kiddie is.

Anyway, I got a phone call from Brisbane saying they got there safely but it was terrible on the boat and everyone got seasick. They must be on the train and I hope they are nearly back in Adelaide by now. Only the way the powers that be are running this war, they could be anywhere. At least they're not in Darwin and that's a bloody good thing, because the Japs came visiting last week and left their calling card in a big way.

They hit the post office among other things – which is one of the reasons why you won't ever see this letter and that's why I'm not worried if there are a few swear words scattered around on it – I wouldn't say this to your face, Mum, but it helps a bloke to curse a bit sometimes. The other reason why you won't see it is that our beloved leader, Mr Bloody Administrator Abbott, has put an embargo on any communication with the rest of Australia. He says there would be panic if the rest of you found out what happened up here. He's probably correct, but that doesn't make it right. A bloke needs to get stuff off his chest and his Mum's the best place to get it off too.

Anyway, the Japs did a bloody good job on us, because we weren't expecting them and they sunk the ships in the harbour, Yankee ones and Aussie ones too, and then had a go at anything handy on land. They killed everyone in the post office and hit the Residency too, so Abbott wasn't too happy. Some of us grabbed rifles but shooting at planes with rifles doesn't make much difference to them. Still, Mum, a man has got to have a go. Then they came back the next arvo for another bite of the cherry.

No one seems to know how many were killed. Some people say there were two hundred killed, but others say five hundred. They probably don't count the Abos as casualties because they can't vote or drink. Poor buggers don't really exist as far as the government's concerned.

They used a bulldozer to dig a bloody great hole on Mindil Beach and we put the bodies there before they started to stink. Only that's a temporary measure, Abbott says, and they'll be moved later on when this mess gets sorted out. Unless the crocs dig them up, because crocs like meat that's gone off and, let's face it, flesh goes off fast in Darwin. Especially this time of year.'

Harry put the pen down as Fluffy, the family's cat, strolled in and jumped up on Harry's knee.

'Christ, Fluff, it's a bit hot for that,' said Harry. Then he stroked the animal. 'Poor bugger, I'm going to have to drown you soon. Abbott says all cats and dogs have to be destroyed. And I told the kids I'd look after their pets.' He shuddered and held the cat against his chest. 'Good girl, Fluff. You stay here and relax a bit, OK? I'll just write a bit more of this letter to my Mum.'

Harry picked up his pen again.

There's only four of us cops here in Darwin but Abbott kept at least one of us on duty at the Residency packing up the silverware and crystal so it can go down to Katherine with Mrs Abbott because he doesn't want the Japs to get anything with the official crest on it. Worried they'll drink a toast to Hirohito out of the government crystal. Luckily for him, the valuables were at the back of house. Unluckily for her, the poor little half-caste maid was in the front and she got killed and no one knew she was there. Mrs A thought she'd done a runner. I hope the kid was killed outright but she could have been dying there for a while – we'll never know.

Speaking of doing a runner, anyone who can get their hands on a car with petrol in it or a bike or horse or whatever, is doing just that. They won't get far. Katherine's a bloody long way down the Track and the Track isn't exactly a macadam highway. Most of them came up here on a boat, so they haven't got a clue just how

145

isolated we are here. A few dills hijacked the night cart and took off in that, but they overturned it going too fast around a bend. Talk about the shit hitting the fan…

'Harry, are you in there? Jeeze, is that your cat sitting on your lap? A bit warm for that, isn't it? Anyway, all the cats and dogs are meant to be disposed of by now, mate. You're allowed to keep any chooks you've got because we might need them when the food runs out.'

'Hello, Jonesy. Yeah, I know that. I told the kids I'd look after their pets. I've got a hessian bag on the floor over there and a bucket of water. I'll drown the cat in a minute.'

The cat stood up when it saw the intruder, arched its back, hissed and took off. It jumped onto the kitchen cupboard and sat there, glaring at Jonesy.

'Bugger. Now I'll have to catch her again. Bloody hot and sticky, isn't it?'

'It's the Wet, you nong. It's Darwin. What are you doing, Harry? Got any cold beer?'

'No, there's no ice, you drongo, but I've got lukewarm beer. I wrapped it in wet tea towels this morning and it's just drinkable. I'm writing a letter to my mum.'

'Jeeze, Harry, you can't write letters. Abbott'll have your guts for garters. You'll get tossed in the clink and shot at dawn.'

'Don't reckon he'll shoot me at dawn, would he? Coppers are a bit short on the ground. Well, maybe he would. The bastard. Mightn't be bad to get shot at dawn. Here, grab a beer. They're warm but they're bitter.'

'You're a bit bitter yourself, mate. Did you shoot the dog?'

'Yair, I shot Boof first thing this morning. One of the hardest things I've ever done in my life.'

Harry didn't say that he had given the dog a bath before killing it because Boof always loved water and he thought he would give him one last bit of fun. Then he had put a big bone in front of the animal, pulled its ears for a while, told it that the ears were the best bit on a dog and stroked its rough damp coat before raising the rifle and firing.

The memory gave him the shakes again. He took a deep breath before continuing.

'I won't be posting the bloody letter, but I thought at least I could get a few things off my chest if I wrote to my mum.'

'Mums are good for that,' said Jonesy.

'Mum married a farmer at Orroroo, and she jokes that she needs all the letters she can get because there's only ever two letters in Orroroo.'

'Pretty lousy joke, Harry, but jokes are in short supply up here like everything else, so I'll pass it. Reckon the Japs'll be back tomorrow?'

Harry picked up the sheets of paper, glanced at them, and then screwed them up into a ball. 'I'll put this into the bag with Fluffy when I drown her. Should be safe. No one's going to let a dead cat out the bag. Reckon it'll be hot again tomorrow?'

'Reckon Abbott'll get himself and his wife down to Katherine and leave us to stew here and wait for the invasion?'

'Yair to all the above. Have another beer, mate.'

'Pass it over. Suppose we'll have to get used to warm beer, mate, now that the war's come to Darwin.'

22

20 February 1942
Rose Pask – Orroroo
Amy Walsh – Norwood

'Mum, you've got to come home. Right now. On the next train!' Amy's voice was hysterical.

I held the phone away from my ear because I was being deafened.

'You must have heard the news on the wireless,' she screamed. 'Darwin's been bombed. Yesterday! Adelaide'll be next. You've got to come back, Mum. I need you to look after me!'

'It's awful, I know,' I said. 'It's Harry I'm worried about. He's right there in the thick of it. I tried to phone him, but I can't get through. I haven't heard from him since he phoned and said Mavis and the kids were being evacuated. They got loaded on to a ship and they were only allowed to carry one little bag each with all their stuff. Nathan couldn't even take his teddy bear. How do we know that the boat wasn't sunk by those bloody Japs? And Mavis is pregnant, too.'

'I know that Mum, but I'm terrified and Annie is too. Well, she is when she's not out with her rotten boyfriend, Leroy. He says everything's going to be OK, but he's what Danny would call a bullshit artist. And when she goes out and leaves me here on my own in the dark, I don't know what to do. I've been sitting under the table most nights in case the Japs drop bombs. How are we going to get through this?'

'We're all scared, Amy. But it's a long way from Darwin to Adelaide. You're probably in the safest city in Australia.'

'No, we're not. You're better off up there in Orroroo. The Japs won't bother about Orroroo. But they might bomb us. There's more people here and they might decide to get us just to be nasty. They've probably heard about the munitions factory. We'll be a strategic target! Sitting ducks!'

Amy's voice was shaking, and I could tell she was trying hard not to sob. I wished that I could give her a hug but it's a long way from Orroroo to Norwood. Just at that moment, I would have jumped on a train if there'd been one handy, but there wouldn't be one for a couple of days, and with any luck Amy might have settled down and be thinking about the latest film at the Odeon instead of Japanese invasions.

Of course, if she went to the movies, she'd see the latest newsreels about the war, and that would make her worse. But if there was a good movie, especially one with Mae West or Veronica Lake, she'd probably buck up. At least while the film was on.

She's a bit of a flibbertigibbet, my Amy. Up one moment, down the next. She was certainly down right now, and rightly so. Everyone at Orroroo, everyone in the whole of Australia, was so tense that we all felt like screaming. Only screaming wouldn't help. Or crying, as Pask had told me firmly when I had an attack of the heebie-jeebies after the news about Darwin being bombed came on the wireless last night. There weren't any details given, so we didn't know what exactly had happened. I didn't know if Harry was alive or dead, wounded or safe.

I just went to pieces. It was like getting the telegram about Brian all over again.

Pask put the kettle on and made me the strongest cup of tea I have ever drunk and assured me that Harry would be all right. He said all we could do was to keep on being brave and know that we would get through this terrible time. I believed him because I had no option but to believe and to hope he was right. And I prayed. How I prayed.

'Make yourself a nice cup of tea, Amy,' I said. 'Tea fixes everything. Better than a Bex tablet. Have you still got some tea coupons or have you used them all up?"

'We've still got some, Mum. Tea's not a problem at the moment.

Leroy brings us all sorts of stuff. Tea, coffee, butter, chocolate, you name it.

'That's useful,' I said cautiously. This bloke sounded a bit on the shady side somehow.

'But it's horrible here now, Mum,' Amy continued. 'We've got black-out curtains and we have to have these stupid covers over the light globes to stop the light spreading in case it can be seen from the air. They're selling them for two and sixpence at Myers but Annie made some out of empty milk tins and they look so ugly.'

'That was sensible of her,' I said. 'It's only temporary, Amy. I suppose even Mrs Williams has had to do the same thing. It'll put her nose out of joint, the way she's so house-proud.'

'No, Mrs Williams has got the Myer ones but they don't look much better than ours do. They're still nasty, just not quite as daggy.'

'She would go for the best,' I said. 'She's always been like that. More money than sense. You stick with the milk tin ones. I'm sure you'll get used to them.'

'And even the parklands are ruined. There's air-raid shelters dug up all over the place. Everyday there's more holes. I see it from the tram when I go into work. It looks as if the government thinks the Japs are going to come and get us any minute now. And it's dark at night because there's no street lights, so we wouldn't even see the Japs if they were just outside the house. And Mr Williams is an air-raid warden and he keeps prowling around checking on us. We hear the gravel chinking and we can't put the light on to see whose there and we think its Japs or murderers or rapists out there at night.'

'At least Mr Williams's keeping an eye on you, love. I can't come home now. We're busy up here. Danny's learning to drive and he's been out helping Pask with the sheep every day and I'm scared he'll crash the ute and they'll both be killed, so I have to be here to pick up the pieces if anything happens. How is Annie getting along at the munitions factory?'

'She's OK. This Leroy bloke is in the American army and he gets heaps of petrol, only he calls it "gas", so she's out most nights. I go out with them sometimes too, but I don't like him much. Or his mates. He's loud and arrogant and pushy. Annie's changed a lot, Mum.'

I shook my head, although of course Amy couldn't see it, us having this conversation over the telephone as it was. 'I thought she was still heartbroken over Brian dying. She's really got a new boyfriend?'

Amy sounded a bit peeved. 'Annie's not the quiet little thing she used to be any more. Mrs Williams says it's because she's never been in the big smoke before and she's just excited about being here, but I'm worried about her. Are you sure you can't come down even for a bit? Just to pull Annie into line a bit?'

'No, Amy. Annie isn't the sort to run wild. She's a good girl. Has she applied to the army nursing people yet?'

'I think she's changed her mind. She's having too good a time to want to go off nursing right now.'

I thought I could hear anger in Amy's voice. But Amy and Annie were so close, they never argued. It all seemed very odd.

'She was very keen about nursing before she left here,' I said. 'Although I think I'd rather she stayed with you for a bit longer, at least until Mavis gets back. You'll feel happier when Mavis and the boys are around the corner in their own house. Phil's moved back to her mum's house, now that Charlie's off in the army, hasn't she? So at least you've got Annie. Perhaps it's just as well she's not leaving right now.'

'Yes, Phil's mum's not well. Heart problems, I think. And she broke her hip too. But it's not much use having Annie here because she's never home. She's having too good a time to think about anything else than jitterbugging and driving around in Leroy's jeep. And now she thinks even more about clothes than I do, and you used to complain about me being obsessed with what I wear. And Leroy brings her silk stockings and chocolates. I don't know what to do, Mum. I even thought about asking Father Flaherty to have a word with her, only Annie's not Catholic, so she'd probably just laugh. Or get cross with me.' There was a definite sob in Amy's voice. 'I don't know what to do,' she repeated plaintively. She sounded like a mother who was at her wits' end with an errant child.

'I'm sure she'll settle down in a couple of months, Amy,' I said. 'Ask Mrs Williams to have a chat to her. She'll know how to handle it.'

But of course, Mrs Williams had never had kids, I reminded myself, and she wouldn't have a clue how to talk to a young girl who was out jitterbugging, whatever that was. I didn't like what I had just heard. I really didn't like the sound of this Leroy chap. If only Brian hadn't been killed.

I would never have imagined that Annie would be involved with another fellow as quickly as that. It just shows you can never tell. I thought I was a good judge of character; I always thought that Amy was flighty, and Annie was the sensible one. I had hoped Annie would be a stabilising influence on Amy. Now it looked as if it was going the other way entirely.

After the phone call, I wondered if I should mention what Amy had said about Annie to Pask but I decided against it. He had enough worries with the sheep and with Bob being a prisoner of war. Pask was teaching Danny to drive too, which was a bit of a strain. Best to put the matter of Annie on the back burner, as it were, and let it simmer for a bit. It was probably just the girl letting off a bit of steam now that she was free for the first time in her life. Only natural, really.

I remembered during the Great War some people did act strangely; went a bit wild. You heard stories about wild parties. I didn't, of course, because when Michael had gone off on his Great Adventure with his mates he left me with three young children to look after, and I wasn't brought up like that anyway, but plenty of people did go off the rails. War can make you think that you need to compress all your living into a short time because you don't know how much longer you have got to live. It must be that idea, plus Annie's youthful high spirits, that was making her jitterbug. Everything would work out for the best, I was sure.

23

20 June 1942
Rose Pask – Orroroo

I'd been working out how many ration coupons I needed to do the weekly shop before we went into town on Friday when Pask brought the post in. Colin, our postie, had seen him near the front gate and handed it over rather than make the trek up to the house. There was a telegram for one of our neighbours Colin had to deliver urgently. It wasn't a duty he liked performing, but there it was. We all knew the likely contents of telegrams in wartime. Pask didn't ask who the neighbour was; the whole district would know soon enough.

I remembered how I had reacted when the telegram boy brought the news of Brian's death and hoped Colin would get a better reception than I had given that lad.

Pask had told Colin to call in for a cuppa on the way back if he felt up to it. Tea is the panacea we all need when there's bad news to deliver. Of course, tea's rationed now at half a pound of the stuff per month, so I'd started drying out the tea leaves after we used them the first time so we could get another brew out of them. I know there's a war on, but the bloody politicians should have worked out where tea comes from and that us Aussies need tea before they decided to declare war. Why can't we grow the stuff in Queensland, for example? It's tropical like India and China up there, I'm sure.

I tossed the ration book aside. I'd rather read letters than add up how much tea and sugar I could buy and how long the supplies would last the three of us. As if life wasn't complicated enough without the pollies imposing rationing on us. But as they keep saying, there's a war on.

At least on the farm at Orroroo we didn't have to worry about the two and a quarter pounds of meat per week everyone else had to survive on, not while we still had sheep that Pask could chase out in the paddocks. And of course, the odd bunny whenever Danny felt like taking potshots at them. And there was no problem about the official specified half a pound of butter per week, as long as Petal kept giving milk and I kept milking her and using the churn.

There was a letter (a combined one) from Annie and Amy. The girls always wrote together because it saved on stamps and I suspected doing a joint effort was a way of getting the job of writing out of the way without either of them having to expend too much time and effort. There was one from Mary, who didn't write all that often either, because she was run off her feet with the butcher's shop, little Kathleen, and with her daily domestic battles with Rosemary. And with her worry about Paddy, who kept saying he was going to join up as soon as he could.

And there was a letter from Charlie. 'About time,' I said, seizing that one first. I ripped open the envelope and scanned the contents.

I waved the flimsy sheet of paper at Pask. It wasn't a long letter, but it was precious because it was the first I had had from my son for quite a long time. Charlie was still alive! At least he was still alive when he had written these words.

Pask was filling the kettle with the rainwater that he had brought in earlier. 'The water tank's getting a bit low,' he said. 'If we don't get some rain soon, we'll be reduced to bore water. What's in the mail, Rose?'

'There's a letter from Charlie, but I can hardly make sense of it because so much of it is inked out. He must have really upset the censors.'

'That figures. Charlie isn't the sort of chap who'd take too much notice of censors' instructions,' said Pask, putting the kettle on the stove. 'Although he'd never write stuff that would put Australia in danger.'

He picked up the tea caddy and shook it. 'Tea's getting a bit low. Sometimes I reckon the censors get bored and just ink stuff out for the sake of doing it. I remember my mum complained my letters from the

Great War were more black ink than writing, and I was always careful what I put down.'

'Charlie's got more sense than to say too much in a letter,' I said. I was dying to start reading it, the words were almost leaping off the page in my hand, but it would be rude not to answer Pask. 'Just like Joe.'

I had a quick scan of the page, I would read it more slowly and carefully later. 'Charlie's still on the Track in New Guinea,' I said.

'Well, we knew that, love,' Pask said. 'I reckon it'll take a while going up that track. Bloody big mountains. He was talking about that in his last letter. Just about all the kids are off doing their bit somewhere. I still feel guilty that I'm here.'

I looked up from the page. 'You did your bit last time, Pask. And lost your eye doing it too.'

Pask touched the patch over his missing eye briefly. 'Yair,' he said. 'I used to write home too. It keeps your spirits up a bit, writing home.'

'Joe's letters are so cheerful you would think he was on holiday instead of helping wounded soldiers. He's in England now. Joe, not Charlie. He sounds as if he likes what he's doing. And even Bob sounds as if he's quite happy, although he's probably going crazy being locked up in the prison camp when we all know he wants to be out doing his bit.'

'That's how blokes are, Rose. You have to make things sound better than they are, for everyone's sake. No sense upsetting the family back home. Charlie's nowhere near Lae, is he? Remember how they said on the wireless last night that our lot blasted Lae? Blew thirty Jap planes up that were sitting on the ground? I reckon the tide's starting to turn for our blokes.'

'He doesn't say where he is, just somewhere on the Kokoda Track,' I said, trying to make sense of what Charlie had written. Part of me wanted to race through the letter, to absorb as much of what my son had said as quickly as possible, but part of me wanted to savour his words slowly.

I would read and reread the letter over the next few weeks, so of course I would do both. But now, with Pask looking at me, I needed to tell him what my first impressions were.

I held the page up so he could see all the blacking out and appreciate how difficult it was to interpret.

Pask shrugged and put the cups on the table. He reached for the biscuit tin. I scanned Charlie's words.

'He says parts of the country are dreadful, full of marshes with leeches that get on your legs and you have to burn them off with cigarette ends, and heaps of mosquitos. Lots of the chaps are sick with malaria and diarrhoea. He says he's OK so far, hasn't had too many problems. But then he says other parts of the place are really beautiful and what did he call it – "like the garden of Eden only with more snakes than the original Eden and coconuts and mangoes instead of apples".'

'Is that a letter from Charlie?' demanded Danny, who had just come in from the paddocks. He ran through the door, his boots clunking on the lino.

'Yes, but your mum says the censor's made mincemeat of it,' Pask said.

'Remember in that last letter he said the Japs had bombed Port Moresby back in early February?' said Danny. 'But the censor didn't black out much in that letter. This stupid bloke must have been having a bad day. Can I have a look at it?'

'Do take your boots off before you come in, Danny,' I said. 'I've just washed the floor and you've got mud and sheep shit all over your feet.' I sighed and passed the letter over. I would just have to wash the floor again tomorrow. 'Here, you see if you can work out what Charlie's trying to tell us.'

Danny shed his boots, chucked them in the general direction of the doorway, and settled down on the nearest chair. 'I could murder a cup of tea, Mum,' he said. 'It's getting cool out there. I reckon winter's coming early this year. We'd better finish the crutching as soon as we can, Dad, in case it starts raining. I thought we might ask Mr O'Halloran and some of the other fellows to give us a hand with our sheep and help with theirs afterwards. Then the job'll be done quicker.'

'Right, we'll do that,' said Pask, trying to keep the grin off his face but not really succeeding. 'That's a great idea, son. I'll phone Tim Halloran later on. Might get a start on it tomorrow if he can make it.'

Later, when Pask and I were alone in our room at night, he boasted about what a great little farmer Danny was turning out to be. I tried not to smile myself as I poured the tea. These days, Danny seemed to be chasing more sheep than Pask did. Either Pask had slowed down or he had decided to step back and let the lad take the reins. If it was a deliberate ploy, it was working well. And if Pask was feeling his age, it was just as well we had come back when we did.

Danny put the letter flat on the table and bent over it. Then he held it up to the light. He tried turning the page over to see if there were impressions on the back of the sheet that might help him decipher the words. He ran his finger over the page as if he was reading Braille. He squinted at the paper then tried holding it at a distance and bringing it slowly closer to his eyes. He grimaced, shook his head and then laid the letter back on the table.

At last, he sat up straight in his chair and looked at Pask and me watching his performance. 'I reckon that word is "shit", announced Danny. 'This letter is full of shit.'

'That's not a nice thing to say about your brother's letter,' I protested. 'He went to a lot of trouble writing it, and he must be busy just trying to keep alive up there in the jungle with all those snakes and spiders and the Japs trying to get him. Not to mention the heat. And the cold now he's up in the mountains.'

'I don't mean it like that, Mum,' said Danny. 'It's just that there are all these short bits of blacked out words all over the page, and "shit" fits with what Charlie's said just before a short blacked-out bit. Look at this paragraph. "Bert cut the back out of his shorts because he couldn't get them down quick enough to…" And before that he says someone else had "…" running down their shorts.'

'Why would the censor cut that out?' I asked.

'I reckon the men have all got dysentery and the censor thought it wasn't something Charlie ought to be writing home about. Maybe he

157

was worried the Japs might get hold of the letter and know that our blokes are crook, or p'raps he's just straight-laced and thought it wasn't something a bloke should put in a letter home,' said Pask.

'Charlie says here they've seen Japs running around with no pants on, so they must have the same problem,' said Danny, smirking. 'That'll slow the buggers down.'

'It means everyone's in the same boat,' said Pask. 'Up shit creek with no paddle.'

'Maybe it's the water,' I said. 'They should boil their water. I always do that when there's gastro about. And put a drop or two of kero in it.'

'They mightn't have time to do that,' said Pask. 'If they're on patrol, they would just fill their canteens out of the nearest creek. There could be rotting carcases in those creeks. Dead animals or…' He looked at me and didn't finish his sentence.

But I knew what he was thinking. Charlie and his mates were at war, and there would be corpses lying about in that jungle. Enemy bodies and the bodies of our boys too. That would be enough to give anyone dysentery or cholera.

Danny was still studying Charlie's letter intently. More intently, I thought, than he had ever studied his books when he was at school. Yes, this lad was cut out to be a farmer, not a city kid. I hope he gets to grow up at Orroroo and if and when Bob comes home, they can work together on this farm. Those two boys'd make a great team when Pask really gets too old to chase sheep. God give us the chance for Pask and I to live long enough to see it.

God, save Charlie and bring him home safe. And please don't let Danny go to war. Don't let his body be destroyed and thrown into a river in some green hell. How much longer will this madness continue? God, make it end before Danny is old enough to be dragged into the war. And God, let Charlie come home to raise the baby Phil is expecting. God, give us peace sooner rather than later. Please God, keep all my boys safe from harm.

'What's for tea, Mum?' asked Danny. 'I'm starving.' He got up from his chair and grabbed my arm. 'Jeez, Mum, you've gone all pale. You look like you're having some sort of fit. Do you want to sit down for a bit before we eat? You're not having a funny turn like Dad did, are you? Do you want me to peel some spuds or something?'

'Do you want another cup of tea, Rose?' asked Pask anxiously. 'You're not having a funny turn, are you?'

I shook my head and took my hands off the edge of the table. I hadn't realised I was gripping it so tightly. 'I'm all right, love,' I said. 'Just wondering what Charlie is up to right now and if he's got enough to eat. There was a bit about bully beef and biscuits in the letter. It doesn't sound all that appertising to me.'

Danny, hearing the word biscuit reached for the tin. 'Can I have another biscuit, Mum?' he asked, grinning.

He had already eaten two, but I wasn't about to say no, and the little devil knew it.

'There's a letter from Mary, too,' I said. 'And one from the girls as well.'

But Danny and Pask were discussing arrangements for the sheep, so I was left to read those letters on my own while the potatoes were boiling.

24

19 August 1942
Charlie Walsh – Owen Stanley Mountains,
New Guinea

Charlie followed Kiri through the forest. There were less leeches up here – it wasn't as marshy here as it had been lower down the Track. The only way to get rid of leeches was to burn them off with a cigarette. But the smell of a fag would be a dead giveaway to any Jap sniper athletic enough to climb the trees, so any leeches that attached themselves to a bloke's legs would have to stay attached.

The thought of a cigarette set off his craving for a smoke. At least any Japs waiting in ambush couldn't afford to smoke either. He sniffed, checking for smoke in the air that might give away an enemy position, then shook his head. Funny to think of the enemy sharing his discomfort. Made them a bit more human, perhaps. Although there were plenty of atrocity stories going around. Aussies strung up in the forest, slices of flesh cut from them. Rumours of cannibalism because the Nips' rations were running out. So are ours. The last airdrops were useless. Bags of flour bursting on impact, tins scattered all over the jungle.

Our side's no angels either, he thought, remembering the no prisoners policy. If you managed to ambush Japanese patrols, orders were to shoot the lot. What else could you do? There were no extra rations to feed prisoners, and no spare troops to shepherd the buggers down the Track.

Charlie checked likely-looking spots where a Jap could be lying in wait in the long grass, then examined the ground ahead to make sure he wasn't stepping into a mantrap filled with sharpened spikes. That was another nasty trick the enemy had mastered. And, of course, there was always the chance a snake lay just where you were about to step. Nothing was certain in New Guinea. Just when you thought the whole place was hot and humid, here you were up in the Owen Stanleys, where the temperature could, and did, plummet.

He shuddered as he remembered the white mist that he had woken to that morning. You couldn't see your hand in front of your face. No dawn chorus of birds; the cloud had muffled sound as well as sight. Or perhaps, like the soldiers, the birds were afraid of giving away their positions when they couldn't see well enough to seek cover. Or maybe they were singing as usual, but the white stuff had crept into the patrols' ears and filled them with cotton wool.

A whole platoon of Japs might be out there. They could have crept up, silent as ghosts in the fog and the sentries would never have spotted them.

But it hadn't happened. Not this time.

Charlie had decided to go pig hunting because of the mist. There was less chance of the Japs spotting a couple of chaps on their own when it was foggy. He'd had a quick word to the sarge, who agreed all the fellows were whingeing about the diet of bully beef and biscuits and a nice pork chop would lift morale.

'Take one of the boongs with you, mate,' Keith suggested. 'And watch yourself out there. The native patrol officer says there's a cannibal village not far from here.'

One of the native porters was using his machete to chop up a snake he had cooked in the coals of a small fire. The other chaps squatted on their haunches and waited. Charlie watched as pieces of the reptile were distributed among the group. It had been cooked in its skin, and the men expertly peeled the skin, exposing the pinkish flesh and devouring it with relish.

'Good tucker?' he asked.

Kiri, the man he knew best, looked up briefly and nodded, his crown of fuzzy hair making the gesture seem more emphatic.

'You come hunt pig?' asked Charlie. He produced a packet of

cigarettes and offered it to the native, who stuffed the pack into the pocket of his army issue shorts. Funny how the uniform looks better on these blokes than on us, thought Charlie. They're not as skinny. Better at living off the land, he supposed.

'We fella get meat too?' demanded Kiri

'Of course, you do,' said Charlie. 'We share the danger, we share the meat. You know that, Kiri. You Fuzzy Wuzzies are good blokes.'

'Danger bad in mountains,' said Kiri. 'Not like coast, not like Moresby. Little cannibal man, him eat man. Call 'im long pig. Allasame pig meat.'

'I've got gun,' said Charlie. 'She'll be right.'

Of course, as the day progressed, the mist lifted, and visibility improved. But there were places here where the giant figs shut out the light. Even the ferns were ten feet high in some spots, their trunks covered with moss, and the wait-a-while vines hung at just the right height to entangle a man and trap him with nasty barbs. Lawyer vines, that was the other name for them, thought Charlie. Get tangled up with them and you were finished.

Kiri swung his machete to clear the path, which made the going easier. Charlie carried his rifle carefully. He was ready and primed to fire if a pig (or a Jap) appeared, but Kiri was still trekking steadily through the bush. Charlie thought the native's body language indicated they still had a distance to travel. Charlie trusted the man's judgement.

Mum would love the plants, Charlie thought – well, some of them at least. Only she'd go mad at the profusion. She'd want to thin stuff out. Of course, there were no roses here, not even blue ones. Even the orchids grew like crazy things. He would have liked to pick some of those purple orchids for Phil. She could wear them pinned to that green jacket of hers, an exotic corsage. What this place needs is a gardener to impose some sort of order, Charlie thought, only he knew no one would ever tame the Track. He wiped his brow. Even up in the mountains it was humid and the sweat ran continuously into a man's eyes.

Now that the sun was up, the birds were loud. Raucous. You never knew which direction they were in; the calls came from one direction, then the other. Or maybe the whole forest was teeming with birds, most hidden, but now and then you saw a flash of colour as something, perhaps even a bird of paradise, shot across your line of sight. They were always too fast to identify. Not that Charlie really knew one of these alien birds from the other.

And the smell. There was a certain odour that pervaded this whole country. An undercurrent of mould and decay, yet with it the feeling and scent of life bursting out of the fertile soil, something that Charlie had never encountered anywhere in Australia. Not even in far north Queensland, where the army had trained before embarkation. A smell of resurrection – life from death.

Everywhere on earth had its own smell, he supposed; he remembered the eucalyptus of the bush back home in Australia, the dry smell of the dust at Orroroo that caught in the back of your throat, the stench of the long-drop at the homestead the day he and Brian had helped Pask move the dunny when it got full, the reek of wet sheep when they were shearing and there had been a sudden shower of rain, the rich flavour of Mum's fruit cake, that floral perfume that Phil wore when they were going to a dance.

But New Guinea was different, although equally memorable. This country's aroma would be with him all his life. It was ingrained into his memory.

In some places, the forest was so thick and dark Charlie couldn't understand how Kiri could make out the prints the pigs had left. Everywhere there were great heaps of leaves, so maybe some of them were squashed and showed where the pigs had trodden. Perhaps the native was looking ahead to see the occasional places where the animals had pushed the bush aside. However he was doing it, Kiri looked confident. And his tracking had always been successful in the past, so Charlie was content to follow him.

The men would feast on pork tonight. No bully beef and biscuits on the menu. There would be fresh meat all round.

'Boss, this way,' whispered Kiri. 'Pig, him go straight in that place.'

There was an area like an entrance to a church where great figs with buttress roots clustered together, but then suddenly the forest parted and he and Kiri were in a place where the sunlight poured through a gap that reminded Charlie of a time he had gone to a stage show with Phil back when they were courting, and a spotlight had shone on a soloist playing a violin.

Shafts of light dazzled his eyes so that for a moment he was transfixed. The effect was almost like light shining through stained glass in a cathedral. This was a holy place, a place where God or his angels might suddenly slide down a shaft of glory to alight on the forest floor. Huge brightly coloured butterflies fluttered through the glade. This was a place of infinite possibilities. A sacred place where a man could be transported to a place of peace, to heaven or to home.

But perhaps this was hell, because something stank. The fertile odour of New Guinea had been superseded by an overpowering, fetid stench. Charlie felt suddenly nauseated.

And then he heard it. An unholy orgy of sound. Pigs, many pigs, rooting and snorting in exultation, and bone crunching and a nasty squelchy sound of something being torn and dragged from a tight cavity and a plopping, and then a gulping sound as that something was devoured.

And then he saw it. Long flaccid brown, purple and red tubes gulped into the maws of swine, swine that were covered in shit and slime and blood. Swine that thrust their snouts into green-clad objects, themselves green with corruption. Objects, Charlie now saw, that once had been humans. Legs and arms and heads pushed aside, tossed into the air as the pigs sought the tastiest of morsels, the guts. Sausage-like guts being dragged from the distended bellies of what had once been men.

'Christ!' yelled Charlie. 'Christ!'

He bent double and vomited. He wiped his mouth on his sleeve, looked around the glade and remembered a line his father used to quote. An educated man, his father. 'What did you use to say, Dad?' he shrieked. '*Dolce et decorum est pro patria mori*, wasn't it? Well, it's not! No matter which country you're dying for, it's a stinking, rotting, death, that's what it is! And nothing makes it right or sweet or noble!'

The swine turned towards his anguished voice, paused briefly in their work then serenely resumed tearing at the corpses. This was a good feed and they wouldn't willingly abandon it.

'Pig, Boss,' said Kiri serenely. He pulled on Charlie's arm, tapped the rifle to draw his attention to the hunt. 'Plenty pig. Mates hungry.'

The native seemed unaffected by the horror. Was horror ingrained in his culture? Was he immune to this? Charlie wondered momentarily what Kiri's life had been before the army had recruited him. And did the natives differentiate between the Australians who had invaded New Guinea from the south and the Japanese who had invaded from the north?

This must be the work of Bluey's patrol, he knew. They'd been up this way last week. Charlie had heard talk. A fair bit of action out there, that had been the word around the campfire. Horror's ingrained in our culture, too, he thought. Am I immune to it? And he knew that although he would do his duty, he would never be immune.

Charlie wiped his mouth and vomited again. Then rage took over. Man versus beast.

He raised his rifle and shot the nearest pig. It fell, writhed for a moment, and was still. A pig nosed at its mate's cadaver and part of Charlie's mind wondered whether the animal fancied fresher meat or whether pigs had some sort of family feeling and it had realised one of its number was dead. But Charlie's anger became a vengeful frenzy and he fired again and again, a volley of shots, careless whether it might attract enemy attention, knowing that he couldn't kill all the pigs, but that he must punish them for the sin of desecration of humanity.

It was not just pigs he was shooting; in his blind rage, he sought revenge on all the old men who had sacrificed youth throughout history. Those elders who had murdered young men back in Abraham's day, from the very beginning of time, generations of young men sacrificed for beliefs held by others.

He fired until his rifle was empty. The shots echoed around the glade. It was a fusillade to rival that which had slaughtered the mouldering Japanese soldiers.

Startled, the surviving swine stopped feasting and gathered in a tense group, snarling, hoofs tearing up the ground, clods of earth flying, lowering their snouts, facing the human intruders, tusks at the ready.

Charlie feared the animals would charge him and Kiri. He felt the native tense beside him and from the corner of his eye saw the raised machete. United, the men stood their ground. Charlie reloaded the rifle with an alacrity to gladden the heart of a drill sergeant and fired another salvo at the pigs.

Fleeing like the Gadarene swine, the beasts plunged into the forest. Their angry snorts were loud in Charlie's ears for a long time, then faded. Silence was momentary before the air was full of the sound of insects descending on the fresh blood and on the decayed corpses alike. And the birds, loud again.

'Them Jap man,' said Kiri, seeing Charlie's rage but not quite understanding it, explaining slowly, as to a child. 'Not Aussie man. Jap man kill Aussie man. Aussie man kill Jap man. War.'

'Yair, I know that,' said Charlie. 'But no one deserves to be treated like that. They're still human beings. They deserve a bit of respect.'

He walked slowly, reluctantly, towards the pile of human bodies. His stomach still heaved. He fought for control. 'You use that machete of yours, Kiri. Cut branches and we'll cover these poor buggers. Christ, that lad there looks about the same age as my kid brother, Danny. Bloody lousy war. OK, I know it won't make much difference. If those pigs want to get at the bodies, they'll push the bushes aside. But we've got to try. Here, give me a hand, Kiri.'

Kiri looked bemused but complied. When the corpses were decently covered Charlie and Kiri dragged the dead pigs to the passage down which the survivors had fled and butchered the smallest carcase.

'We'll leave the rest of the meat here for the pigs. Maybe they'll eat that instead of the Japs,' said Charlie.

Kiri shook his head. Sometimes his Aussie mates did strange things. But Charlie let the man take tusks as trophies, so that was good.

They carried the meat back to camp. Both men were exhausted by the time they reached camp. Their comrades gathered around them and backs were slapped in appreciation.

'Bloody grouse,' said Bunny.

'Well done, Charlie,' said the sarge, grinning. 'No bully beef tonight.'

The fire was stoked, and a barbecue began.

The munching noises the men made as they relished the meat reminded Charlie uncomfortably of the way the pigs had torn into that other flesh in the forest glade. He sat alone and opened a tin of bully beef. Couldn't quite bring himself to crunch on a biscuit, though.

'Aren't you going to have any of this lovely pork, Charlie?' asked Curly.

'No, I can't,' said Charlie. 'I'm Jewish.'

Curly thought for a bit. 'You weren't Jewish last week, though, last time you went pig hunting.'

'I thought you were a Pat,' said Bunny. 'You're always singing those Irish songs, "Danny Boy" and "Rose of Tralee", stuff like that.'

'Half and half,' lied Charlie. 'Mum's one, Dad's t'other. Place like this, time like this, a man remembers stuff. It doesn't hurt to keep on the right side of the way you've been brought up, does it?' He thought about the distorted bodies back in the jungle clearing and shivered despite the heat and humidity. 'None of us knows what tomorrow will bring. Or if we'll see tomorrow.'

'Your funeral, Charlie,' said Bunny, licking grease from his fingers. 'Good of you to provide the pork for the funeral feast for rest of us infidels, though.'

25

16 October 1942
Annie Pask and Amy Walsh
with Myrtle and Bert Williams – Norwood

'Mrs Williams,' Amy called. She used her left hand to knock on the neighbours' back door because Annie's arm was gripped tightly with her right hand. 'Can we come in?

'Of course, dear. I'll put the kettle on. We're just back from the Odeon, the matinee, of course. There's a Veronica Lake film on. Bert's got air raid warden duty at night. Not like you girls, out jitterbugging to all hours.'

Pushing Annie ahead of her, Amy entered the kitchen. After days of arguing, the girls had finally agreed to seek help from Mrs Williams. It was a last resort.

'I saw you come in at eleven-thirty the other night, Annie,' accused Mr Williams, looking up from his *Advertiser*. 'When I was out on my rounds. That Yank with the jeep dropped you off. The dusky bloke.'

Annie sniffed hard and Amy nudged her with her elbow. 'We said no crying,' she whispered.

'Hush, Bert. You're only young once.' Mrs Williams reached into her dresser for another two cups and saucers.

The cups, Amy noted, were the second-best ones. The Royal Albert cups with their red roses and gilt trim sat firmly in place. The Royal Albert cups had emerged from their shelf just once, when Bert Williams served ceremonial tea to the Methodist parson and his wife, while Mrs Williams sat pale and shivering, shrouded in a rug in the darkened front room, afflicted by a 'female problem'. Amy and her mum, bearing roses and consolation, had witnessed the visit. Now we've got a female problem too, thought Amy.

'You girls must go and see the latest newsreel,' Mrs Williams gushed. 'It's about the fighting on the Kokoda Track, where your Charlie is. The jungle looks so thick I don't know how the men see where they are going. That Damien Perry chap filmed it.'

'It's Parer. Damien Parer. He's a wonderful photographer. Yes, we saw it last week,' said Amy.

Annie nudged her. Amy realised her stepsister was telling her not to contradict the woman they had come to ask for advice. 'We'll get out of there as quickly as we can,' the girls had agreed. 'Just talk about things generally but don't tell her the whole story. Say it's a girl at work who's in trouble. Let Mrs Williams burble on a bit first, then ease it into the conversation. But don't let her see we're upset.'

They looked at each other conspiratorially and nodded.

'Apparently the Japs are dug in at the Gap, but our boys are giving them what for,' said Mrs Williams cheerfully. 'They'll wipe them out in no time flat.'

'The Yanks lost nine ships in a battle near the Solomon Islands, but the Japs lost thirty-eight,' broke in Mr Williams. 'I reckon things might be looking up for our lads at last. Thank God the Yanks came into the fight when they did. Our goose would have been cooked if the Japs hadn't bombed Pearl Harbor.'

It's fine for them, they haven't got any kids in the war, thought Amy. They never had any kids at all. Maybe that's what the female problem was.

'You girls look a bit down in the mouth. Is your mum all right, Amy?' demanded Mrs Williams. 'Charlie's OK, isn't he? And the other boys? You haven't had any telegrams?' Their neighbour grabbed Amy's arm, pulled her closer to examine her, then looked more closely at Annie. 'You've both been crying. What's up?'

Annie burst into tears. Amy passed her a hanky and then snatched it back and wiped the tears from her own face. Well, so much for the plan. The cat would be out of the bag before the tea was poured.

She sank into Mrs Williams arms. 'I just wish Mum was here,' she sobbed. 'I miss her so much. We can't talk to her on the phone because it's a party line and everyone in Orroroo would find out.'

Even face to face, she wouldn't be able to talk about this to her mum. And besides, Annie had sworn her to secrecy. They couldn't talk to Mavis or Phil either. Or Mary. Mary most of all. She would be horrified. Furious. Disgusted. If only Charlie was here. Charlie always knew what to do. But of course, even if he was there, they couldn't tell Charlie because this was a female thing.

It had taken ages for them to even believe it was true. Weeks, really. When they did believe it, there were three nights of weeping and three days of thickly powdering their faces so they could pass muster at the munitions factory (no one could know at work) before they agreed to talk to Mrs Williams.

Mrs Williams was the only possible person. Not that they wanted to talk to her either. But, as Amy had explained to Annie, at least Mrs Williams wasn't a Catholic. Protestants were different. Annie had reminded Amy that she, herself, was Protestant, but Amy said she was practically a Catholic because she had been brought up by Amy's mum, Rose, which made a difference.

Rose always said Mrs Williams was a 'woman of the world'. Nosy, but capable. Mrs Williams ran the local Cheer-up Hut for soldiers on leave (and she had urged the girls to go to the dances held there, which was how Annie had met Leroy in the first place, so the whole thing was really all Mrs Williams's fault anyway) and she was involved in the Housewives' Association and the Temperance Union too. She organised things. Mum also said Mrs Williams was an interfering old biddy. But perhaps an interfering old biddy was exactly what was needed now.

Only this wasn't the sort of thing you could discuss in front of a man. If only Mr Williams wasn't there. But he was there, and he showed no sign of moving from his chair. He was anchored to that chair, although now he was sitting on the edge of it with his mouth hanging open and *The Advertiser* in danger of slipping out of his hands.

It had to be said. 'Leroy's married,' Amy sobbed.

'Is that all? Never mind,' said Mrs. Williams breezily, patting Amy on the back. 'He's not your boyfriend, though, Amy. He's Annie's, isn't he? Annie, you're better off without him. I still think it's a great pity that Brian died when he did, of course. Brian was a lovely lad.' She smiled reassuringly at Annie over Amy's head. 'Wait until some of our boys get home. You'll find a nice Aussie boy and you'll forget all about that chap. What do they say about those Yanks? Overpaid and over here? The war will be over soon, Annie.'

'Oversexed, overpaid and over here,' muttered Mr Williams, whose mouth had closed into a sort of leer.

Amy glanced at him and felt he suspected what was coming next.

Mrs Williams shot a dirty look at him but said nothing.

'But I was in love with Leroy and he knew I was, and he never, ever, said he was married,' wept Annie. 'And now he's gone.'

'It didn't take you long to get over Brian if you fell in love as soon as that after he died,' sniggered Mr Williams. 'You were practically engaged to Brian, weren't you? It's all that jazz music, all those saxophones and big bands. That bloody Glenn Miller. You young people have had your brains fried.'

'It's not for us to judge, Bert,' warned his wife.

But Bert was on his favourite hobby horse – the morals of the young – and nothing would unsaddle him from that particular nag. 'Good riddance if he's dumped you. I've heard that these Yankee blokes can't be trusted,' he continued. 'I always told Myrtle that you had no business going out with a Yank, young lady. I wouldn't have let a daughter of mine go out with one, if I had a daughter.' He glared at Annie. 'Bribing girls with chocolates and stockings and butter. No respect for women. I hope you didn't do anything you shouldn't have done, did you? A good Catholic girl like you?'

'Annie's not Catholic,' protested Amy. 'I am. All us Walshes are, but Pask and his family aren't. We're a mixed religion family now that Mum married Pask. You're Methodist, aren't you Annie?' She wasn't sure whether she was defending her friend or her faith. Not only female problems were at stake here.

'No, we're Anglican,' said Annie. Her body began to convulse with sobs. 'But that's got nothing to do with any of it.'

'Depends on what IT is,' said Mrs Williams, releasing Amy and grabbing Annie by the shoulders and shaking her hard. 'Are you pregnant, Annie? Did you go too far with that Yank? Oh, my God, you silly, silly girl. Is this Leroy that swarthy Yankie soldier with a jeep that I've seen with an armful of chocolates and flowers? And stockings?'

'And butter. Remember we gave you some of that butter, Mrs Williams,' interjected Amy, annoyed at the snide remarks being made. 'Lots of butter.'

'Yes, I remember,' said Mrs Williams, looking at her husband guiltily.

She'd had rows with Bert over the provenance of the butter. There were rules about the black market, and Bert being an air raid warden made the rules much stricter, as Bert had told her. He was not happy about the butter.

'Forget the butter,' she snapped. 'Are you pregnant? Pregnant to a Yank? The disgrace will break Rose's heart. What's Pask going to say?'

'Dad would kill Leroy. And me too, probably. Only he can't do anything to Leroy because he's been posted to the islands up north.' She choked on the words, but they came out anyway.

'And he just laughed when Annie told him about the baby,' said Amy. 'He's horrible. I always said he was horrible. I never liked him. Too loud, too fast, too bossy.'

'He didn't laugh, Amy,' whispered Annie. 'He just said, 'Tough luck, honey. I've got a wife and two kids back home in the States, so don't even think about getting hitched." And then he said he'd been posted to the islands.'

'And he told you that you're not the only girl who'll be upset when his lot leaves,' Amy blurted out. 'I didn't think you would really let him go that far with you.'

'They don't even do that in the movies,' said Mrs Williams. 'Well, not on screen anyway.'

Amy nodded. 'They never get in the family way. Veronica Lake wouldn't do that, or Mae West. Well, Mae West might.' She shook her head and glared at Annie. 'Mum'll go mad. She'll never trust either of us again. You can't be a nurse now. Everyone will know.'

Annie began to howl.

Amy put her arms around the distraught girl. 'I'm sorry. I shouldn't have said that, Annie. It'll all be all right.' She rubbed the girl's back and hugged her. 'You'll see. We'll get through it. Somehow.'

'So you're really pregnant?' shouted Mr Williams. 'That American bastard got you pregnant? You're that stupid? Haven't you heard of prophylactics?'

'No. What are they?' asked Amy, puzzled.

'French letters, rubbers,' yelled Mr Williams. 'The Yankees would be provided with them. Birth control. So silly little fools like you don't get up the duff. Or catch some nasty disease. I always knew you Walshes were crazy, but I didn't think you were that nuts.'

'Hush, Bert,' said Mrs Williams. She was remembering that she had accepted pounds of butter from the girls. And chocolates. And tea. Despite the rationing. This mustn't get out. There could be all sorts of ramifications. It wasn't just the kids' reputations at stake here. 'Sit down, girls,' she ordered. 'We'll have to think this out. Are you certain you're pregnant, Annie? You couldn't just have made a mistake about your dates?'

Annie, trembling, shook her head. She clapped her hand over her mouth. Surely she wasn't going to be sick again? Not here in Mrs Williams's spotless kitchen? She dashed for the back door and slammed it behind her. Retching sounded outside.

'Well, that proves she's pregnant. I hope she didn't vomit on the veranda,' said Mrs Williams, grimly. 'It's not gastro? Could she have made a mistake about her dates?'

'The mistake she's made wasn't with her dates. I hope she didn't spew on my lawn,' said Mr Williams grimly. 'I just mowed it yesterday.'

'We're both regular as clockwork,' Amy said, blushing. Periods were unmentionable. And so was pregnancy – especially if a girl wasn't married.

'How far along is she?' demanded Mrs Williams. 'She doesn't look pregnant – how many months?'

'She's missed two periods,' Amy whispered. 'At least we think so.'

'It's early days yet then. It's not too bad. Bert, what about your cousin up at Echidna?'

'You can't ask Keith to get involved in this,' thundered Mr Williams. 'He's got a family to think of. And a career. It's illegal.'

'He did it for our niece, Betty. She was two months gone, too.'

'She's your niece. I've disowned her. And he said he'd never do it again for anyone,' her husband yelled. 'Too dangerous. What if something goes wrong and she dies?'

'What else can we do?' Mrs Williams pleaded. 'We can't let the kid have a baby. Rose and Pask would have kittens.'

'Kittens aren't involved. And it's their problem, not ours,' snapped Mr Williams.

'Remember that heart attack Pask had when he heard that Bob was shot down? Now Bob's in a German prison camp,' pleaded Mrs Williams. 'You saw that bit in *The Advertiser* about the Nazis mistreating our RAF boys? This'll be enough to push Pask over the edge.'

'What are the Nazis doing to the air force boys?' demanded Annie, who had staggered back inside and was now wiping her face with Amy's hanky. 'What are they doing to my brother?'

'Keeping them chained up,' said Mr Williams grimly. 'It's against the Geneva Convention to put prisoners in chains but they're doing it because some RAF prisoners escaped. Supposed to be the Great Escape, but they got caught and shot, all except a bloke called Churchill who the Nazis thought was related to the Pommie prime minister. Now the Germans have clamped down so no one else escapes.'

'It's horrible,' agreed Mrs Williams.

'Churchill's protesting to the protecting power – that's the Swiss –

and demanding that the Germans stop doing it. It's in the paper.' He picked up *The Advertiser* and waved it at the girls. 'I was bringing it over to show you tonight.'

'But Bob's in the air force and he's a prisoner in Germany,' gasped Amy. 'Mum and Pask will go mad when they hear this, and then if they find out Annie's pregnant as well, they'll just die.'

'Dad and Auntie Rose listen to the wireless all the time,' said Annie. 'So they'll know. I can't tell them I'm pregnant when they're worried sick about Bob.' Tears ran down her face.

'Ring Keith up. Say we're coming and he'll have to fix the girl up,' ordered Mrs Williams. 'He's a good vet and he's got the equipment to fix Annie up.'

'It's illegal,' repeated Bert. 'Procuring an abortion is a crime. Myrtle, be reasonable, we could all end up in jail.'

'The law gets bent all the time,' said his wife recklessly. 'What about those people who don't observe the blackout properly? You're always reporting incidents. Light showing under doors. Blackout curtains not shut. What about that crowd around in George Street with their incinerator burning at night? You said it could be seen for miles around.'

'That's different. Keith could lose his licence to practice and go to jail. And I'm an air raid warden, I enforce the law, not aid and abet breaking it.'

'What about the pregnancy? The shame of it? I promised Rose we'd keep an eye on the girls. I gave her my word.'

'It's like being a crooked cop. I'm in a position of trust. Besides, my petrol coupons are running low. Do you realise how far Echidna is from Norwood? It's out past Truro. Miles away.'

'We'll manage somehow,' said his wife. 'Drive slowly.'

'Speed's got nothing to do with it,' snapped Bert. 'And what'll you tell Rose if Annie dies?'

'What do you mean, if Annie dies?' screamed Amy. Everyone was yelling at once and she couldn't keep up with the conversation. It was like listening to that jazz music Leroy played on the gramophone, too much noise happening at once. 'You're not saying Annie could die, are you?'

There was dead silence. They were all looking at her.

Amy persisted. 'Killing the baby's a mortal sin, too,' she yelled while she had their attention.

'We've got to get rid of it,' explained Mrs Williams. 'It's not a proper baby yet. It's just a blob of blood that Annie would have passed if she hadn't missed her period.'

'No, I don't think so,' insisted Amy. "I remember someone saying the soul is present from the moment of conception. That's what us Catholics believe, anyway.'

'It is true that it's just a blob at this stage,' interjected Annie. 'I've seen sheep have miscarriages when they're only just pregnant. It doesn't look like a lamb at all.'

'It's still a baby,' said Amy. 'A baby with an immortal soul. People are different to sheep. Everyone knows that.'

'Shut up, you silly little idiot!' yelled Mrs Williams. 'Bugger the Catholic Church. This is the only way.'

'She could go to a home for unmarried mothers. Have the kid adopted out,' said Mr Williams.

'Don't even think it!' shouted Mrs Williams. 'Rose would find out, anyway.'

'Auntie Rose would make me have it. Look how she passed Danny off as Mary's baby,' said Annie. 'All these years I had a brother and I didn't know it. I'm sick of lies. I'm not living with more lies.'

Annie punched Amy's arm. 'Don't talk about private stuff here,' she whispered.

Mr Williams sneered. 'Did you really think we don't know what goes on in your house? We know more about your family than you two do. Rose tries to sweep stuff under the carpet, but she does a lousy job of it. It's Rose that you two get your loose morals from. What about Mary and her baby? Good Catholic families be buggered!'

'Bert,' remonstrated Mrs Williams, 'we agreed long ago our lips are sealed. But yes, over the years there's been some very funny goings on next door.' She turned to Annie. 'Annie, you've got to get rid of it.'

'I know that,' Annie said, nodding vigorously. 'I agree with that. That's what I told Amy from the start.'

'But,' whined Amy, 'it's dangerous for Annie, and it's murder for the baby.'

'We've already talked about it and I said I don't want the baby,' Annie told Amy. 'I only came over here to see if Mrs Williams knew a way to get rid of it.'

'But you'll never forgive yourself, Annie,' said Amy. 'You'd have to live with the knowledge that you've killed your own child. Forever. You'd never be able to forget it as long as you lived.'

'I've had six miscarriages,' said Mrs Williams. 'Why do you think Bert and I never had any children? I've lost six babies. You get over it.'

'You can't do this, Annie,' pleaded Amy. 'Just have the baby and we'll look after it together. We'll say we found it in the street.'

'Rubbish! You'd disgrace your whole family?' Mrs Williams shouted at Amy. 'A good Catholic family! What would Father Flaherty say? Annie's got to get rid of it.'

'Well, if it has to be done, it has to be a doctor, not a vet,' protested Amy.

'It's against the law,' said Mr Williams. 'No doctor will do it.'

'That's right,' said Mrs Williams. 'No doctor will do it, but a vet's as good as a doctor. Better, probably. It takes longer to be a vet, because they've got to learn about all sorts of animals, not just people. Even sheep.'

'But Annie's not an animal, she's a person,' wailed Amy. 'And so's the baby.' She couldn't bear to hear what the others were saying. She covered her ears with her hands, closed her eyes and began to pray under her breath, her lips moving rapidly. She didn't know which saint presided over female matters, but you couldn't go wrong with the Virgin Mary. If only Annie could have a miscarriage, that would solve everything.

Oh, my God, I'm just like Mum, she thought. Only Mum's better at this sort of stuff than I am. I'm just getting muddled. Even Our Lady, the Virgin Mary, is probably confused now. She remembered there was a saint for hopeless causes. Saint Jude. Would he intercede, or would it be better to go straight to God to provide a solution?

'If I have to have this baby, I might as well be dead because I can't face Dad, and I can't face Auntie Rose and I'm so ashamed that I can't face myself either,' wailed Annie, grabbing Amy's hand and jerking her back to reality. 'So even if it kills me, I'll go through with it. I'll go to Echidna and do whatever has to be done.'

Weeping, Amy threw herself into Annie's arms. 'And what if you die? How will I face Mum and Pask? And Father Flaherty would ex-communicate me.'

'Bugger the Church,' snapped Mrs Williams.

'Amen to that,' said Mr Williams. 'And bugger bloody Rose Walsh or Rose Pask or whatever she calls herself now, too. You know what, Myrtle? You've spent too long with Rose from next door. Just as well she buggered off and married that farmer from Wallaroo.'

'Orroroo,' snapped Annie. 'It's nowhere near Wallaroo. I just wish I'd stayed there.'

Mr Williams glared at Annie and then at Amy for good measure. 'And so do I. So help me, you two young floozies, if there are any more carryings on from either of you, I'll take a strap to the pair of you.'

'You can't talk to us like that. I'll tell Mum. I'll report you to the police,' yelled Amy.

'Just try it. You'll both get yourselves locked up in a home for un-married mothers.'

'I'm not pregnant,' shouted Amy. 'Annie's the one who's pregnant. We shouldn't have told you. I thought you'd try to help, not make things worse.'

'We are trying to help,' said Mrs Williams. She glared at her hus-band, but he had his eyes fixed on Annie.

'As soon this is over, young Annie, you'll get yourself off to the army and enlist as a nurse. In fact, you can both enlist. Neither of you is any better than you should be,' he pronounced.

'And you're a rotten fuddy-duddy stick-in-the-mud, nasty old sticky-beak,' said Amy. 'Mum always said you were a dill who didn't have the guts to swallow a cold beer on a hot day because you were too scared of your wife and her Temperance Union to open your mouth.'

Mrs Williams gasped. 'And you expect us to get you out of the mess you've got yourselves into. Ungrateful little hussies.'

'You were grateful enough for that butter, though,' said Annie.. 'You used it to bake cakes to take along to your Cheer-up Meetings and to the Temperance Union too, as I recall. Maybe we ought to tell the ladies where it came from.'

'That's right. We helped you to carry the cakes in, didn't we, Annie?' said Amy viciously. 'We had a quite a giggle about that.'

Annie smirked. 'I bet the ladies would love to hear a bit of gossip about their precious Mrs Williams involved with black market stuff. The story would spread like wildfire.'

'A couple of no-hopers,' muttered Mr Williams. 'A bit of discipline with the army nurses will do you both the world of good.'

'He's right about you, Annie,' said Mrs Williams. 'It's time you joined up and did something useful. They might teach you about pro-phylactics too. But not you, Amy, that would kill your mum. You can go up and live at Orroroo with her. She'll keep you out of mischief.'

'I'm not going to live at Orroroo,' yelled Amy. 'I'm helping the war effort in the munitions factory. I'm staying here or going nursing with Annie. You can't make me to do anything I don't want to. And I won't go to Echidna either.'

'Amy, if I go, you have to come with me,' begged Annie. 'I can't face it without you.'

The two girls clung to each other again, sobbing.

'There might be another way out of it,' said Mrs Williams slowly. 'I've just remembered.' She stood up and rummaged carefully in the cupboard behind the Royal Albert cups. Finally, she pulled out a bottle of gin. 'I knew there was some of this left. Go home, run the hottest bath you can bear, lie in it and drink this. It's probably an old wives' tale, but it might work.'

Mr Williams stood up. His chair fell backwards. It crashed to the floor. He bent forward, pounded his fist on the table. The cups rose into the air. Tea splashed onto the starched tablecloth. The two girls cringed in their chairs, fearing he was about to spring at them.

But Bert's anger was directed at his wife. He snatched a cup from the table, hurled it at her. It missed. The cup reached the floor first, the tea it had contained following fast behind. The cup shattered.

Then he turned and saw the carefully stacked best cups in the cupboard. Myrtle's treasured Royal Albert. Red and pink roses and gilt edging. Roses like the roses that bloody Rose and her bloody boozing dead husband Michael next door grew to perfection while his own bushes struggled to produce a bud and when they did the flowers were guzzled by aphids. And every time Myrtle lost a baby, bloody Rose brought bunches of the things over to console her while her clothes line taunted the Williamses because it was perpetually full of nappies billowing in the breeze. Bert suddenly realised he hated roses. He had never known until now just how much he hated roses. Useless, bloody, prickly things. Just like Rose Walsh herself. And her kids. Like all bloody women, really.

He reached behind him, grabbed some Royal Albert off the shelf and threw cup after cup at his wife's head. They missed narrowly. Myrtle cried out, but Bert was unrelenting in his destruction.

Annie remembered Bob talking about bombs exploding and impact patterns. She remembered how at the time she had asked if he ever thought about the people on the ground that the bombs were killing. 'It's them or us,' Bob had said. His words worried her. She knew it was true, but what about the children? she had asked. 'Tough luck,' Bob had said. 'They're in the wrong place at the wrong time.'

And now Annie could understand his reasoning. This baby growing in her belly was in the wrong place at the wrong time, too.

Then there was room for nothing in anyone's thoughts other than the sound of Mr Williams's voice roaring. 'What about the Women's Christian Temperance Movement?' he shouted. 'Lips that touch liquor shall never touch mine? How did that bottle of poison get into your cupboard?'

'I bought it for Betty when she was in trouble,' whispered his wife, cringing. 'It didn't work for her, but it might work for Annie.'

'Are you telling the truth, Myrtle? Is this why we never had kids? Were you getting rid of them with gin and hot baths? While bloody Rose next door was popping out a bloody baby a bloody year?'

'Of course I wasn't,' yelled Mrs Williams, losing her own temper at the thought. 'How can you even think such a thing? You know how much I wanted kiddies. I just couldn't hold them for more than two or three months. Just clots of blood, that's all they were. You remember all the doctors I saw. No one could help me. I was desperate for a baby.'

'So you say,' roared Mr Williams. 'How do I know if you're telling the truth? All women are liars! Starting with Eve back in the Garden of Eden.'

'Bert, I bought this when Betty was pregnant. Mrs Wendel told me about it.'

'That German bitch around the corner. I always knew there was something fishy about her. Interned now, isn't she? Her and all her family. Bloody Hun murderers.'

'Mum said the King of England's family's German,' said Amy, indignantly. She had liked Mrs Wendel and her family and was upset when they were dragged away by the authorities and detained as Enemy Aliens. 'The Royal family was called Saxe-Coburg until the Great War, then they changed it to Windsor. They've got German cousins.'

'That's right, Kaiser Bill and the old king were first cousins,' said Annie. 'Auntie Rose told me.'

'Just like a bloody Irish woman to drag that up,' said Mr Williams. 'Disloyal bitch. The Irish revolted against England, didn't they? O'Connell and his cronies? They got hanged for their trouble. And southern

Ireland's on Germany's side now. Bastards. We never should have got mixed up with you lot, troublemakers, all of you.'

'Don't talk like that, Bert. You'll upset the kids. The gin didn't work for Betty, but I kept it in case we needed some strong alcohol. For medicinal purposes. Annie might as well try it. It could save us all a trip to Echidna.' She thrust the bottle into Amy's hands. 'While she's soaking in the bath, feed it to her, a glass at a time, until she's thoroughly pickled. And keep topping up the hot water. It might start her monthlies up. But watch that she doesn't fall asleep and drown. That's Plan A.'

She turned to her husband, angry that he had doubted her morals or her wish to have children and determined to have her revenge on him for the destruction of the Royal Albert. She remembered Keith had threatened to punch Bert in the nose if he ever made trouble again. With a bit of luck, that would come to pass now. 'Bert, you get on the blower to your cousin Keith. If the gin doesn't work, and I'd be surprised if it did, we'll fall back on Plan B.'

Mr Williams groaned. 'Keith won't like it. He didn't speak to me for years after that Betty business.'

Mrs Williams ignored him. She intended to ignore her husband royally for some time after what he had done to her best tea set. She'd have him crawling on his hands and knees before he'd be back in her good books.

'I don't like it either,' said Amy, holding the gin bottle gingerly as if it might explode. 'Is it poison? It might be an occasion of sin to even hold this bottle.'

'For goodness sake, girl, grow up. It's just gin,' snapped Mrs Williams. She snatched the bottle back, opened it and waved it under Amy's nose. 'There, it smells like perfume, that French stuff, eau de Cologne. Here, taste a bit.'

Despite Amy's cringing, Mrs Williams stuck her finger in the bottle and thrust it into the girl's mouth. Amy gulped and swallowed. She looked at Annie and pulled a face.

'It'll just bring her period on if it's late,' said Mrs Williams. 'If it works, it will solve everything. Lots of women do it, or so Mrs Wendel said.'

'It's not that bad, I suppose,' Annie muttered. 'It's probably better than the vet idea. It's more natural. Gin's made with juniper berries, I think. Or so Leroy said.'

'Maybe it's just a venial sin, not a mortal one,' mused Amy. 'Maybe you've just missed your period, Annie. You have been working hard, standing up all day packing parachutes. And not eating much red meat.'

'It's just sitting in a hot bath and drinking a bit of booze,' said Annie, squeezing Amy's arm and standing up. 'Let's give it a go.'

'It's the intention, though,' said Amy, also standing up, but still worried about the ethics of the thing. 'And intention to sin is the same thing as actually committing a sin. That's what the nuns used to say. I suppose the penance would probably be just reciting ten decades of the rosary.'

'You're never going to confess this to Father Flaherty?' demanded Annie in horror.

'No, I don't suppose I will,' said Amy. 'But if I don't confess it, it'll be on my conscience forever, won't it?'

'And mine, but I don't even have the luxury of confession, so it's worse for me,' said Annie. 'You Catholics have got it good, really. A clean slate when things get tough.'

'The sooner this slate is clean the better,' said Mrs Williams, opening the back door and holding it open so the girls could leave. 'You two run back home and fill the bath. Let me know straight away if anything happens, Amy. And don't talk to anyone, including your mum, tonight.' She glared at her husband. 'Bert, you get on the phone to your cousin now.'

'Tomorrow,' promised Bert meekly. 'I'll phone him first thing tomorrow.' He had just remembered the Royal Albert had been a wedding gift from his wife's grandma. Where was he going to find a replacement in wartime? And he was also remembering Myrtle's grief after each miscarriage. None of it was her fault. She'd even tried to persuade Betty to have the kid and let them adopt it, but Betty wouldn't agree. Life was a bastard sometimes. 'Let's give the gin and hot water a go first,' he suggested with a wry smile at his wife, which she ignored.

26

5 November 1942
Rose Pask – Orooroo

'Amy, I've heard from Phil,' I said on the phone. I didn't like ringing home to Norwood, because it's more expensive than posting a letter, but last week Amy had sent the shortest note I've ever seen. And not even one word from Annie. I was certain there was something funny going on down in Norwood, so I had to phone and check up on the girls in person, so to speak. Amy's note might as well have been a telegram, really. It just said, 'We are both well and hope you are too.' Not worth the cost of the stamp Amy had put on it.

'She's had a little girl and she's going to call her Elizabeth after Princess Elizabeth,' I went on. 'It's Elizabeth Margaret Rose, so she's being very patriotic. And my name is in it too, which is nice. Or maybe that's just because Princess Margaret is Margaret Rose. I'm not fussed, though.'

I knew I was sounding like a gossiping old grandma, but that is what I am, so what the heck. And if I rambled on a bit, it might get Amy in the gossiping mood too, and I might find out just what was going on back home in Norwood.

'Yes, Annie and I went to see Phil in hospital,' Amy said. She sounded unhappy, which reinforced my feeling that things had gone awry back home. Maybe the kids were just fighting over who was doing the cooking and cleaning, but I could feel strange undercurrents there. Vibrations coming across the phone wires. Anger, misery, grief. But why?

After a long silence, Amy continued. 'Mavis's baby is due soon too. Everyone's having babies.'

I thought I heard Amy's voice break a little, but it was probably just a bad connection. The phone did tend to play up – technicians couldn't be spared to work on civilian lines these days. Unless all these babies were making Amy clucky, and she was feeling jealous, but, as I reminded myself, Amy's the least clucky person I've ever met.

'I know Charlie wanted to call the baby Cecelia because of that song that's so popular,' I said. 'You know the one: "Does your mother know you're out, Cecelia? Does she know that I'm about to steal you?" Never mind, he'll be so happy that they've got a little girl that he probably won't mind what they call her. He said in one of his letters that he wanted a girl, so it would never have to go to war. I've got a feeling that things are worse up there than he's letting on.'

I knew things weren't too good down in Norwood, either. I was sure I heard a sob from Amy. Perhaps she was upset because she was worried about her brother. She's such a sweet, innocent child, my Amy. Both the girls are. Thank goodness they've been spared the worst of the war. I decided to keep talking to cheer Amy up.

'Babies are such a blessing. Phil's writing to Charlie and sending a photo but I don't know when he'll get it. It should buck him up. The fighting's been bad up there in New Guinea, according to the wireless.'

'It sounds like a tug of war,' said Amy in a miserable sort of whisper. 'One minute, the Japs are pushing our soldiers down towards Port Moresby and the next, our side is pushing the Japs back up the Track. *The Advertiser* said our troops have made a further advance, whatever that means.'

'Yes, and the Americans have been helping out at some place called Milne Bay and the Japs have retreated, so maybe we're getting somewhere. Thank God for the Americans, everyone's saying that.'

There was more silence. Then I think I heard her blow her nose. I decided to shut my mouth for a bit to give Amy a chance to talk. Although this phone call was costing quite a bit of money and it was a waste if she didn't take part in it. Just when I was thinking of giving up and saying 'Goodbye', she spoke.

'How is Danny? Is he getting over the broken arm he got from the sheep kicking him?'

'I'll never forget that,' I said with relief. It was good to talk about something concrete. 'Pask said he'd never seen anything like it. Danny went flying up in the air like a magpie after a sparrow. I didn't know sheep could behave like that. Danny will be more careful next time he helps with the mulesing. We knew the arm was broken because of the way Danny landed. He came down pretty hard. But the doctor said it was a clean break and it'll heal well.'

'That's good,' said Amy.

There was more silence, so I decided to keep nattering. I still hadn't learned anything about matters in Norwood, but at least the girls must be all right, or Amy would have said so by now.

'He's still got the arm in plaster, of course. At least he can't talk about joining the army for a while. Speaking of sheep, we've had quite a few lambs up here, too. I'm hand-feeding three of them because their mothers rejected them. I can't understand mothers rejecting babies. It's not natural.'

There was a sound as if Amy was choking.

'Are you all right, Amy?' I asked. 'Have you got a cold? You sound a bit choky.'

'I'm fine, Mum. Just a frog in my throat. I'll get a drink of water.'

I heard the tap running and then she came back to the phone.

'You and Annie would love it here just now,' I said. 'One of the hens went broody and we've got little yellow chicks running around. Annie always loves baby chickens.'

'That's nice,' said Amy, but she didn't sound interested.

I kept gossiping to fill the space where she should have said something. 'We had a little drop of rain, which is just as well because the drought has been terrible. Pask says he's heard it's worse in Victoria. Started there back in January 1939 and still going. There's just a flush of green coming through here now. Danny goes out with Pask every day to check the pastures even though he can't do much with one arm.'

There was a silence that reminded me of the one minute silence that you get on Anzac Day. A fraught and tense silence that seemed to last forever. Then there was a strangled sort of sound. Perhaps Amy had taken another gulp of water and it had gone down the wrong way. But I was worried.

'Are you there, Amy?' I asked. 'Are you all right, love?'

'I've got to tell you something, Mum. You won't like it, though. Annie and me are both going to join up,' Amy suddenly blurted out. 'We're both going to be nurses. We're sick of the munitions factory. We want to do something different. We need to get away from here. See the world. Make a real difference to the war effort.'

I was aghast. 'Both of you? I thought it was just Annie. Because of Brian.'

'Yes. Well, I miss Brian too, Mum. I want to do my bit.'

'We all miss Brian. But nursing wouldn't suit you at all, Amy. Annie might be all right because she grew up on a farm and she's used to blood and guts, but you get the heebie-jeebies when we chop a chook's head off. You wouldn't be able to stand the sight of blood.'

'I've seen some lately,' Amy said.

'Where did you see blood?' I demanded. 'The only blood you would see in Adelaide would be your monthlies.'

'At the munitions factory,' Amy said. 'One of the girls cut her hand on a machine and it bled everywhere. I was the closest to her and I had to grab the first aid kit and patch her up. It was really messy. So I should do well as a nurse.'

Why did I think Amy was fibbing? I had always been able to tell when she wasn't telling the truth when she was a child, but that was because I could read her face. I couldn't see her face now because we were talking on the phone, and yet I really had the feeling that there was something fishy going on here.

'Nursing in a war would be worse than that,' I said. 'Blood and guts and death.'

'Anyway, Annie and I will just be junior nurses. We probably won't get anything too gory to do. Probably just emptying bedpans and sweeping the wards. Making beds. That sort of thing. And the war might end soon, anyway.'

'You wouldn't like bedpans either, Amy. You're squeamish about that sort of thing. Remember when Mary brought little Kathleen down and there were dirty nappies? You ran a mile rather than change her, and that's just baby poo. Nothing like adult poo.'

'We've made up our minds, Mum,' said Amy. 'It won't be just yet because Annie's not really well. She fainted the other day.'

Now I was really worried. 'Why did she faint?' I demanded. 'Are you girls eating enough? I know Mr Curtin's brought in those austerity measures and rationing, and some things are hard to get because food goes to the troops, which is only fair because they need priority, but you should still be eating as much as you can. Maybe you ought to come up here for a bit if Annie's fainting all over the place.'

'It's not all over the place, Mum, it was just once at work,' Amy said. She sounded tired. 'She'd been standing up packing parachutes for hours and she said it just came over her suddenly and she collapsed. They gave her the next day off. Mrs Williams had some bones and she made soup for us. It wasn't as good as your soup, but it was OK. We don't want to come up there just now. We'll be all right.'

'Well, if you're sure.'

I paused. I was aghast at the news but I didn't want her to know just how upset I was. Even nurses, junior nurses, could be killed in a war. And the Japs had sunk hospital ships. Ships with nurses on them. I decided to waffle a bit.

'Did you hear that icing of cakes is prohibited now?' I said. 'Except wedding cakes, and they have to be plain white. It was a good thing Pask and I got married when we did. Do you remember how I coloured some of the icing and made blue flowers to go on top? I used Reckitt's Blue but don't tell anyone. I don't expect Mr Curtin would have thought of using Reckitt's Blue for icing. Apparently pink is definitely out. He probably thinks we all use cochineal and that would have to be imported, I suppose, so the stocks are probably running low.'

'Yes, Mum.'

I could tell she was annoyed with me. I thought for a moment she had hung up. I thought she had been distracted by something more interesting at her end. She seemed to be listening to something I couldn't quite hear. I shook the phone and put it back to my ear again.

But she asked, 'Have you heard from the boys?'

'Bob says he's all right but we wonder how OK he is really. And Joe says he's busy with the wounded soldiers and morale is good. You know how formal Joe's letters are. Charlie's made friends with a cannibal apparently.'

'Mum, someone's at the door. Annie's getting it. It's Mavis's Mickey. Just a minute.'

'Are you there, Amy? What's happening?'

There was a commotion in the background. Two or three voices all talking at once. I heard running footsteps and the door slamming. Then more voices but muffled. If I could have transported myself down there, I would have flown faster than an eagle after a fleeing wallaby. When Amy came back on the phone, she sounded flustered but excited.

'Everything's happening at once, Mum. I've got to go. Harry's been hurt in Darwin in an air raid. He's been taken to Katherine Hospital. When Mavis got the phone call, she went into labour, so we've got to go around there and stay with the kids until Mavis's sister can take over. I'll ring you back as soon as I hear anything else.'

'Amy, wait,' I yelled into the receiver, but she had hung up.

27

12 December 1942
Rose Pask – Orroroo

'Hello, Colin. Nice to see you. Nice of you to bring the mail right to the door for us. Sit down. You look done in. Just ignore the noise.'

'Thanks, Rose.' Colin clapped his hands over his ears. His postie bag slipped down one shoulder, but he grabbed it, jiggled it back into place and edged a chair out using his right leg, then dumped the bag on the floor and sat down with a sigh of relief. 'Can't leave it in the ute, got to keep an eye on it at all times even out here in the donga. Confidential stuff in there.'

'I suppose a hungry sheep might eat a couple of letters but that's not likely,' I said. 'Or a passing magpie could grab a few.'

As always, when Pask's demented sulphur-crested cocky had detected a new presence in the kitchen, it had flung itself furiously against the bars of its cage and began to screech.

'Or a cockatoo. Damn bird. It's always doing that,' I said. 'I'll strangle that bird one day, I swear it. We ought to send it into combat against the Japs. I reckon a dedicated flock of cockies could save Australia. Kamikaze cockies. Beat those Nip pilots anytime.'

I flung the hessian bag we used as a cage cover at the wire cage and missed. I picked it up, said, 'Good night, Cocky,' and draped it more carefully. 'I asked Pask to put the cage out on the veranda this morning, but he forgot as usual.'

'It is a bit loud, isn't it? Sulphur-crested cockies are all the same. My uncle Bill had one. Drove everyone nuts. They live a hell of long time, too.'

'Pask raised it from an egg, or so he says, so we're stuck with it. Bob used to love it and young Danny gets along all right with it, but it doesn't like me much. Bites my bum if I bend over too close to the cage.'

The bird shifted on its perch and managed to find a chink in the hessian.

I saw a beady eye, heard hissing and knew it was building up for another shriek. I adjusted the bag so the bird couldn't see out. 'Go to sleep, Cocky, or I'll throw a bucket of water over you.'

'I was going past to deliver a telegram up the road, so I thought I'd drop by.' Colin grimaced. 'Put off the evil moment for a while. I hate delivering those bloody things. I won't say who it's going to. It'll be all over the district by tomorrow, but right now it's best kept quiet.'

'Fair enough, Colin.' I reached over and patted his shoulder. 'I thought you looked a bit down in the mouth. We all know about telegrams in wartime. I'll never forget when I got that one about Brian. Pask and Danny are out on the ute feeding the sheep. We're down to the last of the hay. The drought seems to have set in.'

'They said on the wireless there's going to be one of those summer storms in the next couple of days, Rose, so maybe there'll be a drop or two in it and some feed for the sheep.' Colin opened his bag and tossed a few letters onto the table. 'There could be a bit of good news for you here – I reckon that's Pask's wool cheque. And there's a letter with an English stamp on it. That'll be from your lad Joe, won't it? And another one from young Mary down at Mount Gambier.'

I rummaged through the mail and smiled. 'You're right, Colin, that'll be the wool cheque. It won't be a big one, but it should be enough to keep us going for a while.' I heaved a sigh of relief. 'And yes, that's a letter from Joe. And this one's from Mary. She doesn't write all that often, too busy with the kids and the butcher shop.'

'What about Bob and Charlie? I haven't seen any mail from them for a bit.'

I sighed. 'I've just about given up on letters from Charlie or Bob.

The fighting's been pretty fierce on Kokoda according to the wireless, so I suppose Charlie hasn't got much time to write letters. We don't know what's happening with Bob.'

'I don't suppose the German mail service would be too good right now, Rose,' said Colin. 'According to the wireless, things aren't going too well for Jerry. Problems on the Western Front, I hear. Was Bob all right last time you heard from him?'

'He said they were playing cricket and the guards couldn't understand the game and the chaps were trying to explain it to them, but it was all too hard. Too cold to play cricket now. I heard on the wireless it's snowing over there. I suppose he might get a white Christmas, although I don't suppose there'll be much celebrating. I just hope he's getting enough to eat. Speaking of which, have you got time for a cuppa?'

'Always got time for a cuppa, Rose. That is, if your tea ration's holding out. Eight ounces per person for five weeks isn't much. The missus and me, we've tried that red clover and lucerne substitute that the government suggested, but it's pretty nasty.'

'We're not out of tea yet, Colin. Anastasia O'Halloran's tried drying the used leaves out and having a go at reusing them, and she says it works, although of course the brew's not as strong as it was the first-time round. Pask said he thinks it's a rotten idea, so I'll put it off unless we get desperate. The kettle's just about boiled, because Pask and Danny will be in any minute now.'

'Mr Curtin says the only way to get rid of restrictions is to get on with the war and win,' said Colin.

'We all agree with that one,' I agreed. 'Only I can't say I like this idea of abolishing Christmas.'

'Yair, that Dedman bloke says we're not to mention Christmas, New Year or Easter,' said Colin. 'Everyone's up in arms over that. Rotten pollies. Might as well let Hitler take over.'

'Dedman, he's the bloke who designed the Dedman suit, isn't he? Single-breasted and no cuffs on the trousers?' I said. 'And now he says women have to use less cotton for their bloomers, too. And less elastic. He's kidding. When you get to a certain age, you need room in your undies.'

'Yeah, that bugger's a Scotsman. Mean as hell. One of Curtin's mates. He also wants women to paint lines down the back of their legs instead of wearing stockings. And you girls have to shorten your skirts. Use less material.'

'All very well for the young ones,' I said. 'Goes well with jitterbugging, I suppose. At my age, I won't be shortening my skirts, Dedman or no Dedman. He'll abolish clothes all together soon. Have everyone walking around starkers.'

Colin sat while I poured the tea and got biscuits from the tin.

'I just made these last night. Biscuits won't be abolished in this house while I've still got butter from our cow. Would you like a bit of butter to take home, Colin? We've got plenty.'

Colin grinned and nodded. 'Good on you, Rose. I'll be in that. Dedman can jump in the lake as far I'm concerned.'

'Don't know where he'd find a lake with much water in right now. The Pekina dam's a bit low. Pask says probably only got about eighteen inches in it right now,' I said, sipping my tea. 'The water tanks aren't too good either.' I gathered the mail towards me, picked up the letter from Joe and kissed it. 'It will be good to hear how Joe's going. The boys always sound cheerful when they write, but Pask says he sent cheery letters home when he was in the trenches because he didn't want to worry his Mum. They all probably varnish the truth a bit.'

'Yair, we all did that in the Great War, and I s'pose the lads do the same now.' Colin sipped his tea. 'Real tea,' He sighed. 'Beats that lucerne muck anytime. So you've got another grandson, have you?'

'Yes, Mavis had a little boy. And you've heard that Charlie's wife had a little girl? Harry's back at Norwood with the family now. He was in an air raid up in Darwin. He got his leg broken in two places. His back's not too good either but the doctors think he should be able to walk again eventually.'

'Bloody Japs,' said Colin. 'They just keep coming back and back. How many raids have there been on Darwin now? And they hit Broome too.'

'They've been busy, the little yellow buggers. They hit Wyndham as well,' I said. 'Harry was taken down to Katherine for a while, then they sent him back to Adelaide, so he got home about two months after the baby was born. It looks as if he'll be out of the war now. Which is one good thing at least.'

The fly screen door opened and banged, and I heard Pask's boots clunk on the floor as he shed them on the veranda. Then two more boots hit the wooden floor. Danny had arrived too.

'Hello, Colin. I see Rose is looking after you,' said Pask. 'Tea's up, is it, Rose? Danny and I could stand a cup. We're both as dry as a dead snake hanging on a fence.'

'I thought you'd be along soon, Pask,' I said. 'We've been catching up on the gossip. Colin's brought some letters from the kids. And the wool cheque.'

'That'll come in handy,' said Pask, grinning. 'Pay a few bills at least.'

Danny walked over to the cocky cage and tugged the hessian bag off, using his left hand because of the plaster cast on his right arm. The cocky gave a tentative screech, then allowed the boy to scratch its head before giving the plaster a peck.

'Don't let that bird do that, Danny,' I said. 'It might mess it up and we'll have to go into town and get it redone. Your dad's wool cheque'll go in doctor's bills.'

'How much longer do I have to wear this bloody thing, Mum?' Danny asked. 'It's hot and itchy and I'm sick of it.'

'Another month at least,' I said. 'If you take it off before the bones are knitted properly, you'll have to have it broken and reset and you'll never get full use of it again. You heard the doctor say that. Just be patient.'

'I'll have to wear it forever. I'll never get to enlist,' the boy whinged. 'I'm going to miss out on all the fun.'

Please God, let the war end before his arm is healed, I prayed. Please God, keep all my kids safe. I'd rather he had both his arms and both legs broken by sheep than have him go off to war.

'The war can't go on much longer, can it, Rose?' Colin said.

He must have been reading my mind. I saw he was looking unhappy again and that he had his hand in his pocket. Probably touching the telegram that had to be delivered to some poor family up the road from us and thinking about the misery he was about to unleash on the dead boy's family.

I poured another cup of tea for him and put another biscuit on his plate. 'Don't know, Colin. It can't go on forever, I hope. We all hope.'

'How are you going, Colin?' said Pask. 'Only good thing about the war, we get more letters at Orroroo than we ever used to get in peacetime. Keeps you in a job, I suppose, mate.'

'There's some things about this job I could do without,' said Colin. He drank the tea, sighed, set the empty cup on the table, got wearily to his feet and lifted his bag. 'I'd better get on with it, though. Thanks for the tea, Rose. You lot look after yourselves.'

28

Later the same day
Rose Pask – Orrooo

After Colin left, I opened Mary's letter while Pask tickled the bird under the wings. It responded by dancing up and down its perch and making little chirping noises. If I'd touched it, it would have taken my hand off. As I say, sulphur-crested cockies could be our secret weapon of war against invasion.

Rosemary would make another great weapon of war. As usual, she had upset her mother, and as usual Mary had vented her anger on paper. The girl had been playing up at school, Mary lamented, and was rude to her teachers. 'I don't know how the poor nuns put up with her!!' Mary had written. And with three exclamation marks after the statement. Which was a bit excessive, in my opinion. I always feel that what you say in writing ought to be able to convey its meaning without the use of exclamation marks.

Rosemary's latest excuse for slacking off was that it was a waste of time doing schoolwork, especially algebra and Latin, because the Japanese were soon going to kill or enslave us all anyway.

'I don't think even the Japanese would be able to sort Rosemary out,' wrote her mother. 'Fred and I have just about given up trying.'

Rosemary was also refusing to help out in the butcher shop. She said she was a vegetarian at heart and couldn't bear to see all the corpses hanging up on hooks in the shop, but, Mary wrote, 'She still has a good appetite and manages to tuck in to whatever was served up even if it is sausages or meat.' All that girl wanted to do was spend time giggling with her friends, who were, Mary said, just as silly as she was.

I laid the letter down and thanked my lucky stars that my two girls, Amy and Annie, were vastly better behaved and had more common-sense in their little fingers than Rosemary possessed in her whole body. I had brought them up well – those two would never give anyone a moment's trouble. I'm not criticising the way that Mary had brought Rosemary up, of course, Mary's a great little mother, but the proof is in the pudding, as they say.

Of course, Rosemary's behaviour could be Fred's fault. Genetics, they call it these days. I didn't know much about Fred's family because I think they came from Victoria. Or it could have been New South Wales, both places being practically foreign countries and no good ever comes from either of them. Bob Menzies was born in Melbourne, wasn't he? I exempt Broken Hill of course, because Broken Hill ought to be in South Australia, even if it isn't. Some politician got that border wrong. No doubt Fred's ancestors snuck across from one of the wilder bits of Australia when no one was looking.

Rosemary might be some sort of throwback to some rebellious convict ancestor of his, transported in chains for stealing a loaf of bread or a couple of pounds of butter, or whatever criminals did back then. Hungry criminals, that is. The ones that weren't hungry stole a handkerchief and were sent out here because they had runny noses and didn't have the sense to wipe it on their sleeves.

Little Kathleen was a good little girl, Mary said. Mary wrote that butter wouldn't melt in Kathleen's mouth. But I remembered how Kathleen had thrown her little flower basket at Pask and me at our wedding, and I wondered whether Mary was wearing blinkers and the whole family was bad seed. Apart, of course, from Paddy, who had always been a lovely kiddie.

But it was Paddy who was Mary's biggest problem just now. It was Paddy she had poured her heart out about when writing this letter. I could see some blotches in the ink where Mary had obviously shed a tear or two while writing.

I had been worrying about Paddy, too. He was growing up. He had been eighteen last birthday and we knew the age of enlistment had fallen. Nineteen this year, but everyone said the way things were going it would be eighteen next year.

Which was understandable, because we were in such peril from the Japanese. I remember Mary saying how those enemy submarines turning up in Sydney Harbour had upset the lad. Back in May that was. Of course, I suddenly realised, it was Sydney that Fred's family had come from.

Paddy was angry because he said the Japs could have killed his cousins. But it turned out that there were only three little subs, and they weren't much bigger than phone boxes, so they didn't do all that much damage. From what I read in *The Advertiser*, most of the Sydneysiders slept through the raid or just thought it was the army practising their shooting.

Still, you really can't tell what the Japs will do next; they are so untrustworthy and unpredictable. Perhaps we should let Rosemary (or Pask's cocky) loose on the buggers. Or send her off to Canberra to tell the politicians how to devise their policies.

I knew Charlie and his mates were forcing those buggers back in New Guinea, but we could still be invaded, if the Nips managed to get down the Track. Find another path through the mountains, for example. or come around by sea. Like Rosemary, Japs are sneaky. Look how Fortress Singapore had fallen. But apparently all Singapore's guns had been facing out to sea, and the Japs had come down the Malay Peninsula on bikes, so that probably said more about the Poms being dills than about the Japs being clever. Or it could have been both factors at work.

Anyway, Mary was really worried that Paddy would soon be conscripted, or join up if he wasn't conscripted. He was really keen to 'do his bit' — as all the young ones felt they had to. Amy and Annie were saying the same thing; they were acting as though there was something they needed to atone for, although they had no reason to feel like that. They were both working in the munitions factory after all, and that was nasty and even dangerous work too.

And they were helping Mavis with Harry, which wouldn't be an easy task, knowing Harry. Amy and Annie were making a hefty contribution to the war effort already; they didn't need to do more.

I didn't want any more of the kids going to war. My brothers had both died in the Great War in the mud in France. My first husband, Michael, had fought for the Empire and come back a shattered man. Well, he must have been shattered or he wouldn't done what he did when he got back.

I had lost my son Brian in the Middle East at Bardia, fighting for a useless bit of desert sand, and now my boys, Joe and Charlie, were away at war. And young Bob, Pask's son, was a prisoner of war somewhere in Germany. Who knew if he was alive or dead or how much he was suffering? Having to live on foreign food was bad enough. Sauerkraut and sausages, I expect. Probably with garlic. And Harry was still recovering from wounds he had gotten in yet another of those air raids on Darwin.

I didn't want Paddy, Danny or my girls to be the next casualties. It was too much. Just too bloody much to ask from any mother.

How much must I, must all the women of the world, have to sacrifice? How many gallons of our tears did God or the bloody Empire or Australia want? If only women ran the world instead of men, common sense would prevail, and we would find a better way to solve political problems than war. Some contest like a game of cricket or football or tiddlywinks or something. Not blood, sweat and tears like that Pom Churchill promised. Nothing was worth sacrificing another generation.

29

13 January 1943
Captain Joe Walsh – London

Dear Mum and all back in dear old Australia,

Another Christmas and another New Year has gone by with many of us scattered far away from home. There is a saying 'all roads lead to Rome', but I rather think that should be changed to 'all roads lead to Orroroo', because that is where so many of our letters converge these days.

You will never know how your letters cheer me up, Mum. And how happy it makes me to know what is happening back home and that the family continues to be strong even in adversity.

And you have no idea how much I miss you all, especially you, Mum. And how I miss the glorious sunshine we take for granted back home in blessed Australia. It's bleak here in Europe. Not just the bleakness and darkness that everyone endures in winter in the northern hemisphere, although I will admit that the lack of sunshine is all pervading. At this time of the year, it gets dark at about three or four p.m., and we don't see the sun again (if indeed the sun deigns to show itself at all) until about nine or ten next morning.

But the bleakness of war and the general pervading human sadness is even worse. It is very cold, and everyone is hungry. Rationing is strict. How I miss your fruit cake, Mum! Even with the austerity measures you talked about in your last letter, I'm sure you contrived some semblance of your usual fruit cake for Christmas. A small crumb or even just the smell of it would be most welcome to your prodigal son.

I apologise for sounding such a misery. As you realise, this is not my usual style, and I am sorry to write in this fashion. I spent

Christmas Day visiting the chaps in hospital and doing my best to cheer them up. Poor devils, they suffer much worse than I do. At least I have all my arms and legs, and even the face I look at when I'm shaving (although never a pretty sight) is not distorted and burned as some of theirs are. Many chaps have been blinded so they can't even see to shave. And they are just as distant from family and friends as I am; even the English ones, because travel is so difficult with the war.

I don't think I admitted to you why I wasn't in the wave of chaps who left Britain and joined the Pacific War, or why there have been so few letters from me for a few months. I think I made some poor excuse (a lie, I must admit, that communications were bad at the time).

I think the time has come to admit the truth, since I have fully recovered from my illness. I purposely did not reveal this before, but I was laid quite low with pneumonia and at one stage apparently it was touch and go. Eventually I did, with the grace of God, the skills of the medicos and, I believe, the encouragement and good offices of my friend, David, pull through. David is Jewish, so we celebrated Christmas and Hanukkah together. He is a lovely chap and has become a good friend. He gave me a bottle of whiskey at Christmas and we drank some together, but tonight I am drowning my sorrows alone. I am not sure it works, but it can't hurt. And if God didn't want us to drink whiskey, he wouldn't have allowed it to be distilled.

I am now deeply regretting that I didn't come back when the Japanese were rattling their sabres and Curtin told the Brits that Australia would be taking her men back, but of course I was too ill to travel at that stage.

Now the church and the army have decided there are many Catholics who need consolation here. Apparently, my presence here is worth more than the trouble of organising transport home for me, so I have been told I must remain where I am. A waif of the storm of war.

Although I did make some fuss about coming south after I recovered from the pneumonia, I was overruled by the powers that be. It was not my choice to cross that Rubicon, but I must accept my fate and perhaps God has other plans for me.

There is something that I must tell you about those dark days when I hovered between life and death. Dear old Brian came to me in a dream (no doubt one of those moments, as Shakespeare put it, 'proceeding from the feverish brain') and asked me to give him absolution for breaking Mrs Williams's window with a cricket ball many years ago. He also begged me to tell you that it had been he who had done it, so I'm not breaking any seal of confession in writing this, if that were possible from a dream event. He said he had written to you about it, but, and I quote his words in my dream, 'You don't know if letters get through in a war and the censor might have blacked it out anyway.' I know the whole thing is a bit silly, and you would be excused in doubting my sanity, but I wanted to get it off my conscience, Mum.

I'm writing this late at night because even though it sounds as if I have spent my time sitting around feeling sorry for myself, I have been travelling quite a bit.

One of our bases (I shan't say which one because that would mean the censor would have to blot out most of the page in case my scribbles inadvertently fell into enemy hands) was bombed a couple of days after Christmas, and I have been helping with the funeral services of a number of chaps who were killed in the raid, and those of some other chaps who were injured but succumbed later. Funerals held under umbrellas seem somehow more poignant than ones conducted in blazing sunlight.

I thought of Dad's funeral yesterday, as I was saying the usual words and watching the usual coffin lowered into the usual muddy earth. I recalled, however, that the earth into which Dad was lowered was hot and baking, nothing like the soggy graves in this 'green and pleasant land'.

And of course, it meant writing letters to the unfortunate men's loved ones, which is heartbreaking for those who receive the letters, but, believe me, harrowing for those who write them, too. I recalled how you told me of the rather impersonal letter that you received from Brian's commanding officer and I always try to make the letters as kindly as possible.

The war appears to be interminable. It seems that we are at a stalemate, although it is heartening that we have retaken Tobruk, and that Rommel has been pushed back to Tunisia. I remember well my time in the Middle East, where, of course, our poor dear Brian died. He will never be forgotten. I know the whole war thing seems absolutely futile to you, Mum, but unfortunately, we are stuck with this dreadful situation, and all we can do is pray that soon this cross will pass from us. Pass from the whole world, indeed. God help us all.

I am sitting here with a glass of whiskey, and I just spilled a bit on the paper. I thought I would admit that, in case you sniff the page and wonder what your errant son is up to. I do not usually indulge, but whiskey is useful as consolation as well as celebration.

I nearly chucked out this letter for fear of scandalising you with the scent of alcohol and indeed with my miserable thoughts, but paper is in short supply and we're taught to husband resources.

I was rereading some of your old letters, Mum, and I saw a reference to Charlie having a friend who is a cannibal and a headhunter. You didn't expand on the story, and I find myself intrigued by the idea of it. How did it happen? I'm all for embracing the idea of common humanity and all that sort of thing, and Charlie always was a fairly intrepid sort of bloke, but it did sound a bit risky to me. I would have thought that Charlie was in a precarious enough position wandering about in the jungles of New Guinea in combat with the foe without making dubious acquaintanceships with fellows who might lop off his head at the drop of a hat. If indeed headhunters wear hats.

I was overjoyed to hear about the new additions to the family. Congratulations to all concerned.

Don't worry about me, Mum. I'm sure I will get over my present state of feeling a bit down. Hitler and his cronies can't keep going forever, and Mr Churchill seems optimistic that we will get through this little debacle soon. God is on our side, or so the politicians tell us! But why would God wish to harm any of his creation?

Love and best wishes to all, and a belated happy and blessed Christmas and New Year.

Joe.

30

6 June 1943
Rose Pask– Orroroo

'I have to go down and see them off,' I insisted. 'I don't know when I'll see them again. It's not every day your girls go off to war. I want to see them in their nurses' uniforms. Our little girls in the Australian Army Nursing Corps! Just think of it, Pask.'

Pask smiled a little ruefully. I knew he was worried about his daughter and worried about Amy too, just as I was. But proud at the same time.

'I have to take a couple of snaps with the Box brownie. And I haven't seen the babies yet, either, Phil's little girl, and Mavis's little boy. I need to see how Harry's getting on, too.'

'You had that phone call from Mavis the other day, love,' Pask said. 'Didn't she say he's a bit better?'

'Apparently he's walking again, although he still limps. Mavis said the doctors think he'll always limp. So I don't think he'll be off to war or even back to Darwin.'

'At least that's one of our kids safe,' said Pask. 'You know, I still feel guilty that I'm not doing my bit to stop the Japs.'

'You are, Pask. You're providing wool for uniforms and meat for food.'

'It's not the same, though, Rose. A man ought to be fighting.'

'Your son joined up, saved London in the Blitz, and now he's a prisoner of war in Germany, and we lost Brian, remember? And now Annie and Amy are going to be nurses and put soldiers' bodies back together. This family's contributing, and don't you forget it.' I patted him on the back. 'I wish you and Danny could come too, but of course you've got sheep to chase.'

'I know all that, Rose,' Pask sighed. 'Danny and me, we'll be all right. The sheep too. It's just that I don't like the idea of baching up here on my own. I like being married, Rose. I'll miss you in bed. I'll miss you around the house. I'll be lonely.'

'You won't be on your own,' I said. 'You've got Danny. He's not going anywhere. Are you, Danny? You're not planning to join up like young Paddy did?'

I was struck by a sudden horrible thought. Back in 1914, my two brothers, who were also called Patrick and Daniel, had joined up for what they had called 'the Great Adventure' and gone off to die in the mud of France. Now another two boys bearing the same names, this time my son Danny and my grandson Paddy, had the same stupid ideas in their heads. Bravery and heroism and stupidity. Was it something passed down in the blood or was it some horrible joke on God's part that caused two generations to share the same destiny? This time, the Pacific mud was warmer, but blood flowed just as fast if the mud was cold or hot. The Pacific islands could be just as fatal a shore as France had been.

'No, I'm not quite old enough yet,' said Danny, a little wistfully. 'They won't take me yet. Paddy's older than I am. You have to be eighteen and they check your birth records these days. And my birth certificate is a bit confusing.'

'Thank God the government rule is that, although Paddy can enlist, he isn't allowed to serve in the Northern Territory or in New Guinea until he turns twenty-one,' I said. 'Let's hope and pray the rotten war ends before he reaches that mark.' I glared at Danny. 'Or you do.'

'We're going to miss out on all the fun,' grumbled Danny.

'If you call losing an eye the way your father did fun, yes, I hope you do miss out,' I said, glancing at Pask, who wore a patch to cover his missing left eye which he had lost in World War One. A wound about which he still refused to speak.

'Any idea where Annie and Amy are going to be posted?' asked Pask, who was obviously changing the subject, although I knew he didn't want Danny to join up any more than I wanted him to. It was one thing to say he wanted to fight, and another to sacrifice your son

Like Abraham sacrificing Isaac, I thought, in a sudden flash of religious memory. But God intervened back then. He sent a sheep to be slaughtered instead. A ram conveniently caught in a thicket of bushes. Were all politicians as bloody-minded as Abraham, willing to sacrifice the young for stupid ideas? What is God doing now? Why isn't He chasing up a few rams and sticking them into bushes to die in place of this generation?

'No, the girls will be sent somewhere up north,' I said. 'I expect it will be New Guinea because that's where most of them seem to be going. Only,' I suddenly thought, 'how come nurses can be sent to the islands when they're under twenty-one? Is there one rule for girls and another one for the lads?'

'Buggered if I know,' agreed Pask. 'I always said the blokes in charge are nuts.'

'They must be going somewhere because Annie said they've been inoculated against all sorts of tropical diseases. She said her arms ached for weeks because they had different shots on different days. I can't remember what they were, but cholera was among them.'

'All sorts of diseases in the tropics,' said Danny eagerly, sounding as if he couldn't wait to go up there a catch a few of them.

I shook my head. Stupid kid. I continued trying to remember what Annie said when she phoned.

'And they have to take stuff to prevent malaria. It probably doesn't work, because Charlie did say he's had malaria a couple of times, although he said he takes pills – I remember, it's called Atebrin. Charlie says the mosquitoes in New Guinea are incredible and his arms are covered with mossies at night and there's not much you can do about them.'

'Can't carry mosquito nets with you when you're out on patrol, can you?' said Pask.

'In his last letter, Charlie was saying how great the Fuzzy Wuzzy Angels are,' said Danny. 'If Amy and Annie are going to New Guinea, I suppose they'll see them. Those blokes carry the wounded men down the Track to Port Moresby, across rope bridges over deep rivers and everything.'

'Charlie has to carry his rifle and all his other kit over those bridges, too. Charlie said some of them are just vines woven together,' I said. 'And they're slippery because it's always raining up there.'

'Could use a bit of rain down here,' said Pask ruefully.

I shrugged. Never mind the war, a farmer's mind was never far from drought or flooding rain, whichever was the current situation.

'The hospital would be in Port Moresby, wouldn't it?' asked Danny.

'They'd have field hospitals all over the place,' said Pask, obviously remembering his own war service. 'You have to treat blokes where they're wounded and then get them somewhere better when they can be moved. Unless they die beforehand.'

'I wonder if the girls will look after Charlie,' said Danny. I could see he was dreaming of the day he could enlist and share the adventure.

'I sincerely hope not. I don't want him wounded.' I snapped. 'Now, I've made a stew for you two that should last a couple of days unless you make pigs of yourselves, and after that you'll just have to fry some chops and toss a few spuds and veg into a saucepan. Or open some tins of baked beans if you can't manage that.'

'That sounds rotten, Mum,' said Danny.

'Austerity measures,' I said. 'There's a war on. Charlie said he eats bully beef and biscuits most of time.'

'We'll be all right, Rose,' said Pask. 'Don't worry about us. Just don't be away too long.'

'Any time is too long, Mum,' said Danny, giving me a rare hug.

31

20 June 1943
Rose Pask – Norwood

'I'm just so proud of my girls,' I said. Well, I wasn't proud of the state they had left my house in, but that's beside the point, and I wasn't about to admit it to Mrs Williams. I wasn't about to mention there was a coating of dust an inch thick on the piano or that the lino must have been gasping for a lick of polish.

You wouldn't think that dust would accumulate on vertical surfaces, but my poor brothers were peering out through very grimy glass when I ventured into the front room. So, of course, was Mick, but I decided obscurity improved his photo, so I left cleaning it till last. Now, of course, they were all restored to their usual condition. Still, I felt uncomfortable in that room because all three men in their military uniforms seemed to be accusing me of something.

Perhaps they were angry that their sacrifice had been in vain – and of course they were right. My brothers and Michael had fought, and my brothers had died, in the war to end all wars, yet the next generation was slogging through sand and mud and dying the same way they had died. And my girls, Annie and Amy, were now officially army nurses, and going off to do their bit for king and country just as the previous generation had done. There were their official photos, sitting on the mantelpiece, a bit smaller than the ones on the wall, smiling out from under their nursing veils to prove it.

Yes, I was proud of my girls, but at the same time I was devastated. I still thought it was all bullshit. The girls themselves seemed oddly defiant when I first arrived, but when the time to leave neared, I could see they were upset. They had this false air of cheerfulness, but the bravado was stretched thin and fraught, and beneath it they were both fighting tears. I wanted to gather them both into my arms and beg them to stay, but I knew it was too late for that.

And the ringing silence in this house when they had finally left! This house that always been so loud with children's voices, with shouts and laughter and banging of doors and running footsteps. Now it was quiet as the grave, shrouded with emptiness and blackout curtains, even the occasional traffic in the street muffled. It was clean, it was neat and it was empty.

I was sorry that I had cleaned away all traces of neglect. It had been messy, but it had been lived in. Then I remembered the high-water mark around the bath that still lingered, and knew I still needed to expend some elbow grease on this house. The ice chest wasn't exactly fragrant either. Neither was the lavatory. Phil and her sister were going to stay here when I went back to Orroroo, so I wanted the place clean. I didn't want them to think our standards had dropped.

Still, I missed Amy and Annie so much, and I didn't like removing all evidence of their presence.

I knew the girls had been busy in the last few weeks, what with helping Mavis out, working at the munitions factory and studying for their entry exams for the nursing course. But even so, you would have expected them to make some sort of effort. And Mick would have spun in his grave if he'd seen the run-down state the garden was in. Weeds a mile high and even the silverbeet had died, despite the fact that I knew it had rained down here much more than it had at Orroroo.

Stuff Mick, I thought, with satisfaction. I should have left the dirt to cover his eyes on that photo so he couldn't follow me around the room. Even so, I would have to prune the roses or they would go to rack and ruin. The girls hadn't given them a thought. Charlie (who had done them last year) was away in New Guinea and Harry certainly wasn't up to the job.

I wouldn't be asking Mr Williams to give me a hand. I'd seen him when I was out the back hanging the sheets (changing the linen was another thing that had been neglected) and I called out, 'How are you going?' to him over the fence, but all I got in reply was a nasty look. I didn't know the problem was, but I wasn't about make enquiries.

I had expected Mrs Williams to turn up in my kitchen almost before I'd taken my hat off. But, to tell the absolute truth, it was three days before she turned up, and I was beginning to wonder if she was avoiding me on purpose, too. I couldn't have offended her, because I hadn't been here for months. But something must have put her nose out of joint.

I will admit it was just as well she hadn't called in because it gave me the time to scrub and polish so the whole place gleamed like a new penny before her arrival. I had been expecting the royal inspection, and I got it.

I'd dropped some mutton chops on her doorstep by way of a calling card as I walked past her place on my way home from Orroroo. They were wrapped in our local paper, *The Orroroo Register*, so she'd know where they'd come from. I felt I owed her something since the girls had said she had helped them out with a bit of soup occasionally.

Now as I poured the tea, I watched her cast a scrutinising eye over the stove. It was up to even her exacting standards now. As I always say, if you think you're going to die, clean the stove. I wasn't planning on dying just yet, but if I did, it really wouldn't matter, because that stove was gleaming.

'So those two are going off to be nurses just when the war is going to end pretty soon,' said Mrs Williams in a scathing way.

I sneered as I poured the tea, but she didn't notice. How dare she cast aspersions on my girls! My heroic girls! They were both so beautiful that they made those dowdy uniforms look almost glamorous. I'd used up quite a bit of film taking photos of them. I'm not much of a photographer, but how I prayed those snaps would turn out. I'd get them developed as soon as the film was full. I still needed more pictures of the two babies, though. Everyone in Orroroo would want to see those pictures.

'Waste of time, really,' said Mrs Williams. 'They should have done it months ago when it was still worthwhile.'

'What do you mean worthwhile?' I demanded.

'Bert says the war's nearly over. The Russians have got back Stalingrad, that Dambusters business in Germany worked well, and Blamey and MacArthur are sorting out New Guinea now. Mussolini's a dead duck. Bert gives it a few more months before Hitler and Hirohito both surrender.'

'I hope Bert's right, but I reckon he's wrong,' I snapped.

'Bert's never wrong,' said his wife piously.

Stupid bitch, I thought. Once, I thought that Mick could do no wrong and look how mistaken I was about that. Thank God (if there is a God) that I'm married to Pask now. At least he's a decent man with a good head on his shoulders. There's not many blokes like that about, and I didn't think Bert Williams was one of them.

'Sugar, dear?' I asked, knowing full well she took two spoonsful.

'You'll see, they'll be back with their tails between their legs in six months' time. Waste of time the army training them, waste of government money,' she said piously.

I glared at her.

'Do them both good, though,' she added rather viciously.

I looked at her. What on earth was wrong with this woman? Probably had a fight with the management of one of her committees, I speculated. The Housewives Association or the Christian Temperance Union. People need a drink when there's a war on. They'll drink anything they can get. There was quite a demand for black market hooch at Orroroo and I bet there was in Norwood too. People needed to forget stuff they didn't want to remember.

Or she might have had a squabble with Mr Williams. I dismissed the idea as being beyond belief. Mr Williams was a cantankerous old devil, but I couldn't see anything disturbing domestic harmony next door.

'A lot of men can be wounded in six months,' I said. 'Or killed. Or get malaria and dysentery.'

I silently prayed that Charlie wouldn't be among the men my girls nursed. Especially the wounded men. Malaria was bad enough and, from what I read between the lines in his last letters, he seemed to have been quite ill with his latest bout of it.

'Although Annie and Amy will be there to nurse those wounded soldiers,' I said in triumph. 'My girls are so capable and caring. You can't deny they're both girls to be proud of.'

I couldn't quite read the funny look on her face. It must have been envy because she had never had children. She wouldn't be able to understand how it was to feel fear and pride at the same time. I knew, though, because I had kids who had grown into wonderful adults who were willing to give their all for their country.

'Did you catch up with Phil and Mavis and see their babies?' Mrs Williams asked.

I smiled and poured her another cup of tea. I welcomed any excuse to talk about my new grandchildren. It was a pity those photos hadn't been developed yet. I couldn't wait to flash them around.

'Yes, and the girls have arranged both the baptisms while I'm down here. The babies are lovely. Both beautiful, bonny babes.' I knew I was gushing, probably overdoing the proud grandmother act, but I didn't care. Bugger Mrs Williams, I was going to rub it in for all it was worth. 'Both of them have got the Walsh red hair. Harry's little boy has a ginger fuzz, but Charlie's girl is more auburn. Masses of hair on that child. Just like Veronica Lake, only a redhead.'

'It's so nice that you've had the chance to see them while you're here,' she said wistfully.

That was when I remembered all the times my neighbour had lost babies. Usually around the three-month mark. If you get past the first three months in a pregnancy, you're pretty safe. I ought to feel sorry for her, really. She had had a bad trot in the baby stakes. No wonder she was bitter.

But then, with what I could only deduce was a peculiar gleam in her eye, Mrs Williams smirked. 'What do Amy and Annie think of the babies?'

'They're over the moon to have a new niece and nephew,' I lied.

In fact, I had thought both girls had been a bit strange about the babies. I was amazed to see that neither of them seemed keen on holding the little ones; but I thought Annie, in particular, was very stand-offish. She absolutely refused to touch either of them. It seemed odd because before Phil had the baby, Annie had pinched silk from the parachute factory to make a frock that both the girls had spent long hours sewing, smocking and embroidering.

The lack of interest must be due to the excitement of leaving their old lives behind and embarking on a career in nursing. Obviously, professional thoughts filled the girls' minds now. All cluckiness had been driven out of them. I knew nurses weren't allowed to marry. They were discouraged from even getting engaged. Career took precedence over everything. Of course, they were young; there would be plenty of time for romance and motherhood later.

'The baptisms will be next Sunday, after Mass,' I said. 'I'll be there with my ears back, even if it means putting up with Father Flaherty having a go at me for getting married at Orroroo instead of down here in St Ignatius' Church.'

'He'll probably just be pleased that you finally got married. I remember Bert saying he met Flaherty in the street and the priest was whingeing about you living in sin up there in the country all these years.'

'Father Flaherty is an old gossip,' I retorted. 'Priests shouldn't discuss their flock, especially with Protestants.'

'He told Bert you won't go to heaven because you've married a Protestant. Of course, that's all Roman rubbish.'

I wasn't interested in arguing theology with her. I had better ways of scoring points. 'I reckon he gave up on saving my soul years ago. Anyway, I'm not going to any heaven that Flaherty's part of. Do have a slice of this cake, dear. It's full of butter. We've got our own cow up in Orroroo, you know.'

Mrs Williams accepted the cake, but she looked as if she was eating lemons. Probably jealous because I was boasting about the butter. I knew how partial she was to the stuff. I suspected she and Bert had been reduced to bread and dripping, the way rationing was going.

'I've brought a few pounds of butter with me,' I said, rubbing my bounty in a bit. 'Freshly churned, just before I got on the train.'

I really did owe her something more than those mutton chops for keeping an eye on the girls, although I doubted that she had really done much. Amy and Annie were independent adults, after all. Mature enough to enlist as army nurses.

I simpered at her. 'You're very welcome to some of it, being such a good neighbour.'

'I couldn't possibly accept it,' she snapped. 'Bert's very strict about observing the rules about black market goods. Although those chops were a very welcome gift and we couldn't waste good meat.'

I shrugged. Silly old biddy. If she didn't want the butter, I'd have more to give to Mavis and Phil.

'I'm going back next week, just after the babies are baptised. Pask will just have to be patient. He said that Anastasia O'Halloran is bringing casseroles and soup over to keep him and Danny going so they won't starve. Of course, he says she's not as good a cook as I am.'

'He would say that,' said Mrs Williams. 'Probably doesn't want to upset your feelings. I stayed with Anastasia when I came up for your wedding and I thought she was an excellent cook.'

What a snitchy woman she is, I thought. Always had been. I don't know why I invited her to my wedding. But then I realised I hadn't actually invited her. She'd invited herself. I bet the stories she told afterwards about my domestic arrangements got her invitations all over Norwood for months.

'Mary's coming up on the train for the baptisms,' I said, just to remind her about my extensive family. 'Fred will cope in the butcher's shop with Rosemary's help. Because of the rationing most of the actual meat goes to the military, so all he's selling is pigs' heads and offal. And sausages. Fred makes wonderful sausages. Mary's bringing little Kathleen with her.'

The shop will probably go bankrupt with Rosemary helping in it, I thought, but I didn't say it.

'I really miss a bit of steak and the occasional mutton chop,' said Mrs Williams, wistfully. 'Of course, you can eat as much mutton as you want to, up in the bush. Bert sucked on those chop bones like he'd never had meat like it.'

That made me feel a bit guilty. But Bert shouldn't have given me that dirty look over the fence if he'd enjoyed the chops, I thought. Strange bloke, Bert Williams.

'The least I could do,' I said sanctimoniously, 'after the way you looked after Amy and Annie for me. It was a comfort knowing that they were safe in your care.'

Mrs Williams sort of glowered when I said that. By now, I wasn't sure what to think. Both those kids had a sort of haunted look about them, although I couldn't put my finger on the reason, and they clammed up when I tried to quiz them.

Had Bert tried something on with the girls? I wondered privately. Surely, they would have told me if anything untoward had happened. Although of course, Mary had never confided in me about Michael's despicable behaviour. I dismissed the idea as soon as it occurred to me. Bert wouldn't have the stamina. My girls were both strong, healthy lasses, and definitely both virgins, I would swear. They wouldn't allow any hanky-panky. And yet, I had a gut feeling something had changed while my back was turned. Mothers know these things.

One thing I had noticed was that Annie often came out in the mornings with red-rimmed eyes as though she had been crying in her bed. She must still be mourning Brian. It was all just delayed grief for her dead fiancée. Amy seemed very protective of Annie, so she must be trying to support her stepsister. Only natural. Lovely girls, both of them.

I suspected they were both glad to be getting away from Norwood and to escape into their nursing careers. As for the past, it was water under the bridge now. The girls would be all right; no harm could come to army nurses. They wouldn't be in the front line; hospitals were safe

216

places, even in war. They had big red crosses painted on their rooves. There was a Geneva Convention to protect them.

I should count my blessings, such as they were. So far, I had lost only one son, while some mothers had lost two or three. Take Mrs Painter around the corner. Her sons John, Andrew and Bill were all either dead or missing in action. Not that I felt my loss was diminished at all. Losing even one son was too much.

I must cheer up. I had something to look forward to – how wonderful to see Mary and Kathleen again, even if only for a short time. And thank God too that Mary was leaving Rosemary at Mount Gambier to help Fred out. Poor Fred.

I poured more tea into my cup. The thought of Rosemary was enough to arouse the need for tea. Then I remembered Mrs Williams was sitting at the table with me, so I poured her another cup too. I wasn't worried about the ration, because there seemed to be piles of stuff here, tea, coffee, sugar, tinned food. Even butter. And chocolate too. The girls must have been starving themselves.

'Phil's going to be living here while we're all away,' I said. 'And Charlie says he's going to get leave soon. I'm not sure if it's because he's had malaria or whether he's just due for leave, but at least he'll be home for a bit. He'll stay here with her. Her mum is a bit better now and one of her sisters can look after her. Her brother Clive's away in the navy, so his wife will stay with Phil to keep her company.'

Good thing, that, I thought. Phil and her new baby would have company. I didn't enjoy staying in this house on my own. Gives me the heebie-jeebies, now the girls had gone. There were funny noises at night. I remember Amy complained about strange sounds when I left her here, before Annie came down to stay with her. Loneliness does peculiar things to you, works on your imagination. I never used to be jumpy when I was alone, but to tell the truth I couldn't wait to get back to Orroroo.

'It's all very disruptive, this war,' Mrs Williams lamented. 'People rushing here and there. You never know how long anyone will be in one place. I'm glad the house won't be empty.' She sighed. 'I can't say I like the idea of Amy going off to be a nurse. That Annie, she'll be all right, she's got a hard edge to her, but Amy's not the sort of girl to be gallivanting around the Pacific.'

I rushed to Annie's defence. 'I've never noticed a hard edge on Annie. I know she can drive a car, but lots of girls are progressive these days. Independent. Amy said she couldn't bear to be parted from Annie. She says she thinks of her as her sister. Which I think is wonderful. One day the war will be over, and we'll all be back together again.'

'Yes,' said Mrs Williams, with a bit of a catch in her voice. 'It will be nice when everyone comes home again.'

Of course, she didn't have children to come home after the war. I wasn't sure any more whether she was better off than me or not.

Was being barren an advantage or a disadvantage? Her kids weren't coming home but they'd never gone away, either. Myrtle Williams would never receive a telegram like the one I received about Brian. No son of hers was dead in the desert. And she had never had sleepless nights worrying whether her children were alive or dead, wounded or hungry because she had never had them. On the other hand, she had missed out on all the joy of watching them take their first steps and say their first words.

I decided, in the end, that conception and childbearing was worth all the blood and pain. One day, Amy and Annie would learn that too. But for now, they had nursing careers to pursue. Annie's car driving could be a big advantage to her as a nurse. There might be ambulances to drive, that sort of thing. The girls would have all sorts of new knowledge and skills when they came back. Inside knowledge of how things worked.

I prayed that Bert Williams had some sort of inside knowledge because of his air raid warden status, and that he was right and that the war would be over soon.

32

28 August 1943
Corporal Charlie Walsh – Kokoda

Dear Mum,

Sorry I haven't written for a bit. We've been a bit busy up here and mail wasn't getting through. I had another bout of malaria last month, but lots of other chaps have had it too. Up here, we've got mosquitoes that could carry off a bus. Either the mossies are on the Japs' side, or the Atebrin isn't doing its job properly. I was hoping to get leave but that's been deferred until we sort out some problems of the Nip variety.

We are up in the highlands now and it gets really cold especially at night. It's warm enough during the day but humidity you wouldn't believe. Water drips off the trees even when its not raining.

Every morning is misty – looks like a white blanket has come down on us and sound gets muffled so you can't see much ahead or hear anything much either. When there's a bit of a stoush going on, you never know whether you've actually hit a target or not. Which is probably a good thing in some ways.

Thanks a million for the photos of little Elizabeth's baptism. It meant so much to me to see them. Phil had a studio photo taken of her and sent me a copy. I can't get over how beautiful that kiddy is. What about that hair? It's so long she looks like a film star. Veronica Lake or Rita Hayworth. And red? She's a real Walsh! Phil said the dress Elizabeth is wearing is made of silk, so I reckon it came from the parachute factory. An offcut, I suppose. Phil said Annie and Amy had done the smocking and there's little pink flowers embroidered on it. The tinting does show that a bit.

I've packed the photos up in oilcloth and put them in the bag where I carry my most precious stuff. Elizabeth will be with me all the way up and down the Track. I keep thanking God that she's a girl and won't ever have to go to war.

Although I reckon going to war is a choice our grown-up girls have made now they're army nurses. I wish to God Amy and Annie hadn't decided to join up. I just hope they aren't posted anywhere near here. It's hell on wheels sometimes. Moresby is fairly safe now, but I won't be happy until I hear that they are both safely home again.

You said Joe wanted to hear the details of how I met the cannibals. One day there was a commotion out the back of our camp. It didn't sound like the Japs but a few of us investigated. There was a bit of a fracas going on between some of the Kukukus (not sure if that's how it's meant to be spelled but that's what it sounds like when they say their name). They are the local native tribe. They're very different to the Fuzzy Wuzzies. The Fuzzies live near the coast and they're tall and sort of golden-coloured and of course they've got that mop of fuzzy hair standing out like a halo. Some of them stick flowers and feathers in their hair or combs that they make out of wood, and colour it sort of orange. Looks a bit funny, really. But they aren't poofs or anything like that, it's just their way of life.

These blokes up in the mountains are pygmies and much darker. And a lot fiercer. The Fuzzies are terrified of them and swear they're cannibals and headhunters.

I don't think the local chaps have had much contact with anyone outside their own area because they don't speak much pidgin (that's the language that's a mixture of the native lingo and English). All us blokes have learned a bit of pidgin, and Kiri, the native fellow who is attached to me, has learned some English which is useful.

Anyway, as I said, there was this terrible noise and we realised there was a real serious battle going on. No guns because they haven't got them, which is just as well, but a lot of yelling and bush bashing.

A mob of natives came tumbling out of the bush, naked as the day they were born, apart from boars' tusks through their nostrils and a few coloured feathers in their hair. They were covered with white clay, which is what they use for warpaint, and they were screaming like banshees and attacking each other with stone axes and spears.

These blokes use bows and arrows for hunting and a few of them were carrying those, but they were the ones hanging back from the actual stoush. The main action looked pretty much the same way we Aussies set to with the Japs when we get to close quarters. Only we use bayonets, not axes.

These fellows weren't planning to take prisoners any more than the Aussies or the Japs do. It was an all-out fight to the death.

We didn't like seeing it. It was like watching kids fight, because most of them don't come up to our waists. We figured the best way to stop it was to let off a couple of rifle shots into the treetops. A flock of birds must have got a shock because feathers came drifting down.

You should have seen the look on the natives' faces. They jumped a couple of feet into the air and most of them took off as if the devil was after them. Probably never heard a rifle up close before. Some of our chaps started laughing. They said it was like watching Charlie Chaplin and his mates acting. I wasn't so sure. The natives weren't acting, they were dead serious, and you could see their war mattered to them just as much as our war matters to us.

One bloke got left behind, though, and a couple of his mates stayed with him. He sat on the ground and just looked up at me as if he had been stunned. I ran over and saw blood pouring down one side of his face. I sent one of the chaps back to get a first aid box, although a couple of my mates said I was mad to waste good supplies on a boong. I said, 'Just do it', and after a bit of grumbling, Bill brought the box.

I gave the native chap a shot of morphine, which cheered him up a lot, and then I sewed up the wound, which looked a whole lot worse than it actually was. There was a bit of bone split, but I reckoned he would survive. Head wounds always bleed like mad. It's the gut wounds that kill you. And I figure any native that lives past childhood must be pretty tough anyway. So I bandaged his head up, and he recovered his wits really fast.

Bunny Cogan and the other fellows were falling about laughing but the natives who had taken off before as if the devil was after them had come back and were standing around looking as if they expected some sort of ceremony, so after I finished the bandaging I sang 'Danny Boy' and followed it up with 'Phil the Fluter's Ball'.

It worked a treat, although of course none of them knew the words so they couldn't join in. But there were grins all round from the cannibals and from our lot too.

I reckon one of our blokes would have collapsed in a heap after the sort of injury the little chap had had, but this man stood up, picked up one of the bows and some arrows that were lying up the back and presented them to me in a formal manner that would have done credit to the king when he was conferring a knighthood. I accepted the gift as graciously as I would have taken a medal from an officer, not that us ordinary soldiers ever get noticed much by officers.

Next day, some natives came down from the hill where they've got their village and brought us some vegetables, yams and green stuff like spinach, which was very a welcome gift. I've been worrying that we might get scurvy because there isn't much in the way of vegies or fruit up here that we can get our hands on.

And after that, I got invited to go up to the village and they had a bit of a sing-sing in their men's house, which is called the *Haus Tambaran* and they indicated we can have as much veg as we want from their gardens.

I told the sarge that it would be best if it was only me and my mate, Paul Richards, go up there because I reckon if anyone looked the wrong way at their women, it would be the chop for us. Paul's not the sort of bloke who's interested in sheilas. Never has been, apparently. I know there are men like that around, not that Paul's not a top fellow or anything. And of course, I'm married to Phil, so I'd never give a woman a second glance. If either of us looked at their women, we would be pork chops for them. Kiri warned me about that. Kiri said they call human flesh 'long pig' and they're pretty keen on it as a food.

The native patrol officer came round a few days later and warned us not to go anywhere near the village because these pygmies are headhunters. But I knew that already, because I'd seen the shrunken heads hanging up in the *Haus Tambaran*.

I don't know how much of this you want to pass on to Joe. I suppose he has seen some nasty stuff over there in Europe but being a priest is different to being an ordinary soldier, and he's probably pretty sheltered from what really goes on in the world.

We've moved on now, so I don't suppose I'll see that particular tribe again, but it was a bit different from the sort of stuff that usually happens up here.

I hope all goes well with you and the family, love from
Charlie.

33

28 August 1943
Corporal Charlie Walsh – Kokoda

Charlie put down his pen and looked around at the camp. A few of his mates were, like him, writing letters home, but others were busy at housekeeping tasks. It was a job keeping clothes anything like clean in this country. But cleaning guns for the next engagement with the enemy was more important. That was a task that could never be neglected. You never knew when the next encounter would take place, only that it would.

It's like a tug of war, this Kokoda Track, Charlie thought. We're pulling at a rope greased with blood and guts and sweat. One minute we're gaining a bit of rope, and the next the Japs are winning. Back and forth, back and forth. Gaining a few miles and then losing them. And all of it costing lives on both sides.

He smiled when he thought back to the beginning of the campaign when he and his mates had climbed what they called 'the golden staircase'. How the fellows had complained about lifting each leg over the logs that were laid up the mountainside, only to bring that leg down into a muddy pool on the next step. The climb had seemed to last forever.

Charlie looked back once or twice and felt dizzy at the height they had ascended, although the men were warned to keep their eyes to the front.

Living at altitude was the norm now. Here in the Owen Stanley range, often you couldn't see the depths of the valleys. Just swirling cloud hiding deep ravines. When the mist cleared a little, you glimpsed the rivers that plummeted through them. It was crossing those streams that was hairy. Often, the bridges were little more than plaited vines strung across the gap. How those bridges swayed and how the men clung to their precious rifles. Lose your rifle and you lost your only defence, and gained the ire of the officers.

Not even the blokes who hailed from the Blue Mountains or from Queensland had seen country like this. And up here you weren't just out for a stroll, for a bit of a wander through the bush, here you were carrying everything you owned on your back and you had to have your rifle ready for the first sign of attack. Not that there were often actual signs that you were going to be attacked. Attacks just happened.

One minute you were bush-bashing, trying to avoid the vines that carried vicious barbs and keeping noise to a minimum so the enemy didn't know you were there, and not smoking although you were dying for a fag because the bastards would smell the smoke, and the next you were down on your belly answering fire with fire. Shooting into the bushes, taking cover behind any trees that offered shelter, watching blood spurt from the neck of your mate that you had shared a joke or a fag with the moment before.

At Isurava, we stopped them for four days, thought Charlie, and we thought we had won the war. But the bastards kept coming; they always keep coming. And we keep on against them. It just never stops, just slows occasionally when we're at stalemate, or they are. And then it starts up again. The hard slog. Always the hard slog.

Up and down the mountains, through swamps and jungle, across flimsy bridges slung over streams – torrential rivers really – that carry more water than fellows who come from a dry country like Australia would think possible, with waterfalls plummeting down cliffs and across boulders bigger than houses. Every inch of land won by men's lives. Lives that were gone in a flash.

Will Australia remember this, if we win the war? Don't even think *if*, Charlie reminded himself fiercely. *When* we win the war. Because we have to win this bloody war. Christ, I never knew war would be as bloody as this. I'm not swearing, I'm just describing it how it is. I've got a wife and a baby to protect. I won't let them be ruled by the Japs. And every man on this bloody track has got a reason to be here. So we must win.

But will we be remembered? Or will we be forgotten as the men who died in the Great War are forgotten? Who will remember the name Isurava in the coming years, for instance? Or indeed the name Kokoda? Or even the name New Guinea. Bloody New Guinea.

But it's a beautiful country if only you had the time to look at it. I'd like to come back in peacetime, take the time to just look about. Mountains, rivers, trees, birds and butterflies. But there's no time to appreciate it while this stoush is going on. It's just survival. Them and us.

One minute your mate's walking beside you, the next he's on the ground with his body unrecognisable, killed by a sniper you hadn't even seen. And if he's lucky, you've got time to bury him. Sometimes you wrapped a bloke up in a blanket and if you didn't get the burial detail and the grave dug in time, his body turned liquid with his guts running out the end of a grey blanket before you've got him safely into the hole. And if he had run out the end of the blanket, you had to shovel what was on the edge of the hole in after the rest of him as best you could.

And you wondered if you were next. Wondered when it would be your turn.

Charlie shrugged. Fate was fate. A man just had to do his job.

'Pack up your troubles in your old kitbag and smile, smile, smile,' sang Charlie, 'What's the use of worrying? It never was in style. So, pack up your troubles in your old kitbag and smile, smile, smile.'

Smoke rose into the air from the cook fires, hanging low over the camp, held down by the moisture-laden air. No breeze; there'd been calm weather for the last week. The trees in the forest were still. Hot, humid and still during the day. Or cold, humid and still at night. Beside other fires, men were washing clothes, boiling their once khaki clothes with leaves to dye them green. This wasn't approved of by the powers that be, but it did make the soldiers a bit less conspicuous in the jungle.

Why uniforms designed to blend in with desert sand were issued to blokes in a jungle environment was beyond Charlie, in fact beyond the comprehension of anyone with a bit of common sense. But perhaps common sense was not part of the equation for the powers that be who were running the show. Of course, the boiling made the clothes shrink a bit, but that was the least of their worries.

How come the Jap commanders had worked out that green showed up less in the tropics than khaki? Charlie wondered. They couldn't be smarter than our leaders, could they? A bloke would be better off just wearing a few woven leaves, like the natives did. And you didn't have to wash them, just chuck them out and get a new lot from the forest. Live off the land.

He thought about the Kukuku village he had visited. The huts looked flimsy and he wondered how they withstood the tropical down pours that occurred almost every night. But they were definitely an improvement on the mouldy tents the army used.

The imposing *Haus Tambaran,* the men's house, stood in the centre of the clearing and loomed over the smaller huts that the women lived in. Each end of it rose to a point, the beams embellished with elaborate carvings. High stilts kept it free of the muddy earth and added to its status. Men lounged on the wooden porch. They looked relaxed, but Charlie had the impression that they could spring into action faster than the Aussie patrols did when threatened.

In contrast to the resting men, the women of the village were all busy. A few did sit on the ground, but those were engaged in feeding babies or, Charlie was startled to see, piglets, from their engorged breasts. A group of them rhythmically pounded something in a hollowed-out tree trunk. Sago, Charlie realised. Sago was made from the pulp of a special palm tree. He recalled reading that it was poison unless subjected to a process that took a lot of time and effort. So of course, the women got that job. And they would get the blame if it wasn't done correctly and someone carked it, so they were diligent about the work.

Women were the workforce here; men had better things to do. It was women who tended the gardens, grew the vegetables and fruit and carried it back to the villages, who wove the fabric for the few flimsy garments they wore, who bore the babies and cared for the old.

All the men did was hunt and wage war on neighbouring villages.

A lot like us, Charlie thought. Only our wars are bigger, and we've got nastier weapons, that's what. And the decisions about who we go to war with and why are made far away from where we live and we don't have any say about it. But when it comes down to it, there's no difference.

He remembered a woman he had seen whose belly was swollen and who looked as if she was about to give birth. She had reminded him of his own wife, who must have looked much the same before little Elizabeth was born. It made him feel homesick and pretty lonely, really.

There was a curious air of peace about the little village, despite what had gone on a few days ago. As though the fierce battle he and the others had witnessed had been no more than one of those tropical storms that blew over, raged as though the world was ending, and then vanished, albeit leaving a path of mayhem in its wake.

One day, our war will be over, and we will have peace, Charlie thought. Time to go home and plant a garden of my own. Watch my own kids grow up. As long as I'm lucky and I'm not the next one to be poured into a hole in this stinky bloody earth.

Will the natives even notice our peace has fallen, though? War is a constant event here, punctuated by days like today. Little wars between neighbours over things that would seem trivial to us. There will never be a lasting peace here. Not when they have shrunken heads hanging in the men's house like that. And revenge to be sought for murder done. He shuddered when he remembered how the chief, proud of the now dirty and tattered bandage he still sported on his head, had invited him into the *Haus Tambaran*, and how Charlie had had to sit and smoke with the tribe beneath those shadowy objects that hung in the rafters of the building.

It didn't do to offend blokes like that, Charlie knew instinctively.

He'd been glad to escape, wondering whether some of those trophies might be heads removed from Aussie blokes. And whether the pig he had been served up in the village and reluctantly eaten might have been 'long pig' from the body of one of the rival tribesmen who had died in that battle behind the Aussie soldiers' camp on the day he had received the gifted bow and arrows. No, this wasn't something he would put in a letter to Mum. It had been horrible and interesting in its way, but it was a story he'd keep to himself. You couldn't talk about everything that happened when you went to war, it wouldn't be kind to the family at home.

34

15 October 1942
Bob Pask – prisoner of war camp, somewhere in Germany

'Are you writing home, Bob?'

'Yair, but I'm stuck. What do you put in your letters, Allen? I mean it's not like there's much news to talk about when you're stuck in a bloody prison camp. I keep getting letters from the family full of news about babies and sheep and stuff but there's bugger all to say from this end. All I can think of to say is we had cabbage soup today and cabbage soup yesterday and we'll get cabbage soup tomorrow.

'It is difficult, I will admit. One day is much like another. You could say it rained today. And the guard dogs are howling for food because they're kept hungry on purpose.'

'And we're kept hungry too. And it rained the day before and it will probably rain again tomorrow. That's no good. It would just upset my dad. Make him jealous. Where I come from, it doesn't rain from one month to the next. Sometimes for six months at a time. Didn't rain for a couple of years at Orroroo, once, my dad says. You Poms wouldn't know the word drought, would you?'

'We'd say there was a drought if it didn't rain for a week, I'm afraid,' said Allen. 'Or call it a long summer and a miracle.'

Bob looked up at Allen and shrugged. 'What else can I say is happening here besides the fact that the food's crook and it's cold inside the hut, and it's even colder outside, and there's barbed wire and searchlights at night? Can I put that in a letter?'

'Your family would appreciate a letter, though,' his friend said. 'They probably just want to know that you're alive and in a reasonably good condition. That's the main worry they have. I don't expect they think you're going to have scintillating news for them when you're in prisoner of war camp.'

Bob nodded. 'You're probably right. I haven't written home for ages because I just can't think of anything to say – anything that the family would want to hear or that would get past the bloody censors.'

'We all have the same problem. Keep this quiet, Bob, but Tom's just heard on the wireless you chaps built that Italy's out of it.'

'What do you mean, out of it?' asked Bob. 'Out of the war entirely? I knew they weren't getting along with their so-called mates. When I was using the radio a couple of nights ago, the German troops were occupying Rome, but I thought the Ities were supposedly still fighting against our side.'

'Things seem to be changing from one minute the next. Tom's picked up a broadcast that said Italy has surrendered unconditionally to the Allies.'

'Bloody hell! That's great news. One more nail in Hitler's coffin. Well, in Mussolini's coffin anyway. Anything else come through? Pity there's not room for more than one of us at a time in the hole under the floor.'

'The Yanks are doing pretty well in the South Pacific. That should be good news for you Aussie chaps.'

'Yair, well, I reckon our own troops have been doing pretty well there, too. There's never much news about what the Aussies do on your bloody Pommie news, though, is there? I reckon my stepbrothers are fighting in the Pacific. Charlie and Harry. That's where I'd be if I hadn't been shot down on the way back to bloody Blighty.'

'Shush, you idiot, keep your voice down or the Huns will wonder what we're celebrating and poke their noses in the door.'

But Bob was excited. 'I'd give my right hand if I could be having a shot at the Japs. I'd push them all the way back to bloody Tokyo.'

'Keep your voice down, Bob. If the Huns find out we've got a wireless, we're all up for the firing squad.'

'My lips are sealed. I wish I could let the family know that we're not completely in the dark over here, though. Auntie Rose – that's my step-mum, I reckon she keeps putting stuff in my letters that are obviously about the war but either it gets censored her end or this end. Her letters are mainly black lines.'

'My mother writes letters like that, too,' agreed Allen.

'Either that, or she's bagging Hitler, which is the sort of stuff Auntie Rose'd do,' said Bob. 'That's when her letters get through. I reckon heaps of them don't, because sometimes she says stuff about something that she says was in a previous letter and I know I haven't heard it before.'

'You'd better get on with that letter or make up your mind to finish tomorrow. It's nearly lights out and there'll be a patrol around soon. And as I said, keep your voice down. You Aussies seem to talk at the top of your voices. I suppose it's those vast distances you're accustomed too over there.'

'I'm not making as much noise as Johnno over there is with his farting. Christ, that sausage we had tonight was off, I reckon. It was putrid when we ate it and now his farts are even more putrid than the snags were. What do you reckon they were made of, dead horses or dead dogs?'

'Shut up, Bob, I can hear the boots outside. The patrol's coming our way. Just put a sock in it.'

'I won't be shutting up when this lot is over, I'll tell you that much. I'll be yelling all over Orroroo when I get back home. Singing at the top of my voice. I'm going to stand in the middle of a paddock and sing so loud the neighbours will complain and they're miles away. I'll be so rowdy my family will keep shoving food down my throat just to keep me quiet. I'll make more noise than the bloody sheep do when we're shearing.'

'Can you two chaps keep your voices down please? Bob, you'll have to finish your letter tomorrow. Our hosts are going to complain if we don't go to bed immediately and we don't want to upset them, do we?'

'Well, I've written bugger all tonight, so I'll have another go at bugger all tomorrow,' sighed Bob. 'I'm going to get a crook reception for not writing enough letters if I ever get home, but as long as there's a mutton chop and a fruit cake, I don't care if I'm made to sit in the corner for being a naughty boy, so what the heck anyway?'

35

30 November 1943
Rose Pask – Orroroo

'There's a letter that's mainly from Amy but Annie has put a bit on the end,' I told Pask.

'Yeah, Annie was never one for writing,' said Pask. 'Remember how you used to sit with her to write her compositions for school? She didn't mind the reading, she just didn't want to write anything herself. How's the nursing going? Hot up there in Brisbane, is it?'

'Yes. Amy says it's getting steamy. I remember Harry talking about the build-up in Darwin. I suppose it's a lot like that.'

'I was in Brisbane once for a couple of weeks and it was humid as hell. I don't know how Harry and Mavis stood Darwin,' Pask agreed.

'Amy says they're enjoying the nursing. She says they've learned to make beds using hospital corners and once you learn how to do it, you'll never make a bed any other way.'

'My sister was a nurse when she was young, and she said the same thing. It's good that they're happy. I was worried how they'd go.'

'She says the sister in charge is firm but fair. A stickler for protocol, whatever that is. Mainly they're cleaning everything with methylated spirits. I reckon kero would be cheaper. They're going to start giving injections next week. Been practising on oranges.'

'Don't like injections myself,' said Pask with a shudder.

'There was a riot in Brisbane a couple of days ago,' I said. 'People are calling it the Battle of Brisbane. Apparently some sort of scuffle started over a leave pass or something with the MPs, and it got worse and a soldier got shot. Thousands of men were involved. That sounds awful. The girls had the afternoon off and they were having drinks on the balcony of the Gresham Hotel with some other nurses and they saw it all happening.'

'You always get a few fights when men are on leave,' said Pask. 'I remember how our blokes used to let off steam. A few punches thrown, that sort of thing. Didn't usually end in anyone getting shot, though. There wasn't anything on the wireless about it, not that I heard, anyway.'

'No, and Amy says it wasn't covered much in the local papers either. The army tried to hush it up but people who saw it happen are talking about it. Amy and Annie and their friends were ushered away by soldiers with fixed bayonets. They must have been terrified. The soldiers came up the stairs when one of the nurses started shouting over the balcony after she saw men being knocked over in the street by the military police.'

'Are the girls all right? They didn't get hurt, did they?'

'No, but they are pretty upset. Apparently somehow the Americans got involved and then the Australians and the Americans had a pitched battle and the fire brigade was called in to use high-pressure hoses but for some reason they didn't. Refused to do it apparently. In the end, there were about five thousand men in the fight. It went on for a couple of nights and you couldn't go into the city because of the battle. Whole streets were just full of men fighting. Amy said the nurses were kept busy treating soldiers with gun shots and broken arms and bloody noses for ages.'

'Bloody hell, Rose. We don't need the Japs invading, we've got enough war here without them. I don't like to say it, but maybe they should cut the leave passes and not let the blokes into the city.'

'Annie says it gave them a bit of experience of what it's like in a war zone,' I said. 'This letter's got more blood and gore in it than any of the letters I've had from the boys. And the girls haven't even left Australia yet.'

'I hope they don't leave Australia. Only I know we won't get them back for Christmas,' said Pask sadly. 'Going to be a pretty bleak Christmas this year, Rose.'

'Maybe next one will be better. Maybe the war will end, and we'll have all the kids back.'

Only not Brian, I thought. Please God, don't you take any more of our kids. One is too many.

'You've been saying that every year for what seems like a hell of long time,' he said.

Hell is the word, I thought. But I didn't say it.

'We'll get through this,' I said. 'Somehow we'll get through it.'

I opened the next letter, one from Phil and nearly fell off my chair. Suddenly I was laughing and crying all at once. 'Pask, we've got to all go down to Norwood. Charlie's coming home on leave. He'll be here for Christmas! We won't have the girls, but we'll have Charlie. I can't believe it. He's been sent down because he's due leave anyway, but he's been ill with malaria so he's here to get over it and he'll be back next week, she says.'

36

20 January 1944
Charlie Walsh – Norwood

'I'd forgotten what a summer at home was like,' Charlie said. 'Bloody hot but not steamy like New Guinea.'

The phone line crackled. That probably meant someone was listening in on the party line, but I didn't mind. There was no such thing as privacy on the telephone when you lived in a country town. We all knew Pearl at the exchange listened in; sometimes you heard her gasp at your conversation, and she had been known to put her own two bobs' worth into the chat. Any gossip worth repeating would be all over the district before you'd put the phone down. It made you careful what you said.

'I suppose it's a different sort of heat,' I said. 'You're used to the tropics now. How much longer before you have to go back?'

'Just another week, Mum,' he answered. 'It was wonderful being here for Christmas, and just seeing everyone's faces was the best present of all. I've really been over the moon just being here. I hadn't expected it. I mean, I was overdue for leave, all us blokes are, but I wouldn't have gotten it if I hadn't had that bout of malaria. Best thing that's happened to me for years. Well, apart from the baby being born. I wish I'd been here for that, but you can't have everything. I still can't get over how perfect she is.'

'Phil's going to miss you when you go back. We're all going to miss you. Are you sure you're over the malaria?'

'I'm right as rain, Mum,' he said.

But I knew he would say that, even if he wasn't.

'I'm starting to feel guilty being safe and enjoying all the comforts of home, though, while lots of other blokes are still at it up there.'

'You've earned your leave, son,' I said.

'Little Elizabeth smiled at me today,' he said. 'I'm really going to miss her. And she holds onto my finger when I bend over her. Next year, I'll be here for Christmas, Mum. Next year, I'll take her to the John Martin's Christmas Pageant to see Father Christmas. I'll sit her on my shoulders and listen to her giggle, watch her wave at the floats as they go past us.'

I smiled. I would be in the crowd, standing next to Charlie, loving every moment of it. Loving knowing that he and all our kids were safe and well. 'I hope you're right, Charlie. I hope the war ends before next Christmas.'

'It has to end soon, Mum. Can't go on much longer.'

'Pask and I never thought we'd have you back in Australia this Christmas. We'd been just saying how horrible Christmas was going to be and then we heard you were coming. It was the answer to a prayer. I'm so glad we came down and had a real family Christmas together, even going to Mass, just like the old days. Listening to you sing Christmas carols, Charlie, I felt I was in heaven.'

'Keep talking like that and you'll be making friends with Father Flaherty next,' said Charlie. 'Speaking of priests, have you heard from Joe lately?'

'Not for a bit. He was pretty much down in the dumps last time he wrote. That's not like Joe. He wishes he had taken the chance to come back south when he could have done. Said he wanted to be involved with our war effort. And the Pommy weather was getting him down. There'd been a lot of air raids too.'

'Speaking of air raids, I had Mr Williams on the doorstep last night. Wearing his tin hat and waving his little baton in the air. Pounding on the front door. Jumping up and down and yelling his head off. Saying we were breaking the law. Mad as a cut snake.'

I could hear the laughter in Charlie's voice.

'What was the problem?' I asked.

'The silly old bugger said there was a chink of light showing under the front door. I went out to have a look and yes, he was right. If you bent over and looked hard from where he was standing and got the angle right, you could just see a crack of light there. I told him that if he thought Tojo was going to come sailing up the gutter in a submarine, he had another think coming. I told him he was mad as a meat axe.'

'What did he say?' I asked.

'Said to get rid of the light or he'd report me to a higher authority. Then he went on about the fact that we haven't got an adequate bomb shelter in the backyard. He wants me to dig out a hole and cover it with a sheet of galvanised iron and pile earth on top. Anderson shelter, he called it. I told him if he thought that would save anyone from bombs, he's nuts.'

'I saw how they've put bomb shelters all over the park lands in Adelaide. They look pretty flimsy to me,' I said.

'They are. I just hope they won't ever be used. I'm glad you're up at Orroroo, Mum. I just wish Phil would agree to go up and stay with you. Anyway, I told old Williams I'd been digging trenches and graves up in New Guinea and I wasn't going to dig them in Adelaide. I put a towel next to the door to stop the light from escaping and told him to go home and hide under his kitchen table. He can jump in the lake as far as I'm concerned. That fellow's crazy, Mum.'

'I've thought that for a while. He's been a little Hitler ever since he got that tin hat. I'm starting to feel sorry for Mrs Williams, but I suppose she can look after herself. She's been married to him for yonks. We all have to make sacrifices.'

God knows this family's made enough of them. It's time we had a bit of happiness. Just seeing Charlie's face was the best thing that's happened for a very long time. I had hugged him so hard he said I had cracked his ribs and hurt him more than any Japs he had met on the Track had done. I just wanted to imprint the feel of his body against mine so that when he leaves I would still have the sensation of him against me, because I know that he'll soon be far away from us again and that I, and we, will have an ache and an emptiness where there ought to be a Charlie.

I longed to ask him about the nightmares Phil told me he has every night. When he was out of the room, she whispered to me that he tosses and turns and screams in his sleep every night. He swears it's because of the malaria, but she says he doesn't have fever and she's certain he's dreaming about whatever horrors he's seen in New Guinea. Charlie swears he sleeps like a baby, but Phil says she's caught the words 'white fog' and 'I don't want to do it', and apparently, he shakes as though he's having some sort of fit. He even fell out of bed one night. She has to wake him up because he'd have everyone in the house wake up otherwise, including the baby.

The only stories Charlie told us are ones about the exotic fruit he's been eating, mangoes and pawpaws and the like, that he says are like swallowing heaven, and funny tales about his good mates and how everyone is doing their best to win the war. But he never talks about the actual battles or the casualties.

Pask told me it was the same in the Great War. He said it took him a while to get over some of the things he saw, and he still can't talk about it. I don't even know how he lost his eye. Pask says war is best left where it happens, that civilians wouldn't understand and there's just no need to bring soldiers' old memories home.

I suppose we'll never know what haunts Charlie in the night. I keep praying to the God that I'd almost stopped believing in until I saw Charlie's face again, that this rotten war will end soon in victory for our side, and that he, and all our kids, will come home to us sound in mind and body.

37

22 January 1944
Charlie Walsh – on train to Brisbane

'It was bloody brilliant seeing the family again,' Charlie said to the soldier sitting next to him as the train pulled away from the station. Never seen the bloke before, but he was wearing the uniform. They were all in this together. Brothers in arms, that's how Harry had described it.

The chap nodded. 'It's a different world down here.'

'Best weeks of my life,' Charlie exclaimed. 'I met my little kiddy for the first time. Here, look at this photo. Six months old. Isn't she lovely? It's hard leaving home, but a man's got even more reason to fight now. I'm not letting the Japs get anywhere near her.'

He tucked the photo back into his breast pocket and sighed, remembering the perfection of his daughter's pink toes and those little hands outstretched to him, demanding a cuddle. Christ, it was hard to leave, but there was a job to do.

Charlie kicked the kitbag beneath his seat to make sure it was still there. Most of his stuff could be replaced by the army if it went missing, but the fruit cake his mum had made for him was irreplaceable. He knew he wouldn't taste another one until this bloody war was over.

'Yair,' said the other digger. 'Does a man good just to get away even if it's only for a short break. It's a whole different world down here. I s'pose you're the same as me, back to bloody New Guinea? Not that you ever really get away from that place. It sort of stays there, in the back of a bloke's mind, even when you're on leave.'

Charlie nodded. 'I know what you mean. Some stuff you'd like to forget but you can't. I've been posted to the landing craft company. Mopping up, they said. Be a bit different to the Track, I reckon.'

Hopefully a lot different, he thought to himself, remembering the horrors of the Track that still lingered.

'There'll be a lot of mopping to do,' agreed his mate. 'Silly bloody Japs have got a funny way of thinking.'

Funny was one way of putting it, Charlie thought.

He hoped Phil hadn't understood what the truth was behind his sleeplessness and his nightmares. Charlie told her it was the malaria that woke him, but he was pretty sure she knew he was lying. He felt guilty about waking her. He worried what he might have said in his sleep. But her presence beside him was such a comfort. Hard to get used to sleeping alone again, but maybe it wouldn't be much longer. Maybe he'd be over the nightmares by the time he saw her again.

He'd tried everything to induce oblivion with the same hot milk and whiskey that his father had drunk every night. Dad had called it 'mother's milk'. Had his father suffered from nightmares because of his own war service? A pity he couldn't ask his mum if Dad had bad dreams. These days, she absolutely refused to talk about her first husband; dead, gone and forgotten, she said. The past was the past and she had better things to think about now.

'Mother's milk' didn't work for Charlie, and neither did reciting the rosary under his breath as he lay awaiting the sought-for oblivion. And when Charlie finally fell asleep, the shroud of white fog descended and Bunny Cogan shrieked again for his mother to save him.

Now, though it was months after Bunny and his torturers had died, Charlie was constantly on his guard. If he fell asleep now, lulled by the rocking of the train, he would be back there standing under the tree while the sarge clung to the branches high above, peering down at Bunny and the five Japs. The ghost of that day haunted Charlie – probably haunted most of the blokes in his platoon.

The patrol had been woken that morning to the sounds of hell. Unearthly screams such as none of them had ever heard in their lives. At times, the noise was half muffled by the white cloud that had descended on the mountains in the night, but then the sound penetrated through the fog and filled their ears.

'Where's Bunny?' the sarge demanded.

'On sentry duty,' Jimmy said. 'I'm taking over in half an hour.'

Bunny hadn't volunteered for sentry duty. Only fools volunteered for anything, but it was Bunny's turn, so he'd been the one to stand at the edge of the exhausted group lying on the soggy ground. Not that anyone expected much sleep.

It's hard to sleep in mud in the drizzle, with your rifle next to your hand covered with your tunic to try to keep it dry, and always wondering if you ought to keep one eye open in case the enemy might creep up in the darkness despite the sentry; difficult to sleep especially when the terrain was sloping, so even though you had used your bayonet to dig a bit of a hole to stop you rolling down the hill, you still slid about. You drowsed rather than slept. But they were all dead tired after slogging through the bush for days on end at high alert, so rest they must.

And the enemy must have come in the night; come and dragged Bunny away from his lookout post. Must have donged him on the head to keep him quiet, dragged him unconscious to the tree just yards away. Tied him up and begun torturing him. Might have been just for the hell of it, but they probably hoped the rest of the patrol would charge into the mist when they heard the commotion and be picked off easily.

Looking back, Charlie realised the night the fog had descended was the night of the deepest sleep he would ever have in his life again.

His dad, who was fond of Shakespeare, used to recite, 'Macbeth has murdered sleep.' It wasn't some old Pommie poet who murdered sleep, Charlie would have loved to tell his father, it was the bloody Japanese who did the killing.

'Mum, Mum,' shrieked Bunny.

And the white mist swirled, and the men could hardly see their hands in front of their faces, let alone work out what was happening halfway down the hill.

'Get up that tree, Art,' ordered the sergeant. 'You might see what the hell's going on from up there. The fog'll be thinner.'

And Art climbed the tree because he was the best of them at climbing, and when he reached the top he started to yell too. 'The buggers have got Bunny,' he shouted. 'I can see them down the side of the hill. They've stripped off his clobber and tied him to a tree. Cut off his balls. Blood everywhere.' His voice rose in panic. 'Oh Christ, they've put out his eyes!'

Bunny's keening filled their ears. 'Help me, help me. Mum!' he wailed.

The sergeant thumped the tree. 'How many Japs?' he demanded.

'Five of them, I think. We've got to get over there. We've got to save Bunny,' yelled Art. 'Those bastards are skinning him alive.'

'I'm coming up,' said the sarge. 'Pass my rifle. Move over a bit, Art, give me room.' He began to shin up the tree, holding his rifle in one hand, then turned to the men huddled below. 'Charlie, sing "Waltzing Matilda".' And the rest of you blokes join in.'

'What?' demanded Charlie. The sarge had gone mad. Charlie had always thought he was a nutter; now he knew it. 'We've got to charge the bastards!'

'Sing "Waltzing Matilda". That's an order. And make it loud.'

'Why?'

'To confuse the Japs and let Bunny to know we're here for him. Get on with it, Charlie. The rest of you join in.'

The men roared the song. A rifle shot rang out. Bunny fell silent.

Foreign cacophony filled the hillside as the Japanese realised their victim was dead.

'You've killed Bunny, you dill,' moaned Art, peering down from his possie in the branches. 'Why didn't you shoot the Japs? Bunny's hanging there, held up by the ropes.' Then, fear in his voice. 'The Japs are looking our way.'

'I had to put Bunny out of his misery,' called down the sarge. 'Only thing to do. We couldn't help him. He'd had it. Now for the Japs.'

There was a fusillade of shots.

'You haven't killed them, sarge,' said Art, 'You've hit them, but they're not dead. I thought you were a good shot. One's got a gut shot. You shot the rest of them in the legs. They're crawling around. Trying to get away.'

'They won't get far,' said the sarge. 'I want them alive for a bit longer. They can suffer like Bunny suffered. Or worse. Grab your guns, boys, fix bayonets. Bring a blanket for Bunny and a shovel.'

They cut the ropes that held Bunny to the tree. Charlie thought about Jesus hanging from the Cross, although the Romans used nails, not ropes. Blood ran down Bunny's face from his ravaged eyes, as if he had worn a crown of thorns. Poor bugger had been sacrificed all right. A sacrifice to carelessness, perhaps. Charlie breathed heavily to stop the sobs that threatened. The other blokes were doing the same, all except young Terry, who was spewing.

'Dig a grave,' ordered the sarge. 'Charlie, did you say your brother's a priest? Padre in the army?'

'That's right,' said Charlie, sniffing hard and wishing to God Joe was here. Joe would know what to do, what to say. He'd know words of comfort, although this situation was beyond comfort. Beyond belief. Beyond faith.

'You'll do the funeral. You're the best qualified. Bunny was a Roman, wasn't he?'

'The Lord's my shepherd,' intoned Charlie over Bunny's grave.

They'd tried to put his uniform on him, but it was impossible because the Japs had torn it to tatters with their knives, so in the end they had just draped it over him and wrapped the ravaged body in the blanket before lowering him into the hole. Bunny's rosary beads were on the ground near the uniform, fallen from his pocket, so Charlie, shuddering, placed them in the stiff hands before closing the blanket over Bunny's bloody face. That face with the empty eye sockets would haunt Charlie forever, he knew.

And the wailing and the groans from the prisoners would stay with him too.

'Charlie, get a grip on yourself. Say the rosary,' ordered the sarge.

'What, the full deal? Takes a hell of a long time,' protested Charlie. 'What are we going to do about the Japs? Shouldn't we deal with them first? I know we can't take prisoners, but can't we shoot them now? Geneva Convention?'

'Fuck Geneva,' said the sarge.

The prisoners were moaning, some crawling about on shattered legs, others curled up like dying cockroaches. It seemed wrong to feel sorry for them, but when you were praying for your mate it made you aware of a God who might be watching. Do unto others as you would be done by, thought Charlie. That's what Joe would say. Although where was God half an hour ago when Bunny was in agony?

'We've got time. The Japs'll wait. They're not going anywhere yet,' said the sarge grimly. 'Take your time, do the rosary and then we'll sing a hymn or two. I reckon "Abide with me". And then that "Ave Maria" thing I've heard you sing. Those bastards can sit there and watch us give our mate a decent funeral.'

'Sarge, let's shoot them first,' remonstrated Charlie. 'It would be the decent thing to do.'

'That young bloke you shot in the arm and leg is trying to get away,' said Terry. 'He's sobbing his heart out.'

'Give him a prod with your bayonet so he stays with his cobbers,' said the sarge. 'And don't be too gentle about it.'

'Sarge,' protested Charlie.

'We do things my way, soldier. That's an order.'

Charlie pulled his rosary from his pocket and intoned the prayer, raising his voice in an attempt to drown out the moans of the youngest Jap. A couple of the prisoners sat stoically awaiting their fate. Charlie knew that they felt they were displaying their courage and their honour. A different culture; a different way of thinking. He had heard about it before.

After the funeral service, a crude cross made from a couple of branches tied together with the rope used to tie Bunny to the tree was placed at the head of the grave and Bunny's slouch hat was hung from it.

Then, at last, the sergeant gave the order to drag the Japs to the edge of the ravine, to lift them and sling them down onto the boulders far below, where the water rushed white through the gorge.

And the Japanese screamed as Bunny had screamed, and the sarge laughed, and said, 'Good riddance to bad rubbish. Give the buggers a swing before you toss them over the edge, boys.'

Then the patrol gathered its gear and continued on its way, and Charlie remembered it all and wished he could forget.

38

8 June 1944
Rose, Pask and Danny Pask – Orroroo

'It'll all be over soon,' I said. 'You heard what they said. The Americans, the Brits and the Canadians have invaded France. A million and a half soldiers landed on fifty miles of beaches in Normandy.'

'Bloody marvellous,' agreed Pask, turning off the wireless. 'The Germans are falling back. They don't know what hit them. Weren't expecting it. They knew the attack was coming, but they thought it would be at Calais. There would have been a hell of a lot more casualties if Operation Overlord hadn't worked.'

'Something else I missed out on,' said Danny ruefully. 'I knew I wasn't going to get a look in.'

'You wouldn't have been there anyway, son,' said Pask. 'None of our blokes were. All our troops were pulled out of Europe and sent to the Pacific. Mr Curtin insisted that we had enough to deal with down here. Just as well too. Bloody wonderful that Churchill pulled this one off, though.'

'It wasn't Churchill really,' I said. 'Apparently he's not too happy because the Americans ran the D-Day show.'

'He was part of it,' insisted Pask. 'It was a joint effort. A lot of Pommie lads died in that landing. Good thing you weren't there, Danny. Your arm's still not right after the sheep kicked you.'

And, I thought, thank God, it probably never will be. Rather a crook arm than going to war. If I knew which sheep it was that had tossed the kid into the air, I'd make sure it never got slaughtered. I'd drape a blue ribbon over, pin a medal to its chest, sit it in the best bit of the pasture on the property, and give it the life of Riley.

'Do you think Joe was there?' asked Danny. 'He's in England. Even priests get involved when there's an invasion, don't they?'

I shook my head. 'We don't know where Joe is, at the moment. He hasn't written for a while.'

I could see he wanted his brother to be part of the action. I suppose that gave Danny vicarious glory, even if all Joe did was to preside over the funerals of fallen soldiers. The kid wanted to say in the future, 'D-Day? I wasn't there, but my brother was.' As the newsreader on the wireless had said, and all the politicians were echoing, this was a pivotal event in the war. The tide is turning, they all intoned, and they weren't referring to the movement of water on the Normandy coast.

And the Russians were on our side now, Pask had explained. They had been in cahoots with Hitler at first, but after that Operation Barbarosa business, when Germany invaded Russia, Stalin got annoyed. Now the Russians were in Poland and headed towards Berlin.

The Germans were on the run on all sides. The Poms, the Yanks and the Canadians were rushing towards Paris. The Italians were caving in too, so soon the Japs would have no allies left. Although Charlie said the Nips were brainwashed fanatics and would fight on to the bitter end.

But perhaps we might see an end to this madness soon. Maybe before long all our boys would come home safe. And our girls, too. I thought about Vera Lynn's song 'Bluebirds over the White Cliffs of Dover'. Charlie had sung that one when he was down on leave. It was lovely.

Charlie was in the Landing Craft Division now. We hadn't heard much from him because he was travelling around a lot, but he seemed happy enough. He said he had always liked boats and it would be nice to see a bit more of the country which he said was very pretty. Lots of mangroves, like the trees down at Port Adelaide, only there were crocodiles in the ones up there. He mentioned names like Lae and Bougainville and said there were volcanoes and beaches with black sand. He would be a long way from Amy and Annie.

The girls were in Port Moresby now, working in the hospital. We hadn't had many letters from them, but the ones we did get told of a steamy climate that made their starched aprons and caps wilt (this seemed to be Amy's sole complaint about the place), although she had also mentioned the slowly turning fans that didn't work well enough to cool the wards, and stoic wounded soldiers, their bandages soaked with blood and mud who were brought down the Track on stretchers by the wonderful Fuzzy Wuzzies. But there were less casualties from the Track now, and more from the Islands. According to Amy, who still wrote most of the letters, the main medical attention the men received in the field was an issue of cigarettes.

Amy had nothing but praise for the staff in the hospital at Port Moresby. Everyone was 'lovely' from the Fuzzies to the orderlies, and the sisters in charge and the doctors. And there was one particular doctor called Peter she mentioned often.

I thought it was all a bit funny, because Amy had never been the type to describe her workmates at the munitions factory, the nuns at school or even our neighbour Mrs Williams, as 'lovely'. She seemed just a little too effusive, too enthusiastic about the whole deal in New Guinea. I couldn't put my finger on it, but it all rang just a bit false to me.

She was particularly glowing about that Peter chap, who was not only a brilliant medico, but loomed large in her social life. They were just good friends, she insisted, but I counted the name Peter six times in one missive. Annie didn't seem to have a boyfriend, and in fact Amy mentioned Annie was known as the 'ice maiden' by her colleagues. Strange, that. Annie had always been an outgoing sort of lass.

Amy said she expected to become a theatre nurse soon. Annie was already working in the theatre and was doing well. After the war, both girls intended to keep on nursing and would probably get jobs at the Royal Adelaide.

Annie, in the brief postscripts she scrawled at the end of Amy's letters, complained about long hours on her feet and the arrogant surgeons. The head sister was a stuck-up old bitch. She said Amy was always playing tennis on her afternoons off with any officers who were well enough to wield a racquet, and she swam on the beaches, although sentries were posted to watch for crocodiles and Japs. Annie said she worried about Amy getting sunburned with her fair complexion and red hair. Sometimes there were concerts or dances under the tropical moon, but Annie preferred to stay in her room at night and study anatomy. I imagined Amy strolling with the mysterious Peter over white sand among coconut trees that bent towards a deep blue sea. Were they also studying anatomy?

I shouldn't even think that, I told myself. My girls were good girls and would be saving themselves for their future husbands and both would wear white at their weddings.

It all sounded very glamorous, but how much of it was true? The girls seemed to be living two entirely different lives albeit in the same place. Was Amy really writing often because she missed home more than she wished to admit?

But none of it really mattered, because now that D-Day had happened, the war couldn't possibly go on much longer. The Russians were on our side now, striding through Latvia, Lithuania and headed, I think, for Poland. I will admit my geography of those little countries was a bit shaky. I didn't really understand one foreign name from the other. Pask kept getting the atlas out and trying to explain what was happening and where, but all I wanted to know was when it would end.

I prayed every night, and half the day too, that soon the war in Europe would be over and for that day when the Japanese would have no allies left and would have to surrender too. And there would be peace, and all my kids, all everyone's kids, would come home safe and well.

39

12 September 1944
Captain Joe Walsh – Paris

Dear Mum,

I don't suppose you have had a letter with a French postmark on it since Dad was away during the Great War. I thought I would be sending one a bit earlier than this but although D-Day was back on the sixth of June (which seems ages now), it has taken quite a while for us to get this far. Of course, Paris has been liberated for nearly a month, but my crowd weren't allowed in at first.

David and I are here as part of the humanitarian relief effort. You've probably heard about the food shortages in Paris because the rail network was blown up by the enemy. I am proud to say that that crisis is over. Our lot has been supplying five hundred tons of food relief a day and the Yanks did the same. Paris is no longer starving. The only food available seemed to be carrots. Don't ask me why, but I imagine the Parisians are somewhat sick of carrots now.

There were some rather nasty goings-on between the Free French and the Vichy which added to the tension here. I won't say anything about it, because I expect you've either heard about the massacres on the wireless and in the paper or perhaps the press covered it up, in which case I shouldn't mention for fear of the dreaded censor's black pen.

There have been some very unpleasant reprisals against those who collaborated with the Germans. Women's heads shaven and people beaten. We aren't allowed to intervene, but I do feel sorry for the poor wretches. I imagine some of the collaboration was just a survival thing. Horrible things happen in war, as I'm sure you realise.

Anyway, the Eiffel Tower is still standing and although Paris is a bit battered, she's in better shape than poor old London is. It's going to take a long time before the rubble is cleared there. The Huns are still firing their nasty doodlebugs over the Channel from a few remaining spots, but I don't think they can keep the effort up much longer. They've got other problems to occupy them at home now.

But I should explain because, thankfully, you might not know what I'm talking about. The doodlebugs are particularly nasty because they don't make much noise, and people don't know they've landed until they explode. I heard one chap say at least people don't have to spend time worrying about dying until they're dead, but that's a typical sick Cockney joke. I told him at least with the other sort they have the chance to make an act of contrition. Thank God Australia has been spared doodlebugs.

Our side is doing quite well at the moment, and I pray the initiative will continue our way. I know from your letter that you thought the war in Europe would be over after D-Day. Unfortunately, the Huns put up quite a fight and the territory was hard won. Sadly, many people died for the victory that now looks secure.

And now things look as though they're going well in the Pacific, as well. Or at least there seems to be light at the end of the tunnel. Thank God for the Yanks – Australia owes the Americans a big debt of gratitude there!

I am so glad Charlie had that leave over Christmas. Even though you're still worried about him going off around the islands with the landing craft mob, and of course worried about Amy and Annie nursing in Port Moresby, I'm sure the worst is over and the tide is turning (to use a cliché and a platitude). It looks as if the girls are enjoying their experience in New Guinea. That business about them giving all the chaps in the hospital lettuce to chew when the big brass came visiting after that nasty general called them rabbits was a classic. Cheeky little tykes, our girls!

I know I've mentioned my good friend David Cohen who is a rabbi. We spend many an evening discussing theology and life in general over a glass of whiskey, for which he shares my fondness. All roads lead to Rome or, in this case, to God, and we find we have more in common than in separation. David is a Pom, but don't let that put you off him. He is a genuinely nice chap and our friendship is a great comfort.

We're expecting to be sent forward as the army progresses across Europe in pursuit of Victory. I've just heard a news flash on the wireless – our chaps have destroyed the German flying bomb sites in France, which is wonderful. So that's one less worry. The doodlebugs are no more.

Keep well, Mum, and give my love and blessings to all at home. Keep hoping and praying that this dreadful war will end soon and that we will all be united once again under peaceful skies.

Joe

40

12 October 1944
Mary Mudge – Mount Gambier

Dear Mum,

I hope you're well. Sorry I haven't written for a bit, but I've been rushed off my feet as usual. You know what it's like when you are a Mum. I keep remembering that you had heaps more kids than I've got and wondering how you managed. And my dad wasn't the easiest man to live with either. Well, that's an understatement, as Joe would say. Fred is an angel compared to Dad.

I've been meaning to say this because I don't know if I've ever told you, Mum, but you're a great mother, in spite of the things that my Fred and Father Flaherty say about you.

We're all well down here at the Mount. Paddy wrote from Brisbane, where he's stationed. He told much the same story as the one you'd heard from the girls about the fighting in the streets, except that he was actually down in those streets, not on a balcony looking at it from above. He got a bloody nose and a black eye but that was all, thank goodness. I'm so glad that Mr Curtin has said the young ones won't be sent to New Guinea or Darwin. I just hope the war ends before Paddy's old enough to be sent up to the actual fighting.

I'm actually beginning to believe that it will end soon and Fred says it definitely will be over before we know it, what with that D-Day thing and Joe being in Paris now.

Fancy Joe being in Paris. That's a place I would love to go. I remember Dad talking about Paris and it sounded lovely even though there was a war on when he visited. Probably it's not too good at the moment either, but it would make a change from Mount Gambier, where it's cold and wet most of the time, although the calendar says it's officially spring now. Fred says he thinks it would be autumn in Paris at the moment. Isn't it funny how their seasons are the opposite of ours?

It must have been lovely to have Charlie back, even though it was only for a short time. A pity he's still getting that malaria. Phil wrote and told me how he wakes up screaming almost every night. That sounds awful. I thought they had medicine that cured malaria, but I might be wrong.

I wish we could have come up to Norwood to see him, but you have no idea what it's like down here now that the meat rationing is on. People are so angry!

I mean, you'd think they would have some sense of shame, but all we get is 'What can I have? Not that rubbish again!' No good morning or anything like that when they barge into the shop. They really get cross when all we've got is pig's heads and trotters and tripe and liver, brains, that sort of stuff. As you know (or maybe you don't because I don't think you have real problems with rationing since you are living on the farm), it's one and a half pounds up to four pounds of meat a week per person, depending on the sort of meat. It's not our fault, it's Mr Curtin's and that Mr Dedman's fault. They're the ones who set the rules.

Of course, people can have rabbits, as much rabbit as they want. So Fred has to go out shooting or trapping most nights. Mainly trapping now because bullets are in short supply. I suppose Charlie and his mates need all the ammunition to shoot the Japs. The farmers are happy because Fred has cleared out the bunnies for miles around, but Fred is getting worried because he says he's finding it harder to get enough to supply the customers. I'm kept busy cleaning the things.

After the war, I never want to see another rabbit again. Fred suggested I keep the skins to make myself a fur coat but, really, I couldn't stand it. I'd probably look more like a teddy bear than a film star anyway because I've put a bit of weight on. I don't know how, what with the rationing, but my waist is getting thicker. Must be old age.

Fred has been brewing beer. It's hard to get beer because of the shortages, so he has been making the stuff and selling it under the counter. We know it's against the law, strictly speaking, but the local copper is one of our best customers. He's happy to turn a blind eye to it, so Fred's not too worried.

Rosemary isn't any help, as usual. She says she's too busy with her homework from school to pitch in. And she says she won't be involved in anything illegal because she doesn't want to besmirch her reputation. I think she just doesn't want to get her hands dirty. She thinks she's Lady Muck. Her teachers are still complaining about her, and her report cards are awful, so I don't think all the time doing the so-called homework is paying off anyway. Kathleen is a real joy. No trouble at all.

I miss you, Mum. Look after yourself and Danny and Pask.

Love and best wishes,

　Mary

41

25 November 1944
Rose, Danny and Pask – Orroroo

Pask and Danny had made an early start on their tasks because the day promised to be a scorcher. Part of their plan was to shoot a few bunnies for the pot. When it's hot, the rabbits get up early too, to have a feed before the sun comes up. Pask says dry grass probably tastes better with a bit of dew on it.

Now a brace of freshly skinned bunnies lay curled on the kitchen sink, pale skin shining and looking a lot like dead babies. I was glad they had skinned and gutted them and left the trimmings for the crows, because that saved me an extra job. They were decent-sized rabbits, so I decided to make rabbit stew. Adult rabbits can be a bit tough and stringy, so they need a good boiling.

The bunnies would make a change from the old ewe Pask and Danny had killed that we had been chewing on for the past weeks. That sheep was definitely getting a bit on the nose. The remaining chops smelled of death. Rankness was seeping into the kitchen now from the Coolgardie safe, even though I had doused the flesh in vinegar. I decided to feed the rest of the ewe to the dogs to get rid of it.

Either the men (for Danny had shot up so much lately that I had almost begun to think of him as a man now) would have to hunt more rabbits or Pask would have to select another ageing ewe for slaughter. Or I could kill a chook or two. There were a couple of hens that had gone off the lay and the young pullets were coming along nicely and would be providing eggs soon.

The shot gun leaned between the kitchen dresser and the Coolgardie with the wet hessian bag draped over it. I had told Pask that guns don't belong in kitchens, that I hate guns and it would be easy for someone to knock it over and it could go off with disastrous consequences. I said he should have left it on the veranda, but he said it wasn't loaded, and patted his pocket to show me the shells were safely there. He said he would put the gun away directly. As soon as he had his cuppa.

I was about to pour the tea when there was a short, sharp rap on the door. Colin the postie put his head into the kitchen. Unusually for him, he didn't smile. I decided he had been delivering bad news to someone. Poor bugger, it's rotten for them that give and them that receive telegrams in war time.

'I've just made a cuppa,' I said. 'Sit down, Colin. You look done in.'

'You're early, mate,' said Pask. 'Finished the rounds early, have you? Good idea. The mercury's up already. It's going to be a scorcher again.'

As always, the cocky started shrieking as soon as it spied Colin's face. I put down the teapot and tossed the hessian bag over the cage and a couple of white feathers drifted into the kitchen. I picked up the teapot and began to pour the tea.

Just another hot morning at Orroroo. I saw a couple of blowflies had followed Colin into the kitchen. They headed for the dead bunnies.

'Get the swat, Danny,' I said. 'Bloody blowies.'

I saw an envelope in Colin's hand. I grabbed the back of the chair with one hand, remembering the blowies that followed Danny through the door the day Brian's telegram had come. That had been a hot day too. Heat, blowies, telegrams and death went together.

'Yair,' said Colin, looking like a dog expecting to be kicked. He slumped into the nearest chair and carefully placed an envelope on the table in front of him. A telegram envelope. He leaned forward and covered his face with his hands.

I looked at the envelope and said, 'Bob.' I took a deep breath and repeated, 'Bob.' My fingers went numb. I dropped the teapot. It was my favourite teapot, the brown shiny one that had been in the house when I first came up to be Pask's housekeeper all those years ago. I had found it in the back of the cupboard, scrubbed it out and used it ever since. I wouldn't be using it again.

I saw the spout had broken off. Red tea coursed across the oilskin table cloth and fell in a blood-coloured waterfall to the floor. Tea flowed towards the envelope and the four of us watched the coming inundation. No one moved to stop it.

'Bob,' I whispered again. It was a prayer.

'Bob.' said Colin with a catch in his voice.

'Not Bob,' said Pask, his face crumpled. 'No, not Bob.'

Danny grabbed the envelope and tore it open. He pulled out the sheet of flimsy paper, but it was soaked. Saturated. I could see it was illegible. The ink had dissolved.

'What did it say?' Danny demanded. 'Is he missing? He's a prisoner of war. He can't be missing in action. Did he escape?'

'He was shot,' said Colin softly. Did he think a soft voice would cushion the blow, or had his voice lost its power? 'Shot by the Germans for making and using a wireless. Him and two other blokes in the prison camp. Just before D-Day, it was. The RAF just found out about it. They said there's a letter coming later. The Huns shot Bob and buried him in Germany.' Colin put his head on the table and covered it with his hands as if to shut out sight and sound. He had always been fond of Bob. A good friend to this family, but his news had destroyed us.

'Made a wireless. Bob was always good with his hands,' said Pask quietly. He dragged his hanky out of his pocket and dabbed at his good eye. Dabbed at the missing eye that was covered with the patch too. He must have forgotten that the socket was empty. 'Silly little bugger. Could have just sat it out. Always was an inpatient little devil.'

I thought about the model aeroplanes that hung suspended by fishing line in Bob's bedroom. Bob had made them. Bob was mad about planes. All he ever wanted to do was fly, and that was why he had joined the RAAF, gone to England, worn the blue RAF uniform, flown Spitfires, and been shot down over Germany. Bob didn't want to sit it out. He wanted to know what was happening in the world outside the prison camp. Wanted to be doing something with those hands. He always was an impatient, impetuous kid.

Now the room hung with model planes was Danny's bedroom. Pask had told Danny he could use it until his brother came home. But Bob wouldn't be coming home now. He would never see his model planes again. Or the crystal wireless set that stood on the shelf in the room. I knew that Pask had helped Bob make that.

Was the wireless the Germans had found in the prisoner of war camp a crystal set? Probably not. It would have been more powerful. As Pask said, Bob was always good with his hands. He and the other two men who had been shot with him would have built something good. God knows how they got the parts. They must have scrounged, improvised and devised the stuff to build a proper radio.

It would have been a set that could pick up transmissions from Britain, voices coming out of the ether that gave Bob and his fellow prisoners hope. I knew that they would have heard about the D-Day invasion, about the advances by the Allies across Europe, about the recent German defeats. Did they get cocky and somehow give themselves away when they knew the war was ending? Whatever had happened, the consequences were fatal for the three of them. Was it snowing when they were shot? Did their red blood flow over frozen German soil?

But I couldn't believe that our Bob, our crazy, wilful, loving Bob was gone. It wasn't possible. As Pask had said, 'Not Bob.'

Danny still clutched the envelope. 'There must be a mistake,' he said. 'Bob said in his last letter that he'd be home soon. He said he was going to help us with the shearing. He told me that I'd be turfed out of his room and have to sleep in the sleep-out again when he got home. And I believed it. Bob can't be dead.'

Pask, his face grim, crossed the room and picked up the shotgun that leant against the Coolgardie safe. Aghast, I watched him pat his pocket, checking for shells. He turned towards the door.

'No!' I screamed. 'No, Pask.'

'Dad!' yelled Danny. He threw himself towards his father. 'No, don't even think it! Dad, we've lost Bob, he's not coming home. We need you. You can't do this to us. We can't lose you too!' He wrestled the gun out of Pask's hands and ran outside. 'Guns shouldn't be in kitchens, Mum always says that,' he screamed over his shoulder.

Sobbing, I put my arms around Pask and hugged him as hard as I could. 'God, don't let him have another heart attack,' I prayed. 'Keep me strong so I can help him. Don't let me faint, as I'm sure I'm going to. God, help us all.'

I knew Pask had fallen into a terrible state when his first wife, Elsie, Bob's mother, had died of cancer. He had told me that it was only his kids, Bob and Annie, that stopped him doing away with himself.

I had seen how he had reacted when he heard that Bob had been shot down over Germany. I knew what it was to lose a child. When Brian had been killed, I wanted to die myself. The fact that most of our conversations in the past few weeks after D-Day had begun 'When Bob comes home' made this all so much worse.

Pask, Danny and I had planned celebrations, meals. 'Bob will love a good Aussie roast dinner and a fruit cake after all that sauerkraut and sausage.' And the shearing: 'We can probably manage to do most of it ourselves when Bob's back because there'll be the three of us men to pitch in.' And even trips to Norwood: 'Bob and Charlie and Harry can go to the football together.' And now none of those things will happen. Despite D-Day and impending peace, it would be life without Bob. A desolate, joyless life.

'Bob's dead and I've got nothing to live for,' wept Pask.

I felt the same way. The lad wasn't really my son, he was Elsie's boy, but I had known him since he was ten years old, had loved him, fought with him, stood by him throughout his childhood illnesses and struggles, brought him up as my own. And he was gone forever.

'Yes, you have,' I insisted. I knew my attempt at consolation was inadequate. No one and nothing had helped me when Brian was killed. But I had to try. 'You've got Danny, you've got Annie and you've got me and the rest of the family. And we all need you, Pask.'

Colin had risen from his chair and, his own cheeks wet, was patting Pask on the back. 'You'll be all right, mate,' he said. 'We'll all be all right. This bloody war will end soon. It's torn the whole world apart, but we can't let it beat us. We can't let the bastards win.'

Danny came back, his face streaked with tears, his body shaking. 'Dad,' he said, clinging to Pask's arm. 'Dad.'

'Have you got another teapot, Rose?' demanded Colin. 'I think we all need a pick-me-up. Or maybe a drop of whiskey would be better. Or even tea with a bit of whiskey in it.'

I rummaged in the cupboard and found the huge kettle that we use when the shearers come. I shook my head. Too big. There was a billy next to it. One that I recalled using when we were out mustering the sheep. Pask, Bob, Annie and I.

We sat in the shade of wind tortured trees to escape the heat and hoped for a breeze that never came. And we boiled the billy over a eucalyptus-scented fire. And the dust-covered sheep bleated day and night, and the magpies warbled at dawn and dusk.

Such memories attached to that billy. Memories were all we had of Bob now. No amount of tea would drown our grief. But making tea would give me something to do, and drinking it would restore some semblance of normalcy to us. A drop of whiskey in the cups was a good idea. However, I didn't want Pask to take up serious drinking to dull his loss. He had told me that he had drunk heavily after Elsie's death. It was only the kids that got him through that loss. Yes, we needed courage to recover, but Dutch courage doesn't last.

42

1 December 1944
Rose Pask – Orroroo

The days dragged on and there was still no rain. Though we wept a monsoon. There was no respite from our grief. I sought solace in letter writing and in baking.

Danny decided that work was the solution. He drove himself and Pask unmercifully from dawn to dark. Despite the unrelenting heat, the sheep were chased as they had never been chased before. I didn't ask what the fellows were doing out there, and they never told me.

I knew that there wasn't a fence on the property that escaped inspection and repair. I knew this because I saw Pask's hands and Danny's hands torn and bruised and when I asked what had happened, the words 'fencing wire' were grunted at me.

There were trips into the town to purchase paint, and the house was painted inside and out. All except Bob's (now permanently Danny's room) because Danny said he liked it the way it was and it wasn't going to be changed in any way.

I baked cakes and biscuits and told myself that it is what I would have done if Bob had come home. Only now the food was served up to the community who visited us unrelentingly.

Father Travers came of course, and had long conversations with all of us, Pask in particular. His chats didn't follow a particularly religious theme and certainly were not the sort of talk that Father Flaherty had inflicted on me after Brian's death. Just general chit-chat, really. But somehow, we all felt somewhat consoled after his visits. I say somewhat, because what consolation was possible, really?

The only thing that would have helped would have been for our prodigal son to barge into the kitchen and yell, 'What's for tea, Auntie Rose?' And that would never happen.

The whole community came. Anastasia and Tim O'Halloran were there almost every day, Tim spent a lot of time out in the paddocks with Pask and Danny on their mysterious missions to chase sheep. Anastasia helped me with the baking. Her mostly silent presence was a great comfort. There were always visitors to feed, folk whom I had met often about the place, other folk I barely knew.

We had done the same when their sons had died in this war, the war that I hated now even more than I had hated it before. Visits to the bereaved were a tradition in Orroroo; they probably were all over Australia. All over the world, when you thought about it.

Don't let them have too much time to brood over it, was the philosophy. Was it the right thing to do? No one knew, but it was probably the only way to deal with loss. Even if all you did was to sit and hold the hand of the parent whose life had been shattered by the young life lost.

When I had a moment alone, I wrote letters. I wrote to Annie (that was the hardest letter because it was her brother who was dead) and separately to Amy. I wrote to Charlie, although I didn't really have an address for him, just 'care of the Landing Craft Division AIF, but Colin, speaking from his authority as postmaster for Orroroo, assured me the army would sort it out. I wrote to Harry and his family who, thank God, were safe at Norwood because Harry's wounds still prevented him from active service, and to Mary at Mount Gambier.

I had a letter back from Mary within days. Mary was so sweet, so sympathetic, so wise, that Pask and I wept when we read her words. Even Danny surreptitiously wiped his face. Mary, I realised, was upset about Bob's death not only for Bob's sake, and for Pask and me, but also because she feared for her own son, Paddy, who was in the army, albeit still based in Brisbane. Although the war in Europe after the D - Day invasion might be ending, the war in the Pacific still raged, and as every day passed, the time when Paddy might be sent to the front neared.

I wrote to Joe, although I hadn't had a letter from him since his letter from Paris. I wasn't sure where Joe was or why he hadn't written. Because Joe was a priest, I needed to tell him that Bob was dead. I felt only he could really help. I asked him to pray for Bob's soul. Bob had been a difficult child when I first came to Orroroo, had been angry and resentful that I had invaded his home. It had taken a long time before the kid had accepted me. He was a sullen little bugger then. I knew he would resent being dead and he was probably giving God and the angels absolute hell.

Bob's soul would not be at peace; he would not settle easily into heaven and he would need all the prayers he could get. I wanted Joe to write and comfort me. I needed my doubts quelled. I hoped he would say that Bob was now praising God with the blessed angels in the heavenly choir, even although Bob had the worst voice I have ever heard and he would probably tell the angel choirmaster to get stuffed if he was ordered to sing. And Bob was not a Catholic, so how could he adjust to a Catholic heaven anyway? If heaven was, in fact, run along Catholic lines as the Church insisted it was.

Didn't Jesus tell St Peter that he was giving him the keys to the kingdom of heaven? Bob had probably given Peter a black eye or a kick in the shins as the angels thrust him through the pearly gates.

Even Mrs Williams got a letter. She had barely known Bob, but she knew of him, I reminded myself. Then I remembered long-lost cousins I had forgotten existed until now, and I wrote to them as well. Clutching at straws, I even wrote to Father Flaherty. The answer I had from him was predictable and not particularly encouraging, but I should have known that before I wasted the stamp on the letter to him.

'Don't you reckon you're overdoing this letter writing a bit, love?' asked Pask. 'The stamps must be costing a mint. And what are you going to do with all the replies when they come in? Poor bloody Colin won't be able to fit them in his bag.'

'Haven't you got a sheep to chase?' I snapped. 'If I want to write letters, I'll write letters. Anyway, most of them won't answer anyway.'

But answer they did. As Pask had predicted, Colin poured an avalanche of letters onto our table. Most were from Australia, of course, but among the pile was the long-awaited missive from Joe.

'It's Joe's handwriting on the envelope,' said Colin. 'I had trouble working out where it came from. Funny-looking stamp. I looked it up, and I reckon it might be from Turkey. What's he doing there?'

I put the letter aside to open later when no one was around, although I was aching to read what Joe had written. And when I did read it, I was glad that I was alone in the kitchen. I could not have stood it if anyone was looking over my shoulder when I opened that letter.

I should say 'letters', because there were two letters in the envelope with the Turkish stamp. Two letters dated months apart.

After I had read them, I filed them carefully in the copy of *Ulysses* that had belonged to my first husband Michael. I had brought that book with me from Norwood because I had always liked the novel although I was never quite certain what it really meant. *Ulysses* is a lot like life is, really. It's a long and complicated tale, and there was so much and so little that actually happened in that story. I had read it many times trying to work things out and ended up more confused than when I started. Very much like life is.

I knew that neither Pask nor Danny would ever open *Ulysses*. And there were so many pages in it that Joe's letters could be safely hidden.

When Pask and Danny asked what Joe had written, I said, 'Nothing much, just usual Joe guff.'

When they asked if they could read it, I lied and said I had misplaced his letter amongst all the others. It wasn't that I was ashamed of Joe or what he had done, but some things are best kept private, under a sort of seal of confession.

43

30 April 1945
Captain Joe Walsh

Dear Mum,

Just a quick note to say that I'm in Germany. This is not a place I would choose to be, but I've been here for a while and will be here a bit longer. I have wanted to write before today, but I've lacked the energy or the heart or will to set pen to paper.

David (I've mentioned David to you in the past) and I are attached to a division of the British and Canadian Army to assist with the poor wretches incarcerated in one of Hitler's death camps. There are many camps. It's said that some are worse than others. I personally believe they're all hellholes designed by Satan. The one we have been posted to is called Bergen Belsen.

Bergen Belsen is slightly different from, for example, Auschwitz, because there were no gas chambers used here. Instead, starvation and disease were the methods of murder. A slower method, but cheaper and just as effective. Thousands of people have died in this place. And are still dying despite our best efforts.

There was a crematorium, but it had broken down by the time the British Army arrived. There are still bodies lying around although we are burying them as quickly as we can, to try to limit disease. Typhus, cholera, TB, dysentery. Typhus, of course, is spread by lice. The only thing that is in abundance in the camp is lice, although there are lots of fleas too.

We have seen every disease under the sun, although there's little sun. Just grey cold skies. It's meant to be spring in Europe, but there is no spring here.

No heating, and no showers or latrines for the prisoners. Disease spreads more quickly that way. As I said, very efficient and cost-effective.

I am not sure how much you have heard about this awful business. It must have been reported on the wireless and in the papers and perhaps an edited version might appear soon on the newsreels at the movies. Perhaps you know what I'm talking about, and I hope you do, because it's difficult to write about it.

In case it has been hushed up because of propaganda or squeamishness on the part of the authorities, you should know what happened. The whole world should know about this; and the world must never forget it. This is something that must be remembered with dread, with shame and with anguish lest it happen again.

We were briefed before we came. Shown photographs and film. But nothing could prepare us for this. You would not believe the greyness of the place. Or the sheer ugliness. Or the stench. We had been warned that it would be the worst thing we had ever seen in our lives, but still we were totally unprepared for the stark incredible horror and the misery we encountered.

The stench hit us first. Then the sound, like the buzzing of millions of bees, low and indistinct, a wordless moan coming from many throats. And then the sight. All was grey, grey sky from which fell grey drizzle, grey buildings, grey damp stones on the ground on which grey bodies lay or sat clad in thin grey pyjamas.

A phrase from the Bible came to us both: the abomination of the desolation.

The heaped bodies of the dead were pitiful – most of them naked, limbs askew, no dignity as their erstwhile jailers piled them onto trucks and later tossed them into pits. The guards, now under British command, seemed totally emotionless. I suspect they had been the same under the previous regime.

The still-living near-corpses, mere skin and bones, sat gazing into space, indifferent to their fate, apparently uncaring whether they joined their fellows in the pits.

'They're beyond feeling despair,' David whispered.

We're meant to be ministering to the dead and assisting the living, but we have trouble distinguishing between the two conditions. Perhaps the lice cling more to the living, but it's difficult to be sure. And flies swarm over both the living and the dead.

We tried to feed the survivors, but many died after eating

chocolate given them by our Tommies. The poor souls couldn't digest the stuff. They couldn't stomach bully beef. Then we tried Bengal mixture, a rice and sugar gruel used by the Brits during some Indian famine. That only worked after someone thought of adding paprika to make it a bit more palatable.

But still they die. Starvation and illness continues to take their toll, I heard, even after most of the inmates have been moved away.

We found mothers clinging to dead babies, weeping that they had no milk to feed them. Some have been dead for weeks.

Then the storerooms were opened and they were full of food, including powdered milk. To feed the guards, not the babies.

Another sad story. I held the hand of a dying child, shaven head, eyes sunken into the skull, just one of many. 'When will I see Mama again?' the little one whispered in French. 'Soon,' I lied. But I wondered, as my faith recedes, how in the myriad of lost souls milling above Europe in the wake of this war would that child find its mother? And I confess my tears were not only for the kid. I wonder if I will ever see you again, Mum. I'm so far from home. So much evil in this world. So much time has passed.

Sufficient to the day is the evil therein, I have read. So, to the present.

The crematoria used to dispose of the dead had broken down when we arrived. That was why there were so many corpses lying about. Left to rot, as the living were left to rot.

That anyone could treat a fellow human in this manner is beyond belief.

Of course, the Final Solution, as the Nazis termed it, was a very efficient way for Hitler to rid himself of the Jews who were a convenient scapegoat for Germany's economic problems. And of course, to confiscate their goods to finance the war.

Other people were judged unworthy of life; anyone who was deemed inferior in any way by the Reich. Gypsies (who are Catholic so that is probably why I was sent here) and handicapped people, physical or mental, were targeted, and also religious clergy who didn't agree with the prevailing policies, although I'm ashamed to admit some priests went along with official policy. It's rumoured that the Pope colluded with the Nazis to send Jews from Rome to concentration camps. I hope and pray the rumours I hear are false.

I know the Vichy French sent people from Paris. Freemasons were killed. And Jehovah's Witnesses. And homosexuals. In fact, anyone who was or could be a nuisance in any possible way was targeted.

I don't know how many people have been murdered and burned in the crematoria. I doubt a full accounting will ever be made, although records have been kept, because we have seen lists of names in the offices. I suppose there will be some sort of count made by the authorities if only for use in the war crime trials that will invariably take place when this mess is sorted out

The numbers must be staggering, because when we had a moment, David and I wandered down to what was once a small lake in a clearing where the land sloped down. It was full of grey sludge. Grey sludge, we realised, that once had breathed and lived and loved.

The pool had been bordered by trees. Perhaps it was a place of beauty where people picnicked. Now, in places, stumps projected a few inches above the ground. It reminded me of those truncated pillars you see in cemeteries, denoting a life cut short.

One lifeless pine tree remained, bent under a shroud of grey ash. A grim Christmas tree, festooned with tendrils of dust and ash. I wondered why that particular tree had been spared when all its fellows had been cut down. Had some more pressing task distracted the workmen? Some prisoner perhaps in need of bludgeoning to death?

David sank to his knees on the edge of the depression and I joined him and together we recited the *De Profundis*, a prayer from both Hebrew and Catholic lexicons: 'Out of the depths I have cried to Thee, O Lord, Lord, hear my voice. If Thou should turn from me, Lord, who will hear my prayer.'

Mum, I can't go on because I'm weeping again. It makes it hard to believe in a God who could allow this sort of thing to happen. Why did He turn His face away? Thousands of men, women and children were murdered at this place, Mum. Killed by starvation and disease and hatred. Innocent people who once laughed and sang and wept and walked the earth. And they're reduced to grey, mucky, slimy sludge.

Now that the constant rain has eased, the ash is borne around the camp with every breeze and lingers in the fetid air. The ash stiffens the khaki wool of our uniforms, clogs our nostrils, sticks like dandruff to our hair.

And there are stinking cadavers piled up like so many felled trees. And despite all our efforts, people are still dying. The British have sent out medical students to help because not enough doctors are available, but it's an overwhelming task.

I feel my faith, my God has deserted me. Did I tell you that I've been dreaming of my father lately and that I've finally realised that which I should have realised many years ago? Did I suppress the knowledge of his sin because it was convenient to do so, just as the German people suppressed the knowledge of what was happening behind these terrible walls? Or they said, 'I had to follow orders.' Those are the words the guards keep saying. Now they follow our orders. And they seem completely indifferent to their task; no guilt, remorse or pity.

Mum, I'm writing this letter as a sort of serial event. I cannot bring myself to put this all down at once; it tears my heart to put pen to paper. The letter's disjointed, and the paper (it's hard to get hold of paper in this place) is dirty. But I feel I must continue even though I know you'll find what I write distasteful, perhaps even repellent.

And so I continue…a few days between attempts. I'm not dating my ramblings because I've lost track of the days.

I have a sin which I must confess to you, a sin which cannot be atoned. Oscar Wilde called it 'the love that can never speak its name'. I cannot speak of it, even to you, Mum. I can only hint. David and I know the Nazis would have killed us for it. Killed us for our love.

But neither can I refrain from sin. And I am an occasion of sin for the one person in the world who can console me for all I have witnessed. We have shared that which no man should share. And yet the Bible, in reference to that other David and his friend Jonathon, speaks of a love surpassing that of women. And does not condemn their love.

So will God condemn us? Whiskey has become my other crutch, as it did for my father.

Another entry in this serial letter. As the weather here has begun to warm, the task of disposing of the dead becomes more urgent. I can only think of the plague pits into which the corpses of those who perished in the Black Death were thrown. There is no other comparison. David and I and our colleagues intone prayers over the pits, but there is little other ceremony. I often wonder whether our prayers are for the benefit of the dead or for our own comfort. If God could ignore such evil, does He watch now? Is He watching as His children are tossed into the earth, the limbs of strangers tangled in dreadful intimacy?

I take up my pen a week later in another place. David and I have deserted the army. We could stay there no longer.

Now I have something to report other than misery. Perhaps we can hope for release.

When the dead were disposed of and the survivors moved to better accommodation, the authorities decided to burn the whole place down because of the danger of typhus spreading to nearby villages. As I said, fleas and lice were rampant there. It was in the general confusion as the black smoke billowed into the air carrying with it, I felt, the souls of those who had suffered so grievously, that David and I left.

We stole clothing and papers from the warehouses piled high with the possessions of the perished. We had found the tattooing equipment and we inked numbers from the book of the dead onto each other's wrists. For safety, I will not tell you the names of the men whose identities we took, but I now pretend to South African nationality. There were no Australians among the recorded deaths, and my accent is not European. The poor chap who died and whose identity I have assumed was captured in Holland. He must have been there visiting family. David has become French because he is fluent in that language. There were many French Jews here.

No one noticed our departure. There was so much confusion with people coming and going and so many bodies, living and dead, hastily disposed of, that I doubt we have been missed yet. It will happen, but we will be far away.

I can never return home. Nor can we remain in Europe after this experience. Europe and European ideas have betrayed humanity. The spirit of liberty is dead here and we will seek freedom under other skies. I do not know what the future holds for me, for us, for humanity after what I have seen. Hopefully, I'll post this letter from a better place. Pray for me, Mum.

Joe.

The second letter was dated 18 August 1945. The paper was less creased, cleaner. There was no address.

Dear Mum,

I will not say where we are, only that the journey has been a long one (as this journey throughout the war years has been for everyone) and there has been much agony interspersed with fleeting moments of joy.

David and I have technically deserted the army, although with Hitler's death (one should not rejoice at another's death but that man was truly the devil incarnate) the war is over. And today we learned that with the bombings in Japan the war is over in the Pacific too, so dear old Australia is safe. I truly believe that David and I did all we could to help with the war effort and more importantly with the effort to help alleviate the suffering caused by that war.

We both know the penalty for desertion. But we had both reached the point of no return. We had seen things about which we can still not speak, even to each other. The nights are the worst, because in that liminal time between waking and sleeping, horror haunts us still. And when we sleep, as Hamlet said, in that sleep of death what dreams may come?

But we sleep in each other's arms, even though our bed is often a ditch. I greet each sunrise with prayer and with thanks.

We doubt that we shall be missed because there are so many people missing. There are displaced people all over Europe. We hope two more will not swell the ranks by much. We pray to a God we doubt exists. But yet we pray, and we hope.

We decided there was no future for us in Europe, or I fear, in Australia, and certainly no future if we wish to remain together. We will never be accepted in ordinary society. And we are determined to remain together.

We cannot remain in Europe after the evil we have witnessed. It was the stuff of nightmares. Therefore, we have decided to join the diaspora to Palestine.

Perhaps there will be hostility and battle there too, but we will make the attempt to seek a new world. Like Moses, we will wander the wilderness until we find a home. And wherever we find rejection, we will move on.

The British have blocked official immigration to the Holy Land. In fact, there have been blockades to stop Jews travelling by sea to Palestine. You wouldn't think that they would waste resources when there was a war on, but they did. A lot of Jews have drowned trying to get to Palestine.

There are several illegal Zionist organisations that could help, but we decided to go it alone. It may be safer that way, due to our British Army connections and the blame that would attach to any organisation assisting us if we are caught. This way, any penalty will be paid by us and us alone.

Because it is so difficult to reach the Promised Land, we have travelled mainly overland rather than go by sea, although there is a group called Mossad Aliyah Bet which organises travel by ship. We did get some help to get false papers. You can buy anything if you have cash, which is more than most of the poor wretches on the road have. There are hordes of us; there are displaced people swarming the roads in all the countries we have passed through. We have seen so much hardship. We have been able to help some of our fellow travellers, but we have had to be selective and careful in choosing who to assist.

I wear a hat to cover my Walsh red hair, as that is uncommon, but by and large we manage to blend in with the great ragged unwashed tramping across the waste land. I thank God (and you) that you had all us boys circumcised, as is the good old Aussie custom, for hygienic reasons. Not that I wish to expose myself, but I will pass easier in Palestine with that little matter attended to!

We have a little money and we are both relatively young and strong. We have been able to support ourselves when we can find employment. There will be agricultural work in Palestine, orange groves, vineyards and the like. We have heard of the kibbutz movement which is establishing farming communities in Palestine.

As you know, Brian, Charlie and I picked fruit in the Riverland during the Depression. My memories of that time when we camped by the dear old Murray and lived on rabbits and plums are the happiest of my life. Such wonderful, innocent days before evil was unleashed on the world!

David is a city boy, but he will learn farm work, he is adaptable. As for me, I'm improving my Hebrew and making rapid progress with it.

I will try to contact you again, if, and when, we find the safe haven we crave. Behind lies only despair.

Pray for us, Mum. I will always love you and the family and the country I have deserted.

Your son,

Joe.

44

3 January 1945
Rose Pask – Orroroo

After the telegram about Bob's death, Pask lost interest in almost everything. I know it was only Danny's pushing him to work around the property that kept him going at all. And even then Pask moved like in an automatic, machine-like way. He rarely smiled, and hardly ever spoke.

The most dismal Christmas I have ever known came and went. Danny hung a few paper streamers for form's sake, but they drooped and dangled in the heat, and he also put up a sad little Christmas tree, consisting of a dying branch cut off the apple tree near the septic tank. He and I decorated it with the pine cones gathered by Annie years ago to which flaking white paint still clung. The tree was knocked over by Blue the dog. No one bothered to stand it up again.

An elderly chook was killed and roasted, a plum pudding was boiled, doused in brandy and set alight. Pask endured it all without comment. Well, he did say, 'Bob's missing all this,' before relapsing into his usual dreamlike state. But Christmas passed, as all things pass.

After the telegram about Bob came, Pask even lost interest in the progress of the war. Before the telegram (Danny and I had adopted a sort of 'BC/AD' way of thinking except that it was 'before telegram, after telegram).

Before the telegram, Pask had always rushed in from the paddocks and turned the wireless on before he even said 'G'day.' He would rush in, flick the switch, then greet me and sit, ears pricked, as close to the set as possible to hear the latest news from Europe (for Bob and Joe's sakes) and from the Pacific (for Charlie's sake).

Now I was the one who greeted him, and I was the one turned the wireless on as he slunk through the door and sat on the other side of the kitchen table gazing stony-eyed into the distance. I began to feel guilty after a while and stopped putting the wireless on. Danny must have felt the same way because he stayed out of the kitchen until his meal was on the table and I had called him a couple of times. Then Danny would turn the news on and we would listen and eat in silence.

Pask veered between mourning his lost son (his one eye was often red and I knew it was due to tears although when I mentioned it he swore angrily there must be something in the paddocks he was allergic too. 'Probably getting allergic to bloody sheep in my old age – I reckon I'm allergic to that sheep dip. They've probably changed the mixture.'

Some days, he was angry with Bob. 'Bloody silly bugger, why didn't he just keep his head down and wait out the war. He would have been home soon the way things are going over there.'

'We don't even know where he's buried,' he wailed once. I could have added that I didn't know where my son Brian was buried either, or even if enough of his body had been found to be able to be buried. Officially, Brian was still missing in action. But I said nothing. I knew it wouldn't help anyone if I did.

Other days, he would drag out old photos of his children and Elsie, his dead wife, and lay them out on the table like playing cards and wordlessly move them about.

I just made tea and put the cup in front of him. Usually, it went cold and a skin formed on the surface. I took the cup away and poured another for him to ignore.

It was impossible to predict his moods, and impossible to work out what we could do to help him.

The shotgun had not reappeared from wherever Danny had hidden it. When we ran short of meat, Danny would disappear before breakfast and come back an hour or so later with a couple of dead, skinned rabbits. He told me he did not trust his father with the gun, and it was best that it stayed hidden.

When Colin brought the mail, he gave us news of the progress of the war both in Europe and nearer to home. Tim O'Halloran and his wife came frequently, hoping to cheer Pask up. He seemed pleased to see them, or at least he smiled briefly. They were full of hope and enthusiasm that the war would soon end. Things were going badly for the Germans. There wasn't enough fuel for the Luftwaffe to fly, so the war in the air had ground to a halt. U-boats were being sunk. The Russians were advancing on Berlin.

And in the South Pacific the Japs were in retreat in many places. But there was horrific news of prison of war camps full of emaciated survivors, of dreadful treatment of our boys by the enemy, starvation, beatings, beheadings. I worried terribly about Charlie and prayed he would not be captured. As far as I knew, he was still attached to the Landing Craft Division and was engaged in 'mopping up' around the islands. I didn't know exactly what that meant but I wasn't sure I wanted to know. I doubted it was water that was being mopped and feared it was blood.

The war couldn't end soon enough.

Then Colin brought a letter from the RAF confirming that Bob was dead.

I was terrified when I saw the insignia on the envelope and was tempted to toss it in the wood stove. What if it drove Pask further into despair? But of course, Colin had seen it, so its existence couldn't be denied. Then Danny burst into the kitchen, saw it in my hand and yelled for his father to come and see what had arrived. So I missed the opportunity to destroy any evidence, and it was just as well, really.

The officer who had written the letter praised Bob's courage and how his actions in constructing and using the wireless in the prison camp where he had been held had raised morale, had given his fellow prisoners hope in their 'darkest hours'. He said that without Bob and the other men who had built and operated the radio, things would have been much worse for their comrades. He praised the men's ingenuity and determination. They were true heroes. Bob and his mates would be decorated posthumously for their actions and their enterprise. We would hear more about it soon. The officer also promised that when the war ended, Bob's body would be given a full military funeral in an official war cemetery. This was another matter about which we would be advised in the near future.

Pask's head lifted, his shoulders straightened, and he began to speak of 'my son the decorated war hero'. He poured a glass of whiskey for me, for Danny and for himself and we drank a toast to Bob and his wireless. And we had to go into Orroroo to show off the letter to everyone he knew, to tell the whole town that Bob was a credit to his family, to the community and to Australia. Bob's name, Pask announced, would be inscribed on the war memorial. Pask still mourned his boy, but now he felt that Bob had not died in vain. His death was an honourable one. That and the knowledge that eventually the lad would have an official resting place gave Pask the courage to soldier on.

I was proud of Bob too, but I hoped that none of our other kids would be honoured in the same way. As long as they all just kept breathing and came home more or less safe and sound, I would be content. And although I feared I would never see my son Joe again, I prayed that he would reach the Promised Land and find peace there. The only place Joe's name would be inscribed was on my heart forever.

Joe's letter remained hidden in the depths of *Ulysses*. After a while, even Pask no longer asked if I had heard from him.

45

15 August 1945
Rose Pask and family – Orroroo

'What a pity John Curtin didn't live to see it!' said Pask.

After the letter came from the RAF about Bob, Pask's interest in the war had been rekindled. In fact, his interest in life was reborn. Most of the old spark had come back, although I knew my husband would never be quite the same Pask as he had been before the telegram. Or indeed before the war. But none of us could ever be the same. Time and the war had changed the world forever.

Pask turned the wireless up as loud as he could get it. He was beaming my direction. I stood by the kitchen door holding tightly to a basket of newly collected eggs. Even if the noise didn't shatter the eggshells, I feared I might drop the basket because my ears were ringing hard and my hands had gone numb.

'He shouldn't have drunk as much as he did,' I shouted, releasing one hand to clutch the door frame to stay upright. 'He was a great leader, but he did hit the bottle more than he should have done.'

Pask frowned. He didn't like to hear Curtin maligned.

'Mum's right, Curtin was a drunk,' yelled Danny. His sheep chasing for the day was over, and he was seated at the table awaiting his cup of tea. 'Everyone knows that.'

'It's great news, Pask,' I said, 'but for goodness sake turn it down. You're going to upset the sheep in the top paddock. And probably the ones in the bottom paddock too.'

He turned it down a bit, but not enough. I took my hand off the door frame and covered one of my ears, clutching the egg basket with the other. I could still hear the broadcast loud and clear, and still hear Pask yelling louder than I had ever heard him yell. I crossed to the kitchen table, sat the egg basket down on it so I could cover the other ear.

In the corner by the dresser, the cocky started to screech, so I stood and grabbed the hessian bag to cover the cage. There was enough noise in the room already without a demented sulphur-crested cocky adding to it. I tossed the tea towel over the eggs. I wasn't sure that sound could crack eggs, but at this level it had to be possible. I had heard that Dame Nellie Melba's voice could shatter glass, so anything was possible.

'Japan's surrendered!' Pask yelled. 'Danny, did you hear that? Japan's given up. Surrendered! It was those two bombs that did it. We're at peace. Mr Chifley just said it. He's given everyone two days holiday. They're dancing in the streets in Sydney.'

I gasped. The war was officially over. It had been over in Europe back when that madman Hitler had killed himself, and now it was over for us, because the Americans had bombed Japan.

'They can dance in Sydney. Or Adelaide. Everyone can dance except us farmers,' said Danny. 'We're not dancing. We still have to chase sheep and milk the cow and Mum still has to collect the eggs and cook and clean.'

Pask and I turned as one and glared at him.

'It's over, Danny,' Pask said. 'Really, definitely finished.'

'Our kids won't be getting killed. They can all come home now. Annie and Amy and Charlie will be back,' I said. 'Everyone's kids will come home. We're at peace.'

But Bob won't be coming home, I thought to myself. Or Brian. Or Joe.

'And I won't get a chance to join up and do my bit,' Danny moaned. 'I knew I was going to miss out on all the fun.'

'Thank God for that,' I said. I was smiling so hard that my face hurt. But the tears were running down my face, too. Tears of relief that it was finally over, that most of my family would come home, that Danny would never go to war.

'They are dancing in the streets in Sydney,' Pask repeated, his ear pressed to the wireless.

He'll break his eardrums with that noise, I thought. The last casualty of the war.

'I reckon we ought to have a glass of that brandy I keep in the front room. We had one when the war started, remember? We ought to have one to celebrate the war ending too.'

'It's only ten o'clock in the morning,' I protested. 'The sun's not over the yardarm, as Michael used to say. And he was a boozer too. Not as much as Curtin, but a boozer nonetheless.'

'Bugger Michael. Don't be such a wowser, Rose,' said Pask, headed for the bottle. He looked back over his shoulder. 'Give Tim O'Halloran a ring on the phone,' he ordered. 'Tell him and Anastasia to drop in to celebrate. And get Colin and his wife from the post office too. And anyone else you can think of.'

I could think of plenty of people, but most of them were too far from Orroroo to come. But I contacted everyone I could think of within a reasonable distance, and we gathered in the kitchen at Orroroo and celebrated the end of hostilities.

It was a great pity I didn't have a fruit cake to hand, but I dashed off a batch of scones and as always there was plenty of cream because Petal, the cow, was still in milk. And the fig jam was holding out. I hoped the rationing would end soon, though, because it had been difficult to scrounge enough sugar to make the last batch of jam.

'Mum!' It was Mary on the phone from Mount Gambier. Not like her to ring in the middle of the day; she was a great one to watch her pennies, but of course she had heard the news too. 'Paddy will be coming home. And without a scratch on him! I've been so worried that he'd be sent off somewhere in the Islands. Especially after we found out about Changi and the Burma Railway and all those other awful places. But now the war's really over. Finished. Peace at last! Thank God the Yanks dropped that bomb on that place in Japan. Two bombs, actually. Funny names, but I suppose Japs would have funny names.'

I heard Rosemary yelling in the background. I could hear her all the way from Mount Gambier. Probably, I thought, I would have heard her even without the assistance of telephone wires. Bombs always did excite Rosemary.

'Hiroshima and Nagasaki,' she screamed.

'Yes, that sounds right,' said Mary. 'That's what ended the war, in the end, Fred says. It's a miracle. It happened really quickly.'

Yes, I thought. A happy ending. Deliver us from evil, Lord, amen. A miracle for us. But not everyone has had a miraculous delivery from evil. As Mary said, it would have been very quick in the end. One minute you're here, the next you're vaporised.

Did killing all those other people add up to the same sort of crime that Joe had told me about? The Nazis had killed six million people, the newspapers say. But how many millions of Japanese men, women and children were reduced to ash when the Americans bombed Nagasaki and Hiroshima? I reckon those names are going to be ingrained in our memories forever too, just like Bergen Belsen and Auschwitz and the other killing places like the Burma Railway. And the battles like Kokoda.

So many indelible memories for this generation to bear. As if there weren't enough memories from the Great War, now the world's soul bore even more scars.

But knowing the fickleness of human memory, how many generations will remember the sacrifice this one has made? It didn't take long for the war to end all wars to be half forgotten. Will the memory of this war linger when we and our children are dead? I had read somewhere that unless history is remembered, we are doomed to repeat the same mistakes.

Why didn't the Japs have the sense to give in before the Yanks dropped those two bombs? One of them had been called Little Boy, the wireless announcer had said. Strange name for a weapon that killed lots of little boys and girls. And young people, middle-aged people and old people too.

Was that killing just as evil, as premeditated as the killings the Nazis had done? There must have been a lot of thought put into the construction of the atomic bomb, just as there had been much thought and planning put into the building of the gas chambers and the furnaces.

Why was there so much evil in the world if it was controlled by a loving God who cared when a sparrow fell? Could there ever be any penance that humanity might perform to atone for our collective sins? I don't know any priest I can ask. Father Travers has been sent away up north to look after the boys in the islands. I've been praying that he comes back safely and doesn't come back with the legacy of malaria and the burden of terrible dreams that Charlie carries. Where is Joe? Has he found the Promised Land?

'Stop looking miserable, Rose. This is a celebration. Let's have another toast to peace!' shouted Pask.

'To peace!' everyone in the kitchen said, raising their glasses of beer high.

Pask's brandy and his whiskey had run out, but Colin had brought further supplies from Orroroo. I sipped my beer. I would have preferred a nice cup of tea, but when I reached for the kettle, everyone including Anastasia accused me of being a wowser, that something stronger than tea was called for on this occasion.

'Stop thinking and keep drinking, Rose,' urged Pask. 'We're celebrating the end of the war. Don't get all philosophical and religious.'

I shook my head, both to clear it from the alcohol that was starting to make me feel fuzzy and in disbelief that Pask could read my mind.

Pask turned to his mate. 'Colin, would you believe Father Flaherty, that priest Rose can't stand, rang up from Norwood this morning demanding to know when Joe's coming back? The cheek of it! Rose was out milking when the old bugger rang, so I said she'd call him back later. She said it would be much later.'

Later like never, I thought. I certainly wouldn't be discussing theology, philosophy or especially Joe with Father Flaherty.

Perhaps Joe would have the wisdom to understand it all. I wished I

could ask Joe for answers, but will I ever see him again? I suspect thinking about my questions would only add to the burden the poor kid already carries. I prayed that my son was well and happy and picking
oranges in Palestine. And building a new life and a new nation. He
doesn't need more problems; he probably has nightmares worse than
Charlie's.

46

20 August 1945
Corporal Charlie Walsh – Port Moresby

Dear Mum and all at home,

It won't be long now before I'm demobbed. That last bout of malaria was a beauty, but I am out of hospital now. Not that I'm complaining about being in hospital. I got the right royal treatment in there. It was real bonzer to see what lovely little nurses Amy and Annie have turned out to be. A credit to Florence Nightingale. And to you Mum, for the way you brought them up.

I would have thought the bloody mossies were sick of chewing on me. But according to Amy, you don't have to actually keep getting bitten, once the germ or whatever it is – parasite, I think she said, and she's a nurse so she'd be right – is in your blood, you've got the disease and there's not much you can do about it. Except get the fever and chills and feel as if it would be a relief to be dead. Of course, I don't actually want to be dead. Not now when the war is over.

We're coming home, Mum, we're coming home! No matter how often I say it, I still can't believe it. We're coming bloody home!

But I reckon we've all got to remember the people who've made it possible. There are a lot of blokes still up there on the Track who won't ever come home. A lot of blokes that we'll be saying 'Lest we forget' for the rest of our lives. Who won't get the chance to say that for their own mates. Brian's one of them too. And Bob. I still can't believe that Bob's gone. He was a bloody hero, though. That business with the wireless was over the top. I'm proud to call him my brother. Well, stepbrother, anyway.

And we've all the nurses and the medicos and the Fuzzy Wuzzies to thank for what they've done. Lots of us wouldn't be coming home if it wasn't for them. And our girls are among them.

Amy is a damn bloody good nurse, Mum. And so is Annie. A couple of terrific girls, they are. You would be proud to see them in their uniforms with their little red capes and their starched hats. All prim and proper, almost like nuns. And the chaps treat them like nuns, too. Very respectful.

There's a young doctor whose very attentive to Amy. His name's Peter, and I wouldn't be surprised if a bit of romance didn't bloom there. Amy's very bright and outgoing on the surface, but I think there's something going on underneath, somehow. More going on with Annie, though.

Both those girls deserve some happiness.. I've heard Annie doesn't mix much socially, for some reason. Some of the fellows call her the ice maiden, but they don't know her like we do. I reckon she's still carrying a torch for Brian. I remember hearing her say she wanted to patch up soldiers after Brian was killed.

Neither of the girls say much, but I reckon they've seen some pretty nasty stuff up here. We've all seen some nasty stuff actually, that no one wants to talk about, so I can understand the way the girls are. I can see they've changed, and you'll see it too when they get home, but remember there are blokes walking around who wouldn't have made it if it wasn't for the army nurses, including our two.

I'm out of the hospital now and we're camped on the beach because all the accommodation in Moresby is full.

I had a funny experience the other night. I was fast asleep on my camp stretcher in my tent (and had the mosquito net draped over me although I reckon it's like shutting the stable door after the horse has bolted as far as the mossies are concerned) when the whole beach started shaking.

At first, I thought it was one of those earthquakes we get up here. I don't know if you know it, but New Guinea has lots of volcanoes and so we get earthquakes occasionally just to keep us on our toes. Great spot, this country, apart from the Japs, the snakes, the crocs, the volcanoes and the earthquakes. Only this time it wasn't an earthquake at all.

When I put my flashlight on, the sand was moving (the sand here is black because of the volcano) and there were tiny little turtles coming up from under my camp bed. About the size of two-bob pieces, and all squirming like the devil as they struggled from the sand. It was like the day of resurrection when all the dead shall rise, as Father Flaherty used to say.

I shone my light on them, and saw they were all headed in the same direction, trying to get down to the water.

When I crawled out of my tent, there were blokes and turtles everywhere in the moonlight. Most of the blokes were naked or near to it because of the heat, but no one cared because of the general excitement. We were all shining our torches on those tiny turtles that waddled and wriggled their way down the beach, getting in each other's way and tripping their mates up, in their desperation to reach the ocean.

And us soldiers were jumping about and bumping into each other too, yelling our heads off in a mad celebration of life, because when all you've seen for months has been blood and guts spewing from the fellow you've just bayoneted and you have to pull your weapon out of the man you've just killed and even before the squelching and screaming and moaning is over you have to thrust it into the next one who's coming at you, and twist it to make him die quicker so you can deal with another fellow before you get killed yourself, it was a miracle to see such an explosion of life. We all just wanted to be part of creation not destruction.

The beach was covered with turtles. Some of the poor little buggers got themselves flipped over in the stampede and lay on the black sand with their flippers going nineteen to the dozen in the air but they weren't going anywhere, and I reckon they would have died if we hadn't been there to scoop them up and carry them down to the water.

As soon as they hit the water, they dived in and swam like the very clappers out to sea. There's danger out there, and I know a lot of them won't survive because there's fish and sharks and crocs out there just waiting for a feed. They'll perish, just like a lot of our mates did, the ones who are buried up on the Track who didn't survive long enough to reach this beach. But a lot of those baby turtles will last the distance and one day, apparently, they'll come back to this place and lay their eggs. And so the cycle of life goes on.

Some of the fellows laid bets on which turtle would get to the sea first, and men ran up and down the beach to watch the little ones reach that lacy, foamy bit of the water where the waves first hit the sand, and blokes whooped and cheered when their favourite one got there.

I just stood still and said a prayer, tears pouring down my cheeks like an idiot. I know that sounds like something Joe would have done, but I gave thanks to God that after all the filthy rotten killings and all the death and pain I've seen, something like this could happen. Even thinking about it now brings tears to my eyes.

Maybe those baby turtles reminded me of my own little kiddie back home. So fragile yet so strong and determined to survive. Tough little buggers with plenty of fight in them, but looking like they could blow away in the wind. It made me think there was hope left in the world. Hope for peace, hope for humanity.

You're going to think I'm going soft in the head, but it really did seem like a miracle. Just to see so much life and all those little turtles all with the same idea in their heads, just to survive and go home. It reminded me that going home is all I really want, Mum. I want it with all my heart and all my soul. Not that I've ever forgotten home, all through this rotten war and tramping up and down the Track. Going home is all any soldier can desire, home and peace for everyone everywhere in the world, and to know that this hell we have gone through is over and finished and won't ever happen again. And that the sacrifices made to achieve peace were worthwhile. Justification, I suppose Joe would say.

Anyway, as you know, the war is officially over now and old Hitler and even Mussolini are dead, and because of those two atom bombs Hirohito's seen the light. Apparently, the Japs believed their emperor was some sort of god. They've probably changed their minds now.

So maybe we can all start to live again. The whole world will have a fresh start. Let's hope that the few remaining Japs holding out in the islands will work out that the war is over, although they're taking a bit of convincing about it. You'd think they'd want to go home too, but it looks like they're brainwashed. They think surrendering is dishonourable, silly buggers.

Because that's what we've been doing in the 43rd Landing Craft Division, going through the mangroves in our little boats, persuading the Japs it's over, mopping up. It isn't always nice, because some of the Japs who've still got a bit of ammo left shoot at us, use that ammo, and a few poor dills commit harakiri when they see our boats headed their way. Like I said, brainwashed about honour. But most of them look pretty relieved to see us and they don't take too much convincing, perhaps because they're running out of food as well as ammo.

One way or the other, the job has to be done. Sooner the better too, so we can all go home, Japs and Aussies. And Americans too. We wouldn't have got this far if it hadn't been for the Yanks.

By the way, I heard a joke the other day. Russia declared war on Japan a couple of weeks ago. You wouldn't credit it, would you? Left it a bit late, didn't they? Apparently, it's God's own truth, or so the Yank who told me said.

Sorry I've rambled on like this, but until I'm posted back to duty there's not much to do and you can only sit and look at the palm trees leaning over the blue sea for so long before you get fed up with it. I can't wait to be demobbed and smell a gum tree or a flock of Pask's sheep again.

Love and best wishes to all. See you soon. You've got no idea how much I'm looking forward to one of your fruit cakes, Mum!

Charlie.